The Feminine Art of Revenge

Also by Celine Saintclare

Sugar, Baby

The Feminine Art of Revenge

Celine Saintclare

CORVUS

Published in hardback and trade paperback in Great Britain in 2025 by
Corvus, an imprint of Atlantic Books Ltd.

1 2 3 4 5 6 7 8 9

A CIP catalogue record for this book is available from the British Library.

Hardback ISBN: 978 1 83895 821 3
Trade paperback ISBN: 978 1 83895 822 0
E-book ISBN: 978 1 83895 823 7

Printed in Great Britain by CPI Group (UK) Ltd, Croydon CR0 4YY

Corvus
An imprint of Atlantic Books Ltd
Ormond House
26–27 Boswell Street
London
WC1N 3JZ

www.atlantic-books.co.uk

Product safety EU representative: Authorised Rep Compliance Ltd., Ground Floor,
71 Lower Baggot Street, Dublin, D02 P593, Ireland. www.arccompliance.com

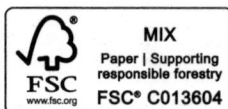

MIX
Paper | Supporting
responsible forestry
FSC
www.fsc.org
FSC® C013604

For George

I am nothing in my soul if not obsessive

– Donna Tartt, *The Secret History*

Revenge, the sweetest morsel to the mouth that ever was cooked in hell

– Walter Scott, *The Heart of Mid-Lothian*

Act One

One

Perfect, Perfect, Perfect

Maria, the ballet mistress, leant forward and began to tell the story. Her dark eyes were wide and gleaming as she spoke, her voice hushed and rhythmic:

'This is a story about love, about revenge, death and sacrifice.

'The tale of a peasant girl who falls for a nobleman in disguise, Albrecht, who is already betrothed to another. When she discovers this, she goes mad and kills herself. Her spirit joins the ghosts of other young girls who've had their hearts broken by men they trusted, and together they take their revenge on any man who wanders into the woods at night. They seduce him with their beauty, and mercilessly they dance him to death.

'But not Giselle; when the one she loves comes into the forest she takes his place.

'This ballet is no Sleeping Beauty, *no* Nutcracker. *It is a ballet with a dark heart and the part of Giselle will require a very special dancer. The role is not only technically rigorous but also emotionally demanding, and it's vital that the dancer can make us believe she's a spirit not a girl.*

'Which of you is up for the challenge? Which of you can answer the call?'

*

'Thanks for coming in,' said Jay. 'I liked your CV.' Sylvie didn't know what there was to like about it; she'd left Willow Way Ballet School four years ago and then tried her luck as a waitress, a barista, a waitress again, an assistant at a tutoring centre, and finally, a nanny. 'What made you want to apply?'

Sylvie couldn't think of anything to say except that her parents were on her case after her mishap nannying for the Wheelers (she kept sneaking Haribos into their sugar-free household) and she'd dashed off a bunch of job applications so that they'd calm down. She didn't actually want a job, least of all as an office admin assistant at a foam finger factory – that would be admitting defeat. That would be accepting that she'd never glitter on stage at the Royal Opera House like she'd always planned. Instead she'd drift into obscurity behind a nondescript desk along with everyone else, the people she'd been raised to consider herself superior to. She looked around at the state of the office and considered how far she'd fallen. By the look of the laminated faux-wood desktops and dust-covered PCs, the yellowing shutter blinds, the dry potted cacti and the large stains on the dark carpet, this appeared to be rock bottom. Worse still, she doubted she was even qualified to work there.

'Uhh . . .' Her eyes drifted to the ceiling as she tried to think. It was hard to think when *he* was looking at her. His good looks had caught her by surprise. He'd come around the corner, this criminally handsome man in his early thirties, and given her a shock. He had no right, Sylvie thought, springing a face like that on someone at this time of the morning without any kind of warning. She could have had a heart attack.

One of the ceiling tiles had come loose from its fixtures and hovered ominously overhead, a dark hole visible through the crack. Despite the stream of cool air emitted by the rickety air-conditioning unit, Sylvie felt her face flush warm with the humiliation of it all.

'That's all right,' Jay said. 'Sometimes I draw blanks too. That's why I hate interviews, they're so formal.'

Sylvie nodded, feeling like an idiot, sure that Jay was just being nice and planned to screw up her application and toss it in the wastepaper basket the minute she got out of the door. He must have known he was humiliating her with his face and his questions, Sylvie thought. He was taking pity on her.

He leaned back further in his chair, crossed one leg over the other and looked at her, his head tilted to one side as he studied her. 'Ever worked in an admin job before?'

Sylvie thought that he was so beautiful. What she meant by beautiful was *right*. He was not only physically striking – curly black hair, green eyes, perfect lips, facial proportions that adhered to all the rules of golden symmetry – but there was something else that emanated from him. She didn't know what it was exactly, but it spoke without words and pulled her in, like a finger hooked through the belt loop of her dress.

'No,' she said. 'I've never worked in an office.'

He nodded slowly, furrowing his brow. 'That's okay, that's okay,' he said. 'We can teach you. It's pretty straight-forward around here. All you need to do is keep track of the inventory. The account managers will make requests, and you just have to order all the materials they need, and then keep track of all the hours the people are doing down in the warehouse. It's a general role we need, some help to pick up the slack.'

Sylvie nodded. 'Sure, I could do that.'

Sylvie didn't know what she'd expected. She hadn't even known foam fingers existed outside of baseball games in American movies. She hadn't been able to find much information about the company online, a registration at Companies House with three or four names on it, a bare-bones website with *South East Foamies: We Help You Give 'Em the Finger!* splashed across the header. There were four framed foam fingers hanging on the opposite wall. One of them with *YOU CAN DO IT!* emblazoned across it. The meeting room had a large glass panel along one side so that you could look out at the rest of the office – a few desks with people sitting at them, the lady who'd let her in, a middle-aged man and a girl in her early twenties, about the same age as Sylvie. They were talking to each other absent-mindedly as they worked away on their computers. The man was picking at a packet of Monster Munch, the girl sipped from a Greggs coffee cup, the woman had a magazine open on her desk beside her keyboard and glanced down at the pages every so often.

Jay smiled, crossed his arms. When he next spoke his voice was lower, softer. 'You know, I . . . Have I seen you somewhere before?'

Was he flirting with her?

'No, I don't think so,' said Sylvie. 'I think I would have remembered.'

He smiled at her and stroked at his lower lip with his thumb, his eyes taking her in from head to toe and back again.

'When can you start?'

'I'm hired? Are you sure?' Sylvie was elated, not by the job offer but by its meaning: Jay liked her, he wanted to see her again.

He shrugged. 'You'll learn quickly and besides, you look right.'

'What do you mean?'

'You look right for the job.'

A few seconds passed as they sat, offering each other small smiles imbued with meaning. Sylvie was alarmed by the way her body responded to his eye contact alone, the quickened heart rate, the growing wetness between her legs which she slid a little further apart under the table, as if on instinct. If this was what it was like, Sylvie thought, just looking at him, imagine what it would be like to touch him, to kiss him.

'I can start on Monday,' she said, pushing her hair over onto one shoulder to expose her neck.

'Brilliant,' he said. 'I'd better take your number then.'

He took his phone out of his pocket and handed it to her across the table. Their fingers met, just briefly. Sylvie typed her number into the contacts page and passed it back.

'There you go,' she said.

'Thanks,' he said. 'All sorted here then, you can go enjoy the rest of the sun.'

'Fantastic,' she said.

'Anything planned?'

'Just some sunbathing,' she said.

Jay raised his eyebrow but said nothing.

It had been a lie. Sylvie didn't have the patience for sunbathing, but she wanted Jay to think about her naked. She wanted to plant the image in his mind, a tiny demonic seed. She wanted the idea of her, of them together, to keep him up that night. Her eyes, black as coal, flickered between his eyes and lips, observing him closely. He gave nothing away. His face was a veritable mask of calmness.

'Do you want some water or a Coke for the way back?' Jay asked her.

'I only live ten minutes away,' said Sylvie. 'But sure, do you have Diet?'

'Yeah, just grab it out of the cabinet on your way.'

'Okay,' said Sylvie. 'Thanks a lot.'

She stood up. She thought they might shake hands, but they didn't. Jay just pulled out his phone while she collected her handbag onto her shoulder, tucked her plastic wallet full of CVs under her arm and shuffled around the edge of the table towards the cabinet. When Jay thought she wasn't looking, he let his eyes wander over her body. Sylvie could tell, and she was pleased. She sucked in her stomach slightly, arching her back. Then she opened the cabinet and frowned at the sight that met her.

On the shelf directly at eye level, pushed back further into the dark recesses, like it had been hidden there, was a small landscape photograph in a swirly, ornately patterned silver frame. In the photo was Jay, his face pressed up next to the cheek of a smiling golden-haired woman, objectively attractive, early thirties. Sylvie's hand shook slightly as she reached for the shelf below which was stacked with cans of fizzy drinks.

'Found it?' asked Jay.

She held up a can of Diet Coke. 'Got it,' she said.

'All right, great, I'll see you next week.'

'Looking forward to it.'

The same woman who'd shown her in walked her down the stairs and out into the gravelled car park where they stood in the blazing heat, exchanging a few perfunctory niceties. Sylvie wondered about the woman in the picture, surely not a girlfriend or wife, he certainly wasn't *behaving* like someone who was attached, least of all in love. It was probably a sister, or a friend, nothing to worry about. She forced any doubts firmly out of her mind and by the time she turned on the ignition in her silver Citroën, she was buzzing again, invigorated by the prospect of a new love affair and with someone like *Jay*. His name was James, he'd explained but *everyone* called him Jay.

It had been so long since Sylvie had really felt anything, anything good at least. It seemed as though her world without colour had suddenly been set alight. When Jay looked at her, Sylvie didn't think about the pregnant, dark cloud of her future, or the overgrown graveyard of her past. She only thought about crawling on her hands and knees under the table towards him. She only thought about unzipping his jeans and taking him into her mouth. After just one meeting she was hooked, obsessed, enslaved.

Sylvie drove home along the A-road. The heat was torturous, the black car seats had absorbed all the sunlight and burnt her, even through her dress. But out ahead of her, the road was almost empty, everything was sunshine and possibility. A procession of white cars whizzed past her on the other side of the road that she took to be a kind of sign. He'll be mine. Jay, she thought to herself. She was giddy with joy, intoxicated with it. It was all starting to make sense now. There was a reason it all happened, that mess at Willow Way. It was a redirection, she was being set on her true path.

She found the house empty when she got home.

Sylvie: Where are you?

Mum: London, going out to eat soon, will be back late

She stripped down to her underwear and went to investigate the contents of the fridge, feeling hungry for the first time in recent memory. She felt as though she could eat and eat and never stop. She wanted to gorge herself on every kind of pleasure she could find. She was awake down to the cells of her fingertips and she wanted to feel. She wanted to eat, drink, to make love. Sylvie stood in the coolness of the open fridge and surveyed it. She picked up thick pink slabs of cold ham and put them into her mouth, piece after piece until it was finished, and then she ripped open a packet of pepper-trimmed roast beef and did the same, enjoying the feel of the meat on her tongue, the saltiness of it.

There was a bottle of white wine in the side of the fridge, three-quarters full, the glass smudgy with condensation. She took down a wine glass, pressed the ice dispenser for a couple of cubes and filled it almost to the brim before taking a swig. The fruity, cold liquid flooded her mouth. She took the glass of wine with her. The ice had almost completely melted before she could climb the stairs. She set it down on the bedside table, peeled out of her knickers and lay down naked on top of her covers. The closed slatted blinds cast stripes of shadow along the length of her body. She was acutely aware of the feel of the fibres of the linen bedcovers against her bare skin. The cool air blown over her body by the fan made her nipples harden. She opened her legs and began to touch herself on top of the covers, thinking of Jay and whispering his name into the dark. She had to have him, she thought, or she might die.

Two

A New North Star

After what felt like an eternity, Monday finally arrived. Sylvie looked around her bedroom as if seeing it through fresh eyes, bathed in the lilac light of a late summer morning. She thought this was a room that belonged to somebody entirely different. Fragments of ballet shoe ribbon pasted onto a collage of Misty Copeland, a dance school acceptance letter mounted and framed on the wall above her bed like a shrine. The logo on the acceptance letter was sage green, two W's interlinking. Willow Way. She didn't talk about what happened there, she'd never breathed a word to anyone and never would. None of that mattered any more.

The past was over with and Sylvie had been given a gift. A new North Star. Something to wish for and my God, was she good at that. She felt as though she'd discovered the secret to ecstatic living, and she wanted to shout it on every street corner: 'Let me show you how to yearn, how to ache with longing! Desire is the most exquisite pain, once you learn how to do it, you'll choose it over easy pleasure again and again and again!'

'You'd understand,' she said, to the framed photograph on her bedside table, a hazy 1980s portrait of a glamorous red-headed woman in a pearl choker with frosted pink lipstick and blue eyes rimmed with eyeliner. Sylvie's great-aunt, Jacqueline Gardiner. *Deceased.*

Aunt Jacqueline had not taken much of an interest in Sylvie until she was eighteen years old and boarding at Willow Way, and then she'd invited her for tea for the first time. To her beautiful three-storey town house with sash windows, one half of a stunning Victorian villa painted cream. When she greeted Sylvie at the door, Sylvie had been struck by her beauty.

Aunt Jacqueline had alabaster white skin and rich red hair that began in a widow's peak at the root and ended in a blunt crop cut at her chin. She had the most striking deep blue eyes and an aquiline nose, a small, almost mouse-like face. The skin around her mouth was finely wrinkled, her lips painted soft pink. Even in her old age she was tall, and as she looked up at her, Sylvie felt herself shrinking with intimidation.

Aunt Jacqueline's silk kimono wafted behind her as she led Sylvie into the parlour. It was embroidered with hummingbirds and petunia flowers in pinks, yellows and blues, a gift from the Prince of Liechtenstein as she explained.

The parlour was decorated in the style of a boudoir with plenty of powder pink velvet and ruched draped curtains, apparently fashioned after something Jacqueline had seen at a burlesque show in Paris. Walking carefully over the assortment of Persian rugs, Sylvie allowed her eyes to rove appreciatively over the leopard print pillows and column candles on gold candlesticks.

Jacqueline sank down into a high-backed velvet uphol-stered armchair, fishing a silver cigarette case out of the depth of her kimono pocket. Sylvie seated herself on the love seat opposite.

'Cigarette?' Jacqueline asked her.

As she held out the case, Sylvie noticed the cigarettes were bright pink, acidic, almost neon. She'd never seen anything like them before but she shook her head.

Jacqueline let out a sharp laugh. 'I thought all dancers smoked.'

She put the pink cigarette between her lips and lit it, exhaling an elegant stream of smoke into the air above her. There was something about her, Sylvie thought, that was as if she had a camera trained on her at all times. Even the way she sat and smoked, one leg crossed over the other, her arm held out in an angular pose, cigarette dangling insouciantly from between her manicured fingers.

Jacqueline took a small sip from her teacup before placing it down on the tabletop beside her, next to a golden candlestick, an ornate box filled with the incense she'd brought back from India and a framed black-and-white portrait of her mother.

'So, Sylvie.' Jacqueline cleared her throat. 'Do refresh my memory, what's it like being young?'

'It's okay,' Sylvie confessed.

'Okay?' Jacqueline was aghast, she shifted forward in her chair. 'My dear, you are a rosebud entering its very first bloom, a beautiful girl like you with the world at your feet. It is not okay, dearest, it's spectacular! When I was your age, I had four boyfriends at once, I went out every night, even if I had to sneak out.' She started to giggle then, and so did Sylvie. 'I wore disguises, you know, if I wanted to go anywhere seedy. I danced all night with a butch lesbian in a three-piece suit once, and a monocle – Caris, she was called. And I took heroin one night at the Moulin Rouge, what a hoot, I was there two days, or perhaps three, I found myself in the dressing room and then next thing I was on stage, shimmying around in the spotlight.' She gestured to her chest through her high-necked black dress. 'Tassels,' she said.

'That's exciting,' said Sylvie, feeling her cheeks warm with a blush.

She couldn't imagine herself ever being brave enough to find herself in situations like those, though she could admit they sounded thrilling.

'So tell me,' said her aunt, collecting her teacup and taking a sip. 'What kind of trouble have you been getting yourself into? You can trust me to keep a secret – I won't say a word, my dear.'

She shrugged. 'Just dance,' she said. 'It takes all my time and attention. We're getting ready for the final showcase now, and that dictates which of us get company parts next year. We're doing *Giselle*.'

As she said it out loud, Sylvie felt the muscles around her throat tighten; she was reminded of the severity of what lay ahead, the crucial importance of the next few months.

'*Giselle* is just right, just perfect. I must come and watch you.'

'That would be nice,' said Sylvie.

'Tell me, Sylvie darling, how does it feel? Dancing, under the stage lights, for an enraptured crowd. Does it feel glorious?'

'It feels . . .' Sylvie hesitated – she had never shared her thoughts out loud before, at the risk of sounding deranged. It was an incredibly vulnerable thing, to be open like this about dance. It felt as though she were betraying herself, letting someone in on a sacred bond. But she looked up at her Aunt Jacqueline, her small mouse-like face, her eyes wide and waiting. She felt sure that she wouldn't judge her, that she would never judge her. 'I always think,' she said, 'it feels like transforming into a daemon, something unearthly. It's . . . alchemical.'

'Yes,' Jacqueline nodded. 'Yes, I think it is.'

*

Sylvie had returned every single week to see her, without fail. She was more than an elderly relative but also a kindred spirit, an artistic soul, a friend. Sylvie knew her aunt would have understood how she thought about Jay. Aunt Jacqueline had lived a life defined by passion, by art, by style. What she lacked in devotion (she had married five times), she made up for with an ever-burning lust for life. If she could see me now, Sylvie thought, she'd be so happy.

She found herself reaching out and touching her aunt's photograph, imagining flesh under her fingertips and not the frigid panel of glass. She missed her.

Sylvie sat up at the edge of the bed with her feet hovering over the floor. As she pointed her toes and flexed them, all the knuckle bones cracked. She stood up and leant into her left hip to pop the socket and then into her right. She had to click all the pieces into place. Sylvie woke up most mornings with a dull pain in both sides of her ribs, with an aching back, sore hips and knees and sometimes a stabbing sensation in the ends of her fingers, under the nails where she couldn't get at them. After an hour or two all the pain would disappear, which led Sylvie to believe that its source was psychosomatic.

But not today. Today she felt blissful. Sylvie took an enormous, delicious stretch, luxuriating in the warm breeze through the open window and the sound of children from next door, laughing as they chased each other around the end of the garden.

Her parents' voices in the kitchen came into focus as she descended the stairs. They lived in a little village on the outskirts of a large, run-down town in the south-east of England. It was an enormous six-bedroom house, renovated to state-of-the-art spec from a crumbling 1970s build that her father, a property developer, had snapped up. But like the majority of his developments, this one lacked any soul and there were too many lights and right angles for it to be comfortable. She passed the professional photos, enormous glossy pictures fixed to the wall. Her family of three: Mum (white), highlighted, blow-dried and with an alarmed look in her eyes, Dad (black), the muscles around his mouth manoeuvred into a bizarre, Joker-like grimace. The three of them were wearing white T-shirts, jeans and bare feet for the photo at the behest of the photographer, who had remarked smugly that he'd once shot a summer holiday campaign for Boden.

Sylvie stopped at the last photo. It was a shot of her alone the year she got into Willow Way. In the picture, she's seventeen years old and dressed in a lilac tutu, standing on the tips of her pointe shoes with her arms curved over her head in fifth position, a small smile on her lips. She could remember one of her teachers saying, 'Sylvie Orange is going to be a principle at the Royal Ballet, you mark my words.' It was all possible once. Never mind, she thought. She had new dreams now. She wanted things again for the first time in a long time. She wanted Jay.

The kitchen was a vast stretch of marble floors, white walls, enormous windows, and professional grade titanium appliances that were rarely used. The white-ness of the room amplified the bright sunlight beaming through the window. She slid onto one of the kitchen island stools, so completely unergonomic in design that it took a fleet of Finnish designers to come up with it. She watched her mum, Nadine, chop up cucumbers and pears. Slender slices of fruit slipped under her fingers, as she filled up her NutriBullet. A handful of spinach, chopped ginger, some coconut water, a tablespoon of Manuka honey.

'It's the working girl!' Nadine exclaimed. 'You're up early! Must be excited for your first day.'

'Yeah,' said Sylvie with a shrug.

'We're so proud of you, aren't we, Clive?'

'Mm,' said Sylvie's dad, Clive, who sat in his favourite leather armchair, scrolling on his phone, submerged in sun's rays. 'You'll be working till retirement paying us back for all those intensive dance courses and Italian costumes.' He laughed then. He was the kind of father who didn't generally take his daughter very seriously. 'Never mind, eh. Kept her out of trouble, didn't it, Nads?'

'You were a beautiful dancer,' said Nadine. 'I always thought the costumes were so pretty, pink tights and ribbons, just *gorgeous*. And it kept you in good shape, didn't it?' She let out a deep sigh. 'Oh, well.'

'What's this?'

Nadine had left a leaflet for adult ballet classes on the kitchen island. Sylvie picked it up at the corner between her thumb and forefinger, disposing of it in the kitchen bin as if it were a dead rat.

'You may as well admit it, Sylvie,' said Clive, smirking, big arms crossed over his chest, 'the real reason you left Willow Way.'

Sylvie was frozen still, glued to the spot. She was sure that the wrong word, the wrong breath, would give her away – any minute now it was going to come rolling out of her like a dam breaking. Finally, somehow, someone had found her out.

'You couldn't hack it in that dormitory, sharing a shower with a dozen other girls, slaving away in a ballet studio with only canteen food to sustain you! No wonder she wanted to come back, Nads, we've spoilt her, only got ourselves to blame,' and then he laughed again.

'Oh, that reminds me,' Nadine said brightly. 'I had a confirmation from Grove Park about Aunt Jacqueline's memorial, it's all booked for next spring.'

She handed Sylvie a green smoothie.

'Brilliant,' said Clive, absorbed once more in something he was looking at on his phone.

'I was thinking, Sylvie,' she said in the same gentle, coaxing voice she'd used since Sylvie was an infant. 'How would you like to do a dance at the memorial? Just a short solo. Would be nice. Aunt Jacqueline loved to watch you.'

'I don't dance any more,' Sylvie responded, taking a gulp from her glass.

'But you could, just once, it's such a shame to let all that hard work, all that training . . .'

'And money!' Clive piped up from his armchair in the corner.

'Such a shame to let that all go to waste.'

Sylvie felt the smoothie curdle in her stomach. There was a tightening in her jaw and an ache behind the eyes that cautioned her she was dangerously close to breaking down into tears. Giving up dance had been like losing a body part, and when reminded of the loss she responded badly. She had spent many nights crying into her pillow, feeling as though her life, her real life, had ended with her ballet dream. She couldn't put any of this into words. If she parted her lips to speak, she knew she could summon nothing but tears, so she gave her mum a small shrug and walked swiftly from the kitchen, into the downstairs toilet where she blinked hard at herself in the mirror.

It's different now, she said to her reflection.

She needed to focus on the good things. Meeting Jay had been a seismic and defining moment in her existence, which could now be divided into two halves. Before Jay and After Him. Before, her empty days had spread out in front of her, long and wide with nothingness. Only last week she'd been so lonely that she'd fucked a stranger in the toilet cubicles at the local park. The isolation was suffocating, it had sprung up around her like a glass dome and she had to do something to shatter it. Sylvie thought summertime must be the loneliest season, when the days stretched out without the punctuation of routine, the bugs hummed and everything bloomed with life, reminding you that you were alone. In the parks and swimming pools and fields, she could feel her own smallness against the wild expanse of the outdoors. That was loneliness. The smell of other people's barbecues, festivals beyond slatted wooden fences. A stranger's laughter vibrating in the evening. A cluster of girls going through the self-service checkout, voices trembling with excitement.

It had happened quite incidentally. She'd just been lying there on the grass and looking up at the sky, feeling as though she were drowning in the blue heat. It had been months since she'd been fired from the Wheelers, the cord had been cut and she was floundering, untethered and, more importantly, unwanted again.

Sylvie had repeated the mantra that had seen her through her darkest times. *I am nothing. I am nothing. I am nothing.* She whispered it over and over like an incantation. The phrase made the pain dissipate like sea foam on wet sand. It made her feel watery, changeable and soft. She felt the numbness cocoon her. Breathe, two-three-four. Like the start of a port de bras, the beginning exercise of every dance class. If you're good enough, her teacher Maria had told her once, you can perform a simple port de bras and bring a grown man to tears.

Sylvie had felt the nudge of a football at her thigh. She grabbed hold of it with both hands. The owner of the ball came chasing after it and when Sylvie tossed it to him, he scooped it up into his arms and looked down at her, grinning. First at her legs, bare in short-shorts, and then the strip of stomach between her shorts and her shirt which had risen partway up her ribs, the triangle of cleavage, damp with sweat, and then, at last, her face.

As it was happening, Sylvie thought to herself that having sex in a cubicle at the public park loos was not actually that odd. Surely, stranger things had gone on there. All the surfaces were metal and when she caught her distorted reflection, she thought to herself, if these walls could talk. He fucked her from behind, hands holding softly on to the flesh of her hips like he was scared to hurt her. Strange hands, Sylvie had thought, so unfamiliar. Then they changed positions, this time Sylvie had her back pressed up against the cool, metal wall with one leg wrapped around his waist. They were face to face and he was smirking. Sylvie wondered if all the time she'd been bent over and he'd been behind her, really letting her have it, if he had had that manic smile on his face. The thought made her chuckle and she managed to disguise it with a well-timed moan.

When it was over, she watched him sprint across the park to join his mates. His face was jubilant, he couldn't believe his luck. I wonder what he thinks about me, Sylvie thought to herself as she wandered home. She trudged through the thick, humid afternoon heat feeling cheated. Easily won pleasures didn't satisfy her, the thrill was in the striving, the agonizingly slow ascent, the dreaming, the fantasy.

It was too hot for office wear. Her polyester trousers were already damp at the seat when she climbed down into the car. As she neared the office, her sudden nerves were abrupt and embarrassing. She felt as though she'd been out of the world for so long, and now she was entering a new world where things mattered again.

Jay was outside the building when she arrived, like he'd been waiting for her. He dashed his cigarette butt into the gravel as she shut her car door. Their eyes met, his green and translucent, hers dark and searching. He was just as she'd remembered him, better even. Shiny hair, a strong nose, lips that could almost be pretty, a heavy brow. She'd never been drawn in by good looks alone. There always had to be something more, something ungraspable. Jay had that something else, Sylvie thought, something dark and gleaming. He seemed to vibrate at a different frequency to the world around him, to ordinary people. He was special.

'You showed up then,' he said, taking a few meandering steps towards her and stopping close.

'Of course I did.'

'Welcome to the mad house.'

Sylvie didn't know what to say to this. Jay gestured for her to follow him inside the foyer. He held the door open to let her pass through first.

'After you, Sylvie.'

She wanted him to say her name again and again and again.

She followed him up the stairs, her hand trailing after his on the banister rail. She could smell him – sandalwood, vetiver, citrus. She wondered what he'd say if he could read her mind or see her weekend dreams. The dreams had been so graphic they bordered on disgusting. The memories made her blush.

The office was the same as she remembered it, that is to say, quite depressing. It was as hot inside as it was outside. Sylvie was sweating, the humidity pooled in her shoes and under her armpits. Meanwhile, Jay looked tranquil. Cool emanated from him.

'You can sit down there –' he pointed to a worn upholstered sofa pushed up against the wall – 'the guys are downstairs. They'll be with you in a minute. We'll start with a production meeting, basically just the schedule for the week.'

Sylvie nodded.

Jay disappeared downstairs, leaving Sylvie alone to take in the surroundings that would become her new habitat for the foreseeable future. She tilted her watch face back and forth under the fluorescents. Aquaracer. A Well Done gift from Mum and Dad for getting the job. While she waited, she watched the second hand tick.

They emerged suddenly, offering her handshakes and welcomes. There was Karen, a middle-aged woman with a platinum blonde pixie cut; Derek, a man who wore his dark hair in a plait down his back; and Sapna, who was close to Sylvie's age but gave the impression, in her buttoned-up blouse and suedette brogues, of being much older.

'Should we get started?' asked Karen.

They wheeled their desk chairs into a circle and the production meeting began. Sylvie, who hadn't been assigned a desk chair yet, had stumbled about uncertainly before sinking into the sofa, which meant she was about a foot below the eye level of everyone else. She sat silently as they discussed deadlines and targets, used technical words that might as well have been a foreign language. She felt intellectually (and vertically) inferior.

When the meeting was over, Jay took his laptop into the meeting room while Karen gave Sylvie the HR spiel about fire exits and break time, career progression, training and industry. Sylvie forced herself to make eye contact for eight seconds at a time with Karen, and then allowed herself to look over Karen's shoulder at Jay in the air-conditioned meeting room. An oasis. *Jay's room.* His face was luminous behind the soft light of his laptop screen.

It was like he was talking to her through the glass. Sylvie felt drawn to him across the office, so much so that her mind drifted mid-sentence and all she could think about was what it would be like to have him put his arms around her and kiss her.

'Sorry, what?'

Karen repeated herself, with great effort and a begrudging sigh. 'Weekends. Would you mind working the odd Saturday? Only when it's really busy.'

Sylvie glanced back at Jay and said sure.

Next, Karen and Derek took her on a tour of the warehouse while Sapna went on a coffee run.

'Latte good for you?' she'd asked Sylvie, leaving without waiting for a confirmation.

Jay stayed behind. Sylvie turned back to look at him and he glanced up, holding the contact for just a second. I want you, Sylvie thought, I want you so much I can barely breathe around you.

Downstairs, they passed through a busy warehouse full of machinery and people in hi-vis jackets. The ceilings were tall, but the heat was stifling. There were electric fans set up and aimed directly at some of the workers as they ushered sheets of foam under the electric printer and queued up with their crates and pulleys in front of the industrial-sized guillotine.

'Maybe just take it all in,' Derek suggested, half-heartedly, giving her a squeeze on the shoulder. He had a friendly face, his dark eyes sympathetic as he noted Sylvie's simmering anxiety. The noise, the heat and the pace of the warehouse were overwhelming. The workers there were cactus flowers who survived in spite of their surroundings. 'There are some training materials in the store cupboard over there.'

'Sure, okay,' said Sylvie.

'I'll come and get you in an hour,' Karen added.

Sylvie let herself into the tiny, dust lacquered store cupboard and collected the ring-bound folder with TRAINING written across the front of it in capitalized Sharpie. She found a quiet corner with plenty of empty crates to sit on, and close enough to a rotating fan to catch a little breeze. From where she sat on the warehouse floor, she could look up at the meeting room and see Jay working at the table, the silhouette of his head. Sylvie flicked through the binder which was full of the stock images of lurid cartoon smiley faces in hard hats and lengthy safety procedures for operating machinery. She watched as the factory workers packed boxes of foam fingers and stacked them in rows by the back door, and she watched as they wafted in and out of the back door for cigarette breaks.

How long had it been? Sylvie checked her watch. Still twenty minutes until Karen came to collect her. She looked up at the meeting room window. Jay was still there. She wondered if they'd get the chance to talk today. Perhaps it had been stupid to take a job because of a man, perhaps he'd only been flirting with her to get her to take it. It was too early to tell, too early to give up hope. She could do it. He was probably just waiting for her to make a move. He was her superior after all, it had to be her, lest HR come beating down his door, or Karen.

A tall man in hi-vis carrying a crate paused to introduce himself. He'd been trying to make eye contact with Sylvie since she came down from the office upstairs. He was very skinny, his arms looked stick thin by contrast to the wide cuffs of his dirtied work gloves. He was in his mid-twenties, which made him stand out among the other factory staff.

'Hi, I'm Brett,' he said.

He had eager, watery blue eyes that took her in appreciatively, like she was the best-looking thing he'd seen in a very long time.

'Sylvie,' she said.

She couldn't have been less interested in Brett. He reeked of gawky, boyish inexperience and over-keenness that repulsed her.

'First day?' he asked her, smiling relentlessly.

'Yes,' said Sylvie, gritting her teeth.

'Working up in the office?'

'Yep.'

'Cool.'

'There's only been one other new start in the office,' he said. 'In all the time I've been here. Sapna, you've met her. Sometimes we go out. Not dating or anything, we go out in a group, some of her mates, some of my mates.'

She wished more than anything that he would give up and leave her alone. She was worried that Jay would see her talking to him and think there was something going on between them.

'How long have you been here?' Sylvie asked him.

'A couple years,' he said. 'I was here when there were different managers, before Jay bought the place.'

Sylvie glanced up in the direction of Jay's room. His figure was gone from the window. She felt a pang of loss in her stomach, a sense of panic.

'There you are!' Suddenly Karen was waving at her from across the factory floor. 'Come on!'

'I'm being summoned,' said Sylvie.

'Good luck,' said Brett. 'Good to meet you.'

When Sylvie reached her, Karen turned and started up

the staircase without so much as a word, humming a tune to herself as her sandals whacked against the stairs.

'Oh, good, you found the folder,' she said, looking at the dusty ring-binder under Sylvie's arm. 'This will be your desk – why don't you just sit there for a bit and go over the health and safety.'

'Sure,' said Sylvie.

Her assigned desk was on the edge of the row of PCs that went Sapna, Karen, Derek and then her, up against the wall. Sapna was nowhere to be seen, neither was Jay but Derek looked up and smiled at her, while he continued his conversation on the phone. He pulled her wheelie office chair out as he said, 'If they're behind on delivery again tell them we won't just give 'em the finger, we'll give them the whole bloody fist, mate. Oh, yeah . . . and I'm six-three, I'm a big fella, big hands. They won't enjoy it one bit.'

Slightly unsettled, Sylvie sank into her seat and flicked open the binder to where she'd been reading about machinery-related injuries. Someone had put a latte in a paper cup on her desk and she picked it up and took a sip that burnt her tongue.

'Sorry about that,' said Derek, once he'd hung up. 'How are you doing? You all right?'

'No worries,' she said. 'Good thanks, just . . . hot.'

Sylvie looked out of the window at the red kites circling. There was a truck reversing around the corner, a woman in a white hijab holding her groceries loose in her arms, stopping to scoop up a stray orange from where it had fallen onto the tarmac on the edge of the road.

There was a quiz playing on the radio station, the radio tingled with static, the presenter's voice was barrelling and melodic. Karen put down her clutch of papers to shout out answers across the room at the radio player.

'Any news about the proofs from Jane?' Derek leant back in his chair to speak to Karen.

'Hmm?'

'Proofs. Jane.'

'Nothing,' said Karen, wiping her lipstick off roughly with a tissue and then reapplying it.

Jay appeared, passing under the fluorescent lights and into his room where he turned off the lights and the AC. He held his car keys in his hand.

'I've got to be off,' he said. 'Have a good rest of the day, everyone. Welcome aboard, Sylvie. Before you leave, Karen will get you all set up on the system. All right with you, Karen?'

'When I've got a minute,' she said.

'Cheers,' said Jay, and then without looking back, let alone a glance at Sylvie, he left the office.

Sylvie felt her heart sink. She looked out into the car park where Jay was getting into the driver's seat of a beautiful, shiny black Jaguar.

'Nice car, isn't it?' said Derek. 'Jay's obsessed with it, can't say I blame him.'

'It's beautiful,' said Sylvie.

She couldn't have cared less about cars but even she could see the Jaguar was a thing to behold, and elevated by being owned by Jay, enchanted almost. She watched as Jay pulled out of the car park in one smooth movement. When he disappeared at the bottom of the road, she felt a sense of loss.

'All right,' Karen said with a heavy sigh, taking off her glasses and putting them beside her on the desk. 'I'll get you set up on the back system, there's a notepad and some pens and highlighters and things in your drawer if you want to get them ready. You'll want to keep a note of your logins and passwords.'

'Yeah, sure.' Sylvie reached under her desk, pulled the top drawer of the little wooden cabinet open.

She got out an A4 Pukka pad and a fresh packet of black ballpoints. Flicking open the cover of the notepad, she almost did a double take at the sight that met her. At first, she thought it was a mistake, and this wasn't a new notepad at all. Someone had already used it, or the first page at least. But then she looked closer – it wasn't a mistake at all, it was a message. Sharp little capitalized letters that read:

YOU LOOK REALLY GOOD TODAY

J

Three

The Other Brother

Sylvie went for a run when the heat had cooled. There was a sizeable wood at the back of the close, it was thick with green leaves in the summer and thinned out to a great mass of ash-coloured branches in the winter, criss-crossing against a white sky. Sylvie loved the sounds of the wood pigeons and the woodpeckers, even the crows. Occasionally, there was a graceful tawny deer that last year brought its baby and Sylvie had watched spellbound from her bedroom window as the creatures, which seemed plucked from a fairy tale, curved their lithe necks to nose in the hedges for berries.

She'd run through those woods a thousand times. If she didn't run, Sylvie's body would become restless with unspent energy that felt like it might turn on her any minute and start to rot away her muscle, gnaw on her bones. The movement of her body had a direct impact on her mind and spirit. Being still for too long, she could feel death drawing in, steely and quiet as a ghost.

Sylvie's feet came down hard and fast one after the other as she picked over the craggy woodland floor. The looped tree roots almost caught hold of her trainers, threatening to drag her down into a pit of crumbly soil. She was running like a madwoman, driven by an electricity that emanated from her core and shocked her arms forward, lifting her by the backs of her knees, propelling her forward. She passed quickly through the wood and out the other side into the park. The sun was shining its last hopeful beams through a fast-amassing cluster of dark, malevolent cloud. The wood pigeons were cooing, and Sylvie was approaching the bridge over the river. She had almost run out of park, and if she kept going she'd find herself pressed up against a wire fence, or she might go over the waterfall, and smash her brains out on the weeded rocks in the water below – the stones were covered in green algae and looked deceptively soft from above.

Then, Sylvie felt it begin, the collective gasp of relief in the air as the heavens opened. She turned over her shoulder in the direction of the green where the tennis courts and football field had opened out. There wasn't even a single hardened dog-walker. It was a matter of minutes before her trainers were soaked through, rain saturated her hair and ran down into her eyes, and her clothes were plastered to her skin.

The downfall was heavy but brief, and droplets of water sparkled like polished gems from the tree leaves that Sylvie passed on her way home. Everything shone new, sunshine lit the rain-washed tarmac.

Her parents were celebrating Sylvie's first official day of salaried employment with party food in the garden, even though they were all exhausted from the relentless heat of the day. Sylvie's dad opened up the folding back doors and hauled chairs out of the shed, propping their wooden legs up on the patio, organizing them like bits of doll's furniture. Sylvie's mum put out artisan crisps, cherry tomatoes on the vine, hummus with sunflower seeds. She folded red paper napkins into triangles even though it was just the three of them. She gave Sylvie a wet sponge cloth and told her to clean the garden table. They barely used it and it was all frosted with scum, sap from the leaves of next door's tree.

Partway into dinner Sylvie realized she was tipsy. She didn't usually drink. Her dad topped her glass up with more wine. Everything tasted acidic, including the breaded mushrooms that her mum spooned tentatively onto Sylvie's plate. More wine, a couple of crisps, more mushrooms, cherry tomatoes, a spoon of hummus. Sylvie spent the whole time dissociating and dreaming of him. Of Jay. It had been a while since she'd unfurled her imagination to its full wingspan. What was it about Jay? He was a big, shiny red button begging to be pushed. He was something with its own magnetic force, a small planet, a demigod.

When the wine was done, Sylvie's dad mixed up some Pimm's and kept refilling her glass like some benevolent medieval king. Sylvie savoured the sweet, fizzing raspberries and strawberries at the bottom of her glass. Fruit juice on her tongue. She looked down at the garden, the wide span of trimmed grass beyond the patio, the birds hopping along the fence at the end of it, animals calling to each other from deep in the woodland. The smell of wet grass and the sun setting over a purged sky, washed with periwinkle watercolour. Sylvie thought that the sky looked the same way she usually felt after a long cry, all damp eyelashes, renewal and peace.

Sylvie was drunk on wine and sunshine by the time she floated up to bed. She lay awake on top of her covers for hours as the light outside her window spun through a spectrum of lilacs and ambers, before settling finally into a deep, star-studded blue. She doubted she'd be able to sleep. Her body fizzed with adrenaline, and she pulled up the blinds so that she could lie down against her pillow and count the stars outside her window. She no longer lived in dread of the morning, she found herself invigorated at the thought of a new day, a new chance to appear in glorious colours to him. To Him. She had been revived with a burning sense of purpose; she was going to find out what he wanted and become it.

What did men want? Aunt Jacqueline had been an expert on the subject and often offered her thoughts unprompted. Sylvie had vivid memories of the parlour room in Aunt

Jacqueline's Richmond town house, the feel of the pale pink velvet upholstery on her armchairs.

'Darling, if you really want to know the truth,' her aunt had told her over steaming cups of Earl Grey from Fortnum & Mason's, poured into delicate blue and white china teacups, 'a man can't resist a woman with a life of her own. No matter what nonsense you might hear, all you really need is to have lived a life. A little scandal, a few secrets, a few love affairs and you don't tell him everything of course, but a well-placed hint and he'll be wound around your finger. You are letting him know that you are the star, and a real-life star is a very rare thing, most people will *never* meet one.'

There had been no doubt in Sylvie's mind that Aunt Jacqueline really *was* a star. Her looks were so striking, so manicured, so eccentric, it was like she was always about to walk onto the set of a Hollywood film. Her confidence was so unwavering that she wasn't really a person at all but more a force of nature. She was theatrical, she liked to be heard and seen whereas Sylvie didn't care for it, unless she was dancing. She wanted to be irresistible to men – well, to one man, to Jay – but she didn't know if she had what it took to be A Star.

She had a 2021 silver Citroën and a gym membership, but not a life. Secrets though, she had plenty of. For instance, the real reason she left Willow Way, that was something nobody could ever find out about. She'd only been close to telling someone once, her Aunt Jacqueline of course, but then she died, and Sylvie took it as a sign to keep her mouth shut.

Of all people, Aunt Jacqueline would have understood, she would have had something smart and pithy to say about it that would have set everything right and put her at ease. But she was gone. It was too late. She'd left Sylvie an exquisite collection of vintage furs, and stories of whirlwind affairs with Hollywood lotharios and European princes. So, Sylvie had no one to confide in, but she could look quite fabulous should she ever feel like it, which was fitting for Aunt Jacqueline, who was known to purr, 'I'm all style no substance, darling.'

Sylvie took a long hot bath, after which she sat in her dressing gown and brushed her hair in the mirror with Aunt Jacqueline's hairbrush. An antique hairbrush with a mother-of-pearl inlay, decorated with flowers all along the back of it and the inside of the handle too. She picked it up and dragged it gently through her strands of curls. She readied for sleep like a bride on her wedding night, with perfume and tinted lip balm and rose-scented body lotion that she applied by candlelight. For the final touch, she leant forward and pinched her cheeks in the mirror to bring the blood to the surface. She was preparing to see him in her dreams. It was a certainty – she'd dreamt of him every night since they'd met.

In one of them, she'd been in a ballet class at Willow Way and Jay was her teacher. He paused halfway down the line-up of students at the barre, turning back to appraise them; they were suddenly all pulled a little higher through the tops of their heads, spines stretching in the hope of meeting the great height of his expectation. There was a smirk on his face. When his eyes met Sylvie's, she looked away, inclined her neck, stretched further, her hip bones and shoulder blades resisting one another as she performed a plié arabesque. She would have appeared perfectly in control, perfectly cool and professional to anybody else, but not to Jay.

Sylvie forced herself to focus on the brushing sound of ten pairs of feet sweeping the floor in unison, as the group performed battement en cloche. Two, three, four, in time to the music. This time, as Jay walked slowly back along the line of dancers, he paused a little longer by Sylvie, so she knew he was watching her. She felt it, the heat of his gaze. She tried her hardest to concentrate on the steps: fondu, back-bend, piqué tourné, but he had invaded her thoughts, her mind, her ability to focus. Suddenly, it was just the two of them in the room. His eyes on her like a spotlight, sweat prickling at her hairline from the heat of it. There was no music at all, no wiry-haired pianist plucking at her limbs. Just the whispered song of their breath. Hers, minute and imperceptible between the bends and folds, while he watched, pulling her towards him with a god-like ease, pulling in the floorboards like a magician with a handkerchief. Sucking in the wooden barre and the wall of mirrors, the dust-crusted chandelier. Sylvie felt as though she was being drawn to him, dragged towards him by a great force. And then she woke up.

The next few days passed pretty uneventfully. It turned out that Jay didn't spend much time in the office, just a few hours each day and, because they worked in different departments, there was never a reason for them to talk except to say 'Good morning', and 'Goodnight' if he was still there when she left for the day. His absence gave Sylvie plenty of time to build a fantasy around him. What was he doing? Where was he going? Who was he with? It was all so mysterious.

Although, Sylvie thought to herself, when he *did* look at her, the odd and precious occasion when their eyes would meet across the room, he really *looked* at her. It made her feel like she was going mad but she held on to the hope each morning that maybe, just *maybe* today was the day where something was finally going to happen between them. What exactly? She couldn't tell. She had the note he'd written her, which she looked at as often and inconspicuously as she could.

To Sylvie's dismay, it turned out that they were actually expecting her to work while she was there. Today that meant proofreading the new foam finger designs for a big corporation's annual paintball competition and calculating the total charge for the job. Sylvie had lost track a while back and was now typing almost totally random numbers into an Excel template that was supposed to spit out the right figures at the end. It was mostly just Derek and Karen in the office. Sapna worked on finance matters and was partly remote, but when she was in, she stuck to Jay's room most of the time. She hadn't made much effort to welcome Sylvie either, and she seemed a little bit frosty towards her, so Sylvie preferred it when she wasn't around. Derek was nice, he liked to chat, he had a teenage daughter, he was patient when Sylvie made mistakes with the stock list, and calmly explained himself once more. Karen kept to herself, she listened to the radio and read her magazines and popped to Greggs at lunchtimes for sausage rolls and cups of tea and sometimes worked late, long hours after everyone had left.

'One o'clock. I'd say that's lunch. See you ladies later,' Derek said, jangling his car keys in his hand and heading for the stairs.

With her glasses on the end of her nose, Karen logged into the back end of the system from her PC and shouted out a series of usernames and passwords for Sylvie to write down, grumbling under her breath if Sylvie asked her to repeat something. When they were finished or Karen was too fed up to continue, she announced that she was going to Tesco and she'd be back later.

Sylvie was alone and finally felt as though she could relax. She stared at Jay's writing, bare and small on the lined notepad. She twirled around on the spinny office chair. She scrolled the news on her desktop, dissociating between lines of an article about 'shrinkflation'.

There was the sudden loud noise of a growling engine underneath the office window. The rumbling of a supercar. Sylvie saw a metallic blue Lamborghini pulling into the car park. She wondered who it could be. She was alone in the office. No sign of Jay either. She hoped the car's owner wasn't here for a meeting the others had forgotten about. Sylvie wasn't going to be much use. She had barely got to grips with how the business functioned. She tried her hardest to look busy, opening a random Excel spreadsheet from the shared system and scrolling to the bottom of it, accidentally replacing a cell with a series of forward slashes.

'Hello.' A man appeared in the doorway, rapping the backs of his knuckles against the open door. 'Hi, haven't seen you before, you must be a new one.'

'I am,' said Sylvie, blushing instinctively. 'A new one.'

The man strutted into the office like he owned the place.

'I'm Greg,' he said, looking her up and down and smiling at what he saw. 'Jay's brother.'

From his appearance, Sylvie quickly gathered Greg was the larger, more muscled, richer and elder of the two brothers, so Jay's business probably felt like something that belonged to him by extension. He had black hair, waxed up at the front into a kind of bouffant, and wore a white polo shirt, tight enough to show his impressively sculpted shoulders and back. His navy chino shorts were tight on the seat by design.

'What's your name?' he asked her.

'Sylvie.'

He stuck out his hand for her to shake, holding hers for a little longer than necessary as he said, 'You from round here? Have we met before?'

'I don't think so,' said Sylvie. Something about him, despite his conventional good looks, gym-honed body and 'sweet ride' was off-putting to her.

'You ever been to Lana's?'

Sylvie shook her head.

'It's the only decent bar around here. I'm there every Saturday night for happy hour with the boys – sure you've never been?'

His head was tilted to one side and Sylvie felt he was trying to look down her top.

'I'm sure,' she said, tight-lipped. 'Never been.'

Greg bent over, leaning on Derek's empty office chair and talking to her at eye level.

'Would you like to go?'

'I don't know,' said Sylvie.

'You don't know?' Greg smirked. 'All right, play hard to get. It's a turn-on, Sylv.'

Sylvie blushed.

'I see through it,' he said. 'But good for you.'

'Umm, no one's in,' she said. 'If you were here to see Jay.'

'Yeah, I see that. All right then, not to worry.' He took a pair of aviator Ray-Bans out of his pocket and put them on. 'Well, I'll see you around then, Sylvie.'

Sylvie nodded. 'Nice to meet you.'

He turned to leave with a final smirk in her direction cast over his shoulder when he reached the top of the stairs. 'If you change your mind about that drink, you know where to find me.'

Sylvie waved at him and realized, as he disappeared at the bottom of the stairs, that she'd been holding her breath.

Derek and Karen returned and the three of them worked in silence for the rest of the afternoon. Derek was sending furious emails about a waylaid pallet of foam, muttering under his breath and sighing heavily as he went back and forth to the kettle to make himself coffees, groaning when he returned to his desk and saw the latest update. Meanwhile, Karen hummed along to the songs on the radio and gave short responses to whatever the presenter was talking about, like she was providing ad libs to a rap song. Sylvie hadn't been assigned a big enough task to fill her afternoon and took to archiving old jobs in the digital system. It was simple and repetitive and satisfying. After a while it was like she was on autopilot and her mind could just drift off.

She wondered what Jay was doing that very moment. She passed several hours like this, and it was quite enjoyable, lost in her imagination with thoughts of him and the two of them together. It was a bit of a shock when four o'clock rolled around and Karen announced that she had to leave early for an appointment. Once she'd gone, Derek looked left and right before shutting down his computer. 'May as well knock off a bit early as well,' he said. 'Get home and enjoy the rest of the sun.'

'See you later,' said Sylvie.

She'd hang around till five. Why not? There wasn't anything exciting waiting for her at home.

She decided to make herself a cup of tea to pass the time. The kettle, white plastic faded to an oyster-shell grey, rattled in its stand as the water began to boil. She crouched down to look in the bottom cupboard, took out a mug and put it on the countertop but she couldn't see any tea. Maybe there was some at the back? Sylvie thought, practically crawling inside the extremely narrow, extremely deep cupboard.

'All right in there?'

She almost jumped out of her skin and banged her forehead on the top of the cupboard. She couldn't see him, but she knew it was Jay.

'Fine,' she said, her own voice bouncing back at her from the cupboard walls. She began to back out, slowly, inch by inch until she was kneeling on the carpet looking up at him.

Jay looked down at her with one eyebrow raised, his lips parted, arms crossed over his broad chest.

'I'm, uh . . . I'm looking for tea.'

'And?'

'No luck,' she said, trying to get to her feet as elegantly as possible and dusting carpet debris from her knees.

As he looked around the office, Sylvie stood quietly, rolling her empty mug between the palms of her hands as Jay took his phone from his pocket and scrolled for a bit. He refocused his attention on her. 'Are you hungry?'

46

Four

Big Macs and Blackmail

Sylvie stood outside with Jay in the office smoking area, watching him puff on the end of a cigarette with total nonchalance. She was trying her hardest to achieve two objectives: the first was to keep her joy from overflowing, from spilling out from her face via an enormous cheesy grin, and the second was to use this precious time they had alone together to take a definitive step forward in their relationship. He'd suggested they go to get something to eat. He didn't have much time, he said, but they could drive up to the retail park and go to one of the drive-thrus and then he could drop her home.

She was too wired to even think about food, but she thought that the drive, twenty minutes each way, the two of them alone together, was probably more intimate than going to a local restaurant or pub. She could understand why he didn't want to go out in town together so soon. It wouldn't look good, him out with his new, young employee. She would take what she could get.

'Ready?' he asked her, flicking his cigarette butt onto the gravel.

She followed him to the car park. When Jay got down into the driver's seat, Sylvie ran her hand along the lacquered black paint of the Jaguar's door.

'I love your car,' she said, climbing in.

He didn't respond.

'Seat belt,' he said.

She reached for it and clicked it into the buckle. He was hard to read. His face was stony, almost expressionless as he started up the ignition. He made her second-guess herself constantly. She'd expected for him to be chatty and flirtatious now that they were alone. She thought he'd invited her because he wanted to spend some time just the two of them, but now it looked like he'd just been hungry. As they started down the road, Sylvie put her hands in her lap and watched out of the window. With the air-conditioning on full blast, she could forget about the heat. It was as if the outside world had melted away and it was just the two of them, alone in this cool bubble together. She looked at him, as subtly as she could manage, the handsome profile of his face, his hands on the steering wheel, a mysterious tattoo that peeked above his collar.

'Where did you go today?' she asked him.

His eyes flicked in her direction, taking their focus off the road for just a second. He looked surprised. 'That's for me to know.'

'Mysterious,' said Sylvie. 'Aren't you?'

'Not really,' he said, turning the right-hand indicator on. 'I just think we all know too much about each other these days, don't we?'

Sylvie shrugged. 'Suppose so. But I don't know *anything* about you.'

'We're strangers,' he said.

'You like that? Us being strangers?' She could feel the blood pulsing through her, thudding in her ears.

'No,' he said. 'Not for ever, at least.'

'You don't want to know me?' said Sylvie. 'I want to know you.'

'And what would you like to know?'

'Anything,' said Sylvie. 'Literally anything.'

Jay looked at her then. 'And what makes you think there's anything worth knowing?'

'I don't know.' Sylvie ran her fingers along the interior of the car, the metallic detail on the door handle. 'I just had a feeling, when I met you, that maybe you were someone worth knowing.'

He stifled a smile. 'That's why you took the job, I take it?'

'Of course,' she said. 'The only reason.'

'Well, you know why I offered it to you.'

'Why?' asked Sylvie, intrigued.

Jay didn't answer.

Talking with Jay felt like playing chess, as if they were both manoeuvring around something significant and unsaid, the tension palpable but each of them afraid to be the first to cross the line. Jay fiddled around with the car's audio settings, connecting his phone. The speakers, situated all around the body of the car, throbbed with the urgent rhythm of the music, which wasn't anything Sylvie was used to. It was instrumental, pounding drums with rattly macarena-like accents.

'What kind of music is this?' Sylvie asked him.

'You don't like it?'

'I don't know,' she said, truthfully.

But the more she listened, the more the jungle-like rhythm seemed to match the rate of the passing street lamps and the road markings whizzing out of view under the car bonnet. It sent her into a trancelike state beside him in the passenger seat.

'We're here,' he said, pulling into a large car park between four or five different fast food joints. 'Where do you want to eat?'

'McDonald's,' said Sylvie because she'd had a McDonald's but never a Taco Bell or a Popeyes and worried that the food there could be unexpectedly messy or smelly and ruin the seductive, sophisticated air she was trying to cultivate.

They pulled up to the speaker of the drive-thru which Sylvie found a little dark and ominous on account of its anonymity, the stark metal pole sticking out of the ground.

They were greeted by a very buoyant, very loud Welsh voice: 'What's occurrin'?'

They ordered two Big Macs, large fries, one normal Coke and one Diet. Jay pulled up into a nearby parking space.

He began to divvy out the contents of the paper takeaway bag. Sylvie didn't know how to tell him she wasn't hungry, so she said thank you and began to gnaw on a chip. They ate in embarrassed silence for a few minutes before Sylvie got up the courage to ask him a question.

'So, someone downstairs told me you bought the company quite recently?'

Jay paused to swallow his mouthful of burger. Sylvie noticed that despite the considerable size of his hands he only took small bites and ate slowly.

'Yes,' he said.

'So . . .' Sylvie went on. 'Why?'

He frowned at the burger for a few seconds before picking out a slice of gherkin and flicking it into the open burger case below.

'Business was doing well,' he said. 'But the owner wanted to sell.'

Sylvie nodded. 'That the only reason? You didn't dream of making foam fingers when you were a kid?'

'You didn't dream of proofreading PDFs for a living?'

Sylvie winced. 'Not really, no.'

'Sorry,' he said, putting the burger down. 'Was that mean?'

'No,' she said, though it had felt like a jab. 'I actually wanted to do something else, but I had to give it up.'

'Care to share?'

'Maybe later,' said Sylvie, quietly.

She felt as she always did when she thought about the old days: wistful and on the verge of crying. She had to be careful or she was going to come to pieces on the passenger seat and scare Jay off for good.

'Why'd you stop? Whatever it was you wanted to do instead.'

There it was, the question she had been asked so many times and always struggled to answer. She looked at Jay's face, thought to herself how much she wanted him to know her, how much she wanted to tell him the truth. But it was too soon, she knew that; she felt him slowly drawing closer and she would never forgive herself if she did anything to ruin it and make him pull away. He'd never speak to her again if she told him what had really happened at Willow Way. She didn't want to lie to him so thought it best to say nothing, to borrow Jay's habit of avoiding the question.

'That's for me to know,' she said, smoothly.

Jay had reached the end of his burger and put the tip of his thumb in his mouth to lick off a remnant of sauce. Sylvie had only managed a couple of chips. She had no appetite whatsoever and the oversized burger glowered at her intimidatingly from its open wrapper, a corner of chemically produced cheese winking at her under the car light. What *would* Aunt Jacqueline have to say about that? Sylvie doubted her aunt had ever heard of a McDonald's, let alone eaten one. She reached out and tore a little bit of bread out of the bun.

'I met your brother today,' she said.

'Oh, yeah? He called me earlier.'

'He seems nice,' said Sylvie.

'You reckon?'

'Nice car,' said Sylvie.

'Yeah.' Jay put his empty packaging into the bag. 'You're not gonna eat that, are you?'

'I'm not that hungry,' said Sylvie.

'Here.' He held out the bag for her to put it in.

'So . . .' Sylvie was fast running out of ideas for conversation. 'Why did you ask me to come with you?'

Jay shrugged. 'Dunno.'

'We wouldn't get in trouble for this, would we?'

Jay looked at her in his intense way, as though he were undressing her with his eyes. 'You tell me.'

Sylvie blushed, feeling the contrast of her hot cheeks against the coolness of the air-conditioning. 'How would I know?' she said, her voice little more than a whisper.

The oppressive heat of the afternoon was cooling to dusk. Above them, a few birds sang out from the tree branches. The car park was still pretty empty, though every so often a pair of headlights would turn the corner slowly and pull up into the queue for the McDonald's window, or two people would get out and head into Taco Bell together. They were alone in their little corner of the car park.

'Well,' he said. 'This could be blackmail.'

'You're joking, right? Getting me a McDonald's is blackmail?'

'Could be.'

'But you invited me here.'

'And you accepted.'

'Should I not have?' Sylvie asked, perplexed. 'Was it some kind of test?'

'I don't know,' he said, with a half-smirk that made Sylvie question whether or not he was serious. 'You just happened to apply for the job, really low pay, sort of menial, with a private education behind you, so I ask you to come in for an interview and you turn up looking like . . .'

'Like what?'

'Like exactly my type.'

Sylvie couldn't have fought the smile if she'd tried.

Jay shrugged but he was smiling too. 'It happened to my brother. Blackmail, that is.'

'Why would anybody blackmail you?'

He didn't answer.

'Well, I'm totally innocent, I swear. You want to pat me down for wires?' she asked him, laughing.

The smile had dropped off Jay's face and he watched her with his brow furrowed, thinking intently.

'Oh my God,' Sylvie squeaked as a realization dawned on her. 'You want to pat me down for wires!'

Jay scratched the back of his head.

'Sort of, yeah, if you don't mind.'

'I've got nothing to hide,' said Sylvie, surprised almost at how defensive she felt, hurt that he was suspicious of her. 'But fine.'

She opened the car door and got out. Jay did the same, walking around to the passenger side, until they stood opposite each other with a foot of space in between them.

Sylvie held her hands up in surrender. 'Well, how do we start?'

'Turn around and put your hands on the car.'

Sylvie turned to face the car, putting her hands flat against the roof.

'Spread your legs a bit wider,' he said.

She obeyed.

'All right,' he said, as he pressed his hands over her body, squeezing her firmly, over her shoulders, her back, her waist.

It exhilarated her, the sound of his breath when he was close behind her, his touch dulled through the thin fabric of her white blouse. She wished he would slip his fingers inside the cuffs and stroke the insides of her wrists. Sylvie knew that even this small touch would send a shiver down her spine. She waited for him to reach for her inner thighs, to put his hands between her legs, but he didn't. His final touch, the touch that Sylvie would think on for days afterwards, was a squeeze around her waist with both his hands, his fingers feeling through the wrinkled folds of her shirt fabric to get a firm grip on her.

'Satisfied?' she asked him, summoning all the feigned nonchalance she could muster.

'Far from it,' he said. 'But you're not wearing a wire.'

'Did anyone ever tell you you're really paranoid?'

'Once or twice.'

They each got back into the car.

Jay checked his phone before saying, 'About time to head back.'

'Sure,' said Sylvie, her arms instinctively folding around her waist as she tried to recreate the warmth of Jay's touch. They began the journey back home and as they pulled out of the car park Sylvie realized that she only had twenty minutes. Twenty minutes left to make an impression, to do something, say something, push things forward. After that, God only knew when she would get the chance to be alone with Jay again. 'So what is it really?'

'Excuse me?'

He didn't look at her, just ahead at the road, at the scarcely populated dual carriageway and the amber-coloured street lamps, which blurred into streams of orange light in the damp corners of Sylvie's peripheral vision. She looked at his hands on the steering wheel, his lips. This has got to be dangerous, she thought to herself, wanting someone this much.

'You're afraid of being blackmailed,' she said. 'Are you a secret billionaire or something?'

'Not quite,' he said. 'And if you don't know, I'm hardly going to tell you, am I?'

'You don't trust me?'

'We're strangers, remember?' Jay looked at her, a brief smile in her direction.

'I'll tell you what I think,' said Sylvie, swallowing her anxiety, aware that perhaps it was now or never. 'I think you like me. I think you like me a lot.'

He didn't look at her. 'Of course I like you,' he said.

'And you didn't want to be lonely,' said Sylvie.

'I'm used to feeling lonely,' he said.

'Me too,' said Sylvie. 'What's your tattoo?' she asked him, reaching out and running her fingertips along the edge of his collar, as gently as she could, like she didn't want to tarnish him.

He didn't answer.

'Do you like to go fast?' he asked her.

'Yeah.' Sylvie nodded. Something about him made her feel open and alive to the world, hungry for sensation.

He smiled, the smallest twitch of a smile, and with a tug of the steering wheel, he pulled the car into the fast lane. Jay put his foot down on the accelerator, the car roared to life beneath her as the speed increased, like a plane taking flight. Sylvie felt the pressure in her back, her neck, her head which was pushed back against the headrest. Adrenaline coursed through her body. Jay looked over and they smiled at each other. Emboldened by this, she reached across the car with her right hand and put it onto his leg.

'How was that?' he asked her, as they pulled up to a red light. 'Scared?'

'No,' said Sylvie.

Jay took her hand from where she was resting it on his thigh and entwined his fingers with hers. She could barely breathe, it was like a dream.

'So you don't scare easily?'

'No,' said Sylvie. 'I don't.'

'You'll have to tell me where you live,' he said.

Sylvie told him her address.

'I'm almost sad, actually,' he said. 'That I've got to take you home.'

You don't have to, Sylvie wanted to say. *You never have to take me home, you can take me with you, wherever you go. For ever.* But she didn't say this. Instead, she thought very carefully before saying, as casually as she could, 'I thought you were going to kiss me.'

Jay didn't look at her, just drove on steadily. 'Maybe I am,' he said.

'I don't think so,' said Sylvie. 'I think you want to but you're scared.'

Jay scoffed at this, shaking his head.

'What's your aim like?' he asked her.

'My what?'

'Open the glovebox,' he said.

Curious, Sylvie pulled the lever handle. It was a gun. A small black handgun, the shaft blue-black under the tiny automatic glovebox light. Sylvie shut the little door, her heart beating like a drum.

Jay looked at her, quick glances, a smirk at her obvious shock. She said nothing, unsure of what he was trying to tell her. He said nothing, only stared at the triangle of flesh where her blouse had unworked itself from the top two buttons, the goosepimply flesh of Sylvie's chest and the quiver of her ribcage that betrayed her attempts to appear calm. She was as frightened and as curious as if she'd been locked into a cage with a tiger. They left the dual carriage-way and drove through town to Sylvie's village. They joined the back of a small queue of cars that had built up at the traffic lights. Sylvie could see the people in the four-by-four in front, the driver's face in the rear-view mirror, or her eyes at least, two grey enquiring eyes.

She felt Jay's hand at her neck, and then his face up close, those pale green eyes with something desperate in them, and the heat of his breath. This is it, she thought, he's really going to kiss me, right here in the middle of town in front of all these people. He held her, almost roughly, by the back of the neck, and kissed her hungrily, sucking at one lip and then the other, his tongue over hers. It felt like more than a kiss to Sylvie: it was everything she'd hoped for and more, electricity, a cosmic alignment, a fire spark. Proof that it was perfectly right, that she was exactly where she needed to be, with him.

A loud honk of a car horn from behind them spoilt the moment.

'Shit,' said Sylvie.

'Don't worry.' Jay drove on and as the car pulled through street after street, he put his hand across the car and undid the button on Sylvie's work trousers, deftly and without looking. Then he pulled down the zip and poked his fingers through, stroking at the thin fabric of her underwear while she held her breath and watched the road.

'People can see us,' she whispered, as he pulled her knickers to one side, emitting a soft, helpless little gasp as he stroked her.

They were still behind the four-by-four and the woman with grey eyes was looking at Sylvie. They watched each other as Sylvie sat, petrified of being brought to orgasm there in the front seat of the car for all the town to see, but perhaps more petrified of asking Jay to stop. She didn't want him to stop, couldn't bear the thought.

But he did.

'This way, right?' he asked her, putting both hands on the wheel.

Flustered, Sylvie shifted her underwear back into place and zipped up her trousers. They were nearly at her house. She straightened out her blouse and raked her fingers through her hair, certain that her parents would take one look at her and know what she'd been up to.

Jay gave her a brief smile, a small squeeze of the leg. As they turned down the entrance to Sylvie's road, the street lined symmetrically by manicured trees, Jay's phone began ringing. She glanced at the name on the screen when he turned it over. Annabel. He grimaced dismissively.

'Who's that?' she asked him.

'No one,' he said. 'Work.'

Before she left, starry-eyed and practically floating up from her car seat, Jay grabbed a hold of her hand. Sylvie anticipated a goodbye kiss, but he only looked at her earnestly, his mouth a stern line across his face.

'Don't tell anyone about this,' he said. 'Promise.'

'I won't,' she said. 'Promise.'

He nodded then, letting her go and starting up the ignition, frowning at his phone screen as he said, 'People ruin things, Sylvie. Best to keep them out of it.'

Five

Please the Boss

Jay: You look fucking hot today

Sylvie blushed at the message on her phone screen. She was still giddy from the night before and had worried, upon waking up that morning, that perhaps it had all been a dream. It seemed as though things were really happening, moving forward.

Sylvie: I'm trying to work

They'd been messaging like this for most of the morning, Jay in his office and Sylvie at her desk. She had a growing mountain of proofs to check and emails to send, passed on helpfully by Derek to 'give you some good practice, Sylv', but every ten or fifteen minutes she'd get up to make a coffee, or go to the loo, to reply to his message. Or she'd answer at her desk as inconspicuously as she could.

For the meantime, she had her phone tucked between her legs as she researched an email query Derek had received and passed on to her.

The email subject line read: **Personal Request**

Hi, just found out my pig of a cheating husband has been sleeping with our son's Year Three teacher. He's about to run a half marathon and I'd like to meet him at the finish line with a giant foam finger that says 'CHEATING TWAT' before I ask him for a divorce.

Please will you send me a quote.

All best,
Cynthia Blatt

Sylvie felt the phone vibrate between her legs and a surge of desperation ran through her body as she fought herself from answering. It was too risky right now, with Karen pacing the floor behind her on the phone to her son, berating him for forgetting his key again. She'd have to wait.

Sylvie sighed to herself and opened up Google Chrome, typing into the search bar, Is there a legal ruling against profanities on foam fingers?

'No,' said Derek, looking over her shoulder as he came back from his midday Starbucks run, 'it's not illegal.' He took a bite out of his pastry. 'But it's definitely frowned upon. We made that discovery after a stag party job. "Kiddie-Fucker", I think, was the slogan.'

Karen paused from her carpet-pacing and pressed her phone to her neck, glaring at Derek.

'Sorry, sorry,' he said, holding his hands up. 'You approved it.'

'*You* approved it,' Karen snapped, and then talking again into the receiver of her phone. 'No, no, sorry, love. Listen, take Mrs Dolittle's wheelie bin and use it to stand on and get into the bathroom window. What? No, I don't care what it smells like . . .'

By this point, Sylvie was desperate.

'Right back,' she said quietly, excusing herself to the loo for her eleventh pee break of the day.

She opened Jay's message: **Thought it was your job to please the boss**

Sylvie wrote back: **I'm doing that already, aren't I?**

The response was immediate: **I can think of one or two things you could do to impress me**

Sylvie felt a chill up her spine. She wanted him badly. She couldn't wait for the day when they could consummate their relationship. She thought about it constantly. She imagined the two of them together: his lips, his tongue, his skin. Last night she'd woken up around 4 a.m. from a dream of him that resulted in orgasm. She was naked and breathless, her body slick with sweat and her bedsheet wrapped in a tangle around one of her legs.

'So, new girl . . .' Sapna perched on the edge of Sylvie's desk.

Sapna and Sylvie hadn't yet had an actual conversation. Sapna worked in the finance department, but the department only consisted of two people so it might be more accurate to say she *was* the finance department. Together with Jay. Sapna was one of those girls who always seemed older than they really were because of her seasoned, brusque quality, booming laugh, and her ability to make smooth, unawkward small talk for forty minutes with middle-aged women like Karen. Sapna had a round face, a dimpled smile, her cheeks were plump, and her chin wobbled when she laughed. Sylvie thought she must have recently had a haircut because she kept flicking her shoulder-length hair around like she couldn't get it to fall right. At some point she would, without fail, wrap her hair up in a tight little bun, revealing a set of small ears that stuck out slightly and a short neck with a crease at the back that reminded Sylvie of pleated velvet.

'Do you live local?' Sapna asked her.

'Yeah,' said Sylvie, giving a vague description of her drive to work.

Sapna nodded and smiled, her eyes glazing over with barely veiled lack of interest. 'So you grew up here?'

'No, not exactly.'

'Oh,' she said, screwing up her nose.

'We moved here from Cookham Dean when I was a teenager,' said Sylvie.

She felt as though she was missing something. Sylvie hoped Jay would still be there in his room when she was done, and she would get the opportunity to talk to him later. The fire escape door was flung open but there wasn't any through-breeze, just more stifling heat. Sylvie marvelled at Sapna's ability to look cool in her black polyester office trousers while she sat overheating in a floral sundress. She's making me anxious, Sylvie thought. Sapna looked at her as if every utterance out of Sylvie's mouth was a disappointment. She'd never been good at this. At people, especially women. Too many variables. Too unknowable. The only person whose company she'd genuinely enjoyed and who had seemed to genuinely enjoy hers in return was her Aunt Jacqueline. It was as if Sylvie could never say or do or, indeed, think the wrong thing around her.

'So,' Sapna said, looking at her studiously, 'we're going for drinks tonight at the Three Butts, do you want to join?'

'We?'

'Yeah, me and a few of the guys from downstairs.'

'Sure, yeah, thanks,' said Sylvie.

She wasn't keen but couldn't think of an excuse and didn't want to offend Sapna.

'All right, sweet,' said Sapna. 'Let me get your number and we'll talk later.'

'Sapna,' Jay called out then. 'Can you bring the VAT folder?'

'Got to go,' said Sapna.

Sylvie felt a flush of jealousy as she watched her disappear behind the doors of Jay's room with her cup of coffee and her folder.

About fifteen minutes later, Jay left the office without a word to anyone. Sylvie watched as he disappeared down the stairs, car keys in hand. Sapna stayed behind in his office, hunched up close to the laptop screen, her finger tracing down a column of numbers on a page which lay open on the desk.

Sylvie: Are you gone for the day then?

No response. She hated when he did that, ignored questions he didn't want to answer. She was wired whenever Jay was around, but when he left, she felt herself crashing, as if she were coming down from a drug. She whiled away the hours answering emails and then took a long meandering 'stock check' visit to the warehouse downstairs. She saw Brett who waved at her from across the warehouse floor and put his thumbs up, grinning.

Around four o'clock, Karen announced her departure and then fifteen minutes later Derek looked over his shoulder before letting Sylvie know he was on his way out.

'See you tomorrow,' she said, checking the time.

'I'm off.' Sapna came out of Jay's room rather quickly once Derek had left. 'See you in town about seven-thirty?'

'Yeah, cool.'

She opened an email that her mother had sent a few days ago, titled: **Grove Park Memorial.**

Hi Sylvie,

I've forwarded the details of the booking for
your Aunt Jacqueline's memorial next spring. I'm
copying in Janet, the lovely lady who's going to
help us organize and run things on the day.
If you have a little think about the piece of music
you'd like to perform to, you can let her know and
she'll source it and get it all loaded up onto the
system ready to go. Plenty of time still of course, I
just wanted to put it on your radar and make sure
you have everything you need in time for . . .

It wasn't that Sylvie didn't *want* to do a dance tribute for
her great-aunt, it was that she wasn't sure she *could*. Her
technical ability would have plummeted to nothing after
all this time. It would be a miracle if she could lift her leg
above 90 degrees, let alone balance en pointe. She couldn't
bring herself to put on a sad imitation of the dancer she'd
once been, like an old beauty queen clinging on to former
glory, strutting around like mutton dressed as lamb. Yes,
her aunt had loved to watch her dance, had believed in her
career, when she was young and determined and in her
prime, but that was over now.

Aunt Jacqueline had once compared Sylvie to a priest-
ess. 'Your life devoted to an art,' she'd said. 'I think it's the
noblest pursuit a human spirit can take. Mastery. It goes
against our nature as flawed, imperfect, prone to illness

and defect, mortal after all. It goes against our nature but somehow obeys the call on our spirit, the challenge, I suppose, to rise up beyond the mire of mediocrity and ascend unto something greater, something *perfect*. And that is why, my darling, the masters are immortal. That is why, every time you rise up onto the tips of your pointe shoes it is a defiance against the bounds on the human body and a joyful leap into the possibility of what can be achieved with dedication, precision and an outpouring of the soul.'

Sylvie missed it. She craved the feeling of being encompassed by music, of flying through the air, of turning her body into an instrument, a vessel for art, grace and beauty, but the perfectionist inside her couldn't bear to be anything less than what she had been.

A few moments later she heard someone coming up the stairs, heavy footsteps belonging to a man. Jay walked into the office. He carried a plastic bag with a big packet of ice in it and under his other arm, a crate of beers in glass bottles. Sylvie stood up. She felt her slightly damp skirt against her calves.

Jay cast his eyes over the office. 'Where is everyone?'

Sylvie shrugged, not wanting to gain a reputation as the office grass. 'I don't know,' she said. 'They were here just a minute ago.'

Jay shook his head as if dislodging the concern, tucking it away to be addressed later.

'What are the beers for?'

'My brother's coming down, I'm looking to expand the business, hopefully get him on board.'

'He'll want to help.'

'Why do you say that?' Jay frowned.

'Well,' said Sylvie. 'He's family.'

She didn't have any siblings, but she imagined they were obligated to help one another.

Jay scoffed and shook his head. 'You don't know my brother.'

Sylvie swiftly changed the subject. 'And you're drinking here?'

'Yeah,' he said. 'Why not?'

It struck Sylvie as quite a formal meeting point for brothers. Why wouldn't they go out somewhere, or meet at one of their homes?

'Well, is it . . . allowed?'

Jay laughed at her. Perhaps he found it strange that the same girl he'd put his fingers inside while sitting in busy traffic was afraid of breaking the rules.

'Allowed by who?' he asked her. 'I own the place.'

Sylvie noticed that he liked saying it, talking about the things he *owned*.

'I dare you,' he said, using the bottle opener on his keyring to open a beer before passing it to her.

Sylvie took the chilled bottle and held it to her chest.

Jay opened a beer for himself and leant up against Sylvie's desk to drink it.

'Go on,' said Jay. 'Have some.'

Sylvie froze.

'I'm not trying to drug you,' Jay said. 'Paranoia. Not good.'

'I've never patted anyone down for wires,' she said, coolly. She didn't know why the hazy seasickness of being near him gave way to cool resolve when it was just the two of them. It reminded her of performing, how she'd be nervous in the wings but confident on stage. It was like that with him, another thing Sylvie took as a sign that they were meant to be together. She was her best self, sharp and witty, under the spotlight of his attention.

'Shame,' he whispered, and she felt his hand grab her tightly by the flesh on her left hip. 'I would enjoy it.'

'You're not supposed to enjoy it,' said Sylvie, smoothly brushing him off, though she secretly hated to stop him touching her.

Watching him steadily, Sylvie tilted the beer bottle to her lips. Jay reached out and tipped it up from the base so that it spilt over her chin.

'Hey!' Sylvie put the bottle down, wiping at her face with the back of her hand.

Jay drew closer. Sylvie looked at his beautiful lips amongst the dark bristle of his beard, remembering how it had felt rough against her cheeks and her chin. The look of his face up close, his piercing green eyes that felt as though they saw right through you. What a privilege to see him up close like that.

'Here?' she asked him, her heart fluttering in her chest.

There were still factory workers downstairs finishing off their shift. Any minute one of them might appear in the office with a question about a payslip or something, not to mention they were standing at her desk in full view of the window. Sylvie knew they would be visible from the street below. Jay grabbed her hand and pulled her behind him into his air-conditioned office, pinning her against the wall and kissing her before she had a chance to catch her breath. She felt the carpet underneath her shoes was loose from the floor. She was so hungry for him, so desperate that she murmured, 'Fuck me,' between kisses, surprising herself with the bluntness of her request.

Jay wrapped his arms around her waist. 'I will,' he reassured her. 'I will, soon.'

'Now,' Sylvie pleaded.

'No,' he said, beginning to kiss her neck, pressing his lips to her skin.

'Do you want me to beg?'

Jay put his hand around her neck and looked into her eyes.

'You never have to beg me,' he said. 'When the time's right, I promise.'

They kissed once more, but they were interrupted by the supercar roar from below the window.

'That will be Greg,' said Jay, a touch of sadness in his voice. 'I'll go meet him downstairs.' He wiped his mouth as he left.

Sylvie straightened her clothes and wandered dreamily over to her desk, closing the open windows and logging out of the stock tracking system. Beside her on the desktop were their half-filled bottles of beer. She ran her finger over the rim of the bottle that Jay's lips had touched and then she pressed it to her mouth in a cool glass kiss, before collecting her handbag onto her shoulder and heading downstairs.

Out in the brightly sunlit car park, Jay and Greg sat on the bonnets of their respective vehicles and talked to each other as they smoked. Sylvie put her hand up to wave at them.

'When are you coming for that drink?' Greg called out, standing up and grinning at her.

Sylvie shrugged, her eyes flickering nervously in Jay's direction, but he sat as cool and unreadable as ever.

Greg laughed and waved at her. Sylvie permitted herself one more glance, one look back in Jay's direction at him and his beautiful black Jaguar. She loved watching him leave in it, starting up the ignition and pulling slowly out of the office car park. She didn't know where he was going, only that it was probably somewhere important. Jay had that authoritative quality that Sylvie needed. He could contain her, guide her, allow her to breathe. Sylvie felt another huge surge of need that washed around her body, and she knew that she would do anything to be with him. Every step she took across the car park was a harrowing sludge against gravity, away from Him, the only person in the world she wanted to be near to.

Jay: What are you doing tonight?

Sylvie: Out in town with Sapna and co
Sylvie: The Three Butts
Sylvie: Why do you ask?

Jay: No reason, have a good one

That evening, on her run, Sylvie found herself chanting Jay's name in time with the thud of her feet against the woodland floor. After a shower, she lay down, still wet and naked, and brought herself to orgasm thinking of him inside her. She fell asleep with the images of the two of them together. She closed her eyes and imagined he was in bed next to her. As she wrapped her arms over her chest and pressed her hands to the backs of her shoulder blades, she imagined it was him touching her instead.

An alarm woke her just in time to get ready and she found she had no aches and pains, just a churning in the pit of her stomach, a void that screamed out to be filled. Sylvie showered, dressed and applied her usual minimal make-up. She planned to arrive in town a little after 7.30, the agreed-upon meeting time.

Six

Bones, Blood and Ballerinas

Sapna looked at Sylvie strangely when she first approached her, as if she recognized her but couldn't quite place her. Sylvie felt the familiar pang of social anxiety as she neared the group. There were six of them in a little cluster by the bar including Brett, who worked in the warehouse and who she knew had a massive crush on her; Jordan, another warehouse worker; and two women whose ages she couldn't decipher.

'Hi,' Sylvie said to no one in particular.

She expected Sapna to introduce her to the girls but she didn't. None of them showed her much interest except for Jordan who put his arm around her, and even though she usually hated to be touched by strangers, she was grateful this time.

'What you drinking?' he asked her.

'I'll . . . I'll get her drink,' said Brett.

It was endearing, Sylvie thought, the flush of red at his neck, the nerves catching in his throat. She had no real interest in him but still, it was nice to be liked, wasn't it?

'All right, all right,' Jordan laughed.

He removed his arm from where it had been resting, heavy over Sylvie's neck, and she felt strangely exposed, as though a safety blanket had been removed.

Brett sidled over, his watery blue eyes wide and alert, as if he was trying to take in as much of Sylvie as he could, scanning her face for the smallest reassurance.

'What do you want to drink?' he asked her.

'Uh, anything. What are you having?'

'Get a round of baby Guinnesses!' said Sapna loudly and the other two women cooed their approval.

Brett looked at Sylvie and she said, 'Sure,' even though she hadn't got a clue what a baby Guinness was. When he handed her the shot glass, she noticed the bitten skin around his fingernails. As he knocked back the drink, she watched the bobbing of the Adam's apple, the goosepimply skin there, scuffed up by a semi-blunt razor. Brett noticed her looking, and hastily wiped the corners of his mouth with his hand. Sylvie averted her eyes.

'You'll love it,' said one of the girls, referencing the full shot glass in her hand.

Sylvie thought it looked like dishwater. She knocked it back. It took two gulps to drain the glass. It was disgusting. The pub was getting busier. Clusters of people shuffled in, announcing their arrival with booming, sing-song voices like they were members of a pantomime cast. It was a small town, and everyone knew everyone there.

'You seem a bit out of place here,' Brett said, and he bent closer, putting his hand at the small of Sylvie's back, rather innocently, like he just wanted to be heard.

'Do I?'

'Yeah, you've never been here before, have you?'

Sylvie shook her head and then added, 'It's not so bad.'

It was impossible to follow the conversation of the group. Partly because of the alcohol and partly because she had no idea of the people, places or events they were referring to. It was as if she'd arrived three seasons and two episodes late to their favourite show.

'Oh my God, Tara's here . . .'

'Did you speak to her? I heard about her brother getting locked up.'

'Serves him right. Honestly, did you hear about the thing with Wajid?'

'No, I saw Connor and Mo last week, but they didn't say anything. Connor was fucked. What happened?'

Sylvie gave up trying and just let their words wash over her as she finished what was left in her glass. Jordan took the empty glass from her hand and replaced it with a Long Island Iced Tea from a magically self-replenishing tray of them.

'Happy Hour,' he explained, grinning.

Brett kept eyeing her, up and down her legs in the linen tunic dress she'd taken out of her mum's wardrobe. Sylvie felt like she was wearing a potato sack but the dress was from an expensive designer boutique, and it showed off her legs so she figured it was probably a good choice. She'd always had exquisite legs. Dancer's legs. The muscle tone had held up remarkably well. Every part of her leg was defined, ankle to calf to thigh, lithe and smooth and perfect. He was looking at Sylvie's face now and she was looking at his.

He inched closer. 'You . . . you want another drink?' he said, feeling his wallet in his hand as if mentally weighing it.

'I'm good,' Sylvie told him.

Then, Sylvie saw Jay behind her in the mirror that wrapped around the back of the bar. The outline of his face, cheekbones, the colour of his skin and the hair in his beard as specific and evocative to her as if they were the flag of her own personal nation. Was she hallucinating? He emerged more fully, his eyes hypnotic as he watched her, smiling slightly.

Sylvie whipped around to face him.

'What are you doing here?' she said.

Jay shrugged.

'Jay!' Sapna squealed demonstratively.

She wanted her friends to know she knew him, this handsome stranger. Brett and Jordan nodded half-hearted hellos. The last thing either of them wanted was for their boss to show up on their night out. The other girls hovered a little closer, eyeing him up like fresh meat.

'You want a drink?' Jay asked Sylvie, and then he added, 'I'll get a round.'

'Gin and tonic, please,' she said as he turned towards the bar.

The look he gave her then sent a chill up her spine and prompted the blonde girl to tug on Sapna's arm and pull the other girls into a huddle to whisper amongst themselves. Brett, considering himself bested for the time being, took Jordan off in the pursuit of more promising targets for the night. When Jay turned around again it was just Sylvie, standing there deserted.

'Where did they go?'

'I don't know.' Sylvie shrugged.

Jay laughed.

'Where's your boyfriend?' he asked Sylvie quietly.

'*Brett?*' Sylvie remarked with disbelief. 'He isn't my boyfriend.'

'That's not what he's been telling everyone.'

Sylvie thought he must be joking but he didn't smile.

'Let's go for a smoke,' Jay said. 'Come on.'

Sylvie followed him through the crowded bar out into a paved courtyard area with strung up fairy lights hanging from the walls over their heads. There were a few people sitting out at the benches but not many, a couple of men talking loudly over their beers, legs splayed, cigarettes hanging from between their fingers.

'You didn't seem surprised to see me,' he said.

They stood by a little wooden podium that had been affixed to the tree. He took a sip of his beer and put the glass down. He looked at Sylvie very intensely. His eyes stroked at her lips, her eyes, the outline of her body through her dress.

'I'm surprised you're not on a date or something,' he said.

'I'm not dating right now,' Sylvie said.

'I'm disappointed to hear it,' said Jay.

'You want me to go on dates?' she asked him. 'You know you don't have a say in that.'

'You're right,' he said. 'Because we're strangers, right?'

'Exactly.'

'And I take it Brett was lying then, about you two. Judging by the way you just abandoned him to come with me? A bit harsh, Sylvie,' he said, trying not to smile. 'You should have brought him along.'

'I didn't abandon him,' said Sylvie. 'He wandered off.'

'You didn't want to take him back to yours then?'

'No,' said Sylvie, looking down.

'Because he doesn't do it for you,' said Jay. 'He's not what you want.'

'He's a nice guy,' said Sylvie.

'But you don't want to rip his clothes off of him,' Jay said, quietly. 'And you want someone that makes you feel like that, don't you?'

Sylvie shook her head at him and took a sip from the top of her G&T.

'Yeah, you do,' he said with a mournful sigh of recognition, like he and Sylvie were the same.

It was not in her nature, all her life she'd exercised control, but since she'd met him, she often felt she was being eaten alive by lust. She felt it late at night when she lay awake and thought of Jay and he spilt over into her dreams. So many dreams of him and the office, of his hands, his lips, his voice. Orgasmic fantasies, waking and dreaming, that were so powerful her body responded of its own accord. He had wormed his way into her subconscious, an overpowering seduction, seduction that went down to the wood of her bones.

She smelt the vetiver of his cologne as he inched closer. She could feel the warmth of his body, so close to hers. He looked at her like he wanted to devour her. What a pleasure, to be eaten by him, Sylvie thought, to feel the rough under-edge of his molars, the sharpness of his incisors pressing the flesh at her upper arms, her thighs, her stomach. To see her crimson blood in the ridges between his teeth, pooling at his bottom lip like he'd taken a punch to the face.

'You do,' he repeated himself. 'And this Brett guy doesn't do it for you.'

'Are you jealous?' Sylvie said coolly, her expression as placid and emotionless as she could manage. 'Some guy's got a crush on me, so you had to come out looking for me on a Friday night? Couldn't wait till Monday?'

He laughed. 'Nah, I was heading back from somewhere. Thought I'd come for a quick pint before going home.'

'Heading back from where?'

'Somewhere,' he said.

'You can't tell me?'

'No.'

It was maddening.

'You're happy, aren't you?' He smiled. 'I did really want to see you, I wanted to make sure everything was all right between us, show you I was serious about liking you, because I am and soon it's all going to be easier. We just need to keep things quiet for now. Low-key, all right?'

'Well, this isn't really what I had in mind, meetings in the pub. It's sort of impersonal, isn't it?' Sylvie said.

'Yeah, it's a bit lame here,' said Jay, looking around the courtyard. 'Just be patient, Sylv, you need to trust me.' He took a swig of his drink and said, 'So what don't I know about you?'

Like all seductive people, Jay knew to talk little about himself and steer the direction always in Sylvie's direction.

'You know I was training to be a ballet dancer,' she said.

'A ballerina?' He smirked at this.

Since she stopped dancing, Sylvie noticed that men responded with especial interest to the whole ex-ballerina thing. It was sexualized: the svelte thinness and the extreme flexibility. She thought of ballet as something brutal and beautiful because of its brutality, like the ocean, a storm. However, while dancers act out the entwined lives of the great loves of literature and history, for the viewer there is no invitation of sex in ballet. Sylvie was consistently surprised and almost impressed by the male ability to find some ripple of sexual promise where there was none.

'Yeah.'

She hoped she hadn't been wrong about Jay. In her mind he stood alone, away from other men, more sensitive, more awake to the acute vibrations between things and people. He yielded some extraordinary supernatural power, over her anyway.

'Like Darcey Bussell?' he asked her.

He moved closer. The soft pink of his top lip was wet from his drink. His lips were something violent to Sylvie, she worried about the power they had over her. More than ever, she was dying to kiss them. She had never in her life wanted someone like this. She would have consummated her desire for him on first meeting, but these days stretched out like years with no promise of release.

He took her silence for surprise, saying, 'Are you shocked I know who that is? You are, aren't you?'

She confessed, 'A little bit.'

'I know a lot of things,' he said. 'Perhaps some things you wouldn't expect.'

Sylvie realized that he wanted to impress her. Despite his authority, his calmness, his coolness with his colleagues in the office, he held her in some kind of esteem. A small piece of him was as insecure and in need of assurance as anybody else. This was excellent news. She could find out what he needed and become it. She could discover exactly how to scratch the itch, the unsatisfied part of him.

'You know more about me than you let on,' she said, nodding at the cigarette he offered her. She put the filtered end between her lips and accepted the flame, blowing smoke into the air. 'You've seen my CV. You know where I went to school, you *knew* already that I went to ballet college, you know everything.'

'I don't think so,' he said, lighting his own cigarette and putting the lighter into the front pocket of his dark jeans. 'I think there's much more to you, Sylvie.'

I feel the same way about you, she wanted to say, but didn't. She tried to mimic his cool mystery. In the silence, she imagined them having sex, rough, right there on the varnished top of the outdoor bench, Sylvie's legs wrapped around his waist with everyone watching. She was thinking it, he was thinking it. A couple of girls came out into the courtyard and with the opening of the door, a swell of the music from inside reminded them of time and place. And of the consequences perhaps. Jay stubbed out his cigarette underfoot.

'Wanna go back in?'

Sylvie nodded. She followed him in, her knees shaking as she noticed the way the girls looked at Jay as they passed. He looked back at them, though Sylvie couldn't see the expression on his face. If she could, she'd be the only woman on earth for him.

'Oh, there you are.' Sapna seemed annoyed and approached them like an angry mother dealing with a pair of unruly kids. 'These guys want to move on to Mitchell's. Do you wanna come?'

Mitchell's was an even smaller, even divier bar further out on the outskirts of town, but they had karaoke on

Fridays and the drinks were dirt cheap. The other girls looked at Sylvie threateningly, as if to say, *Try and come with us, we dare you.*

'No,' said Sylvie. 'I think I'll head back.'

'Jay?' Sapna asked him.

'Got to get home,' he said.

The blonde girl tugged on the sleeve of Sapna's jacket.

'We're gonna get going,' said Sapna. 'See you at work, Jay.'

Sapna gave Sylvie a half-hearted squeeze around the neck and then the three of them headed off out of the door. Brett and Jordan were nowhere to be found, swallowed by the crowd around the bar.

'I should go,' said Sylvie. More out of nerves than anything else.

'How are you getting back?' Jay asked her.

Sylvie shrugged. 'Walking. It's not that far, maybe like twenty minutes.'

'That's too long in the dark,' he said. 'It's not the safest round here. I'll drive you.'

She followed him out to the nearest car park. Jay walked ahead, playing with his keys, a soft metallic jingle as they fell over and over into his palm. The headlights flashed a greeting.

'Get in,' said Jay.

Sylvie put her hand over the black handle as the Jaguar rumbled to life, lighting up across the dashboard. She pulled the door closed behind her. It was heavy. She felt the coolness of the leather seats under her bare legs. Jay lowered the window, his hand hanging down over the edge of the door.

He didn't look at her until they'd pulled out of the car park and the cold night air came in through the wide-open window in a rush.

'Do you want me to take you home?' he asked her, softly. 'Or do you want to drive?'

'I want to drive,' she said, without thinking.

Seven

Dancing Men to Death

Jay was different that night from the last time. As they raced down dual carriageways and sped through just-changing lights, Sylvie noted that there was something violent about him, a desperation perhaps, a need. She liked the way he grabbed her face like he owned it when he pulled up on the side of the road at the next street along from hers. His fingers dug into her jaw as he whispered that she was dangerous. Sylvie didn't know what he meant by this, she didn't want to be a danger to him, she only wanted to love him wholly. He goaded her, teased her, pulling away from her kisses, as he dared her to reach out and grab him, as he tested how badly she wanted him, and she did. More than anything. She wished she could put her hands around his neck. She wanted to bite him, to scratch him, to draw blood.

Jay gave in with a smirk, satisfied by Sylvie's desperation for him. He kissed her like an animal, with heat and longing on his breath. She could taste him, his spit, feel the warm slick contours of his tongue. She felt along the ridges of his teeth with the tip of her tongue and a shiver sparked up her spine. Sylvie would have liked to kiss his bones, and this was the closest she could get. He told her she was trouble before he bit her, hard little bites all along her jaw, her lips, her tongue. He pressed his lips to her ear and told her how bad a girl she was for tempting him, how gorgeous she was, how hard he was going to fuck her.

When Sylvie woke up around 10 a.m. the next day, she already had a message on her phone from Jay. The sight of it elated her. It made her feel as though she were so featherlight that she was going to float away.

Jay: Meet me at this address at 11pm

From the outside, the bar was fairly inconspicuous. It looked like any old dive bar nestled between a Subway and a pub with shuttered windows. But as Sylvie walked down the dark set of stairs, she began to hear the music, a thumping bass, and she saw lights, swirls of green and purple. The staircase opened up into a long narrow bar with one uninterested woman waiting behind it, who looked up from her phone as Sylvie passed. Then she saw Jay, waiting in front of a dark door without a sign. He put his hand through his hair and smiled as she approached.

'This way,' he said, pushing the door open for her.

It was a strip club with women dancing on poles and podiums, and booth tables upholstered in black leather arranged around the floor. Two men stood up to greet Sylvie and Jay with warm, cologne-drenched hugs. They introduced themselves as Abdyll and Simon. Jay put his arm around Sylvie's waist and, guided by him, she slid into the booth seat and he sat down beside her. Finally, she thought, we're side by side.

From the leather seats, they watched the dancers on the podium above them and, as the bassy music pounded on, Sylvie found herself entranced. It was hypnotic, the rhythmic snake-like undulations of the women's bodies, an arm sliding gracefully through the air, a woman gliding to her knees, her back against the pole. Her hair was illuminated under the stage lights, blowing softly under the air conditioning, a few strands blown back against her face, across one eye, over her softly parted lips.

Sylvie enjoyed watching them, although not in a sexual way. She'd never felt any sort of romantic or sexual pull towards another woman, but she had a great appreciation for the erotic and sensual beauty of the feminine form, and all the promises it seemed to hold. For the strength disguised by softness. She imagined the pain, years' worth of abdominal pain under softened tummies, now adorned with silver waist chains. The supple skin that curved like velvet over breasts and hips and buttocks and thighs. And their feet – she always found bare feet so vulnerable to look at – the dancer's small feet with sparkly painted toenails strapped into sky-high, transparent PVC stripper heels.

Sylvie watched and drank quietly, thinking that the women were beautiful. And that this kind of dance, the type that went on in the darkened private room, was an exercise in intimacy, in connection, in an exchange of energy between people who had no past and no future together. It was contained within one song. Sylvie felt that being a dancer captured something true about being a woman, performance, but also surrender to the performance and she missed it.

'Get a private dance for the new girl,' said Jay's friend Simon, noting Sylvie's interest in the dancers and mistaking it for desire. He nudged her arm playfully with a loose fist. 'Want one?'

'No, thanks,' Sylvie said, blushing.

'Jay will go with you.'

Sylvie looked at Jay. He smiled, a crooked, one-sided smile, and watched her steadily before taking a swig of his beer.

He shrugged. 'Come on, Sylv,' he said, 'it'll be a laugh.'

She could hardly protest. When she stood up, she hoped nobody would notice that her legs were trembling. She watched as Jay walked over to a dancer – she was not on stage or on a podium, just standing at the edge of it waiting her turn. She had blonde hair, shoulder-length and flicked over onto one side so that her neck was exposed. She wore a black thong and a translucent black lace triangle bra, so that her nipples could be seen through the fabric. Her body was like the women depicted in Greek statues, abundant and Venusian with no hard edges. She wore thick black eye make-up with silver glitter smudged over her lids, like the Milky Way. She had a tattoo on her forearm of a sunflower, which Sylvie felt was at odds with her overall impression of the dancer. She was sexy, and Sylvie felt a stab of jealousy when Jay engaged with her. The dancer pushed her chest towards Jay and her butt out back. It was a small adjustment, but Sylvie noticed it. She also noticed the dancer watching Jay's lips when he talked with slow-blinking, lustful eyes.

He looked back and gestured for Sylvie to come over.

'Take this before you go.' Simon held up a half-empty glass.

Sylvie knocked it back.

Jay and Sylvie followed behind the dancer as she walked to the private room. Sylvie felt Jay touch her hand. He entwined his fingers with hers. That feeling, the sensation of being palm to palm, of being interlinked, interwoven with him, was more intimate than sexual intercourse could ever hope to be. She felt the effect of the drink she'd just drained. It was not a buzzy, tipsy feeling but a low, smooth one, as if she were wading through caramel. She savoured it, her breath fragile with anticipation. She imagined her skin was like water-softened paper, just beginning to flake away, and her muscles so tender they might slide right off her bones. She felt closer to the animal side of herself than she had in years, since she could lace up her pointe shoes and become a daemon.

The dancer closed the door behind them, the three of them shut into a dark box of a room, with a seedy-looking black leather seat all along one side of the wall. There were spotlights over their heads which, filtered through Sylvie's blurred vision, became illuminated opals, white light melting into pink, into purple, green. Jay and Sylvie sat down with a bit of space between them. Sylvie wanted to look at him and see the expression on his face but she couldn't bring herself to, not yet. She looked down at her hands: her skin was buffed into something alien-like under the bright coloured light.

Music started playing loudly through the speakers over their heads and the woman's hips rolled in time to the beat. The dancer slid onto Jay's lap and leaned her head back against his shoulder, looking into Sylvie's eyes and reaching out to run her fingertips along the side of her face. They watched as she slowly peeled her bra straps from each shoulder before unclipping the clasp. She took off her knickers and got down to her knees in front of them, her torso and hips undulating as she ran her hands over her breasts, and stared deeply into their eyes, first Jay's and then Sylvie's.

Sylvie felt Jay shift closer towards her on the seat. He put his hand between them and pressed the tips of his fingers gently against her thigh. It was a light touch but the intention of it made her twitch between the legs. A glance in his direction confirmed it: he was gazing at her, eyelids heavy with want, drowsy on lust.

They left the private room and returned to the booth where the others were chattering loudly and ordering more drinks. Jay sat between Simon and Abdyll, and Sylvie perched on the end. While the men talked, she watched the dancers with fascination. Taking their money. Another, another. Dancing men to death. One man had three dances, one after the other. The women took his money emotionlessly, thanklessly, into the inner elastic of their garter belts.

'You all right?' Jay switched places, coming to sit beside Sylvie.

She felt him grab at her thigh under the booth table.

'Did you like the dance?' he asked her.

Sylvie nodded.

'I knew you would,' he said. 'I liked watching you in there.'

Sylvie felt his hand draw further up her thigh.

'I love that I can bring you here. It turns you on like it turns me on.'

He leant over and puts his lips against her neck. Sylvie stiffened in response to his touch, aware that the dancers, and his friends, could see them.

'Does it?' he asked her, between neck kisses. 'Docs it turn you on?'

'Yes,' Sylvie confessed.

'You're dangerous for me,' he said before putting her finger in his mouth and biting it gently.

His teeth nudged against her bones. She felt a sinking feeling, a sadness, when she questioned whether the space she occupied in his life, the role she fitted into, was one of a bad girl, a temptress. He would never bring a respectable women here whereas she, Sylvie, was a bastion of depravity. She didn't want a fling, she wanted him to know her – the raw, pathetic parts of her. She assumed he would want to know all of her because she wanted to know all of him. She wanted to know everything about his childhood, his first love, his first part-time job. She wanted to know every part of him that had been wounded or hurt in this lifetime and she wanted to love it, mend it, breathe life into it. She didn't know how to tell him this. She didn't want to be forbidden fruit, something to long for in the small hours and regret in the daylight. She wanted to nourish his bones, stick there like a metal rod to strengthen his spine.

But then Sylvie looked at him, into his hungry eyes, and she saw clearly that he loved her darkness. He loved that she was there in the black underground with him, his hand between her legs under the table. He loved that she could meet him, his dirtiness, and match him. Sylvie was willing to take his love in whatever form she could get it. For now, at least.

The only nearby hotel was a Best Western on the out-skirts of town. Jay said they couldn't go to his because his mum was there. She had to get a flight in the morning and Jay lived nearer than she did to the airport. As they climbed the stairs and walked down the brown paisley-patterned carpet, Jay with his arm around Sylvie's shoulders, she was happy but she felt inexplicably as though it couldn't last. She had waited for this moment for a very long time and she knew, as it was happening, that she would always remember it. She tried to store every part of it away in her memory. The light from the street through the waxy blinds, the rain outside the window, the lamp by the side of the bed, her feet, nails painted deep red, on the dark grey carpet. The tiny coffee table and the love seat where they sat and kissed for almost an hour. She was delaying things and what exquisite torture it was.

There was the shrill, intrusive sound of Jay's phone ringing but he silenced it and left it turned upside down on the bedside table. Sylvie let him unzip the back of her dress, plant kisses along her stomach and down between her thighs where he paused and looked up at her, saying softly, 'Do you like knives?'

Sylvie didn't know that she did, but she nodded anyway, afraid of disappointing him.

Jay took out a folding knife from his back pocket; she'd seen him use it before for cutting open boxes in the warehouse.

'Open your mouth,' he said.

She opened it.

He ran the knife-edge along her tongue, over her chest, pressing it gently into the flesh of her stomach. Sylvie waited for the sharp sting of the blade, but it didn't come.

She trusted him, she surrendered. Her body was his to use however he liked, and he knew this.

Jay's face hovered over hers. The light was dim. His expression was serious, analytic. Sylvie reached up to kiss him, eager to maintain the momentum, her neck and her shoulder blades curved away from the mattress towards him. She felt the sharp edge of the blade across her throat, a pressure forcing her head back onto the pillow where she was caught up between its softness and the hard edge of the knife. She looked into Jay's eyes, and he looked into hers. She felt the knife edge press even harder against her throat, and she would have gasped had she dared to move an inch. Suddenly, the pressure released, and Jay tossed the knife onto the bedside table and grabbed Sylvie by the wrists, pinning them over her head against the back of the headboard. He held them tight in one hand while he worked open the zip on his jeans with the other. Sylvie didn't care that her wrists were being crushed in his grip. Her mouth went dry with anticipation.

'I've had dreams about this,' she said. 'So many dreams.'

The rain beat on the outside of the window. Jay held tight to her wrists. Sylvie's neck curved up away from the pillow once more, she couldn't help it. She needed to kiss him. He saw this and denied her, told her gruffly to open her legs.

'Wider,' he said.

She obeyed him. Sylvie gasped as he entered her, an electric spark that started between her legs and ran like a lit wick along her spine.

'Are you okay?' he'd ask her occasionally, answering her silent nod by going deeper than before.

Sylvie badly wanted to kiss him, to complete the circuit of fire that raced through her. Seeing this, Jay paused.

'Look at me,' he said.

Sylvie looked at him, his beautiful face. His forehead was beading with sweat and she wanted it all over her skin like rain, she could have licked it from his brow. At the thought she felt herself tightening around him, an internal flex that pulled him in tighter. Jay groaned. He released her wrists and put one hand around her neck instead.

'Open your mouth,' he said.

Sylvie looked up at him, opening her mouth. Jay leant closer, his grip tightening around her neck. He spat into Sylvie's mouth before he kissed her. Sylvie grabbed hold of the back of his neck, holding him there with his open mouth against hers. She worked her hips as hard as she could, faster, back and forth until she made him come. They were both breathless and dazed. It was the culmination of so much dreaming and more than even she had imagined.

And then he held her tight up in the crook of his armpit, her cheek against his chest as he stroked her hair.

'Should we . . . get to know each other?' she ventured.

Jay laughed, planting a small kiss on the crown of her head.

'I'd say we know each other pretty well now, wouldn't you?' he said.

'No.' Sylvie blushed. 'I mean, like *really* get to know each other, like things no one else would know.'

Jay yawned. 'I'm a very private person.'

'Why?' she asked him.

'Why am I private?'

'Yeah.'

'Well ...' Sylvie saw that he was thinking, and this pleased her, the idea of finally getting inside his head, the chance to dig around in his mind and unearth the real him. 'Once you accept that no one cares about you but yourself, you lose interest in letting people in.'

'You think no one cares about you?'

'I know it,' he said. 'I learnt the hard way, growing up. Don't feel sorry for me,' he scoffed. 'I'm fine with it – if anything I feel bad for all the people who live in a state of delusion. Better to face the reality and get on with it.' He changed the subject then. 'What about you, what was your childhood like?'

'Idyllic, sort of,' she said. 'I'm lucky.'

'You don't sound pleased about it.'

'I don't want to say boo-hoo, poor me, my parents didn't get me, because that's a cliché but ... I don't know. The most important things in my life, the whole way I exist, I don't think they could ever understand. And that's ...'

'Lonely?'

He kissed her forehead again.

'Yes,' she sighed. 'It's lonely.'

They lay in silence for a few minutes.

'Can I ask you something personal?' Sylvie said.

'This hasn't been personal?'

'What do you want?'

'To eat?' he asked. ''Cause I'm starving, should we go to the drive-thrus again?'

'No,' Sylvie said, mock-punching him on the arm. 'I mean, what do you want in life? What would *really* make you happy?'

There was a pause as he pondered the question.

'When I was younger,' he said, 'I used to come home from school every day, my mum would be crying about the bills, the debts we had racking up since my dad left. I was too young to work but I'd put my head down on the pillow every night and dream about money. Not just enough of it but a lot, like a cupboard full of gold bars and a pirate's treasure trove of all these rubies and diamonds. It was like, money was the most important thing in the world, it could solve anything, cure anything. I knew if I could get enough of it, I could fix things.'

He took a laboured sigh then and looked at Sylvie, studied her face, a questioning look as if he were considering how much to tell her, whether or not he should let her in. He continued, 'I started working a paper round at twelve, at fourteen I got a job at a shooting ground, about the same time I fell in with a group of local boys. They were all older than me, involved with dealing and gangs and all that, none of it scared me. They gave me more money than I'd ever seen for the odd gun smuggled out from the range.

I felt invincible then. I would have gone straight to juvenile prison if I'd been caught but I was careful. The owner's son would check guns in and out but he'd quite often forget. It was easy to blame it on him.

'And then I was dealing for a while. I was smart with that too, saved everything I made and got out as soon as I could.'

'And the gun in your car?'

He shrugged. 'I like guns. I have all kinds, some legal, some not quite. I shoot rabbits on my property. You've got to, or they infest the place. The first time I felt guilty, but I'm used to it now. Whenever it all gets too much, I take this shotgun I've had for years, out into the back fields, and I wait, all day if I have to, for just the right moment to pull the trigger and I feel this incredible release.'

There was a shyness in his expression. 'I don't know why I'm telling you this.'

'I'm glad you are,' she said.

'Why?'

'I want to know everything about you. I want to study you,' she laughed. 'I want to write the book on James Lakemore.'

'You really think I'm worthy of all that?' He looked at her like a little boy, uncertain, hopeful.

Sylvie kissed him very gently on the lips.

'I think you're everything,' she told him.

Sylvie wanted more than anything to be close to him, closer than close, she wanted to unzip his skin and climb inside it. If only, she thought, if only you would just let me love you, you have no idea how happy I could make you.

'There's something I've never told anyone,' she said. 'The reason I stopped dancing, the reason I had to quit ballet school.' She rolled her eyes. 'Well, I didn't exactly quit, I was expelled.'

He stroked her shoulder and looked deeply into her eyes in a way that urged her to continue. 'You can trust me, Sylvie.'

'I know I can, and I want to tell you.'

'I'm listening.'

'I had a great-aunt, my Aunt Jacqueline, who was like a goddess to me. But anyway, I was in my final year at ballet school, at Willow Way, and we were doing *Giselle*, and I was going to play the main part, and everything was going to be perfect and then out of nowhere, Aunt Jacqueline told me she was sick and then a few months later she was gone.'

Sylvie paused, choked up by the memories. She felt Jay squeeze her shoulder though she couldn't see him clearly through the bleary-eyed haze.

'It destroyed me. I felt myself declining every day, the days I could actually bring myself to go to class. The grief was all-consuming. I was getting worse, I couldn't perform. There was another girl in my class, Ffion, and she was breathing down my neck, just waiting to take my place. It was driving me insane. Ballet was the only thing I'd ever wanted, and she was getting ready to snatch it from me. It wasn't fair.' Sylvie looked at him, tears streaming from her eyes. 'I won that part, it was mine. It was supposed to be me.' She wiped her tears with the back of her hand. 'I knew if I didn't do something they were going to take away my part and give it to her. I had to do something. So I hurt her.'

'What happened?'

Sylvie shook her head, trying to dislodge the long-buried memories from crawling out of their graves. 'It doesn't matter. Plus, I was expelled so she got my part anyway. They didn't want to risk any bad press or their reputation or anything, so they quietly asked me to leave.'

'Did you hurt her badly?' Jay asked her, a soft growl in his throat.

'Yes,' said Sylvie. 'I would have done anything, tried *anything* to get her out of my way.'

Jay nodded like he understood, pulling her in tenderly by the back of the neck and giving her a deep kiss.

As they lay on their backs, looking up at the ceiling, Sylvie said, 'I have this rage inside. It's buried right here.' She put her hand to her stomach.

'I see it,' Jay said, he took his finger and ran it gently under each of her eyes. 'I see it in your eyes, you know how to want things, to really want them. Me too.'

They lay still in silence for a few moments, Sylvie warmed with the feeling that she had found *the one*. Her soulmate.

'What was it about ballet that you loved so much?' he asked her.

Sylvie thought about it for a few seconds, before saying, 'The freedom, the ecstasy ... the pain. Really, it's about conquering yourself, embracing the pain. The pain is inevitable, the pain is the cure. There's something about me that needs to hurt.'

Jay hoisted her on top of him by the waist, pulling her into a straddle.

'Where have you been all my life?' he said. 'You were fucking made for me.'

'Jay,' Sylvie whispered. 'I love you.'

There was a pause before he said, 'I love you too.'

Sylvie gasped, she couldn't help it. She couldn't ever remember being as happy. She committed it to memory, tattooed it onto her heart. I-love-you. She would remember Jay saying those words for ever.

Jay went on, 'You just have to trust me, okay? We're going to be together one day soon like a normal couple, I promise. We just have to keep things under wraps for a while.'

'I trust you,' Sylvie said, relieved, certain that Jay just needed some time to figure out the right way to break the news to everyone at work.

They fell asleep beside each other for a few blissful hours. Then Jay's face was over Sylvie's and he was gently shaking her awake, telling her they had to go. Sylvie dressed sleepily, still dazed and perhaps half-asleep. Outside, dawn was breaking. The car was icy cold, their breath formed clouds in the frigid air.

'You should have worn something warmer,' he said, as Sylvie shivered in the passenger seat. 'Summer's over now.'

The journey was just five minutes from the hotel to the road next to Sylvie's where he'd dropped her off last time.

'You could give me your jacket,' she said, quietly.

It was a leather aviator jacket with a sheepskin collar.

'You know I can't,' he said, softly. 'We're almost home.'

Sylvie started to cry then. She didn't know why exactly, something about his tone of voice, the seediness of driving around town in the early morning, the fragility of their hopes and plans. She was so happy and yet the tears fell thick into her lap, one after the other.

'Don't cry,' Jay said, turning up the hot air in the car and tilting the vent to aim it at her. 'It's gonna be fine. I'll see you at work, okay?'

'Okay.'

When he pulled the car over at the side of the road, he put his fingers under her chin, tilted her face up towards him and kissed her.

When he moved back, he said in a gentle coaxing whisper, almost as if he were speaking to a child who'd just woken up from a bad dream, 'If you ever tell anyone what we did, I'm going to kill you.'

Sylvie nodded, observing the blazing intensity in his green eyes. She unclipped her seat belt and got out of the car. As soon as she'd shut the door, he drove away without looking back.

Eight

My Kind of Girl

'Hey!' It was Brett, smoking a cigarette outside the entrance with his warehouse friends, the group of them on their lunch break.

'Going to Tesco Express!' Sylvie said, showing him a wide smile and walking swiftly past him to show she really *didn't* want to talk.

'Hang on!' He started a little jog and caught her up.

'Yes?'

'You haven't responded to my texts,' he said. 'You've been avoiding me.'

Sylvie hadn't even given him her number. It must have been Sapna. So when she'd received a 'Hey, Sylvie, it's Brett from work. How are you doing?' at 11 a.m. on Saturday she hadn't felt obliged to respond. And anyway, she'd been distracted.

'I haven't been avoiding you,' she said breezily, although she didn't think he was buying it.

'Are you gonna come out with us again soon?' he asked her. 'Or . . . just out with me. We could get dinner or go to the cinema. What do you reckon?'

'Yeah maybe,' said Sylvie with a sigh. 'I've just been so busy, and I don't think I'm ready to date right now, it's not you. I'm sorry.'

Brett frowned. His whole demeanour changed, his tone was hostile when he said, 'That's funny, because I've heard some rumours about you. People talk, you know.'

'Excuse me?'

'I'm not getting involved,' he said. 'But you should be more careful, you don't want to get yourself a reputation.'

'I have no idea what you're talking about.'

'You don't, do you? So you're not hanging out in town with the boss? He's not driving you around everywhere?'

'Look,' Sylvie said. 'I don't want to go out with you. There's no need to get nasty about it.'

'But there's something you should know,' he said. 'Hey, look, maybe you already know but just in case—'

'Brett, I don't want to hear it,' said Sylvie. 'Don't embarrass yourself. I don't want you, okay? End of.'

Sylvie walked to her car as quickly as she could. It was nothing, just Brett being jealous and bitter and trying to mess with her. Nothing to worry about. But she would mention it to Jay just in case.

*

That Thursday Jay invited Sylvie along to his mate Abdyll's bachelor pad (or palace, rather) in the countryside. The party consisted of Abdyll and Simon, who Sylvie had met at the strip club, and a couple of women with long dark hair and pointy acrylics, who were quiet and dedicated most of their attention to snapping selfies by the pool. The swimming pool was indoors in a log cabin with wooden walls and overhead beams. It was about twenty metres in length and lit from below so that the rippling water cast sparkling white spots onto the ceiling. Sylvie and one of the women, whose name was Claudia, floated about on lilos. The wrinkled pads of Claudia's toes passed by close to her face. The men, reduced to boys, catapulted themselves into the deep end and Abdyll doggy-paddled over, hair slicked down over his forehead.

'Here comes trouble,' said Claudia.

Her friend Gianna sat up at the edge of the pool with her legs dangling in the water and watched with intense focus.

'Ladies.' Abdyll gave them a grin and then Sylvie startled at the feel of his hand around her ankle. Immediately her eyes searched for Jay. 'You like the pool?' he asked her.

Sylvie nodded. 'It's really nice.'

'Yeah?' Abdyll's eyes scanned up and down her body, her legs and stomach, her black lacy underwear drenched through and slick against her skin.

'Lovely place,' she said. 'Remind me, I don't remember what you do for a living.'

Abdyll winked at her. 'Jay didn't tell you? He's done a couple jobs for me.'

'Foam fingers?'

'He don't do nothin' legal,' said Claudia.

'Come on, Claudia, man. You're scaring our new friend.'

'I'm not scared,' Sylvie said. And she wasn't, she was just curious.

But she didn't pry any further. She looked up and saw Jay standing by the side of the pool in a black robe, smoking a cigarette and talking to Simon. Jay looked at her every few seconds, at Abdyll. The tightness in his jaw betrayed his discomfort despite the frequent smile he tossed Simon's way. Sylvie was pleased, the idea of Jay's jealousy made her warm inside.

Claudia nagged and nagged Abdyll until he disappeared off into the main house and returned with a portable speaker. Claudia played her Spanish music so loudly that you could hear it under the water – Sylvie knew this because at one point, Abdyll grabbed a hold of the edge of the lilo she was lying on and flipped it upside down, so for a few seconds, she was floating at eye level with his Versace-clad bulge. When she regained her balance and emerged from the water, she splashed him, angrily.

'Hey, hey,' he said, putting up his hands and smirking. 'Just a joke, sweetheart.' And then, in a whisper, 'My kind of girl. Maybe we'll spend some time together when you and Jay are finished.'

'Don't talk to me,' Sylvie snapped. She climbed out of the pool and put on one of the waiting black robes.

Jay approached and put his arm around her waist. They kissed. A small but meaningful one.

Someone had set up a dartboard on the far wall and Simon was taking his turn, swinging the dart back and forth through the air in a practice throw. Abdyll stood by his side and cheered mockingly.

'Will you shut up?' said Simon through gritted teeth.

He threw the dart, a spectacular miss. Abdyll applauded him, slowly, and slapped him on the back of the shoulder.

'Nice try, mate,' he said. 'My turn.'

Much to the annoyance of everyone else, he scored a perfect bullseye.

There were plenty of drinks, more darts, loud music, and they were all tipsy and weak-bodied from the sauna, steam and swimming pool. Jay put his hand around the back of Sylvie's neck, gripping it firmly, his hand over her water-slicked hair.

'Come with me,' he whispered into her ear.

His whisky-laced breath sent a shiver down her spine. She put her hand into his and he led her back to the driveway where he opened the glovebox and presented Sylvie with the pistol. He laughed at the frightened look on her face.

'It's locked,' he said. 'Here, hold it.'

She held her hands out, her two palms open flat and held together as if she were a child receiving a gift. It was heavy. Sylvie peered up close to it like it was some alien creature she'd just discovered, observing the mottled cast on the handle, the horizontal lines along the barrel.

Jay's eyes shone as he watched her. 'It's a Beretta nine thousand,' he said. 'You want a go?'

'Where?'

They went through the gate into the garden, out of view of the swimming pool. It was a modern garden, a small patio of light grey slate and then a long expanse of fake grass that backed onto open fields.

Jay unlocked it for her, cocked it and showed her how to hold her arms; he stood behind her, wrapping his arms around hers, his finger over hers on the trigger. Sylvie was trembling. She would say it was from the frigid night air on her scalp, her wet hair in the cold, but it was because of the gun, which both frightened and excited her.

'Aim up into the trees,' he said.

They pressed the trigger together. A ripple of energy shocked along Sylvie's arms and vibrated the bones against the walls of her chest. Jay took the gun from her – it hung in his hand by his side – and pulled her towards him with his other hand to kiss her. Sylvie was wary of the loaded gun in his hand, but she kissed him back.

'Did you feel it?' he asked her, excitement in his eyes, the corners of his lips curving upward into a smile.

'Feel what?'

'The release.'

Sylvie nodded. 'Yes.'

'Let me fire a few on my own,' he said.

'Sure.'

She watched him, his stance, the muscles flexing along his back. The cold, distant look in his eyes as he pulled the trigger reminded her of the threat he'd made after their night together in the hotel. Surely a joke, she thought, but there was a darkness in him. It was why she'd been so drawn to him in the first place. The sound of the gunshots ringing out in the dark emptiness reminded her that things would never be simple with Jay. With him, love and suffering and violence and sex were all hopelessly tangled up together and would never be unpicked.

'Come here.' Jay pulled her closer.

He tugged at the belt of her black robe and pulled it down to her waist, leaving her chest bare in the night-time chill. The cool air prised goosebumps from her flesh and made her heart race. Jay took the gun and ran the shaft over her chest, over her nipples which were hard from the cold. He pressed the gun gently to the side of her cheek, watching her, his shallow breath ragged with arousal. He put his left arm around her waist and drew her in towards him, their clouded breath mingling in the air. With his right hand, he put the gun up under the bottom of Sylvie's robe between her legs. She startled as the cool metal met her skin, but the pleasure soon overran her and she jutted her chin up to meet him, her lips pursed, seeking a kiss. He refused her lips.

Jay's car crawled slowly along the street next to Sylvie's, the usual spot where he dropped her off. They stopped under a street lamp. He leant across the middle of the car to kiss her, pulling her in by the back of the neck. When Sylvie looked down at the glovebox it was as if she had X-ray vision; she saw the contours of the gun glowing through the container.

'There have been rumours about us, apparently,' she said, nervous.

'What?' Jay's green eyes blazed.

Sylvie felt herself shrinking smaller and smaller in the passenger seat of the car. She resisted pulling her knees up to her chest and ducking her head down between them.

'Brett from the warehouse, he said people know about us.'

'So you've been bragging to your boyfriend about us?' he spat.

'Bragging to my . . .?'

Stunned into silence, Sylvie squinted hard at the dashboard, trying to think of the right thing to say.

'What do they know?'

He was so hostile and seemed so angry that Sylvie was at a loss for words. There was no trace of the man who'd held her in his arms and told her he loved her. He'd been cold towards her before, but this was different. It was like he hated her.

'I don't know, I could try and find out,' she offered.

'What, are you stupid? That's the worst thing you could do.'

'I'm sorry, I'm just trying to help.'

'Don't.'

All she could think to do was get out of the car as soon as possible and hope that things would be better in the morning.

'I've got to go,' she said, shutting the car door behind her.

Jay's car sped past her down the road. As she walked home, her shoulders hunched up to her ears to brace herself against the cold, Sylvie kept envisioning Jay's eyes, glaring green eyes, like a mirage at the end of the road. She crawled into bed and begged God, the universe and all its angels, and failing that, her own mind, for a solution. She needed to reassure him. She didn't think about losing him, the thought was too much for her.

Act Two

Nine

The Emerald Insult

Something was off. With Jay. It was too soon to say she knew him inside and out, but she'd observed enough to see that something was amiss. Sylvie had hardly seen him in the week since Abdyll's, barely communicated with him apart from a few texts, and he'd only been in the office a couple of times. Sylvie was desperate to see him, and he promised her she soon would. He was busy working on something away from the office, but he'd make time. She believed him, how could she not? It was all she wanted to be true.

But that morning it was clear something was wrong. Jay was already there when she arrived, sitting in his room with the door closed. Sylvie thought he must have been busy with some kind of urgent matter that had brought him into the office so early. She sat at her desk and tried to busy herself with little tasks Derek and Karen had passed on to her via email. 'Chase this colour foam up with the manufacturer.' 'Start working out the factory staff rota for the first week of next month.' 'Urgent: We've been out of mint Club biscuits for a whole week now – will somebody please re-stock them!' By 'somebody', they meant Sylvie. She got up from her chair and put her handbag over her shoulder.

'You might want a jacket.' Karen swivelled on her chair to look her up and down over her glasses. 'It's a bit nippy out there. Autumn's here.'

'I didn't bring one,' said Sylvie.

She permitted herself one more look into Jay's room as she passed him on the way to the stairs. He was on the phone, standing in the corner of the room, his neck bowed into the wall. Sylvie felt a sickly sensation in her stomach. Something *was* wrong. It was as though an enormous dense black cloud had blown overhead, blocking out the sunlight, her whole world gone dark. She hoped to be able to make eye contact with him, for a small smile across the office, for something, anything to put her mind at ease. As she pushed open the door and walked out into fresh air across the car park, she realized that Karen had been right, it was colder than it had been in months. Sylvie's arms prickled with goosepimples as the cool air engulfed her. Thankfully, it was only a short walk to the Tesco Express.

Sylvie: Hey, is everything all right?

As she roved the aisles hunting for Derek's biscuits, she took her phone in and out of her pocket several times in response to an imagined vibrating sensation. Brilliant, she thought, picking up three packets of mint Clubs, I am actually losing my mind. Once she'd paid, Sylvie checked her phone again, opening her messages with Jay to see whether he'd read her text. Jay *had* read the message (at 10:09 to be exact) and four minutes had passed without a response. Sylvie hurried back to the office. She was too wired and walking too briskly to think about the cold. It's over, she thought as she climbed the stairs. It's over already. The thought made her feel helpless, as though the thread that connected her to sanity and purpose had been severed and now she was floating, aimlessly, through the cosmos.

'Here.' She practically threw the biscuits at Derek. Although he was embroiled in a heated phone call of his own (welcome to the high-pressured, dog-eat-dog world of foam fingering), he received them gratefully, tearing open the first packet and taking an enormous bite out of the chocolate-covered biscuit.

'I'm making a cup of tea,' Sylvie muttered, turning as she passed Jay's room to see that he was back at his laptop.

He still didn't look up. Sylvie checked her phone as she turned the kettle on. Nothing. Desperate times called for desperate measures and Sylvie was not above admitting that she was desperate. She wandered over to Jay's room and knocked on the door frame, holding up the kettle in response to Jay's hostile expression.

'Do you want tea?'

'No,' he said. And then after a pause, 'No, thank you.'

Sylvie shut the door and returned to the kitchenette, flicking on the kettle and leaning against the wall as she waited for it to boil. A white-hot flush of panic circulated her veins. She must have done something. It was over before it ever even started. But the way he looked at her just days ago, the way he'd kissed her. She pressed her fingertips against her lips at the memory. Sylvie wondered if she'd imagined it all, the messages, the touches, the kisses. It all felt so distant and unreal.

'Annabel!' Karen rushed up from her chair to greet someone. She ushered her into the office with her arm over her shoulder like they were old friends.

Sylvie abandoned the kettle and crossed the office floor to her seat, intrigued by this unexpected visitor. This woman was sleek, her appearance was so polished it gave the impression of a high gloss finish, like she'd been painted all over in enamel varnish. She was young, maybe just a few years older than Sylvie. She had shiny, golden blonde hair bouncing at her shoulders, as if she'd just walked out of a salon. She wore a blue and white striped shirt under a light, quilted navy Barbour, white trousers that stopped just above the ankle, and tan leather boots. She was tall, her legs were long and her wrists, visible below her jacket cuffs, dripped with silver bracelets on fine chains.

'Oh, Annabel,' Karen gasped, her typically uninterested drawl suddenly infused with enthusiasm, 'you haven't met Sylvie, our new start.'

The blonde woman turned over her shoulder and flicked her hair back out of her face. Sylvie was met with a waft of Jo Malone English Pear and Freesia and a stark realization that made her heart drop to the bottom of her stomach. This was the woman from the photograph, the one she'd found at the back of the cabinet in Jay's room. She'd put it out of her mind but here she was in the flesh, beaming at her with very white teeth, and holding out her hand for Sylvie to shake. Her skin was cold and soft.

'This is Jay's wife,' said Karen, announcing with cheerful gusto the worst news Sylvie had ever heard.

She felt her stomach curdle, the bile churning in the pit of it. Sylvie looked down at the woman's left hand and sure enough, there was a marquise-cut diamond on her ring finger that glinted, taunting her, under the fluorescent lights. It took all her muster just to squeak hello and keep herself upright.

'I'm Annabel,' she said. 'Nice to meet you, darling.'

Sylvie thought she had one of those aristocratic, almost feline, faces with small eyes and a lot of cheek. Her face was covered in fine down like peach-fuzz, with a South of France tan. Around her neck she wore an emerald on a fine silver chain.

'I like your necklace,' said Sylvie, her mouth dry.

Annabel looked down at it like she'd forgotten it was there, then back at Sylvie, flashing her white smile.

'Have it,' she said.

'What? No, I couldn't.' Sylvie felt herself blush, humiliated twice over by this woman's presence and her generosity.

The value of the necklace – it certainly looked like a real emerald – made it feel like an insult.

'No, really.' She unclipped the fastener with ease. 'I've just bought a new version of practically the exact same thing. Take it. It will only go into the back of a drawer and stay there.' She grabbed at Sylvie's wrist with her right hand and pressed the necklace into her palm with her left. The metal was still warm from her skin, and the intimacy of this made Sylvie's stomach turn.

'It will suit you,' Annabel said, still smiling, and then, her attention switching suddenly, 'Where's James? Anyone seen him about?'

'I'll go and have a look for him downstairs,' said Karen.

'I'll come with you,' said Annabel. 'He's always disappearing, that one.'

Annabel smiled at Sylvie again before she left, a closed-mouth, sympathetic smile. 'Nice to meet you! See you around.'

Sylvie waved goodbye and then looked down at the emerald in her hand. She didn't know what to do with it. She had half a mind to throw it in the bin. She didn't want it. She put it in her trouser pocket and sank into her desk chair on shaky legs. She entirely forgot about making a drink. She was stunned; her thoughts raced so quickly and loudly through her brain that it felt like they were echoing around her. He has a wife, of course he has a wife. No ring though. This changes everything. This changes nothing. I love him. Shut up. How can you love him? You don't even know him. But the way he touched you, the way he kissed you. I need to speak to him. What is there to say? He lied. He's married. It's over. Sylvie was dizzy with confusion, her stomach gurgled. She worried that she would throw up.

Sapna appeared then, passing quickly through the office and gesturing at Sylvie to follow her.

'Me?' Sylvie whispered, putting her hand to her chest.

Sapna rolled her eyes. 'Who else? Come on.'

Derek raised an eyebrow but said nothing.

Sylvie followed Sapna into the kitchenette where they were safely shielded behind a screen of frosted glass. Sapna looked Sylvie up and down, 'Are you all right? You look a bit . . .'

'Not feeling great,' she said. 'Think I'm getting a cold.'

Sapna screwed up her nose and took half a step backwards.

'I've just come from downstairs,' she explained, her eyes shining with excitement. 'I bumped into Jay's wife. Have you met her?'

'Yes,' said Sylvie. 'She seems . . . nice.'

Sapna shook her head, smiling. 'That poor, clueless woman.'

'What do you mean?'

Sylvie felt her heart drumming against her ribcage like the timekeeper in a marching band.

Sapna looked left and right over her shoulder before reaching over and turning the kettle on. 'To mask the sound,' she said with a conspiratorial look in her eye. 'Come on, Sylvie, don't play dumb, you thought she was coming here to confront you, didn't you?'

'What?'

Sapna rolled her eyes. 'Everyone knows he's got a thing for you.'

Sylvie blushed. 'I don't know about that.'

'But I guess that should be the least of her worries, considering.'

'What do you mean?'

'Well, Jay has a double life, sort of.'

'What?'

'Oh, yeah, he hangs out with Simon Pelham and Abdyll Murati all the time. They're like local gangsters, I guess. Abdyll's his best mate and he only just got out of prison.'

Sylvie remembered Abdyll's grin, his hand around her ankle while she bobbed about on the lilo in his swimming pool.

'Really? What for?'

'Mhmm, pretty sure it was assault, or dealing or whatever. He's definitely involved in something dodge.'

'Who?' Sylvie breathed. 'Jay?'

Sapna nodded.

'How do you know?'

Sylvie was practically on the verge of collapse.

'Everyone knows everyone in this town. Word gets around. Jay and his mates always go to this place. What's it called, what's it called?' She pressed her middle and index fingers to the side of her forehead as she racked her brains. 'Some place in town anyway with a rooftop and you can smoke shisha and apparently –' her voice dropped a few decibels – 'get this, right. Apparently, there's some back room for big spenders with strippers and poles and all that.'

'Round here? That sounds unlikely.' It was a great effort for Sylvie to force words out of her mouth, but she knew that an overreaction would give her away, and it was important to keep up the semblance of impartiality. She could piece it all together again when she was in private.

'Yeah, and it's thirteen quid for a double JD and Coke,' Sapna said, with disgust in her voice.

'Criminal,' said Sylvie, before adding, as casually as she could muster, 'How do you know his wife's in the dark about it?'

'I can just tell.' Sapna said this with such certainty that Sylvie immediately accepted it. 'You've met her – tell me that woman's cool with her husband hanging out with the drug dealers in a strip club every week? She's bougie as fuck and she's from proper old money.'

'Mm, maybe,' said Sylvie.

'She is. They have vineyards in France or something and that's just *one* of the businesses. Jay never talks about it, but I looked her up when I first met her. Her dad has a whole Wikipedia page, it's crazy. It's proper jarring,' she said, shaking her head. 'I'm a girl's girl though, so whenever I see Annabel, I actually feel bad for her, which is so stupid because she's like a millionaire and I'm basically on minimum wage.'

'Mm.' Sylvie had to agree with her. Annabel hardly looked like the type to accept her husband consorting with local gangsters in underground strip clubs.

'And then there's the girls,' Sapna said, flicking the switch on the kettle so that it juddered alive once more.

Sylvie flinched. 'What girls?'

'The girls he sees. One of them has a sister who went to college with my mate. She was seeing Jay for like six months a couple years ago, and then it ended, and she had a nervous breakdown or something and had to move in with her mum in Portsmouth. Though kind of serves her right, messing around with a married man and all that.'

'Crazy.' Sylvie could only manage the one word.

'You want one?' Sapna shook the carton of PG Tips at her.

'No, thanks,' said Sylvie. 'I've got loads of work to do.'

Sapna shrugged.

Sylvie, stunned, sank into her seat, unable to focus her vision on the screen. She was flooded with thoughts; she felt as though she were drowning in her own mind.

Leave it alone, Sylvie, she thought to herself, forget him. Why would you want to get mixed up with a person like that anyway? Except it was too late. She was already mixed up with him, or he was mixed up in her. All the molecules of her body sang out for him.

By one o'clock she was practically climbing the walls. She couldn't take it any longer. She took herself outside for a 'smoke break' although she didn't smoke. She turned back to look at the storage shed behind the warehouse and saw Jay and Annabel there talking. Jay smoked a cigarette and Annabel wore a reflective pair of sunglasses, her chin turned up into the sunlight and her arms crossed over her chest. The scene was sombre, Sylvie thought. There was no giddiness, no trace of romance, no laughter. It was impossible at her distance to gauge what they were talking about. She wanted – but strongly resisted – to rush over and confront Jay, asking him why he'd let her feel like the only girl in the world, what it was that he'd wanted from her, surely he didn't think he could have kept his wife a secret for ever. She didn't know what she thought.

'Too much caffeine,' was Sylvie's excuse for pacing the stained carpet like a caged big cat. Around two-thirty, she opened a packet of fig rolls from the biscuit cupboard and ate six of them. This behaviour surprised her, but the hunger was deep and gnawing. She knew she could eat and eat and eat the entire contents of that biscuit cupboard even though her stomach was already bloating with the sudden, foreign influx of wheat and sugar. The afternoon groaned on and for the first time, Sylvie left the office that evening before anyone else. She had done nothing but tap her foot and replay everything in as much detail as she could, combing over the contents of every message, every conversation. As soon as the clock on her computer flashed

4:36, she muttered an excuse about feeling ill, gathered her things and bolted.

Her heart was a fragile quiver in her chest when she pushed open the foyer door and strode out into the car park. Jay was there. She'd expected him to be long gone but there he was, leaning against the bonnet of his shiny black Jag smoking a cigarette. There was no sign of Annabel. Sylvie had to stop herself from rushing at him, her pain becoming anger. She was overwhelmed with the desire to hurt him.

'What the fuck,' she said, her voice cracking.

'What?' He looked at her like he didn't have a clue what she was talking about, like she was a mad woman accosting him on the side of the street.

'You're married.'

'I thought you knew,' he said, a note of irritation in his voice.

'I didn't.'

He shrugged and tapped ash onto the gravel.

'Nothing's going to happen between us,' said Sylvie, her cheeks burning hot. 'Ever again.'

'Fine,' said Jay.

Sylvie felt herself begin to crumble then. 'You said you loved me.'

Jay looked at her with pure, seething hatred that cautioned her to tread carefully.

'I *never* said anything like that,' he said. 'Don't lie.'

Ten

Darkness in the Shape of a Girl

No one was home when Sylvie got back. She headed straight for her room, stripped out of her work clothes and pulled on a pair of running leggings. She put her trainers on by the door, tucked her key into the zip-up pocket in the back of her leggings and headed for the woods. She knew that if she didn't start running soon, she was going to scream. So she ran and she ran through the woods and out into the clearing on the other side where she began to cry. The tears were ugly and accompanied by convulsions that made her body shake uncontrollably. It was a fit of despair that blinded her, and she sat on the park bench waiting for it to subside, wiping her tears on the back of her hand. She looked over at the darkening landscape, the distant yellow lights of the homes on the hill. She hiccupped softly. She felt embarrassed though there was no one around to see her. Sylvie wondered if any of it had been real. The car rides or the dance in that seedy nightclub room with the walls painted black. The hotel, the notes, any of it. Perhaps she wasn't even a real person after all. The way Jay had looked at her, as if she'd made the whole thing up, as if he'd never spoken more than two words to her before. She looked down at her palms, imagining them translucent; her legs too, as if she could see straight through them to the wooden bench slats with their scuffed edges.

It was dark when Sylvie began to walk home. She felt numb as she trudged through the inky gloom. It was freezing. Her ears were so cold that there was a deep cramping pain inside her head. She rubbed her hands together, trying to ply some warmth out of her skin. She walked on, taking the footpath that led through the centre of the wood, her wood, and would spit her out at the mouth. It was different at night, more ominous with its spindly trunks and the anonymous animal noises that surrounded her. Something – a flash – in the corner of her eye caught Sylvie's attention and she froze. What had it been? She didn't know. There was another flash then, of something white that dashed between the tree branches several metres ahead of her and then disappeared without a trace.

'Hello?' Sylvie whispered. 'Anyone there?'

She was afraid of whatever it was but more afraid perhaps of hearing a response. She waited for a few moments, but nothing came. She rubbed her eyes and blinked hard, exhausted from the crying. She must be seeing things. Sylvie knew she couldn't stop, she couldn't turn back. She had to walk through. It was already too dark to be wandering through the woods alone. She could barely see four feet in front of her. The moon loomed like a ghostly stage light up above her. She saw it again, that flash of white in the silvery moonlight, and then she could have sworn she heard her name whispered through the gaps in the tree branches. It sounded like the rustle of dried leaves blown across the woodland floor.

Sylvie, Sylvie, Sylvie

Join us!

There was something there, something powerful watching her from the darkness.

Perhaps, Sylvie thought, it's the moon herself. She felt like darkness in the shape of a girl. She remembered the feeling. Memories of violence, the guilt that followed. She had locked them up and triple-bolted the door, ugly, ugly, ugly. It was all going to spill out everywhere. She thought of Jay's gun, the relief that she'd find in a single pull of the trigger, the barrel of the gun between her lips. *I am nothing, I am nothing, I am nothing.* She longed for the void, to disappear into the black hole of nothing. To never feel again.

Finally home, Sylvie closed her bedroom door and flopped down on the bed. She took Annabel's emerald necklace from the bedside table and held it up close to her eyes, so close that it blurred across her vision into three emerald necklaces instead of one. She hated it and wanted it gone. Not only hidden in the back of her underwear drawer or thrown out with the rubbish but gone, vanished from the earth, the atoms of it broken apart and dispersed as if it never existed. She uncorked a bottle of wine she'd taken from the kitchen, unhooked the clasp of the necklace and put the emerald pendant on her tongue. Then she took a swig from the bottle and swallowed it.

She drank as quickly as she could and then she lay down on her bed. As she looked up, waiting for the wine to get to work and put her under a hazy blanket of loosened consciousness, her eyes were drawn to the framed Willow Way acceptance letter. She felt like a squatter in the land of the hopeful. None of the dreams of a future that she'd had from this bed were ever going to be any more than that. Dreams.

All night she dreamt about the Willow Way *Giselle* stage set. The great cardboard trees and the sad little house painted on a slab of wood and propped up at the side of the stage. She dreamt that the theatre was empty, and it was pitch-dark except for the pathway lights in the auditorium, glowing with their small white offering from between the rows of seats. And then suddenly, a spotlight and Jay came walking slowly out of the wings.

Sylvie's heart raced but before she could say a word the music began. An invisible pianist played the opening chords and Sylvie performed her curtsey, shoulders slumped, palms open and upward. She looked up towards the sky, eyes full of resigned despair. She rose with ease onto the tips of her toes and hovered there, her arms, white as sheets, rippled at her sides like they were boneless and made of silk. Sylvie could actually feel the cold of the dark forest and then the warmth of Jay's body as he drew closer. She raised her left leg into an attitude position, balancing on her right. She bent backward, her back curving like a lithe tree in the wind. Sylvie held her breath as Jay grasped her waist. His presence startled her, intruding on her impression of a wafting nymph. Jay's feet were planted to the spot. He was the earth to Sylvie's air.

She was Giselle and he was Albrecht. They moved as one, as magnets, closely synchronized, pulling apart and drawing closer. When their cheeks touched, Sylvie was aware of the heat of his breath mingling with hers. He lifted her up over his head and she extended her spine backwards, her neck a swan curve. She felt his hands grasping her, the inside of her thigh, her waist.

As suddenly as he'd arrived, Jay was gone and his gun was in Sylvie's hand. She held it up and examined it under the stream of stage light, the mottled handle, the gleaming shaft.

The music of that singular piano was replaced by an orchestra swell. Sylvie crouched down and crawled over on her forearms to the edge of the stage above the orchestra pit. There was no one there but the music was so loud, so urgent, that it sounded as though it was being played right there by a phantom band. She recognized this part especially, 'The Mad Scene', when Giselle loses her mind after she discovers Albrecht's betrayal.

There was the deep, juddering percussion of the cello strings, minor note to minor note like a swarm of bees. It was so loud it pained her, echoed through her. She stood up, made a start for the wings of the stage, the direction of the stairs and the dressing room, but there was nothing there, just a dark mist around the edge of the stage, as if she was floating through a vacuum. The gun quivered in her hand. *Use me*, it urged her. And she had to, she had no choice. She kissed it before she opened her mouth and pushed the barrel between her lips, against her tongue. She pulled the trigger.

Sylvie woke up ice cold and gasping for air. As she lay staring up at the ceiling, she felt like a husk of a person, like she was barely alive. She felt as though she'd given Jay her soul and he'd devoured it.

She'd had dreams once, she'd wanted simple and sweet things. To dance, that was all. A life filled with music and the wood-paint smell of the theatre. She closed her eyes and tried to remember what it was like before the mess she made, and a single tear rolled warm down her cheek. Where had it all gone wrong? Sylvie wondered if there was a part of her that was destined for tragedy. Some kind of character flaw so deeply entrenched that it would always sabotage her every bid for happiness. Truthfully, she didn't know if she was capable of happiness. Maybe if she'd been born in a different era – but the way things were, she was always longing for something she couldn't put into words. What was it about being in a state of obsession that satisfied her soul? It satisfied her soul and ruined her life at the same time. *I am nothing. I am nothing. I am nothing.* Sylvie didn't want to be nothing any more.

Eleven

The Treasure Chest

Sylvie woke up with a terrible pain on the left side of her jaw, as if she'd dislocated it over the course of the night. Her whole back and hips ached as if her joints had been locked with rust. She checked her phone: nothing from Jay. Yesterday nothing, today nothing; she would begrudgingly hold out hope for tomorrow though she knew it would be painful when again nothing came. She sat with old words to comb over, rock pool conversations to mine for treasure, sand to sift. She reread their past texts over and over again until the minutes cycled into hours and half the day had passed with no respite from thoughts of him.

She remembered something her aunt had told her once. Sylvie recalled the silk tendril of smoke that curled over their heads as Aunt Jacqueline puffed on the end of her pink Sobranie which she held aloft by a cigarette holder. 'My darling, there's something you should always remember,' she said. 'A love affair with a married man is sour cherry – that's what it's like. When it's sweet, it's sweet and when it's sour, it's corrosive – your tongue burns with acid and ulcers scar themselves onto the slick insides of your mouth.' Sylvie wished more than anything that she could speak to her great-aunt now.

Sylvie began to search in her wardrobe through all her old things, as if the key to her future was buried somewhere among the dusty artefacts and mementoes of her past. Eventually she came across her old dance kit, a duffel bag bulging with spandex leotards, pale pink tights, pointe shoes and split-shoes, and soft blocks. She sat cross-legged on her bedroom floor and pulled every-thing out of the bag, one item at a time. She fingered the split-sole shoes, made of canvas, soft informal warm-up shoes. She'd wear through a pair in a week or two. They'd be grey from the rehearsal room floor, holes worn under the toes. She poked her index finger through the familiar hole in the bottom of the canvas, to feel the fraying fabric. She held the pair of shoes together against her chest, the rough fragility of them on her skin. She smiled, she felt warmly about the memory, and this surprised her. A different stage of grief, she supposed. Next, she pulled out a glut of satin pointe shoes; some of them were all tangled up by the ribbons and she had to prise them apart. The pointe shoes smelt like rehearsal, like theatre. The insides were stained with brown, dried blood. Most of them were too worn to wear again, she kept them as personal trophies. Rarely in ballet was your suffering acknowledged, but she liked the look of old pointe shoes, blood-soaked satin.

The smell and feel of her old ballet shoes brought back Willow Way memories. Sylvie remembered how she used to stretch in front of the Oak Room mirror every morning. How pleased she'd be to find that her calves and hamstrings felt exactly as they should, the comfort of delicious and familiar pain. The only thing to do was lean deeper into the pain, to go where it hurt. Pain was good, she thought, pain meant progress. She'd talk to her reflection in the mirror as she stretched: *We have no choice, do you understand? We've got to be the best, or we're nothing. Our whole life has been building to this.* Sylvie knew this in her soul, as true as her own heart beating.

The air was different in her final year, sharper, less friendly. When the girls had first arrived, they had eyes shining with stars, but their final year was different, it was serious, it was war.

In the office behind reception, the girls queued up to be weighed and measured after class. They stood shivering in their leotards and tights with goosepimples on their arms, waiting for their turn. When Sylvie stepped onto the scale, she would cringe at the creak of it under her feet. Most of the time ballet made her feel embarrassed of weighing anything at all. Next, she felt the teaching assistant's cool, hard fingertips on her leg as she wound a tape measure around her thigh. Everything was noted down in an enormous, navy leather-bound folder.

Then it was lunchtime. Between the synthetic overhead light, the dim cloud outdoors and the smell of overboiled tomato soup hanging bittersweet in the air, the canteen felt oppressive. Leg warmers and sweatsuits were left hanging open to reveal the ridged edges of bony chests – pale and hard – nipples visible through the lycra, angular kneecaps in pink-white tights. A land of bones. The less meat the more grace, that was the mantra.

Sylvie found safety in so much control: eat, sleep, move, shower, stretch, what to wear, how to do her hair, how to do her make-up. She feared the vastness, the great funnelling of the masses towards mediocrity, towards okayness. She hated ordinary, she wanted to be special and she was prepared to do whatever it took. Ballet. She dreamt of it, worshipped it. When she danced, she felt unhuman, more than human, she felt as though she were brushing the edge of heaven. When she leapt high into the air, she felt as though she had transformed into a daemon of magick, into an angel.

Maria, Sylvie's dance teacher, was Spanish with thick eyebrows and a dark red mouth even without lipstick. Like most teachers she wore dance gear even though she never danced full out: leggings, a leotard, a black ribbed knitted romper over the top of it, leather split soles.

'All right, let's see about a port de bras,' said Maria, and then she'd choreograph it in a matter of seconds. 'Breathe, one-two-three, first, one-two-three, open to second and down …' She'd demonstrate for them with reserved, professional coolness.

The demonstration was the girls' only opportunity to retain the sequence. They would mark it out for their brains, moving their hands in place of their feet to memorize the movements. Maria gestured to the pianist and they had to begin, ready or not. While they performed the exercise, she inspected their line-up like a sergeant. Out of the corner of her eye, Sylvie would watch Ffion's reflection in the mirror as they performed the exercise side by side. Ffion and Sylvie had always been in competition for the top spot in their class. Ffion's back bend was good, her arch was high, while Sylvie bent further and pointed harder.

It was after one allegro class in September, when they were sweaty and breathless, hearts pounding from the rapid jumping sequence, that Maria sat down on her chair and told the class to gather round for an announcement.

'The ballet I've chosen for you girls as your final show-case performance is *Giselle*.'

Sylvie could envisage the dark stage set, twisted teal and midnight blue, the other ghosts, sultry and weightless, as they wordlessly summoned their male prey. A single cool spotlight, herself in the long white tutu, complexion whitened to a ghostly pallor, gliding by way of bourrée across the stage, ethereal and inhuman. She imagined herself, of course, as the lead role, the titular role. It was imperative.

Sylvie could remember the day the cast list went up, the bustle and excitement in the hallway. Some of her classmates had their eyes downcast, others' were wide and gleaming like prophets who'd seen the future. Their eyes flickered between Ffion and Sylvie, sensing their anticipation. They were the only two in real competition for the main part. Sylvie's heart had swollen to twice its size and was threatening to pop inside her like a balloon.

'Well,' said Ffion, 'I can see the list on the noticeboard.'

Giselle – Sylvie Orange

Something else caught her eye, there in the back of the wardrobe, tucked away beneath a vacuum-packed bag of her old competition costumes. The chest. The domed lid of the wooden chest was covered in a fine film of dust. It had sat undisturbed at the back of her wardrobe for years. Sylvie laughed out loud to herself then at the irony of it all. She'd wished for so long that she could speak to her Aunt Jacqueline again and all the while she'd had these diaries. Thousands of words' worth of her stories and thoughts. Sylvie hauled the chest into the middle of the floor, opened the clasp and began to rifle through its contents with all the desperation of a thirsty man coming across water in a desert.

Sylvie remembered the night she'd been given the chest. Aunt Jacqueline wore a floor-length robe made of pale purple velvet and embroidered with tiny beads on the shoulders and back. Beneath it, she had on a deep purple satin drop-waist dress and a pair of kitten heel slippers which clacked loudly down the tiled hallway as Sylvie followed her into the parlour.

Aunt Jacqueline passed Sylvie her cup and saucer, the gemstones on her wrinkled hands gleaming with fire. Sylvie drank the hot tea with slow, tentative sips, nibbling the edge of a rose macaron only at Jacqueline's behest.

Jacqueline put down her cup and saucer and picked up her cigarette holder, nudging a flame from a gold vintage Cartier lighter that looked like something belonging to the end of a regal sceptre. She exhaled reams of smoke from the corner of her pursed lips. The satin sheen of her pink lipstick had left a ghostly kiss on the rim of her teacup and the remains of it on her lips were slightly smudged.

'There's a box on the floor to your left,' said Aunt Jacqueline. 'Pick it up and have a look. Open it,' she urged her.

Sylvie lifted the lid of the chest and looked up at her great-aunt who sat with her head resting against the back of the armchair, watching Sylvie with a thrill of pleasure in her dark blue eyes and a small, satisfied smile on her smudged pink mouth. Sylvie could only make out a clumsy-looking stack of old books, some leather-bound, some cloth-bound, with yellowed pages and photographs and slips of paper sticking out at various angles.

Sylvie picked up a leather-bound journal and ran her fingertips over the engraved design on the front cover before unhooking the buckle and letting it fall open. As Sylvie began to leaf through the pages, she realized she was reading a personal diary – Aunt Jacqueline's to be exact – and she found herself blushing. Even the letters of the elegant fountain pen scrawl were lusciously slouched against one another as if they were drunk on champagne.

16th December 1968

Last night I finally succumbed to the prince's frankly embarrassing attentions, somewhere off the coast of Anguilla, in the superyacht master-cabin. There were copious amounts of rum followed by some rather clumsy sun-drunk fumbling. When it was over the prince fell asleep immediately and I took advantage of his raucous snoring as I slipped out from his room and took myself for a cigarette and a dirty martini on the sun-deck where the deckhand almost collapsed at the sight of me, poor lad. I looked spectacular, if you'll permit me to be a little vain: my red hair flowed long down my back and I was naked underneath this fabulous translucent blue and green kaftan, the plunging collar embroidered with sequins and diamantés so that I glittered under the startling sunlight, shining against the crystalline blue of the Caribbean Sea. I'd designed it that way, of course, it never hurts to sparkle. The way he looked at me, at my body, well, I positively melted on the spot. Have you ever seen the crew cabins on a yacht? They're such poky, funny little rabbit holes but I didn't mind a bit. I much preferred the deckhand, agile, young and handsome. The princes are easy pickings.

Sylvie blushed and hastily clamped the journal closed.

'You mustn't read them in front of me,' Aunt Jacqueline said. She patted a self-conscious hand to her red waves. 'At least not any of my journals. You must take them home and guard them with your life and for God's sake if anyone called Herbert Germin from Universal tries to get hold of you, you must tell him NO and nothing else. He's been after the film rights for my journals for decades and I simply cannot stand to see the intricacies of my personal history mined for cheap thrills and kicks for this bloodthirsty, attention-deficit generation. Guard them with your life,' Jacqueline urged her.

Down in the chest, the gleam of the dimmed chandelier light overhead on the leather-bound journals with their gold clasps looked like exotic treasure.

Sylvie pulled the lid shut and closed the hinge.

I will, she assured her aunt.

Good girl.

Now, Sylvie picked up the first of the journals and ran her fingertips over the worn leather cover. She unfastened the clasp and blinked hard at the sight that met her. It was a cream-coloured square of an envelope with 'Sylvie' written across the front of it in Aunt Jacqueline's handwriting. But what could it be? A birthday card she'd forgotten about? Why hadn't she noticed it before? Why hadn't her aunt told her she'd written her a letter?

Twelve

Steel Fist in a Velvet Glove

Sylvie sat on the edge of the bed and peeled open the flap on the envelope, hunching close to her bedside lamp to read it.

Dearest Sylvie,

I hope this letter finds you well. I wanted to write it because I believe some things are better read when we need them than heard when we do not, and I would like you to be able to return to this letter should you ever have the need, though I truly hope you never will.

My darling girl, I must confess something to you. When I asked you if you had a young man and you said that you hadn't, I was relieved, but I know that one day you shall and the thought of that frightens me. You see, it is love that makes even the strongest among us weak and vulnerable. We are blinded from the truth, we see what we want to see and believe what our beloved chooses to tell us.

I hope that the love you experience will add to your life in rich and wonderful ways, I hope your young man is honest and true but if it transpires that he is not, if you find yourself broken-hearted and alone, I hope you will find the strength to believe in your own resilience and be brave, my darling, be brave.

I did fall in love once, truly, when I was young and the man that he was, was nothing like the man I'd imagined him to be. The version of him that I wanted did not exist. He was just a figment of my imagination, a character I conceived of on a lonely night in a state of wine-induced whimsy when my bed was cold. He was nothing but a faded grey impression of something I invented and that saddened me, and it made me doubt that God can truly love his own creation. I'd forgotten myself, that I am golden. I needed to remember that a kiss is a kiss, not a Midas touch. I loved a phantom, a man who never existed, I had a love affair alone.

He was a cruel and unimaginative man looking for something to feed on. What did he have to offer me but emptiness? What did he bring to my temple but illusions and victor-less games? He wanted to recreate me in his image, his misery and rage. He sensed the softness and knew I could be pliable, his kisses were intended to leave marks. For a moment I thought he saw me but then I realized he was simply searching for his own impression on my skin. He was pleased to hear his words from my mouth, but I decided no more and never again.

I recovered, as will you.

Darling Sylvie, please remember this: my sweet little angel, you are loved. Never mind that you're quieter, darker, more introverted than the others. There's life and there's death and then there's women like you and I who have the potential of whole worlds within us – and courage. Courage is the most important.

Aside from this there's something else you must promise me. You must never allow yourself to be walked over, to be made into some man's pet or fool. Never forget that you are a Gardiner, you are a steel fist in a velvet glove. We bow to no one and never allow a man to diminish us. I hope you will find some comfort and amusement in the diaries and a little inspiration in the art of feminine warfare.

And for now, sweet Sylvie, I leave you with a poem and the sincere wish that wherever you are right now, however you feel at this moment, you will always remember who you are.

A pretty girl with a soft soul barely stands a chance
    of living
she is a target, draws the world to her, flies to her
    light.
Break if you must and then arm yourself
There are ways to make weapons of your lovely eyes,
your voice dripping honey.

My sweet girl you can live for ever on this island
    with us
eating the souls of men and screaming into the air

With love always, unending and without question, my special one.

Your Jacqueline

Sylvie picked up the framed photograph of her Aunt Jacqueline that sat propped up on her bedside table and planted a small kiss on the cool glass.

'Thank you,' she whispered. Hopeful that her aunt could hear her.

Somehow, she had delivered the perfect words at just the perfect time and managed to bolster Sylvie's spirits even from beyond the grave. She shed a few happy tears at the beauty of her aunt's words which were like a tonic to her weary soul. She unclipped the glass from the framed picture of her aunt and tucked the letter behind the photograph. She would not be able to see the letter, but she would know it was there, feel its fortifying energy beside her.

There was more in the diaries, there had to be. She rushed downstairs to steal a bottle of wine and a glass from the kitchen and then Sylvie lay back on her bed with a glass of red and began to read. It rained hard outside her window, the wind howled, the dark sky crackled overhead with intermittent flashes of bright white electric lightning, and she felt the whole house shake with thunder. The power of the storm stirred something in her, a minute version of the feeling she'd had when she danced all those years ago. A feeling she had convinced herself would never be found again, except during sex with the world's worst men. It made her feel as though the power of the whole earth was gliding into her veins, as if her bones were fortified with steel and that she could shatter all the glass of the windows of every house on the street with sheer will alone.

17th April 1978

My mother would be very disappointed in me. She always said that revenge is a feminine art. It ought to be well thought out and executed with elegance. I'm afraid I seem to have lost my head completely, it's quite unlike me, I've always prided myself on my pragmatism in matters of the heart and bank account.

Sylvie squinted up closely to the page. This was her Aunt Jacqueline's diary but it didn't sound like her at all. She'd always imagined her aunt had been born knowing the ways of the world and exactly what she thought of them.

Never mind. There's no going back. What's done is done and I'll be damned if I show a flicker of regret where Cornelius is concerned. I'm afraid it's going to be another divorce. Well, not afraid, rather glad actually if I'm going to be totally candid. And what's the point of a diary if one can't be totally candid? So, call up Geraldine

at Hummingbird on Fifth Avenue and order a cake,
we're celebrating tonight, my darlings! I have quite the
talent for divorces it seems, and this is how it happened:
the end of marriage número cuatro. Just give me a
second to pour myself a drink.

Sylvie sat down on the edge of her bed and turned the page. She ran her fingertips down it, over the lines of her aunt's extravagant scrawl, the rich indigo ink and the looped letters, the tails of the g's and y's swooping back on themselves. She could imagine Aunt Jacqueline in one of her long velvet robes with a champagne coupe in hand and her gold cigarette holder between her lips as she scribbled away with her signature passion, pausing only to flick ash into the waiting crystal ashtray.

Aunt Jacqueline had always been somewhat reluctant to discuss her marriages with Sylvie; she referred to her ex-husbands as a monolith of businessmen, heirs and playboys, to the point that when she talked in an offhand way about 'my ex', Sylvie pictured a kind of monster with four heads and three sets of arms, each of the hands clutching a bulky eighties-style brick phone or a cigar or a Cartier ring box, and she pictured the body of the monster to be as wide as a tree trunk and dressed in a pinstripe waistcoat. There'd been so many husbands and so many lovers that it was hard to really pin them down as individuals and easier to just imagine them as one bumbling entity.

I can't quite believe that what was supposed to be a wonderful solitary evening of relaxation ended in such hideous destruction.

I'd just come out of a glorious bubble-bath in the lovely pink bathroom suite I've recently had installed – the bath (big enough to swim in) was filled to the brim with rose-scented bubbles – when the telephone in my bedroom rang loudly, trespassing quite insistently on my blissful evening. I trod dripping, foam-edged footsteps across the fluffy pink carpet, as I wrapped myself tighter around the waist in my floor-length, feather-trimmed silk dressing gown and went to answer it.

'Hello?' I said, pressing the receiver of the corded phone to my ear.

'Is Cornelius there?' came the voice on the end of it.

A female voice, can you believe it? It gave me such a start. The moment I heard the woman's voice, with a touch of Long Island in the accent, I knew, oh boy, did I know.

'No, he is not,' I said, with my jaw wound so tight with fury that I could barely get the words out. 'This is his wife.'

The line went dead. Can you imagine it? Having the gall to ring my home, at 9 p.m. no less. Characteristic, if you ask me, of exactly the kind of classless hussy Cornelius would take up with, terribly disappointing, I'd rather have expected him to have raised his standards. I can joke about it now that I've exploded, but last evening I was feeling decidedly less jovial.

I saw red then. I don't know what came over me, but I ran straight for the safe. All I could think of was the gun. The metallic .357 Magnum revolver he kept in the safe in case of emergencies.

I held the gun in my right hand and stalked through the apartment, taking aim and shooting (POW!) at anything of his that he'd miss. Those hideous paintings he'd picked up at auction when he fancied himself a connoisseur of modern art (BOOM!), a clean hole right through to the brick of the wall. That disgusting sculpture his sister had given us as a wedding present (BANG!) shattered into shards of cream ceramic all over the carpet. I went on until the gun was out of bullets. And then, when I felt sure that I'd caused some considerable damage to his property, I put the gun down and began to apply my make-up, painstakingly, ready for Cornelius's arrival: everything had to be perfect from my smoky blue eyeshadow to my peach lipstick, with my hair set with curlers and brushed out just so. I'd be sure to have the gun aimed right at the doorway the second I heard his key in the lock.

Oh, and let me state clearly that I had zero intention whatsoever of killing the man, I only wanted to give him a fright, and what a fright he had. Ha. But after all that the whole business gave me only a temporary sense of satisfaction . . .

Sylvie read on.

. . . as I watched him reposition his hat atop his large, round, bald head with trembling fingers. His sausage-like fingers glinting with gold rings. I knew that in a matter of minutes he'd be seated at a bar in a darkened, smoke-filled nightclub, and those sausage fingers of his would be stroking the bare back of a young woman dressed in a plunging gold halter-neck with hair like Farrah Fawcett, as he bled out money on overpriced drinks and moaned about his crazy bitch wife. And I walked right into it. The Trap. We women must avoid the Trap, the very best we're able. The Trap is playing into their hands, the stereotyped perception of an over-emotional woman. It is far better to keep them guessing, to keep one's feelings to oneself and one's diary, to make a plan and then execute it with stealth.

Revenge is necessary, of course. If one does not achieve appropriate revenge when wronged then the injustice wreaks havoc on one's complexion. I simply cannot allow myself to be disrespected and in such a public fashion, and do nothing about it. Oh! My veins are positively tingling with the venom I feel towards this man. But this time I must go about things with a bit of guile. When I'm finished with him, Cornelius Dormer is going to rue the day he was born, and that he ever met Jacqueline Gardiner.

Suddenly it was so obvious to Sylvie, as though a mist had cleared, exactly what she needed to do to set the world to rights and recover herself, the vital spark in her that had been extinguished twice over. Sylvie pictured Aunt Jacqueline, the stern cast of her made-up face as she said with her blue eyes ablaze, 'Get revenge.'

She'd reached the part of Jacqueline's diary that detailed in exquisitely incriminating detail how she'd sought revenge on her cheating husband.

The first thing to know about revenge is that it must be tailored to your subject and not to yourself. Remove yourself from the equation and become an objective observer. Identify the things that matter most to your subject and invent ways to take them away, play on their weaknesses, discover them if you do not know them already. Trigger their deepest insecurities, unsettle their soul, mire their very image of self, shake them to their core. That is revenge. My mother explained it to me once like this. We women may be no match for the brute strength of a man on the battlefield, so we must make our own battlefields, choose our own weapons.

Sylvie's mind began to tick with replayed memories, with glances, with words. She *knew* Jay. She had taken great care to observe as much as she could. She'd noticed his liberally applied cologne and perfectly styled hair, the pride he took in his freshly waxed car which shone down to the alloys, his failure to mention his wife and his predilection for extra-marital affairs, the disdain he felt for his brother which was so strong he couldn't help but show it. He was proud, he was image-conscious. Sylvie could work with that.

Cornelius Dorner is passionately in love with just one person on this planet, and that one person is Cornelius Dormer. He treats every straggly blond hair on his balding head like it's made of gold. His clothes are custom, bright colours, burgundies, yellows, deep purples, blood red, alligator shoes, alligator wallet.

Once a week he goes for a sauna and steam at the Russian bathhouse where he sits for hours with his belly out and his legs splayed, displaying his thoroughly unremarkable cock and balls for all the world to see.

He loves his car, naturally.

He eats too much. I imagine his diet will eventually kill him in the end and do my job for me. Ha! If I only had the patience to wait for the inevitable cardiac arrest that will strike him one day when he's midway through a tomahawk steak at Vito's. A butter-basted, peppercorn sauce-smothered steak, of course, with a side of dauphinoise potatoes with extra cheese and a plate of spaghetti Bolognese on the side that will have left red splatters down the front of his shirt. And he'd wash it all down with a bottle of red wine and a couple of whiskies. God in heaven, if anyone should ever read this you must swallow your judgement. Crude, vile classlessness looks an awful lot like authenticity when you've spent a few months locked up with an overgrown schoolboy of an ex-priest. You completely lose your sense of centre.

Naturally, after the debacle with the gun, things were rocky for a while. Cornelius stayed for a night in a hotel, he called me grovelling the next morning and

*I'd had time to cool off. We met at the plaza where
he apologized profusely and promised to be faithful. I
pretended to believe him, I even managed a few artful
tears. For a week I let things go on as normal, though it
was difficult. As he lay snoring beside me, I fantasized
about suffocating him in his sleep. Sometimes, sacrifices
must be made, there's simply no other way. I must equip
myself with the mind of a soldier marching into war,
there's no way but through.*

*His hair (what remained of it) was my first target. He
was drunk. Naturally, these things are so much easier
when one can rely on their target to maintain a near-
constant state of intoxication as I can with my dear
darling husband. He came back mumbling and swaying
with a moistened red glow about his heavy cheeks. I
heard him scraping his key back and forth across the
keyhole, swearing and stuttering and mumbling to
himself. I was ready for him. Lying in wait in the living
room with the curtains drawn, stretched out on one of
the sofas like an alligator in the swamp rushes. Except
I was a different kind of predator, a different animal.
I was dressed in cream silk, a sheath nightdress that
kissed my hips and breasts before falling like water to
the floor. My perfume was jasmine flower, my face was
powdered, rouged, my lips applied stroke by stroke with
a tiny lipstick brush. The outline of my cupid's bow
drawn on a little sharper, two angular peaks above my
mouth, an extra pair of teeth.*

I poured him a drink from the trolley in the living

room, a crushed sleeping pill. Nothing too sinister. When he fell asleep, his head tilted back, his mouth hanging open, snoring loudly, I prodded him a few times, fairly hard. I had to make sure he was fast asleep, you see. I walked back and forth, stamping my slippered feet on the floor. He didn't stir. So I fetched the clippers we kept in the bathroom and I buzzed that well-tended, elaborately crafted comb-over right off his head, trying my hardest not to laugh out of sheer delight.

The next morning, I was woken by a spine-tingling scream that lurched through the apartment. I crossed the hall to the bathroom and saw sheer terror in Cornelius's eyes as he stood craning up to the mirror, pressing his fingers into his scalp as if he could prise the hair back out of the follicles, as if somehow by manipulating just the right pressure point, he would suddenly sprout a full head of abundant, flowing golden locks. I had to excuse myself and go to my own bathroom where I locked the door and turned both the bath taps up all the way, the sink too, to mask the noise of the laughter that erupted out of me, so violently that it shook my whole body.

Sylvie decided that she would find it within herself to destroy Jay no matter the cost. With her Aunt Jacqueline's diaries to guide her, she had a manual to ultimate revenge. She would begin at once.

Thirteen

Bloody Armageddon

Sylvie was wired during her drive to work. Her mind danced with all kinds of pictures of revenge, tableaux of Jay in various states of distress. Revenge. She didn't know how exactly she was going to do it. All she knew was that she was going to do something. She *had* to do something. Her muscles were twitchy with it.

'Feeling better?' Karen raised her eyebrow, scanning Sylvie for any lingering signs of the mysterious illness that had rendered her unable to come to work the day before.

'Much better,' Sylvie said.

'Nasty stuff going around,' said Derek, his fingertips jamming against the keys as he whacked out a furious email. 'It's the weather change.'

The three of them looked out of the window at the crisp autumn day, the bluish morning light reflected up at them from the windscreens of the parked cars. Jay was nowhere to be seen. Sylvie scrolled through her emails, then pausing she turned in Karen's direction and asked as inconspicuously as she could, 'Do you know if Jay's coming in today? I need to check something with him.'

'What's that?'

'Horton Views have had some problem with their accounting department. They think they might have paid us twice. I need him to check.'

'Ah,' Karen said. 'Well, as far as I know he's due to come in this afternoon. He's got to sign off a job with the warehouse manager, it's being collected tonight.'

'What is it?' Sylvie asked.

'Leeds University charity fundraiser,' said Derek. 'It's one of our biggest jobs, happens every year. This time we're running a bit behind though, it's right down to the wire, they need the fingers for this weekend.'

'Why's it so late?' Sylvie asked.

Derek shrugged. 'Some mess-up with the production schedule. You weren't here when Jay found out about it, so you missed out on the hubbub yesterday morning, lucky mite. Mad, wasn't it, Karen?'

Karen gave a small grunt of agreement.

'Like bloody Armageddon.' Derek shook his head and returned to his email.

Sylvie had an idea. Like most good ideas, it was both primitive and effective. She busied herself with various tasks all morning, occasionally her face would light with a smile as she envisioned the chaos she would soon create. When it was time for lunch, she watched out of the window until all of the factory workers had filed out of the door downstairs, and she made her excuses to Karen and Derek.

She knew she had to be quick. The fingers for Leeds University had been packaged in crates by the back door, where the Transit vans and lorries backed up to be loaded. Sylvie ran her fingertips over the sheets of bubble wrap that were laid on top of them like a veil of frosted glass. She peeled it away, casting an eye over her shoulder in the direction of the office to make sure no one was watching. The foam fingers beneath were a rich royal blue, the paint was yellow gold and screamed *Go! LEEDS! Go!* in sunny capital letters. Sylvie heard the voices of the warehouse workers outside the door, men's voices and laughing. If she couldn't pull it off in five minutes or less, she'd almost certainly be caught. Now, where do they keep the paint? Sylvie wondered. She began to rush around the edge of the warehouse inspecting cardboard boxes filled with sheets of foam and spare machine parts but no paint. She opened the door to the storage cupboard and saw them there, five or six tins of paint, covered over in layers of dust, stacked against the back wall.

She didn't have time to waste. She dropped to her knees and inspected the tins. She chose the acid green. It seemed most appropriate for her purposes. She took her house key out of her trouser pocket, and she stuck it under the lip of the paint-tin lid and began to work it. It popped off and

Sylvie lifted it away. The paint inside glowed like a pool of opaque uranium. It looked like something that would strip all the flesh from your finger if you dipped it inside. The surface of the wet paint was as glossy as a glazed cake. Sylvie picked up the tin and rushed over to the stacked crates of foam fingers. She paused, paint tin primed, counted to three, before she poured acid green paint all over the first box; then she lifted it away and poured paint all over the second box, and then the third and the fourth until her arms were exhausted and she was very nearly out of paint. Having done that she discarded the paint tin and rushed out of the warehouse and into the upstairs bathroom, scrubbing furiously at the remnants of green paint that had stuck to the skin around her knuckles and the edges of her nails.

'What do you mean they're fucking destroyed?'

Jay had arrived within the hour. The news about the ruined foam fingers had been broken to him by the crowd of bewildered factory workers.

'I'm sorry, Jay, I've got no idea how it happened.'

Karen, Derek and Sylvie watched open-mouthed as the interrogation took place in the middle of the office. The warehouse supervisor was a big man with a shaved head and neck tattoos who was reduced to the state of a trembling child in the full glare of Jay's fury.

'I know how it happened,' said Jay. 'It's not fucking rocket science, someone's sabotaged it. So the question is who?'

'I don't know,' said the supervisor. 'It wasn't any of my guys. I've got a few new starters, but everybody needs this job. Should I pull them in one by one?'

Jay glanced across the office floor, his eyes settling on Sylvie's face. The look he gave her chilled her to the bone.

'Go downstairs,' he said to the supervisor. 'I'll come and find you later, I need to think.'

The man trundled off, his work boots heavy on the carpet. He looked ashen and Sylvie was flooded with guilt. She hadn't wanted to hurt anyone but Jay, and he'd been a casualty.

'What can we do to help, Jay?' Karen piped up.

'Nothing for now,' he said. 'I need to speak to Sylvie in my room, please.'

Sylvie shut the door behind her, hovering in front of it. She felt as though she'd been locked up with a wild animal. She could feel the hatred coming off him like steam.

'Sit down,' he said.

Sylvie sank into the nearest chair. She was disappointed to realize that she still found him beautiful. She'd thought maybe with a break and a little mental adjustment, she would have been able to break the spell. She'd been wrong.

He paced back and forth along a two-metre stretch of carpet with his head ducked and his brow furrowed before he finally sat down across from Sylvie. He didn't look at her. He took a packet of cigarettes out from his pocket and began to roll one against the desktop.

'I could call the police. This is vandalism.'

Sylvie panicked.

'I'll tell your wife,' she said.

Jay's typically stoic expression barely flickered.

'Why would you do that? You'll make yourself look bad.'

He took the cigarette and tucked it behind his ear, leaning back in his chair and crossing his arms.

Sylvie simmered with anger. Why wasn't he afraid of her? She wanted him to be afraid of her.

'Worse than you? I've got texts, Jay, dozens of them. Fuck it, maybe I'll just post them to LinkedIn, let everyone know what you're really like.'

She meant every word of it. She didn't care how she looked.

'I don't think you want to be threatening me,' said Jay; his green eyes gleamed and his voice was low, quiet.

Sylvie tried not to let it show that she was frightened. All the memories of his knife, his hands around her throat, the black handgun, seemed poisonous. She'd thought they'd been expressions of passion, of a desire so vital and urgent that it bordered on violence. But now she wondered if he'd been warning her, showing her his weapons, letting her feel the span of his hands, the way his fingers had so easily wrapped around her neck. She recalled the feeling of her wrists caught up in his grip, pinned to the headboard. Her mouth went dry.

'I know things about you,' he said. 'Your past, don't forget that. I'd hate to have to tell everyone here, your family. I'd hate to have to report this little incident to the police, wouldn't look good, would it?'

Ffion. Willow Way. They were like corpses buried in shallow graves, enough rain and the earth would melt away.

The thought of Sylvie's mum and dad finding out what had happened was unbearable. The thought of the world knowing what a monster she was. Being unmasked. She couldn't let it happen. She'd be marked for ever, perhaps she already was.

'No more nonsense,' said Jay. 'You behave yourself and I'll let you keep your job, all right?'

'Okay,' said Sylvie. She felt there was no alternative, it was as though she'd already reached a dead end, a stalemate.

Sylvie collected her bag without a word to Derek and Karen. She focused on the carpet, the stairs, the worn wooden flooring of the foyer, the car park tarmac. So much for revenge, she thought as she started up the ignition. She'd barely left a scratch. Jay had dealt with her as if she were a toddler having a tantrum, a naughty child who'd made a mess and needed telling off. It's my own fault, Sylvie thought. She'd allowed herself to become emotional, she'd fallen into 'the Trap'. She needed to be strategic. She needed to be organized. She needed to wait patiently and strike when the time was right.

Inspired by her aunt's diaries, Sylvie made a mental list for seeking revenge on Jay. She would target four key areas. Jay's looks, his business, his pride, his marriage. It was back to the drawing board and this time she would not fail.

Sylvie remembered something Ffion had said then, years ago during the *Giselle* auditions. Ffion had asked her what she thought about the choice of ballet to which Sylvie responded that she liked it.

'You do?' The expression on Ffion's face was one of shock, maybe even a little horror.

Sylvie felt the need to defend herself. 'Well, yeah, it's got passion, devotion, death. What more could you want?'

'A different message?' Ffion said, lowering her voice but failing to hide her disgust.

'The message is about the power of love,' said Sylvie. 'How it endures even after death.'

'No.' Ffion shook her head. 'It's about how women sacrifice themselves for lying, cheating men.'

'Giselle loved Albrecht,' said Sylvie.

'I don't know why,' said Ffion. 'I would have stopped loving him the moment I found out he'd lied to me and then, if he ever wandered into my damn forest, I'd haunt his arse to death. Let alone stand in his place.'

Sylvie thought maybe Ffion had been right after all. Jay had made her into Giselle but who was he to say how the story ended? When Giselle danced in Albrecht's place that was *her* choice, but she could have killed him instead. Sylvie was happy to right the wrong for both of them.

Fourteen

Fox Fur Red

It was late. Sylvie had spent the evening reading the diaries and drinking a bottle of wine. She didn't feel like fighting the warm sleepiness that emanated through her. Tomorrow she would work on her plan. She needed to deliver a personally tailored revenge (bespoke, if you will) exactly as her Aunt Jacqueline had described. Sylvie imagined herself laughing, a laughter so strong that it shook her body violently from the core, the feeling of victory, sweet and whole. She could almost taste it. She closed the journal and reached down to tuck it under her bed. She yawned before burrowing her face into her pillow and closing her eyes, she fell asleep easily. Just the thought of *revenge* was like a balm for her fractured heart and frayed nerves.

The first idea arrived almost by accident, like something blown in on the crest of the wind, a feather or a crumpled five-pound note. As she lay in the dark, Sylvie let her hazy half-sleeping mind wander through all kinds of open landscapes, through pits and peaks, entire meadows of revenge, of poppies sprung up from Jay's blood and rivers of his tears.

In her imagination, she began to walk a winding path and at the end of it she saw a man. Not Jay, surely? No, it couldn't be Jay, the tall well-built figure with black hair cut close to his neck. Sylvie wandered nearer, cautious, intrigued, and the man turned over his shoulder and grinned at her, eyeing her hungrily, mischievously. She saw it was Greg, Jay's older brother.

It was obvious and practically foolproof, the seduction of Greg Lakemore. A natural beginning for Sylvie's quest, one her Aunt Jacqueline would surely have lauded. The Gardiner women were expert seductresses, after all. Jay would hate it, Sylvie knew. It would be an insult, a wound to the heart, or failing the existence of a heart, it would be a wound to the ego. It would be easy too. Greg was a flirt and it would only take a short nudge to seal the deal.

The only possible pitfall of the plan would be if Jay had told Greg about what had happened between them. She thought hard, so hard it hurt her brain, back to all their interactions, to the times Jay spoke about his brother, to the few times his brother was around. What had she sensed? Resentment, a little envy. Jay envied Greg's freedom, that much was clear. Jay probably thought he was one-upping his brother in the beginning, marrying Annabel, becoming a real family man, and with a woman of status no less, only to find it all so very disappointing. Greg had never been married, but he'd had long-term girlfriends. She'd heard Sapna talking about one of them, a while ago now. She'd been called Sophie. Ditzy, that was what Sapna had said, and she'd rolled her eyes. How had it ended? Sapna had said something about that too: 'Greg got bored again.' He'd be dating a new girl next week, someone petite after Sophie's ample curves. That was how he did it, always craving the opposite, something different, something more.

Sylvie didn't think Jay would have risked polluting his image as the family man. Regardless of the reality, it was the only thing he really had against Greg, who was a much more successful businessman. He'd made an extraordinary amount of money working in SEO and domains, so much money that aside from the occasional glamorous business trip to woo potential clients, he didn't really need to do much work at all. Runs like a machine, Greg had said, on a crisp autumn day when he'd popped into the office.

When the sun came up that Saturday morning, the birds were singing outside her window, welcoming in the day and, with it, a new sense of purpose. Gregory Lakemore.

Sylvie entered the run-down arcade of shops with a small Boots, a shop selling plastic toy models, and a sandwich shop that was permanently empty except for a lone old man with a Morrisons plastic carrier tucked under his table and an enormous mug of hot chocolate in front of him. She felt a pang of sympathy, ridiculous maybe, whenever she saw him. Maybe he had a wife and a whole stable of children and grandchildren at home, and this was his only respite from the madness. Maybe he was totally alone. Maybe Sylvie's sympathy was actually guilt about not spending as much time as she could have with Aunt Jacqueline at the end, her beautiful Aunt Jacqueline who never would have allowed herself to fall under anybody's control, least of all a fraud like Jay.

She had so much to learn from her that she couldn't even comprehend it at the time. She assumed that Jacqueline's fierceness, her dazzling confidence, was something innate. She'd spent so much time reading the diaries that the more she thought and the more she learnt about Jacqueline's divorces – from a man who beat her, from a relentless lothario, from a sickening 'mama's boy' and from a man who in the end just 'didn't excite me' – Sylvie saw that she had earned every bit of her strength, that she forged it for herself.

Even when she was sick and Sylvie had been afraid to visit her, she'd hear her voice coming in, muffled over the receiver, 'The hairdresser's just been, darling.'

'Aunt Jack, you don't need a hairdresser! You just need to focus on getting better.'

'Sylvie, darling, I am eighty-two, I am *not* getting better. I want to look my best when I meet God.'

She'd said it with such conviction that Sylvie couldn't disagree with her then, nor when she saw her body lying in the open casket at the funeral, like she'd insisted. Sylvie cried at the beauty of her because while ballet was her religion, and each detail of it the burden of Sylvie's life, beauty and style were Aunt Jacqueline's. In beauty, she found her liberation and identity.

Sylvie found herself taking a right-hand turn before the enormous dusty Christmas tree propped up, slightly prematurely, at the end of the arcade and ducking into Boots. It smelt ancient. The once-white tiles were yellowed. There was an assistant behind the till, a girl in her teens, who looked up half-heartedly before returning to her plastic basket full of mascaras, a giant roll of red 'Discount' stickers next to her on the counter. Sylvie took herself in the direction of the hair dye aisle, feeling like a woman possessed.

Back in the safe isolation of her ensuite bathroom, Sylvie returned with an old paper she'd found to cover the tiles on the floor with. When she began to tear off pages from the local press, a lilac-coloured A5 leaflet fluttered to the ground.

LINDA GRAYSON ADULT BALLET CLASSES
MAPLE VILLAGE HALL
MONDAY – BEGINNERS 7pm
THURSDAY – THOSE WITH PRIOR EXPERIENCE 8.15pm

She'd heard of the classes before, crumpled up the leaflet her mother had left beside her morning coffee. Adult ballet classes. Part of her wanted to dance again. She'd have to accept that she would have declined massively, her legs wouldn't go up as high, she wouldn't plié as deeply or turn as fast. But wasn't there something left that would make it worth putting on a leotard and a pair of tights again? Lacing up a set of ballet ribbons, taking that glorious anticipatory inhale and exhale as the pianist performed his introduction. Did adult ballet classes in village halls even *have* pianists?

Sylvie held the flier, taking in the burgundy font, slightly blurred, pixelated against the background. The clip art cartoon image of a pair of ballet shoes, erect on their points like they were being danced by a ghost. This time, instead of crumpling it up and throwing it away, she pinned it to the empty corkboard on her wall, the first thing she'd pinned there since she threw everything else away.

Sylvie carried on ripping pages from the paper, pulling the leaves out of the staple grip and papering the bottom of the bathroom floor like a bird feathering its nest. She stood over the sink and mixed up the box dye according to the instructions. She'd never dyed her hair before but this looked simple enough. She put on the thin plastic gloves and gave the bottle a good shake. She set it aside to part her hair with the tail end of a comb into four sections, clipping the top two to the crown of her head with claw clips. Maybe she should have done this before she mixed the dye up, she thought, it was all so fiddly. She felt the back of her neck start to prickle with sweat, the pressure of it all.

She applied the dye as evenly as she could all over and then made sure she'd covered the front of her hairline.

She massaged it all in from top to tip and clipped it up at the back of her head. Her collarbone, neck and ears were smudged with red dye and she poured some micellar water onto a make-up pad and rubbed at the marks as hard as she could, until she got them to fade. They looked like bruises, like love bites. She sat for a while on a stool by the bathtub and scrolled on her phone. She hadn't messaged Sapna back even though she'd texted her asking what happened with work and if she wanted to go out in town that night.

She took a deep breath in through her nose and out through her mouth, and stared down her own reflection. The dye was working its magic, transforming her from black to red like glowing coals. She was going to make Greg fall in love with her. She'd be round the office on his arm in no time. She'd be at his mother's house, at all Jay's family gatherings, smiling sweetly, planting kisses on Greg's cheek, his lips, his hands. She couldn't wait to see the look on Jay's face.

As she washed the hair dye off in the shower, she watched it pool, red as blood, in the water at her feet and she imagined it was Jay's blood. Is that sick? she wondered. Maybe I'm sick. Maybe I'm not. Maybe there should be some consequence for destroying a person you claimed to love. How else can you deal with someone like that? she thought. You can't appeal to their higher nature for sympathy, you can't ever expect them to learn and grow unless you discipline them like the dog that they are. This is for Giselle, she thought. Sylvie held up her hands to watch the red-tinged water run between her fingers, down her chest, her stomach. She closed her eyes and let it run over her back. Jay Lakemore, I'm going to destroy you, Jay Lakemore, I'm not going to stop until you're begging for mercy. When she stepped out of the shower and saw herself, that rich fox red, she felt a thrill through her body. She smiled so hard it hurt but she couldn't stop.

Tinselly decorations hung overhead in the coffee shop, lights in the shapes of bells, ribbons and Christmas trees. It was busy, perhaps the only time of year that the town had any semblance of buzz.

She cleared her throat, took a sip of her coffee and turned to the next page in the diaries.

With Cornelius newly bald, he is rarely seen without a hat. As a result of that simpering milliner's flattery combined with Cornelius's vanity, we are positively drowning in hats, so plentiful and ever-expanding is his collection. There are enormous white hat boxes stacked all over the wardrobe, our bedroom, and NOW they have graduated into the hallway.

There are hat boxes sprouting up everywhere like a quickly multiplying mould. He has cowboy hats made of leather and suede, straw hats, fedoras and trilbies in a rainbow variation of wool and felt, pork pie hats and bowler hats and Greek cotton captain caps, walker hats and berets and big apple caps. Far more hats than

I've ever owned. My life is simply overrun by hats, the situation is untenable and yet, I have not voiced a single word of complaint. I am on a mission for revenge and must maintain the demeanour of a doting wife and the sense that our relationship is going smoothly. So I compliment his ridiculous hats and rub Quick-Gro hair ointment onto his scalp each night until my fingers ache. It will all be worth it, I think, it simply has to be. I've been waiting for exactly the right moment and I believe it has finally presented itself.

You see, last night when we were lying in bed (yes, I know, but if I slept in a different room it would arouse his suspicions) Cornelius told me that we'd been invited to dinner on Saturday night with an old friend of his, Joe Morelli, a well-known mobster and a notorious bigot, whom I simply can't stand. I have protested the business relationship between him and Cornelius at every available interval. I don't know exactly what they do together but I have my theories. Cornelius has always insisted that it's 'just business' and then added, 'Leave it to the men, honey,' in an exasperated tone if I ever pushed him on it. Whatever it was, it seemed to require numerous late night phone calls and emergency meetings in various nightclubs around town. And lately Cornelius has been going on about some 'huge new deal' that Joe promises will make them both millions, though I suspect their friendship is about more than just money. Joe is exactly the kind of macho figure Cornelius loves to idolize, whose approval carries weight.

I've met Joe once or twice, and the impression he made on me was (unfortunately) rather memorable. Amidst a gaudy, penthouse party he came over to introduce himself with a mouth full of hors d'oeuvres and managed to insult 'the Jews, the blacks, the gays' and all of womankind by the time he had the good grace to swallow. A vile man, I immediately despised him. If Cornelius is a toad then this man is the king of them all, ten times the size and simply covered in pus-oozing boils. Well, any other time, I'd have made an excuse and wriggled my way out of dinner with that oaf. I'd sooner go to the salon and have a bikini wax ten times over, but on this particular occasion I was delighted and my mind began to tick with a multitude of possibilities.

Sylvie tilted the coffee cup at her lips and found that she had finished it. As she queued at the till for another, she pondered Jay's whereabouts, wondered what he was doing and with whom. She hoped that somehow, the course of her revenge plan would bring them face to face again. She wanted him to hurt, *needed* him to hurt, and she also wanted him to know that it was she who'd caused the pain.

The next page of her aunt's diary was written in slightly larger font than her typical handwriting. It was punctuated with numerous exclamation marks and various additions of 'hahahaha' that hovered some way above the ruled lines. It was clearly a victory lap, a gloat. The jubilance of its authoress could be felt even half a century later.

Well, I've done it! Hahaha! It went even more splendidly than I could have anticipated. Again, I come to the crucial importance of knowing your subject – or victim, perhaps, is a more appropriate term. My plan was only successful because Cornelius acted in exactly the way I'd anticipated. We met Joe at Emilio's on Bleecker Street, taking a driver from the usual service, ordered by the concierge in our building. As we sat in the back seat, he wore a yellow suit and the hat I'd gifted him for this exact occasion, a floppy-edged felt hat from the women's department at Bergdorf's. He looked at my glorious plunging dress in deep purple, and my impossibly high heels and my skin all glossy and fabulous and he really looked for a moment as if he might cry of pride and remorse. This is the importance of dressing for battle. You see, if one is intent on establishing oneself as a bitch, then one may as well become a bitch of the undeniably fabulous variety. A stylish bitch, if you will.

The importance of dressing for battle. The phrase hung like a string of Christmas lights at the forefront of Sylvie's brain as she picked through clothing racks and folded piles of identical garments. Greg was in town, Sylvie knew this from his LinkedIn, and it was a Friday night so with any luck he'd be at Lana's, the bar he'd claimed to frequent. This was it, her chance at last. She'd been waiting almost a month to strike her opportunity with Greg.

Preened, plucked and perfumed, Sylvie sat up at the bar and waited for Greg. She'd prepared herself by taking a very long, very hot shower and staring for thirty minutes at that tapestry of inky lies she'd made, like it was some kind of hideous experimental, modern art piece.

'What can I get you?' the bartender asked her.

'Vodka soda.'

She was heavily made up with red lipstick and a top with a low scoop-neck.

Underneath, she wore a padded bra to draw attention to her cleavage. Too much, probably, but it was important. She was bait, and everyone knows the bait has to dance, it has to look lively, it has to tempt. So tonight, she was dressed as a matador's flag.

She knocked back her first drink in a few gulps and ordered another; this time she'd nurse it, slowly. She adjusted her posture, shoulders back, one leg crossed over the other in dark jeans. She appraised herself in the reflection of the mirror behind the bar, under the blinking Christmas decoration lights hanging from the ceiling. It was a nice-ish place, an attempt at a plush bar in a rotten area. On closer inspection, you could see that the finishes were cheap imitation, the leather seats of the bar stools were already flimsy and the crowd, late-twenties and thirties mostly, were playing make-believe, wearing their glitziest clothes for a night out at the 'posh place'. Sylvie thought she'd even seen some of them before at the Three Butts but here they were now, buttoned up and looking bewildered, a stiffness to them like they were going to be escorted out any minute for breathing in the wrong way. The bar was made up of an enormous island, where she sat now. Booths made up the rest of the floor space. There was a DJ deck, though no one had arrived to man it yet and instead there were just chart hits playing out of the overhead speakers. It was not especially busy, but it was promising: gaggles of women, mixed groups, an older couple or two.

Sylvie tried to look interested in something behind the bar, not so interested as to actually draw a bartender's attention, but not so lost in her own dreamy thoughts as to look insane. It's an art, as Sylvie soon discovered, looking just *right*, when you're out on your own. Too melancholy and everyone assumes you've had a break-up or been stood up and they give you a wide berth, careful to avoid the contagious stench of failure that seems to steam off you in all directions. Too happy and you look unhinged. No, it's got to be just right, a pleasant almost-smile like you're luxuriating in the bliss of a very weak and overpriced cocktail, the occasional glance at one's phone or at somebody else, a quick scan (and Sylvie was careful to limit these) at the door to see who was coming in. No sign of Greg and it was almost ten o'clock. What time do people go to bars? Sylvie wondered. Sapna's lot just went to the pub, and you could pitch up there whatever time you liked, noon if you really fancied it.

By the time Sylvie got on to her third drink, the place had really livened up. It was packed from wall to wall with office Christmas parties, people booming and beaming at each other across large tables. Several were wearing tinselly decorations on their heads, bobbling snowmen, glittery Christmas trees, their faces reddened with the merriness of it all. The DJ arrived and started playing Wham! A couple of women got up to dance, holding glasses of prosecco over their heads, their lips parting as they scream-sang along, wide-mouthed, red tongues lashing. Sylvie sighed. It looked like fun. But she wondered if she'd ever really derived enjoyment from *light-hearted pleasure.* No, she didn't think so. It had to be more than that for her. Real enjoyment, real satisfaction came from answering an internal call, a gnarled, twisted desire, that had lived in the darkness between her ribs. They were ugly because all hidden human desires are a little ugly, even the ones with pretty faces. To uncover these desires, to interrogate them with torchlight, and then to hunt them down. *That* is what Sylvie enjoyed. Hunting the thing or the person that would bring her closest to her desires. Yes, she could see that now in the pattern of her life.

Had she been living her life like prey when all this time she had a predator's nature? A solitary hunter like a leopard, entirely focused, low to the ground, visible only through the long grasses as her yellow-green eyes narrowed in concentration on the nearby herd of impala. Hunger. Isn't that how it felt? Those low, sure-footed steps before a galloping speed, when she turned her fouetté pirouettes? Like an animal. Sharper, faster, more precise than just anybody, than any normal person. Her leg slicing like a knife in the air, her back perfectly straight, her head whipping around at the neck, her eyes returning always to the same, single spot on the wall ahead, with such focus it was like she could laser through it. That point, for her, represented the point of desire, the want that burnt in her stomach and sent warmth all through her body.

'Vodka tonic and a . . . what do you want, mate?'

'Peroni.'

'And a Peroni, cheers.'

It was Greg, finally, right next to her at the bar. She could smell the cologne coming off him, something with citrus. She looked up at him as he loomed over her. She made sure it came out just right, surprise and flirtation that wasn't desperate but loud enough to be heard.

'Greg?'

He turned to his right and then to his left, searching out the source of the voice and then his eyes caught her, and he grinned, a bright, white smile.

'Sylvie,' he said, 'what are you doing here? Red hair, wow. Almost didn't recognize you. You look unreal.'

He leant over and kissed her on the cheek, one hand pressing at her lower back. He was freshly shaved but still a little rough, the burgeoning stubble scratched at her cheek. He checked her out properly when he drew back, her lips, her chest, her legs.

'Just took myself for a drink after a bit of Christmas shopping,' she said.

Greg made a big deal of looking around for her bags.

'Not a successful trip, then?'

'Your drinks, mate.' The bartender put a glass and a bottle of beer on the countertop and Greg paid with his phone before giving his friend on the other side of the bar a sharp nod and saying, 'I'll be over in a minute.' The nod said, *I'm taking this girl home.*

Sylvie knew she had his interest, but she needed to be careful about what happened next. She had to pivot this into something relatively long-lasting. Sure, Jay would be annoyed if he heard she had slept with Greg, but a one-off festive bonking is nowhere near as triggering as a relationship, as Sylvie infiltrating his family, his inner sanctum.

'No,' she said. 'I gave up. I'm going to do it all online. Where's your girlfriend?' she asked him, looking around earnestly.

'I'm single,' he said. 'I know, I know. It's sad, right, all alone for Christmas.'

'I'm sure you'll survive.'

'Maybe,' he said, leaning closer, 'maybe I'll find a pretty girl to keep me company for the night.'

'Maybe you will,' she said, and then looking right past him, she pointed at a woman standing in an awkward slump on one leg like her dress didn't fit right. 'You could try her.'

Sylvie glanced up at him, he was squinting at her.

'Nah, I couldn't.'

'Why not?'

'I think you'd be jealous.'

'Me?' She allowed herself to look shocked. She pressed her hand to her chest, plumped up by the padded bra.

'Yeah,' Greg said. 'I think so.'

She took a sip of her drink. 'Why don't you try it, and we'll find out.'

He turned to look at the girl. 'Don't think I'll bother.'

'Why not?'

'Waste of time,' he said, with a wink. 'You're so much better.'

Sylvie sighed like his interest was wearing on her. 'Are you all ready for Christmas, then?'

'Of course,' he said. 'Got a Christmas tree and everything. Let me get you a drink. What are you having?'

'I think I'll have something festive next,' said Sylvie.

Greg raised his eyebrows at her and snatched a small, crimson, gold-trimmed piece of card off its stand on the bar.

'Hmm,' he said, scanning the five or six festive cocktails the bar had customized together for the season. He looked up at her once more before gesturing to the bartender. 'One gingerbread martini, please.'

'A gingerbread martini?' Sylvie said quietly, screwing up her nose. 'What made you choose that?'

'Best of a bad lot,' he said, leaning on the bar countertop with his forearms and looking at her.

Sylvie looked back at him with wide glistening eyes. 'Was it very lonely?'

'Excuse me?'

'Decorating your Christmas tree, I mean. I assume you live alone.'

'You assume right,' he said, 'but no, it wasn't, actually, my mum wanted to come by and give me a hand, you know, make an afternoon of it all.'

Damn, Sylvie thought, she was supposed to be seducing him and now they were talking about his mother. She had to find a way to steer them into definitively sexier territory. Or perhaps . . . As she observed Greg, she noticed a sudden forlornness, a sense of sadness, as if he was being transported back to the distant loveless terror of his childhood.

'Do you see her often?' Sylvie asked him, her voice soft. 'Your mum.'

Greg had a strange look in his eye.

Sylvie accepted the drink from the bartender, put it down on the counter in front of her and looked at its murky, milky brown colour with suspicion.

Greg chuckled. 'Look, you don't have to drink it, but I'll be disappointed if you don't even give it a try. And no, I don't see her often, I'm certainly not high on her list.'

Sylvie lifted the martini by the stem and took a small sip. 'Mm, well, you're not exactly high on *my* list after that.'

'That bad, eh?'

'I'm kidding,' she said, touching his arm, squeezing it gently at the bicep. 'It's delicious, surprisingly delicious.'

And she let her hand linger there. Sylvie knew it was an important part of seduction. Forming an emotional connection. Normally you had to wait patiently for your subject to break open and then when you see a little chink you can get in. You can manufacture intimacy, connection, by mirroring, by giving validation, by being the one who sees a person the way they really want to be seen. She was always good at that, Sylvie realized, she'd done it before with Jay. Only her own emotions had always been too wrapped up in things for her to make the most of her abilities.

They talked about families. Greg thought it was sad Sylvie was an only child. Even though he didn't get on too well with his own brother, he said it was still better than not having one at all. He was closer with his dad and his step-siblings now, he said. He talked about his big family Christmases, all the dutiful driving around and errand running and box hauling he had ahead of him for the season.

Sylvie drank the rest of the martini down to the last few sips and then Greg reached out for the glass and tipped it back at his lips.

'Pahh.' He stuck out his tongue, a thick, large tongue, and wrinkled his nose. 'That's disgusting.'

Sylvie shrugged at him and then she gestured for Greg to look over his shoulder. 'I think your friend's gotten tired of waiting for you.'

Greg lifted up his hand to wave goodbye to his friend, who was winding a scarf around his neck and staggering out the door.

'My fault?' she asked him.

'I'll give him your apologies,' he said. And then, 'So . . . Sylvie, what do you think?'

'What do I think about what?'

Leaning on the bar, with his other hand he began to trace the length of the index finger of her right hand.

'All looks a bit naff actually, doesn't it?' he said, looking up at the bottles of liquor lined up on shelves over the bar.

'I thought you loved this bar.'

'It's all right,' he said, the soft underside of his fingertip stroking her hand. 'But I've got much nicer drinks at my place.' The way he said it was rather disjointed, soft, as if he knew with each word that he was wandering further into dangerous territory, up to the edge of a cliff. It was a tiptoe of a sentence.

Sylvie had to act like she didn't want to when it was the only reason she was there. She rolled her eyes and smiled, curling her tongue briefly up over her top teeth so that he could see it, pink and wet in her mouth, like she was tasting herself.

'Are you any good at making cocktails?'

'The best,' he said, flashing those veneers again.

Fifteen

Good Little Wife

Greg's place was on the top floor of an apartment building that had been converted out of a Victorian-style mansion; it was just the one building and there was an enormous gate at the top of the drive that opened automatically as they approached in his electric-blue Lamborghini. There must have only been three or four apartments in the whole building, and Sylvie wondered what kind of person would choose to live there. She guessed someone like Greg, a perennial bachelor with zero interest in tending hedges. She followed him into the plushly decorated lobby, overwhelmed by the heat of it as they passed through the threshold and shut the door on an icily cold night.

'Is it always this hot?' she asked him.

'Nice, isn't it?'

The marble tiles were warm beneath her feet. There was an enormous geometric chandelier hanging over her head, beams of light at various angles, hanging from a silver metal frame. They crossed the floor to the lift. Greg pressed the button and smiled at her, and she smiled back at him, shyly. Sylvie felt Greg's hand at the small of her back, guiding her gently and firmly into the lift. She saw her reflection in the interior mirrored wall and for a moment she didn't recognize herself under the light. You're going to do this, aren't you? You have to do this, she thought. The woman in the mirror was tired, with dark circles under the eyes and a wild lost look in her irises, wearing a coat that seemed too big for her. Her brown skin was almost grey, washed out under the overhead light.

Stop it, she told herself, stop picking yourself apart like that. It was the lighting, that's all. Stay focused. Sleep with Greg, humiliate Jay. Greg. In the mirror she saw his wide square jaw hovering over her head. She had a sense of finality when the lift doors closed behind them, and then the heavy whir of the lift taking off, rising up. She felt her stomach shift. She thought she'd feel triumphant. The first step in her revenge plan, a bold and pragmatic move, but instead she felt something different. Something sour. Regret? Resentment? When Jay found out about this, he was going to hate her, really hate her. Any chance of the two of them would be gone for ever. But that's not why she was doing this, right? She hated Jay. Yes, she hated him. She wouldn't want to be with him even if he crawled towards her over an ocean of shattered glass, with a four-carat ring. Would she? Would she?

'Sorry, what did you say?'

They'd arrived. They had somehow drifted out of the lift and to an open front door, white with a brass number 4 hanging up against it. Would Sylvie like Greg to hang up her coat?

'Yes, please.' Sylvie shook off her earlier reservations, trusting her previous determination over momentary doubt. She wouldn't get this chance again. She handed it to him. 'And, uh . . . shoes?' She pointed down at her feet.

He shrugged. 'Up to you.'

Sylvie began to unzip her heeled boots, hunched over, inelegantly, for balance. She managed to rid herself of them in a few awkward pulls and then she stood in her black cotton socks in the hallway, awaiting instruction.

'Drink?' he asked, beckoning for her to follow.

'That's why I came.'

He looked back over his shoulder and grinned at her. 'Thought you came for the Christmas tree.'

'That too,' she said. 'This is a really nice place.'

And it was. The hallway was long, with white marble floors and overhanging light fixtures, in a similar style to the one she saw in the lobby. They passed several closed doors on each side and she wondered which one was Greg's bedroom.

The end of the hallway opened up into an open-plan living space, with an all-white minimalist kitchen fitted up against the wall on the far left. Despite the Victorian architecture of the outside, inside it was extremely modern. There weren't any appliances on show, any spoons or spatulas, they were all cleverly tucked away somewhere and probably popped out when you pressed on the large white cupboard doors in just the right way. There was a small island and a vast expanse of white and grey marble floor, and there were a couple of sofas, sort of slimline, like something out of a James Bond film from the late sixties. There was a coffee table that looked like a sheet of glass balanced atop a polished grey stone, and an enormous flatscreen TV, hanging like a black mirror on the far right wall.

And there it was, squished up right in the corner looking neglected, a black synthetic Christmas tree with scant white baubles nestled in among the plastic bristles, a length of silver tinsel wrapped around it, and a silver metal star balanced on top.

'Hang on,' Greg said, rushing over to the tree and bending down to scrabble behind it, swearing quietly under his breath as he struggled to reach whatever it was.

'So this is the magnificent tree?'

'Never said it . . . was . . . magnificent, almost got it, hang on!'

Sylvie wandered over to the kitchen area and ran her fingertips along the surfaces. It was extremely tidy. The white countertops were freshly wiped down and there was the faint smell of lemony detergent hanging in the air. It was too clean, like it had been prepared for visitors, prepared for a woman, and here she was. She didn't think it would be difficult to get into Greg's bed, but it might be harder to get him to want to date her. To convince him she was worth investing time in. That was her mission.

'All right, look at it now,' said Greg.

The tree twinkled to life with white fairy lights, honestly too many. Greg stood back from it to appraise the sight.

'Wow,' she said, drily.

'Worth the trip?'

'Definitely.'

'I know it's a bit naff,' he said. 'But it suits me fine. I'll make you that drink.'

As he began to pull glasses and various half-filled bottles out of cupboards she stood up close to the cool windows, and looked down at the driveway and the dense hedges that lined the road beyond it, merging into black. Sylvie tried to think of what was going to happen next, exactly how she wanted things to progress.

It turned out she didn't have to think much at all. Greg was experienced enough for the both of them. They sat together on the sofa and had a few more drinks each, their conversation becoming slowly more incoherent and suggestive, Greg coming closer and closer by the minute, his hand on her leg and then her arm, then her shoulder and then they were kissing.

'Do you want to go into the bedroom?' he whispered, putting a hand through her hair. Sylvie nodded, before adding, sheepishly, 'I don't normally do this.'

'Neither do I,' said Greg, a twinkle in his eye.

They both laughed.

'No really,' she said. 'I don't want you to think . . .'

'I don't think anything,' he said, pulling her in for a kiss. 'Just that I like you.'

They had sex on Greg's super-king bed with 1,500 thread count Egyptian cotton sheets and when it was over, all Sylvie felt was tired. She was so sleepy that her head was heavy and her eyelids burning to close. She shut her eyes, with her cheek resting on Greg's chest and her arm wrapped over him. Her tiredness made her weak. Weak to lingering old feelings of sentimentality, of love that she felt for Jay, feelings that had survived somehow within her, like cockroaches after a nuclear disaster. She breathed in and allowed herself to imagine it was Jay beside her, the two of them lying there together, warm, sated, peaceful, and she was so happy. She was in heaven. She imagined that when she looked up, she would see Jay's face there, the rough-edged, gorgeous beauty, his deep green eyes. But when she opened her eyes, she saw Greg, as beautiful perhaps, more beautiful to some, but too simple to be perfect to her. There was no taking this back.

Sylvie got up and took herself into the bathroom. To the shiny sheen of its rectangular mirror, with bright spaceship-style lights in a rectangular frame. Everything smelt like lemongrass and all the glass was free of smudges or fingerprints, so she knew it had been professionally cleaned. She caught one look at herself in the mirror, naked with mussed-up hair, and she started to cry. She pulled the door shut behind her. Trying her hardest to quieten her sobs she held a towel over her mouth. I love Jay, she thought. She leant forward to look at herself in the mirror, with the red lipstick kissed off her mouth. She took her hand and slapped herself hard in the face with it, once, twice. *He never loved you, he never loved you. It was all a lie and a game, do you understand? You mean nothing to him. He was only special because you applied the breadth of your imagination to him, you embellished his absences and you knitted together every phrase he uttered your way, every glance, every touch like it was a great sign in the sky. He is nothing, yes, he is nothing.*

Sylvie felt hurt and stupid but alive, like there was fire in her veins because she was nothing if not focused. She was nothing if not devoted to a goal. That goal had become Jay's destruction and she wouldn't stop until his life was in pieces and she could pick them up and throw them over herself like confetti.

Sylvie woke up hours before Greg in the morning. She lay still, careful not to disturb him, and looked at the narrow shaft of light peeping through the gap in the curtains. When he finally stirred, he looked at her and smiled gently, beckoned for her to nestle in to him and she wriggled back, pressing her body against his.

He made her an espresso in the kitchen, the two of them dressed in hotel-style robes, Sylvie swamped by hers.

'You're really prepared for these sleepovers, aren't you?'

Greg looked embarrassed. 'Bachelor life,' he said. 'What can I say? I used to be a Scout.'

Sylvie raised an eyebrow.

'You really don't want any sugar in that?' Greg asked her.

She shook her head, sipping her espresso from the tiny ceramic cup.

'You know the Italians would say you're a psycho,' Greg said.

'I'm not Italian,' said Sylvie. 'Are you?'

'Not even a little bit. But they say only dark personalities drink coffee like that.'

Sylvie laughed. 'Who says that?'

'I don't know,' said Greg, as he pointedly heaped two large spoonfuls of sugar into his mug of coffee. 'Scientists.'

'Sure they do.'

'Look, I know you're probably keen to get out of here now that you've had your way with me and everything but do you fancy sticking a movie on, ordering breakfast?'

'Is this what you do with the other girls?' Sylvie asked him. 'Because I have to say, it's very well-rounded, the Premium Bachelor Experience.'

'Hey,' said Greg, softly. 'Who says I want to be a bachelor for ever?'

They ate breakfast muffins from a café down the road while they lay on the sofa in their dressing gowns and watched *The Holiday*. Greg put his head into Sylvie's lap and though the intimacy of the action threw her at first, she

194

found herself running her fingers through his hair, twirling a small lock of it around her finger. He had the same dark hair as Jay's.

He dropped her home in the early afternoon.

'What did you think?' he asked her as they pulled up outside her house.

Sylvie could see her mum peering through the glass panel in the front door, watching.

'Below average tree,' said Sylvie. 'Decent drinks. Great film.'

'No,' said Greg. 'About me.'

'Undecided,' said Sylvie before pulling him in by the back of the neck and kissing him. 'See you later.'

Sylvie got out of the car without looking back. She smiled to herself; it had been a triumph and she knew it.

'Yes, you will,' said Greg as he watched her go.

Sylvie almost gave Nadine a concussion when she opened the front door.

'Mum! What are you doing pressed up against the door like that?'

'That car sounded like thunder when it came down the road,' said Nadine, her eyes sparkling. 'Who was that?'

'No one,' said Sylvie. 'Someone I'm seeing.'

'He doesn't deal drugs, does he?'

'No, Mum, he does not deal drugs.'

'Well, then I'm happy for you.' Nadine really smiled then. 'That's wonderful, darling. And have you given any more thought to the memorial service?'

Sylvie had pushed any thoughts of her Aunt Jacqueline's memorial service firmly into the shadowy, outer recesses of her mind. But now with the diaries, she felt her aunt's presence more keenly and vitally than she had in years. Shouldn't she do something for the service? As a thank you to the one person who'd helped her so much in life and even in death.

'I don't dance any more,' she said, quietly.

'Just one dance,' said her mother. 'Something short?'

'It's not like that,' said Sylvie, frowning. 'You can't just leap right into it after years of nothing.' She looked at her mum: Nadine's diamond studs glinted in the light. Sylvie knew she could never understand. She couldn't call to mind a single memory of her mum working hard at anything, she didn't even wash her own hair.

'Will you think about it, Sylvie?'

'Yeah,' she said, giving a short sigh. 'I'll think about it.'

In truth, she had been thinking about ballet ever since she'd uncovered her old shoes and leotards; part of her was desperate to go to the adult ballet class on Thursday, if only for old times' sake.

Nadine beamed and gave Sylvie a kiss on the cheek.

'Nadine!' Clive's bellowing voice echoed along the staircase and Nadine gave Sylvie a helpless look.

'I'm being summoned,' she said.

'Yes, you are.'

As Nadine sped off to the kitchen, Sylvie hauled her weary body up the stairs.

As the day dwindled away, Sylvie's fear only grew. She dreaded the morning. She dreaded seeing Jay after the destroyed foam fingers, seeing Jay after Greg. What if Greg had said something? She couldn't imagine how Jay was going to react and that frightened her. But she'd done it, she'd really fucking done it. She'd achieved exactly what she'd set out to do. All evening, she bounced between ecstasy and terror. She rested her head against her pillow and tried to lose herself in her aunt's diaries, desperate to be out of her own head just for a minute.

As we sat in the back of the cab, I began talking to Cornelius about a young waiter who had served my friend and I the last time I'd been to Emilio's only a month or so ago.

'Lawrence, I think his name is,' I said, looking out of the window with a deliberately pensive expression on my face.

'Well, what the hell's that got to do with me?' said Cornelius, opening his cigar case and putting one between his lips.

'Not much,' I said. 'Only he's got his first boxing match coming up soon at the Palladium, and he's rather nervous. Last time he told us all about his training, it sounded so brutal! I wonder how he's been getting along.'

Cornelius puffed out a thick cloud of smoke. 'What's he got to talk to you for?'

I looked at him then, with awe in my eyes. 'Because of you, darling! You're the whole reason we had the conversation in the first place! He said hadn't he seen me at Emilio's before, with a gentleman who looked as though he had a boxer's build? And I said yes that's my husband and he was a rather good boxer in his younger years, incidentally.'

Cornelius softened then, the cigar hanging from his lips when he said, 'Good? I made Johnny "the Wall" Johnson's head spin. The guy was like a goddamned owl.'

'Yes, that's what I thought,' I said. 'Well, will you have a word with him about it? He's such a meek young fellow I'm sure he'd appreciate your advice, he'd be ever so grateful.'

Cornelius put his hand up to stop me, as if he didn't want to discuss it a moment longer, but a smug smile played on his lips, and I knew he'd do exactly as I asked.

Joe was already there when we arrived, and halfway through a bottle of wine.

'Tonight's real important,' he hissed in my ear as we approached the table. 'Once we sign this deal, babe, we're made. Don't embarrass me, all right.'

'I'll try my best not to, darling heart,' I said, as I trailed behind him.

'Cornelius, why the fuck are you wearing a lady's hat? You look like a fairy!' Joe laughed as Cornelius snatched the hat off, revealing his shiny bald head.

'He loves that hat,' I said, quietly, as Joe pulled me in for a kiss.

His hand wandered very low down my back when he greeted me, his breath was alcoholic and his teeth dyed a crimson hue in the edges.

'Where do you wanna sit, Lady?' he asked me.

He insists on calling me Lady because I'm English, but the noble connotations are scrambled on his tongue, and it comes out sounding more like a term for a female animal than anything else. He poured me a glass of wine and before I could swallow it, he announced, 'Can you believe we've got a fucking foreign waiter?' and I almost spat it out all over the white tablecloth.

I sat quietly while Cornelius asked Joe about his current girlfriend, a woman called Sally Hedges who had almost left him for good last week when she'd discovered him in bed with a prostitute.

Joe wiped his fingers on a napkin before jabbing them in the air at an imaginary Sally. 'I said, listen, honey, this is the way things are gonna be or you can find another sucker to pay off your tab at Barneys.'

Cornelius laughed entirely too hard. 'And what did she say to that?'

Joe grinned, his face shiny and red in the low restaurant lighting. 'What could she say? She shut the door and walked out, and we never mentioned it again.'

I cleared my throat, before standing up from the table. 'I'm going to go and powder my nose.'

'Sorry, Lady,' said Joe. 'Didn't mean to offend you, sweetheart.' He gestured with his hand in the air beside his mouth as if imitating turning a key in

a lock. 'I'll be a good boy when you get back, don't
wanna catch a spanking.'

I turned away so he didn't hear me groan and then
I started in the direction of the bathroom as Cornelius
laughed, again, far too hard, at Joe's awful joke.

In the ladies I patted my face with cold water. I had
to endure this until the moment was exactly right, and
the right moment arrived shortly thereafter when the
entrées had been taken away. Cornelius stifled a burp
before wiping his fingers on his already soiled shirt
and stood up from the table, excusing himself, before
swaying away in the direction of 'the shitter', drunk on
a bottle and a half of good red wine.

I felt the edge of Joe's buckled shoe slide towards me
under the table – he's that kind of man. He asked me,
eyelids hanging low with lust, if I'd been being a good
little wife to his friend, keeping him satisfied and so on.
I saw my chance and I took it.

Jay did not come in to work the next day, which gave Sylvie
an enormous sense of relief. His presence always impeded
on her resolve, which was as resolute in his absence as fire-
forged iron. Revenge, revenge, revenge. Derek spent most
of the morning 'wired-in' to a manufacturer call; Karen
excused herself at ten o'clock to go to a dentist's appointment and didn't seem in any rush to return; and Sapna
made a coffee and shut herself away into Jay's room, though
it looked to Sylvie as if she spent most of the morning

scrolling TikTok rather than engaged in anything remotely work-related.

Sylvie was too agitated to direct her energy in any one particular direction. She kept thinking about Greg and wondering what was going to happen when Jay found out about the two of them. He might get violent. It was a thought that both thrilled and soothed her, the idea that she was still able to rile him, to get at him, under his skin. He could hurt her, sure, he *had* hurt her, but he couldn't prevent her from reaching into his hidden, tender core. He might have killed her once but there was nothing he could do to stop the haunting. Sylvie decided that she shared her Aunt Jacqueline's gift after all, something like a second sight, the ability to understand a man more acutely than he understood himself.

'How's it going?' Sylvie opened the door of Jay's room and peeked through the inch-wide gap in the frame.

Sapna looked up at her, a watery smile barely masking her irritation at being interrupted.

'Yeah?'

'I'm just a bit . . . bored,' said Sylvie. 'Don't have any tasks, do you mind if I chill in here for a bit?'

'Sure,' Sapna shrugged. 'Red hair, nice. Very . . . Little Mermaid.'

'Felt like a change.' Sylvie pulled out a chair and Sapna returned to her scrolling.

'Busy day?' Sylvie asked her as she sank onto the rigid plastic seat.

'Oh, yeah,' said Sapna. 'Absolutely stacked. I'm glad,

to be honest, ended up going out last night, got a banging headache.'

'Where's Jay?'

Sapna shrugged.

When it was obvious that Sylvie wasn't going to be able to coax a conversation out of her that morning, she got up from her seat and began to wander around the room. She remembered the shadow-cast sight of Jay's face hovering above hers in the dark, the kisses, the sweet cold beer bubbling over her tongue, the rough insides of his palms under her blouse, calloused fingertips stroking against her skin, pinching her puckered nipples. The daylight, together with the overhead synthetics, sanitized and castrated the scene. Sylvie ran her fingertips over the piles of paperwork on a desk tucked into the corner, the red binder with INVOICES written across the front, the plastic cup filled with identical black biros, most of them unused, their perfect plastic caps still firmly in place and the barcode labels undisturbed. Factory fresh. Her eyes fell on the filing cabinet, and she crossed the carpet partially on tiptoe, cautious of disturbing Sapna who had her phone resting on the desktop and was hunched over it, dead-eyed and doom-scrolling. The cabinet was locked. Strange, Sylvie thought. She turned the key in the lock and the door creaked open. Sylvie looked over her shoulder to see that Sapna was still engrossed in her scrolling and paid her no mind.

The bottles of water and cans of Coke were nowhere to be found, and the cabinet was filled with uniform black files. Sylvie crouched down in front of it. She noticed the grey clusters of dust that had collected around the metal feet, and her knees began to tremble as she fought the urge to rest them on the floor. She ran her hand over the stack of folders on the bottom shelf; the black binders were unlabelled and unmarked.

'What are these?'

'Huh?'

'These folders.'

'Oh, Jay's projects.'

'Jay's projects,' Sylvie repeated. She hooked her finger around the top of one binder and pulled it towards her, sliding it out of its place on the shelf.

'No one's supposed to touch those,' said Sapna. The note of urgency in her voice made Sylvie turn over her shoulder and look at her.

'Why not?'

'They're like VIP or whatever, he's the only one who's allowed to look at those accounts.'

'And you don't think that's a bit . . .'

'Dodge?' said Sapna. 'Yeah, it's dodgy as fuck but he's the boss and he pays me, so . . .' She shrugged. 'Can you put that back? He'll know if someone's touched them, I had a look before and he went mental.'

Sylvie pushed the folder back into place. 'How would he know?'

'No idea,' said Sapna. 'But I do know he used to store them somewhere else and since he brought them here, I have to lock the filing cabinet when I leave every night.'

'Interesting.' Sylvie got up to her feet, shaking out her tired legs. 'Very interesting.'

'What's going on with you and Jay anyway?' Sapna asked, locking her phone and putting it face down on the table. Her eyes gleamed, she was ready to gossip. 'You haven't seemed so buddy-buddy since his wife dropped in that time.'

Sylvie made eye contact with the framed picture of Jay and Annabel at the back of the filing cabinet shelf, which had been left in the exact place she'd seen it that first day she'd come in for the interview.

'I don't know,' she said. 'Just don't think he's that nice of a guy.'

'Oh, come on,' said Sapna. 'You never thought he was nice. Like, he's a lot of things but he's not that.'

'Maybe you're right.'

'Honestly, babe, I think you dodged a bullet. Like, I didn't want to get involved or anything, but you do *not* want to get tangled up with that fucking psycho.'

Sylvie forced herself to smile.

'Did you fuck Brett? I thought maybe that's why you didn't want to come out with us any more.'

'What?'

'Doesn't matter if you did, it's just one of my mates really likes him so if you *are* fucking Brett then can you do me a favour and just *not* fuck Brett any more?'

'Sure,' said Sylvie. 'No problem.' She closed the filing cabinet door and turned the tiny key in the lock. 'Better get back to my desk,' she said. 'Before Karen shows up.'

*

Sylvie rested her chin in her cupped palm and watched the sun set outside the window. The factory workers trailed out into the dark under the flickering acid-yellow glow of the street lamp at the end of the car park, breathing out clouds of cigarette smoke and laughing condensation into the cold air. She was alone. She'd been waiting, patiently and then less patiently, like a caged animal pacing back and forth behind bars. She had not been able to stop thinking about the rows of black files and what they might contain. She remembered Abdyll's swimming pool, slicked black hair, slicked black underwear, Claudia's accented English when she said, 'He don't do nothin' legal.' Could it be possible, Sylvie pondered, that the folders contained the smoking gun? She could ruin Jay's life, his career, his business. It was almost too good to believe, and she was cautious, suspicious of the optimism that flowed over her like warm honey.

It was time. Ten minutes at least since the last worker had left. She'd heard the door downstairs clang shut and there'd been nothing since. Jay's office was ghoulish in the dark. Sylvie planted her feet on the same patch of carpet where she'd stood when Jay pinned her to the wall and kissed her. She closed her eyes and remembered it, felt the same threadbare patch underneath her shoe, the bit where the carpet sagged away from the floorboards. She tilted her head back against the pane of glass and felt it cold where it pressed to her scalp. She gasped as she recalled the intensity of the memory, and then she drew herself back, fought against the tide of feeling that threatened to sweep her away and overwhelm her. She focused on the hatred. She didn't dare to turn the light on but switched on her iPhone torch instead. Sylvie put her fingers against the lip at the edge of the cabinet door and pulled it. There was no movement. Locked, but this time the keyhole was empty. Sapna must have moved the key.

'Fuck,' she whispered in the gloom as she began to feel frantically over the contents of the desk. She picked up the pot of pens and shook it, once and then a second time to confirm that what she'd heard was real. The chime of a small metallic object hitting the interior of the cup. It could be a pencil sharpener, she reasoned as she put the pot down and grabbed the pens in one hand, feeling the bottom of the pot with the other. The key. A key at least, perhaps the spare. It didn't matter why it was there, all that mattered was whether it would open the filing cabinet. It was a fragile, flimsy-feeling thing like the kind of key that might belong to a journal or a toy. Sylvie squinted up close in the gloom and thought that she could have bent it, twisted it up in one hand. She thought it was strange how something so feeble could be so crucially important.

A noise downstairs in the factory startled her and she froze, her heart racing as she strained her ears to listen, but nothing more came. It was likely a machine resetting itself, or the metal stem of a mop, left precariously resting against the wall, that had succumbed to gravity and hit the cement with a whack. Even still, she sank to the floor and crawled on her hands and knees towards the filing cabinet, reaching up to fit the key into the slot and rejoicing silently when it turned in the lock. She chose a file at the end of the row, tucked it under her arm and locked the cabinet, put the key back into the pot and collected her coat from where it hung on the back of her chair. She locked all three locks on the office door before skipping out into the dark.

When Sylvie got home, she discovered that she had scud like pond-scum, dust and debris stuck to her tights over her knees. She sat on the edge of her bed and opened the folder. She was disappointed to find at first glance that the invoices looked legitimate. They were addressed to Black Star Ltd and contained details of monthly projects dating back the last year, starting around the same time Sylvie knew Jay had joined the company. The contents of the invoices were always different and seemed obscure. *3,000 apple green foam fingers. 2 lines electric pink print. Overnight delivery.* Weird, Sylvie thought, for this company to need foam fingers of a different kind every month but she supposed it could have been some kind of cheerleader supply company. That would sort of make sense. She was starting to feel deflated. There was nothing obviously amiss here and she'd been looking forward to showing up to work the next morning and throwing the file down on Jay's table like a young, mixed-race, female Sherlock Holmes in a pair of heeled ankle boots. But alas.

But then she thought again, Black Star Ltd, had she seen the name before? Heard it somewhere? When she googled it, results spat out a registration at Companies House and named Abdyll Murati as the director. Abdyll. Sylvie smiled, vindicated. She returned to the Google search page, scrolling for a company website, and found a plain website template with **Black Star Ltd** in a banner across the header and then an email address and a landline number with a local area code. There was no description of what the company claimed to do. Sylvie's thumb hovered over the number, a moment's hesitation before she pressed it. She held the phone to her ear, ready, anxious but she heard nothing but the beep of a dud line and the sound of her own blood rushing in her ears. Either the line was dead or the number was fake. *He don't do nothin' legal.* It was more than likely, she thought, that Jay was washing money through Abdyll's company. And possible that the other black files contained even more fabricated invoices for even more shell companies.

Sylvie clutched the folder to her chest and lay back on her bed, breathless with the thrill of her discovery. Remember Aunt Jacqueline, Sylvie cautioned herself – it was vitally important that she handle this discovery with care, that she not make any rash decisions. She slid the folder under her bed. It was like a latent explosive, a bomb she'd deploy when the time was right.

Sixteen

Act of Rebellion, Act of Love

Greg: When can I see you again?

Sylvie: So soon?

Greg: Thursday night I'll buy you dinner. 7pm.

Sylvie glanced across her bedroom at the ballet class flier pinned to the corkboard.

Sylvie: I'm busy Thursday night

Greg: Wednesday then?

Sylvie: Wednesday it is

Jay didn't come into the office on Tuesday either that week. Sylvie waited with bated breath as the hours drove on, fully expecting him to pull up into the car park or come striding up the stairs. When she returned from lunch, she thought he'd be there. She readied herself to make eye contact with him across the office, but he didn't show. She asked Karen, as inconspicuously as she could, whether Jay was coming in and Karen would shrug. Family stuff, apparently.

On Wednesday night, Greg picked Sylvie up. Sylvie's mum watched from the reception room window with an unmistakable look of pride on her face. He took her to a small town, thirty miles out on the riverside. They went to an upscale French restaurant and ate oysters and drank white wine looking out on the water. It was dark but the riverside was lined with lights. Sylvie thought it looked like a great lake of black ink. She pressed her foot against Greg's leg under the table. He talked a lot about his hopes for the future, where he wanted to live, the kind of house he wanted. He wanted kids, he told her, two boys and a girl. Sylvie thought it was a pretty intense conversation, seeing as it was only their first official date, but she did her best to mirror him, widening her eyes and smiling with recognition as he described his dream future, as if to say, *Me too, aren't we just made for each other?* He was making it easy for her, she thought. She'd worm her way into his heart in no time and then Jay would have no chance of getting rid of her. She'd be there, in his life for ever if she really wanted.

'You're a good listener,' Greg said as he paused to take a sip from his wine glass, a little embarrassed at having gone on for such a length.

'You're easy to listen to,' said Sylvie. 'You're not what I expected.'

'No?' he asked, smiling.

'You're a lot more,' said Sylvie.

She knew he'd like that one.

Greg gave her a lingering kiss when he dropped her off outside her house. She wanted to stay over at his, she told him, but she had to be up early for work. Another day soon, she promised him. He said he'd hold her to that. He blew her a kiss from the driver's seat before driving off. Sylvie had him exactly where she wanted him. Phase one was coming together rather nicely. Soon it would be time to step things up.

Thursday. Sylvie woke up, with the ballet class at the forefront of her mind. The lilac-coloured flier almost luminescent on the corkboard. She'd put it to the back of her mind, open to it as a concept. Herself at an amateur adult ballet class was an act of rebellion against the pressure she'd put on herself to be perfect, but an act of love as well, for the art form and the thousands of hours she'd dedicated to it. She woke up that morning with a sense of resolve that had materialized overnight. The first thing she did after making herself coffee was go through her duffel bag of ballet things and take out what she needed.

She found an unopened packet of pink ballet tights zipped into the inside of the bag and she picked a pair of ballet shoes, ones with the sturdiest soles, ones that hadn't been worked to a flimsy, papery state. She slipped them on over her bare feet and, with her hands on the railing of the bed like it was a ballet barre, she worked them through. She tried to articulate some movement out of them, bending her legs in a knock-kneed plié with her feet together and then rising onto the ball of each foot one at a time. The stiff glue under the soles creaked with her movement. Not bad. She stood in front of her mirror. She looked so strange in her sweatshirt and knitted leggings with pointe shoe ribbons wrapped around the ankles. She'd never expected to see herself in a pair of ballet shoes again. She put her arms out either side of her body in second position, and rose onto the tips of her toes, holding it for a few seconds and then lowering herself down again. It didn't hurt exactly, but there was a strain. As she sat down on the floor to take the shoes off again, she felt a burgeoning cramp across the bottom of her right foot. Her muscles remembered, but they were tight and stubborn.

She untied the shoes and examined the bottoms. Every dancer prepared their shoes differently. It was incredibly personal. Ffion and Sylvie were the only two in their Willow Way class who didn't like to wear toe patches or stuff the bottom of their shoes with animal wool or cotton. Perhaps it was a little competitive, which of them was the most *serious*, which of them felt less pain, but after a while Sylvie preferred it, feeling the rough abrasion of the shoe through the tights. She could identify each part of the shoe, find her balance, rather than feel an all-over, cotton-encased numbness. That's not to say that toe pads made pointe work pain free, there was no escaping pain in ballet. Most dancers roughed up the bottom of the pointe shoe. It was almost impossible to get a good grip otherwise and you risked slipping over. You could rough up the satin itself or paste a suedette patch onto the bottom of the box, the hard, reinforced part of the shoe around the toes, like Sylvie did.

The suedette on the pointe shoes she held in her hands was smooth as anything. She took a pair of scissors out of her bedside table drawer and began to scratch a cross-hatched pattern on the leather. It hurt her hand a little, the metal of the scissor blades pressing into her skin, but she had to get a good pressure or it didn't work. It brought back memories, this action, of Willow Way but before that too, the tense atmosphere of ballet school auditions, sitting in musty changing rooms in oversized warm-up clothes, of her local ballet schools and the holidays and weekends she spent at Central School of Ballet. Preparing pointe shoes, just one of many rituals in the ballet church. Sacred.

Work went quickly. Sylvie busied herself the best she could with all the odd jobs Karen and Derek passed her way. She ate sausage rolls and drank lattes with Sapna at lunchtime. Sapna told her stories about people she knew from town and Sylvie pretended to listen though she didn't recognize a single name Sapna mentioned. She nodded to give the impression she was listening intently even though she spent the whole time dissociating, thinking about the ballet class and Greg and Jay and Annabel.

Maple Village Hall was set back from a long road that connected Sylvie's town to several other small villages on the way to Oxford. Sylvie drove in silence. It was an eerie drive, the winding country road almost empty and some of the bushes overgrown so that she heard them brush against the side of the car. They were like arms, like fingers reaching out and trying to get a grip on her. As she considered the possible danger of her plans to fuck with Jay, some retaliation, her gaze flicked up to the rear-view mirror – someone following her, perhaps? – but there was nothing but empty road, dense hedges, trees with low-hanging branches, the expanse of dark sky. Would he hurt her? Surely not. She shook her head to dislodge the thought.

When Sylvie pulled up into the hall car park, she noticed most of the spaces were full and felt a pang of anxiety. What if maybe Maple Village Hall was a secret hub of balletic middle-aged prodigies? She pulled down the car sun visor and slid open the flap to look at herself in the light. She remembered looking at herself in the enormous mirrors at Willow Way before class, before auditions, before a solo. She didn't know why it calmed her down, but it did. She'd look into her own eyes, look at her neck, throat, chest, pulsing gently with breath, with life. She thought of all she'd done before, accomplished, endured, and feel a sense of steadiness because no matter what else, she knew she could rely on herself to make it through. She was surprised to find that even now the feeling remained, weakened after a bit of a battering, but it was still there. The red hair helped, she thought, and in the bright orange-yellow light it looked even brighter, aflame. Her hair was the first thing she noticed in her reflection and it was an emblem of courage, reminding her of her goal. Jay's head on a platter and his balls, pickled, served up beside it as a side dish.

Sylvie wandered in through the main door. It was an old Victorian build with brick walls painted over thickly in pale pink paint. There was a small desk stacked with different leaflets in piles. Prenatal yoga and massage. Painting and Pottery for Tots. Chair Aerobics. And of course, the lilac adult ballet flier. It seemed strange to see it there, as if it was something personal and specific to her, out on display like a page of her diary, the way she'd been looking at it pinned to her corkboard for so long. A quickening in her chest. Thursday 8.15 p.m. Well, here she was.

She heard women's voices talking and laughing from somewhere behind one of the closed doors. She dawdled in a little circle, searching out the source of the sound. There were four different doors, all of them closed. One of them was easily eliminated, a neat little **WC** sign nailed to the door.

She pushed open one of the other doors and saw that it opened onto a small wooden-floored hall. The women, six or seven of them, turned to look at her when she shuffled in.

'Adult ballet?' she asked them, feeling herself blush.

'You're in the right place, love,' said one woman who Sylvie presumed to be the instructor. She was nothing at all like elegant, imposing Maria, draped in black and tossing withering looks about. She was a fairly unremarkable-looking woman in every way, her mousey hair tied back in a scrunchie. This woman wore gym leggings and a long-sleeved T-shirt.

'Welcome! I'm Linda. We're about to get started. Does everyone want to introduce themselves? What's your name, love?'

'Sylvie,' she said.

The women introduced themselves and talked about their dance history. One of them, Geena, had danced to a high level, planning to go professional but choosing law in the end instead. She was in her late thirties and stood in a dancer's posture with her feet turned out. Their eyes shone with recognition when Sylvie talked about Willow Way.

'Do you want to demonstrate for the others, Sylvie?' the instructor asked her. There were some encouraging oohs and aahs from the women.

Sylvie felt, instead of the cringing shame she'd imagined, a little pride as she demonstrated the exercises at the front of the class and helped make corrections at Linda's encouragement.

'Get a bit further forward over your supporting leg, Geena,' she said.

'Yes, exactly,' Linda echoed.

Geena pulled it off. A quick, tight turn with a neat finish. 'Much better,' Sylvie assured her.

At the end of the class Linda beckoned for Sylvie to come over.

'How did you enjoy that?' she asked her. 'You were great, honestly, it's lovely having you.' Linda had a friend who was looking for teachers. She ran a big, successful children's ballet school in Oxford. Linda asked her if she would consider it. Sylvie said she wasn't sure.

'Well, here are her details.' Linda copied out a number from her phone onto the back of a business card, then wrote SUSANNA DARRENSON under it in boxy capital letters and underlined the name twice.

When she got home, Sylvie showered and lay out in her towel to dry. She put her hand down the edge of the bed and felt the black folder, exactly where she'd left it. She stroked the plastic edge of it with her fingertips. Soon it would be time to use it. She pushed it further under her bed for the time being. She lay back, staring up at the framed Willow Way acceptance letter. If her seventeen-year-old self had been able to see her now, what would she think? She'd despair, probably, Sylvie thought.

She'd enjoyed the class. She promised herself to go again. She thought about Linda's suggestion that she start teaching. She couldn't imagine it. She turned the thought over and over in her head as if it were an object she could examine and then she gave up and reached for Aunt Jacqueline's diary. She'd left it on her bedside table with her hair dye receipt tucked between the pages like a bookmark. She'd gotten up to the part where Aunt Jacqueline was sitting alone in the restaurant with that creep Joe Morello.

'Oh, Cornelius is ever so independent,' I said, casually, taking a sip from my wine. 'He spends so much time out of the house, I hardly see him.'

'If you were my wife I'd never leave the house,' said Joe. 'Hell, I'd never leave the bedroom.'

I swallowed my disgust with the wine.

'Cornelius spends a lot of time at the baths,' I said. 'I believe he's got some very dear friends down there, which is lovely, I suppose.'

Joe nodded. 'Yeah, I know the place.'

'He adores the baths,' I said. 'He goes most evenings.'

'I know the place,' he said, gruffly. 'On Twenty-third.'

'Oh, no,' I said, with a cool little laugh. 'Not that place, somewhere different. Ah, Velvet Harbour Saunas, I believe. It must be good, he always returns rather tired. Far too tired for anything else than sleep.'

Joe's eyes were as wide as saucers and then we both swivelled our heads in the direction of Cornelius's voice. He'd emerged from the toilet and was engaged with the handsome young waiter. Joe's eyes filled with horror. We watched as Cornelius squeezed the young waiter's shoulder and looked him up and down as if awed by his form.

Joe got right up from the table then and stalked off in the direction of the cloakroom, saying, 'Fucking homos. I'll be damned if we do business together again.' Goodness me, was I pleased to watch that awful bigot go. I was almost ready to shout out, 'Promise?' after him but felt it best to hold my tongue.

Cornelius returned, shiny, bald and perplexed, to the table.

'What the fuck happened?' he asked me, and I just shrugged and said, 'Darling, I have no idea.'

When the car pulled up to the kerb outside our apartment building, I said to Cornelius, 'You go on up ahead. I think I'll go out dancing.'

When the car drove on, I stuck my hand out of the window and gave him a little wave. The truth is that his misery was like an aphrodisiac to me and I was resolved that evening to finding a lover of my own. The sanctity of our marriage had already been compromised and if there were going to be lovers involved then, darling, two of us can play that game and one of us can play it better.

Sylvie's phone began to ring. She heard it buzzing somewhere nearby, muffled by her goose-down duvet. Greg. She answered it, careful to sound sexy. She practically purred down the line.

'Greg? What are you doing calling so late?'

He laughed. 'Don't worry,' he said. 'It's not a booty call.'

'Shame,' said Sylvie, examining her nails.

'What are you doing Sunday afternoon?' Greg asked her. 'I'm going for a pub lunch with your boss and his wife, if you fancy it.'

Sylvie could have sung out with delight, but she controlled herself.

She yawned. 'Suppose I could.'

'Perfect,' he said. 'I'll pick you up around two.'

'All right,' said Sylvie. 'Looking forward to it.'

'And uh ...' Greg's voice changed, lowered an octave. 'What are you wearing?'

'Bye, Greg.'

Sylvie hung up but she couldn't help grinning. This was it, the next phase of her plan. She was going to make Jay's life a living nightmare.

Seventeen

Ice in her Veins

The pub was out in the middle of nowhere, but it seemed to have a devoted following. Judging by the state of the car park it was the destination of many a Sunday pilgrimage. Greg pulled up into the only empty parking spot in the rect-angle of asphalt outside after five or six minutes of circling the occupied bays like a vehicular vulture. Sylvie got out and looked at the witchy bare branches of the trees that lined the footpath ahead. She unzipped her jacket halfway, the back of her neck was damp with sweat. She was nervous.

'Ready?' Greg asked her. 'I'm starving.'

They held hands on the walk across the car park. The brick-and-flint pub was called the Old Key. Big brass-coloured letters were pinned up over the door. Inside, it was bustling. The smells of potatoes roasted in duck fat, of roasted beef, of beer, of burning firewood, together with the stifling warmth of the place engulfed her.

'There they are,' said Greg, loudly in her ear.

His words were moist. His lips tickled her earlobe. Sylvie turned her head to follow the direction he was pointing in. She saw Jay's hair over the edge of a booth-seat on the far right side of the room. She felt her breath catch in her throat. Sylvie, don't you dare, she cautioned herself, remember why you're here. She slid her arm under Greg's top and wrapped it around his waist, pulling him against her hip as they began to cross the pub, their steps in unison. Sylvie saw Annabel, who sat opposite Jay, put her hand up and beam at them as they approached. Sylvie tilted her forehead against Greg's chest. She kept watching the top of Jay's head, anticipating the moment he would turn around and see her, but he didn't. Why didn't he? Sylvie thought, why couldn't he do what she wanted just once?

'Sylvie! Look at your hair, goodness me! It's great to see you.' Annabel stood up and pulled Sylvie into a floral embrace. 'I had no *idea* you two were dating,' she said, releasing Sylvie and moving on to Greg. 'I'm so pleased. It's so lovely to have a fun couple to go out with, isn't it, Jay?'

Finally, Jay looked at her. His green eyes locked on to hers for just a second.

'Hi,' he said. And then, 'All right, Greg?'

'Yeah, I'm good, mate.'

Sylvie's jubilation at having discovered the folders in his office, her thrill at Greg inviting her to a family lunch, was crushed to nothing at the sight of him. I hate him, she thought, I fucking hate him. She was consumed all over again with need, the need for revenge having overrun her need of his love. Greg kissed Sylvie in the parting of her hair. Sylvie was glad that Jay was watching. She hoped that beneath his irritatingly calm exterior, he was seething with jealousy. I'm here, she thought, and there's nothing you can do to get rid of me.

'Sylvie, come and sit next to me,' said Annabel, patting the empty part of the cushioned bench beside her.

Sylvie sat, obediently, and listened as Annabel told her how they'd first discovered the pub, how *wonderful* the stuffing in the roast was and how she *had* to have the sticky toffee pudding for dessert. As often as she reasonably could, Sylvie let her eyes flick across the table; she tried to decipher some of Jay and Greg's conversation, but it was impossible to unpick from the rest of the racket. They talked in low voices, leaning in. They looked alike today, Sylvie thought, when they were side by side.

'From PR to MR, that's what the girls used to say,' said Annabel and then she laughed and took a drink from her glass of white wine.

Sylvie didn't know what she'd been talking about. She kept zoning in and out, lost in thought. She'd been looking at Jay and thinking about the black folder and how easy it would be to report him.

'Sorry,' she said. 'What was that?'

'Oh,' said Annabel, blinking rapidly as she tucked a strand of hair behind her ear. 'Just a silly little thing they used to say at the PR firm I worked at, that we were all there just until we got married and then we'd hand in our notices.'

'And were you?'

'Umm . . .' Annabel tilted her head, and her eyes drifted up to the ceiling as if she were trying to summon the distant past. 'Gosh, do you know, it turns out that I was!' She laughed. 'They were right after all.'

'You got married?'

'Yes,' she said. 'I met Jay through one of his old businesses. He hired me and before I knew it . . .' Annabel held up her left hand and wiggled her fingers, making the diamond on her ring-finger dance.

Sylvie was determined not to wince. 'What was the business?' she asked.

'Any more drinks?' A teenaged waitress with greasy hair enthused from the edge of the table. She unhooked a notepad and pen from her utility belt, noting Sylvie's request for wine, anything red, yes, a whole bottle, why not, two pints of Guinness and ooh-just-a-sparkling-water-with-lime-for-me-please.

'One glass of wine is quite enough for me these days,' said Annabel. 'The business? Oh, gosh, he had a bar in those days. It was a natural fit for me, I'd done a lot for my parents' company. They make wine. It's just a small vineyard in Bordeaux but the wine is very good.'

'That's quite ironic, isn't it,' said Sylvie.

'Sorry?'

'You'd think you'd be a bigger drinker, considering.'

Annabel smiled. 'It's true.' She picked up her half-drunk glass of white wine and swirled the remains around the bottom of the glass, staring into it as if she were trying to divine her future in the whirlpool of Sauvignon Blanc, as if she were a fortune teller who read wine glasses instead of tea leaves. 'It was a classic workplace romance. We started dating while I was working on his account,' she went on. 'I couldn't help it, he was so ambitious, determined. I'd grown up around all these incredibly privileged men who didn't *do* anything, who had no motivation to make anything of themselves. He was different, and so handsome.'

Annabel looked wistfully across the table at Jay; there was something nostalgic in her gaze.

'What are you girls talking about then?' said Greg.

'Jay,' said Sylvie.

Jay's eyes narrowed. He coughed to clear his throat. 'All good things,' he said. 'Right?'

'Wonderful things, my love.' Annabel finished her glass.

Jay gave a small nod, satisfied with her answer. He turned back to Greg.

'So,' said Annabel, raking a hand back through her blonde hair, flicking her long fringe into place and fluffing up her curled-out ends. Her attention, with one hand propped under her chin as she looked at Sylvie, was focused, friendly, inquisitive. 'How do you like working for my husband?'

'It's great,' Sylvie squeaked, bobbing her head up and down in an effort to convey some enthusiasm.

'He's not too hard on you, is he?' asked Annabel. 'Just give me the signal and I'll have a word with him. I'll get him in line for you, don't worry, darling.'

'Thank you,' said Sylvie, her voice slightly hoarse.

'And you live near the office, I hear. In town, right?'

'Yes,' said Sylvie.

'I always think,' said Annabel, 'there's not much for young people around here, is there? What do you think? Were you ever tempted to move up to London?'

'I like the quiet,' said Sylvie, truthfully. 'I live near the woods, can't stand cities.'

'You and me both,' said Annabel, her eyes alight with a spark of recognition. 'I love the countryside, looking out of the window and seeing nothing but green. Of course, it's much more social to be in the city but I'd trade all that five times over for the peace.'

'Me too,' said Sylvie.

'Sylvie, you want to come for a smoke?' Jay asked her.

'I don't smoke,' she said.

This wasn't part of the plan, she thought. She was there to look good, to make him jealous, to torment him. The thought of being alone with him was unsettling.

'Yes, you do,' Jay said. 'I've seen you.'

'Ah,' said Annabel. 'The boss is always watching.'

'You don't have to do anything, Sylvie,' said Greg. 'You can tell him to fuck off whenever you like. I do.'

Jay's green eyes glowered at her from across the table.

'I'll keep you company.' Sylvie shrugged. 'If that's what you want.'

Jay went out first into the cold, with his hands in his pockets and his shoulders hunched up around his ears. They were the only smokers. She thought she detected a slight tremble as Jay felt in the pocket of his jacket for his packet of cigarettes, his lighter. She remembered, suddenly, where she recognized the jacket from – he'd worn it the night they spent together in the hotel. She'd asked him for it that morning when she sat shivering in the dawn light. He'd refused.

Jay held the cigarette carton out for Sylvie. She could see now that he really was shaking and she could admit that she was enjoying it, his agitation, his discomfort. She hated that despite it all, how pathetic she had begun to find him, he really was beautiful. His skin was like marble and his eyes, lined with black lashes, made him look like some kind of arctic wolf, some snow-dwelling predator.

She shook her head. 'I told you, I don't smoke.'

Jay shrugged. He let out a long exhale. It was an isolated place, just the pub and the rows of silvery frost-kissed fields, the car park beginning to empty as the lunchtime rush tapered out. A couple of crows swooped overhead, departing the mossy pub roof for the spindly naked trees in the field beyond. A woman bundled up in hat, scarf and duffel coat to her shins, trailed after by three fat Labradors. Sylvie hung back by the entrance. She only had this fashion jacket, this hip-length double-breasted black tweed thing, more of a blazer and not a proper winter coat. She crossed her arms over her chest and waited with anticipation. She could see that Jay was thinking, his eyes roving around. He hadn't planned what he was going to say when he got her out there. He only saw his chance to speak to her alone and knew he had to take it.

Finally, he spoke, from a safe distance with one hand in his pocket and the other holding his cigarette, from which he took a final puff and then discarded down into the black drain.

'Are you enjoying this?'

'Yes.'

The expression on Jay's face was contorted, unreadable.

'He's not serious about you, you know that, right? He's not serious about anyone,' said Jay.

'I'm not serious about him either,' said Sylvie. 'Yet.'

Jay clicked his tongue against his teeth and looked up at the sky and then he put another cigarette between his lips and lit it.

'So, what happens now?'

'What do you mean?'

He took a step towards her, the hatred rolled off him like hot steam.

'You keep showing up until what? Until you decide to tell everyone what happened? Is that it?'

He was panicking, Sylvie thought, he was desperate. She could see it in his eyes and in the deep, hungry inhales he took from his cigarette. She felt it, power, and she liked it just as much, maybe even more than she'd expected to.

'But nothing happened between us, remember? That's what you said.'

It was a half-smile, half-grimace on his face when he looked at her, a mixture of wonderment and terror as he struggled to comprehend her. He wondered, perhaps, where the helpless, lovesick girl had gone. The Sylvie who'd loved him had been replaced by this red-haired bitch with ice in her veins.

'What do you want?' he asked her.

'What do any of us want?' she replied.

'All right, enough with the fucking riddles, Sylvie. Listen, I've got money.'

'I'm not for sale.'

'But some people are,' he said, and his eyes danced with green fire. 'Some people will do terrible things for money, they do them every day.'

'You mean like inventing companies that don't exist?' she said. 'Because then I would have to agree with you, Jay. People do all kinds of *terrible* things for money. I wouldn't threaten me if I were you.'

Jay said nothing.

Sylvie smiled.

'It's good to see you,' she said and before she pushed open the pub door, she turned over her shoulder and said, 'I always liked that jacket.'

'There she is,' said Greg, grinning. 'Sit next to me now, Sylv, I'm absolutely sick of him.'

'I agree,' said Jay, quietly. 'Thirty minutes is plenty.'

'Boys,' said Annabel, she winked at Sylvie. 'It's a wonder these two didn't kill each other when they were little.'

'We came close to it a couple of times,' said Greg. 'Didn't we?'

As Jay and Sylvie took their seats, Annabel's eyes roved between them. There was a discord between her taut smile and her slightly frenzied stare. Sylvie could tell that she suspected something, and if she didn't suspect it, she was certainly curious. Sylvie's bottle of wine waited in the middle of the table. Someone had poured her a glass. It was deep ruby, scarlet. She took a large gulp.

The boys had pint glasses of dark Guinness. Sylvie watched as the contents settled, as the oat-coloured foam wafted through the glasses like sand in an egg timer. Greg put his arm around Sylvie's shoulders, his fingers stroking at the fabric over her upper arm. The fire danced in its blackened cave. The conversation of the table washed over her, discussion of Christmas celebrations, of traffic, of the dangers of AI and a news presenter freshly accused of sexual assault. Sylvie couldn't stop thinking about Jay, how badly she wanted to hurt him. She hated him, not only for his lies and deceit, his manipulative games, but for how he kept it all from Annabel and maintained this perfect husband façade. It was sickening, Sylvie thought, how he could live his life this way, take his secrets to his grave knowing this woman who had devoted herself to him was playing pretend at her own life. He used people, women, he used them up. And when he'd finally sucked the life out of them, he simply moved on to another.

Sylvie knew she could have killed him if there was any way to get away with it. The fire poker hung from its holder in the distance, a seductive iron spike. Through the heart like a vampire, she thought, that was probably the only way to get him. She sipped her blood-red wine and fantasized about driving the iron rod into his body, over and over again.

The food arrived. Sylvie's plate of roast chicken glistened with gravy. Jay stabbed the crackly shortcrust lid of his steak and ale pie with the end of his knife.

'What are you guys doing after this?' Greg asked Annabel and Jay, before putting a whole roast potato in his mouth.

'We'd better get back to Aurelie,' said Annabel. 'Hadn't we?'

'How is the little angel?' Greg asked between chews.

'Wonderful, thank you, Greg.'

Sylvie froze. Aurelie. Who was Aurelie?

'You've got a daughter?' she asked. She'd wanted to sound casual but the shock strangled her words.

Annabel gave a short, hard laugh. 'Yes, little Aurelie. She's eighteen months.' Annabel put her hand on top of Jay's which lay resting on the tabletop, and intertwined her fingers with his. 'She's our life, isn't she, darling?'

Jay looked at Sylvie, chewed his mouthful slowly and then swallowed. He'd never said anything about a child.

'She's sweet,' said Greg.

Sticky toffee pudding next. Sylvie cut the corner piece with the edge of her spoon and scraped a curl of ice cream from the scoop of vanilla on top. She felt sick, too sick to eat, but the others were halfway through their puddings, and she couldn't just sit there, staring at the plate and watching the ice cream melt, ivory-coloured cream weeping onto the bowl.

'*So* good, isn't it?' Annabel enthused.

'Delicious,' said Sylvie, though the syrupy sweetness made her want to retch.

Sylvie couldn't believe he had a daughter. She was sure now more than ever that he never had the tiniest intention of leaving Annabel for her, there'd never been any love at all. Just a sick and twisted little game.

When it was time to leave, Annabel put her arms around Sylvie and hugged her tight. Sylvie felt her, the sinew of her bones and muscles, the rigid clips and fastening hooks of her bra through her thin cashmere jumper as Annabel's body pressed against hers and she wanted to recoil in protest. Annabel was an inconvenient fact. It would have been easier had Annabel been nasty, but she wasn't, she was delightful, and even worse than being delightful, she was genuine. She took one of Sylvie's hands between hers and pressed them together, enclosing her soft palms around Sylvie's hand. Annabel studied her face closely. Sylvie wondered if she suspected anything and she knew that even if she did, she wouldn't say a word. She was too classy, too eager perhaps to see the best in people.

Greg and Jay clapped their hands together in a rough handshake.

'See you at work tomorrow, Sylvie,' Jay whispered into her ear when he pulled her in for a hug. 'We'll have a chat.'

We'll have a chat. The phrase was a threat. A challenge. She sat in Greg's passenger seat and as the car rumbled to life beneath her, she tried her hardest to put Jay's words out of her mind. But she couldn't. Something bad was going to happen, she was sure of that.

Eighteen

Truce?

Jay's car was already there in the car park when Sylvie arrived on Monday morning. She pulled down the overhead mirror and spent a few moments just staring at herself, at her red hair, her dark determined eyes as she tried to ready herself. She was afraid to see Jay in the office. It was his territory and as long as she was there, she worked for him. Part of her questioned whether she'd gone too far by going for lunch with Greg and Annabel; part of her knew she hadn't gone far enough and would go further still. What would Aunt Jacqueline do? Sylvie felt in the glovebox for an old forgotten tube of lip gloss. She twisted off the lid and applied a few slick coats of it to her lips. It was fragile armour but all she had.

Derek was on the phone when she arrived but put up his hand to wave at her. Karen was hunched over a steaming cup of tea, examining an Excel spreadsheet, her glasses down on the tip of her nose.

'Good weekend?' she asked without turning around as Sylvie passed her by.

'Yes,' said Sylvie. 'Thanks.'

She craned her neck to see that Jay was sitting in his room on his laptop. He didn't look up. A cool panic thrilled through her. She sat down at her PC and input the wrong password four times in a row. Her hands trembled as she opened up her emails and scrolled through them. There was no hope of her doing any actual work. She got up and put the kettle on, pacing a circle in the kitchen as she waited for it to boil. She made herself a coffee, strong and black. She remembered what Greg had said about her unsweetened espresso as she sat in her office chair and took a sip of her drink. The Italians would call her a psycho. Not just the Italians, she'd wager. What was there to do but try to look busy and wait?

Time dragged. An hour passed agonizingly slowly and then another limped on after that.

A quiz played on the radio station.

'In what year was the pop song "Modern Love" by David Bowie released?'

The radio tingled with static. Karen shouted, 'Nineteen eighty-three,' at the radio player. The actual radio show contestant was umming and aahing, Karen clicked her tongue disapprovingly and said it again, 'Nineteen eighty-three.'

'*Nineteen eighty-six?*' The radio show contestant's voice wavered with indecision and static.

Sylvie felt certain she was going mad.

Finally, at about eleven, Jay's door swung open. Sylvie heard it, the bottom of it grazing the rough carpet. Her heart rate quickened. She felt her stomach tighten. And then she heard him: slow, heavy steps, that came closer and closer until he was right behind her.

'Sylvie, can you come into my office for a minute?'

She stood up, taking her time. Summoned at last. She followed him across the office floor. Neither Karen nor Derek looked up. Sylvie wondered if they already knew what was going to happen. As she followed behind Jay, she was overwhelmed by the scent of his aftershave. Sandalwood, vetiver, citrus.

Jay held the door open for her.

'Have a seat,' he said.

Sylvie brushed past him and sat down on one of the chairs.

Jay closed the door and then sat down opposite Sylvie. He scratched his beard and stared at the table for a few seconds as if wondering where to begin, and then he crossed his arms and leant back in his chair.

'Yesterday,' he began, 'you crossed a line and it never should have happened.'

'I was invited,' Sylvie said, her high-pitched squeak of a voice contradicting the defiance she otherwise felt.

'Should have said no,' said Jay.

He'd gathered himself since the day before, Sylvie thought. This Jay was cool and unbothered. Maybe he was, or maybe he was taking great pains to mask the panic.

'I know we've had this little back and forth,' he said. 'I know you're pissed. I can admit I've been a dick but that's just what I do, all right, Sylvie? What do you want, do you want me to say I'm sorry?'

'Yes,' said Sylvie, desperately fighting back the tears that stung her eyes, which were beginning to form.

Jay looked at her, a half-smirk on his lips. 'I'm sorry. All right? Now can we just let this whole thing go?'

Sylvie studied his face. She hated his smugness, she hated the way he lacked any sense of integrity, any moral centre. He simply pushed all the buttons, like a toddler with a TV remote, trying anything to get what he wanted. Deny, threaten, apologize. What did it matter as long as Jay was okay? As long as Jay got what he wanted. She blinked back her tears and steadied an icy gaze on him.

'No, Jay, we can't,' she said. 'And you don't get to decide where the lines are or whether they have or have not been crossed. You gave up that right a long time ago.'

He stared at her as if he couldn't believe what he was hearing, as if a dog had just stood up on its hind legs and started singing the alphabet song.

'I don't know what you want,' he said.

I do, Sylvie thought. She wanted him and his life in tatters. She wanted to punish him, she wanted to break him.

'If you're looking for a truce you won't get one,' she said. 'I won't stop seeing Greg.'

Jay gave a laboured sigh. 'I'm sorry to hear that,' he said. 'Because you know I can't have you working here if this is how you're going to act.'

Sylvie shrugged. 'Fine.'

'And I know you think you have some information about me and my business,' he said.

'Yes,' said Sylvie. 'That's right.'

'But I'd bear this in mind if I were you, before you decide to act on it. We can end this nicely, you can go home, I tell everyone you found a different opportunity. You can keep seeing my brother if you like, fine, I can tolerate a few more lunches before he gets bored of you and moves on.' Jay put both hands on the table and leant forward, lowering his voice to a husky whisper. 'But if you report me, if you tell *anyone* about what's in those files, I will tell everyone what I know about you.'

Sylvie watched him, unblinking, waiting.

'Maybe you didn't leave so amicably, you know what I'm saying? After all, you have a history of violence. You might have been looking into me, but I've had someone looking into you too. You didn't just *hurt* a girl at Willow Way, you put her in the hospital over a part in a ballet production. You could have killed her. You're a fucking psychopath. They didn't press charges because you were grieving. Do you think everyone else would be so understanding? I'm sure Derek and Karen would be interested to hear about it, your parents too, maybe even the police. The school report said it was "out of character" – but what if it wasn't? Maybe you attacked me one night when I rejected you, maybe you need help.'

Sylvie stuttered as visions of her worst fear come to life danced across her mind's eye. 'I've got messages,' she said. 'Proof of things between us.'

'Well then,' said Jay. 'I guess we're at a stalemate.' And then he waved his hand in the air as if tossing the whole idea away. 'Anyway, the point is this, don't throw your whole life away because you're angry. You're not the first bitter little girl who thinks she can take me on, and you won't be the last. Think about the consequences, because I can assure you things always go my way in the end.'

'You're right,' said Sylvie.

'What's that?'

'I'm thinking,' she said. 'About the consequences.'

'You can get your things and go,' said Jay, obviously satisfied that he'd put the world to rights. 'I'll tell the others later that your employment contract has been terminated, effective immediately.'

'Sure,' said Sylvie, getting up from her chair.

As she pushed the handle on the door, Jay called out to her softly and she turned over her shoulder to look at him.

'Hey Sylvie,' he said. 'I'll play nice if you will.'

'Sure,' she said. 'Truce.'

Sylvie collected her things.

'Going out,' she said.

She'd leave the awkward explanations to Jay. She felt strangely liberated. She wouldn't have to drive to work and wait and wonder any more. He was no longer her superior, they were equals. As for the truce, she had no intention of honouring it. Any notion of her leaving him alone had been firmly destroyed by their last conversation and the way he'd tried to manipulate her. She was frightened of him telling everyone what happened at Willow Way but she had so much on him it would be mutually assured destruction. Was he really going to risk his reputation and family? Maybe, she couldn't be sure.

As Sylvie pushed open the door of the ground-floor foyer, she almost bumped straight into Brett. He was smoking a cigarette, still wearing his warehouse gloves; his pale face was bluish in the cold, hollow cheeks freckled, the white of his watery blue eyes were red at the rims.

'Hi,' he said.

'Hi,' said Sylvie. 'Are you on break?'

'Yeah,' he said.

He was still angry at her, she could see that. But he'd been right about Jay, when he tried to warn her.

'Thank you,' she said. 'For trying to warn me.'

Brett's brow crumpled into a frown.

'About him,' said Sylvie, gesturing towards the first floor of the building behind them with a jut of her chin.

Brett shrugged. He was a decent person, Sylvie thought, he wasn't taking any pleasure in it.

'I didn't know,' Sylvie went on. 'About his wife.'

Brett discarded his cigarette.

'I still like you,' he said. 'If you want to get together some time.'

'You're a nice guy, Brett,' she said. 'But I really think I'm meant to be alone.'

Brett stared at the floor for a few seconds and then gave Sylvie a resigned look. 'Yeah, sure, fine.'

'Come here.' Sylvie gestured for him to come closer and as he took a step forward, she rose up onto the balls of her toes and kissed him on the mouth.

The kiss lasted a few seconds. He tasted of smoke and his lips were rough and chapped from the cold, but she'd suddenly felt like she had to kiss him. She left him there, slightly dazed on the tarmac. Then she climbed down into the driver's seat of her car and drove off.

*

Outside in the crisp cool on her walk to the Oak Room, Sylvie found that the dried leaves beneath her feet had been crushed to the point of auburn-coloured dust on the walkway path. The sun was readying itself to set, a blazing stage light across the pinkening sky. Birds over her head cawed the warning of approaching nightfall. Sylvie shrank further down into her thick crocheted scarf and woolly coat; her hands encased in pale pink wool gloves may as well have been bare, the way the cold bit through them to her fingers. As she approached the mouth of the building, heard the excitable chatter of the other students and the pianist playing the keys, the cygnet dance in Swan Lake. *Sylvie wondered what would happen if she just kept walking.*

But perhaps because she lacked the courage and perhaps because her feet had walked the path so often that they took her there on their own accord, she found herself in the Oak Room, unwinding the scarf from around her neck, unbuttoning her coat and crouching on the floor to tie up her pointe shoes. She smelt it, the sourness that told her she'd forgotten to wash her tights, the slight stickiness on the fabric stretched over her knees. A whiff of yeastiness from between her legs, originating from the unwashed gusset of last week's leotard. She sighed to herself, felt the warmth of the humiliation blooming at the back of her neck. She wished the ground would swallow her up.

'Let's begin from early in the second act,' said Maria, her arms leant on the edge of the piano as she addressed the pianist and the dancers, the slick-haired, pin-thin girls; clad in various shades of pastel, clutching their veils, they looked like little girls playing dress-up with their mothers' wedding gowns.

Sylvie rose to her feet with a sickly feeling in the pit of her stomach as the girls pulled the veils over their faces, balancing them on the crowns of their heads in anticipation of the music. Sylvie knew that in the last few weeks her performance had plummeted. She'd lost her sense of balance, of rhythm, her musicality, and flexibility. It was as though her muscles were hardening and shrinking into themselves, as though she'd been replaced by someone else.

She was a shadow of what she'd once been, and she dreaded the rehearsals, the knowing looks exchanged around the classroom, the disappointment in Maria's eyes.

The girls, imitating the virgin ghosts, ran soundlessly across the stage in a mesmerizing interweaving motion and round and round in a circle so tight and fast, it was dizzying to observe and then they froze, still and sudden, and Ffion emerged from the centre of their cluster as Queen of the Willis. Maria raised a hand to stop them there.

'Okay, girls,' she said. 'Better. Let's stop there. Clear the stage, please, so I can see Ffion properly.'

Ffion executed a flawlessly clean performance while Sylvie watched on, forlorn, and the other girls toyed with their long white veils; some of them wore them around their necks, others over their heads, some had tied them like sashes around their waists.

'Well done, Ffion.' Maria praised her before turning her dark eyes to Sylvie. 'Sylvie, let's see yours.'

She only made it through a (rather dismal) count of sixteen before Sylvie felt her ankle roll over itself and the hard under-edge of her pointe shoe bang clunkily onto the floor. Her veins surged with the adrenaline that accompanied the sharp uneasy feeling of a bone jolted out of place.

'Are you all right?' Maria rushed forward to offer her arm.

Sylvie reluctantly took it, trying and failing to put weight on her left leg. 'Just a twisted ankle,' she said.

Maria tutted, in sympathy rather than disapproval. 'Sit,' she said. 'Rest. Ffion will dance the rest of your part.'

Sylvie sat, disgraced, at the front of the classroom with her back resting against the cool mirror. She focused her efforts on maintaining the shallow rhythm of her breath, afraid that if she did not, she would be in danger of breaking down in front of the class. Sylvie burnt with shame. She felt her lungs gasping for air, her heart struggling to recover itself. Her calves and feet were too weak for another repetition, while Ffion breezily and elegantly performed her part. So smooth was her recollection of the steps, so polished was her timing, that Sylvie knew Ffion had practised her part over and over again. Was it that obvious, she thought, that she was declining? Willow Way was all she'd ever wanted, all she'd ever worked for. Sylvie reached back behind her and pressed her fingertips against the glass, a wishful attempt perhaps at holding her own hand.

'This is not good, Sylvie,' said Maria, when the rest of the class had filed out of the door, pretending not to look back over their shoulders, morbidly curious about Sylvie's fall from grace. 'This is not good at all.'

Sylvie felt the jealousy through her body. It was a sharp-edged deep-sea thing that tugged at her throat and caught over the bones of her ribs. She knew then that sooner or later she was going to do something terrible, something she would likely regret for ever, but she'd be powerless to control herself.

*

'Hello?' Greg sounded surprised when he answered the phone.

'What are you doing tonight?' Sylvie asked him as she hurried upstairs and began to pack an overnight bag of things.

'Nothing that can't be cancelled,' he said.

'Good, pick me up in thirty minutes.'

Sylvie didn't want to be alone. She wasn't afraid of Jay, but of her own mind. She thought that left alone she'd overthink and overthink until she'd talked herself out of her plan for revenge and convinced herself the whole thing was futile. She needed a distraction. She needed Greg. She quite liked his company, Sylvie thought to herself. He was good in bed and didn't seem to notice when she zoned out, taking her general lack of interest for intense focus. She imagined he thought she was smart, well-educated, which she wasn't at all. Ballet had been her life since her mid-teens. He seemed, dare she say it, serious about her.

He took her to an upscale Mexican restaurant in Oxford where all the cocktails were spicy, and the lighting was exceptionally low. He held her hand across the table when he'd had a few tequilas. He told her she was pretty.

'Everyone's pretty in this dim light,' she said.

'Even me?' he asked, grinning.

'Even you,' she said.

It was time to seal the deal, she thought, time to thaw a little and hook him in with warmth and romance. The icy act couldn't work for ever. It was all very simple, sooner or later a man wants you to treat him like a king, a generous, worthy man who's fundamentally good while being irresistibly sexy. That's how you *really* hook them. Sylvie had read as much in Aunt Jacqueline's diaries. Occasionally, you had to throw them a bone if you wanted to get anywhere.

'Thank you,' she said when Greg paid the bill, her eyes wide and gleaming with admiration.

He sat up straighter and smiled, delighted by her obvious gratitude. It's working, Sylvie thought. When they walked to the car, slightly tipsy, Greg had his arm over Sylvie's shoulder, and they stopped under the twinkling Christmas lights and silvery moon to kiss. He was so tall he had to hunch over and she had to crane her neck. It was uncomfortable but Sylvie didn't want to end it prematurely. She sensed that Greg was bonding with her and she didn't want to do anything to disrupt this. At the moment he was all she had, the only in into Jay's inner circle.

'What do you want for Christmas?' Greg reached for Sylvie's hand as he drove, and pressed her knuckles to his lips.

'I'll send you my list,' said Sylvie.

'Anything you want,' he said. 'It's yours.'

'Wow,' she said, teasing him. 'Guess this is what it feels like to be flavour of the month.'

'This month,' he said. 'Maybe next month too, we'll see.'

Sylvie giggled. 'You're so funny.'

Greg seemed to grow a foot taller as he sat beside her in the driver's seat.

Back at Greg's apartment, he uncorked a bottle of red wine. They were already drunk but each nursed a glass, taking occasional drowsy sips as they lay on the sofa. They watched nonsense on the 75-inch TV in the living room, reality shows and late-night gameshows that were indistinguishable from one another. Just like a real couple, they lay wrapped up in each other and covered with a blanket.

'I quit my job today,' she said.

'Why did you do that?' Greg asked her, tucking a stray strand of hair behind her ear.

'Not for me,' she said. 'Think I'll go back to nannying after Christmas.'

'Did my brother do something to piss you off?'

'No.' Sylvie couldn't help but flinch. 'What makes you say that?'

'Nothing.' Greg shrugged.

Sylvie changed the subject. 'Dreading telling my parents.'

'They'll understand. You'll be a good nanny,' he said, pulling her closer.

Sylvie laughed. 'You think so? Because last time I was pretty shit at it.'

'Definitely,' he said. 'You're kind and you listen and kids love that.'

'How do you know what kids love?' she teased him.

'I know what they *don't* love,' he said. 'You can trust me on that one.'

'Your childhood?' she asked him, softly. She stroked his cheek.

It had been hinted at, this terrible childhood that Greg and Jay had endured.

'It was . . . it was all right before my dad left. Not perfect,' he said. 'But less of a fucking shit-show than afterwards – sorry.' He apologized for swearing.

'It's fine,' said Sylvie. 'Tell me if you like, tell me what happened.'

Greg sighed. 'My dad left our mum for another woman when I was ten, Jay was eight. My mum was hollow after that, just . . .' He waved his hands in front of his eyes. 'Just not there. She tried to commit suicide a couple times, the first time it was pills. I found her in a pool of vomit. Called the ambulance.'

'I'm so sorry,' said Sylvie, stroking his cheek.

It was startling, the thought of what those men went through as boys, and it gave her pause, sympathy for Jay where there'd been none before. Perhaps inside he was still this little boy, frightened, terrified by the idea of being alone in the world. But did it justify what he'd done? The way he treated people?

'I wasn't there the second time. That time it was Jay who called the ambulance and after it came to take her he disappeared for days, no one could find him.'

'Jesus,' said Sylvie.

'So yeah, not exactly what you'd call stable. She was always fragile, our mum, but it was like one day she just snapped.'

Sylvie saw that his eyes were shiny with tears. She reached up and pressed her lips against his.

'Sorry,' he said.

'Don't be sorry,' said Sylvie, kissing him deeply.

'It was a long time ago,' he said, between kisses. 'My mum's fine now, she's recovered. In some ways it's like it never happened.'

'Maybe,' said Sylvie, 'you should stop talking about your mum now.'

'Maybe you're right.'

Greg returned the passion of her kiss, his tongue slipping over hers. He was hers if she wanted him. That was clear. And he was her key to Jay who deserved everything that was coming to him, damaged little boy or not. She just had to play her cards right and make it last until she had the chance. She could do it. She could do anything she set her mind on. When she removed her emotions from the equation, she was a sniper. Sylvie pushed Greg back onto the sofa and straddled him; he looked up at her with a rakish, wonky grin on his face as his fingers unpicked the buttons at the front of her blouse.

'Cheetah,' he said, his voice low and hoarse as he admired her lingerie.

'Leopard,' Sylvie corrected him.

She'd seen the underwear set in an advert online and knew on first sight that she just *had* to have it. She lowered herself over Greg so that they were face to face and looked deeply into his eyes. She felt it, *want*, *desire*, and she knew that if she needed to, she could eat him. She really could, suck the meat off his bones.

As they lay naked on the sofa wrapped in a blanket, Greg put his fingers through Sylvie's hair and rested his chin on the top of her head. Sylvie watched the silver-coloured moon, almost full, glimmering in the distant dark. She watched it until her eyes lost focus, and it blurred into an orb of bluish-white light, shining like an opal. *Sylvie,* the women's voices whispered, *Sylvie, Sylvie, join us!* The same voices she'd heard when she stalked home in the woods after dark, the day Jay had broken her heart. She knew what they wanted, the girl-ghosts. The women who'd died of broken hearts, been betrayed by men, lain down in their beds and cried until it felt like something in their chests had broken, so anxious and distraught that their hair had thinned, shedding from the crowns of their heads to reveal smooth patches of scalp, hollows under their red-rimmed eyes from sleepless nights spent awake crying, the ridges of their ribs visible from lack of nourishment.

Now, as ghosts, they were restored, gleaming, their hair glorious, bountiful afros of endless curls or falling to their hipbones in swathes of silk. They were ageless, their faces serene, their bodies graceful; something within them had been answered, fulfilled. They amassed together under the light of the moon. They drifted between tree trunks, their feet suspended above the rock and root of the forest floor, the dark depth of the forest visible through their iridescent, vapour bodies.

They were waiting, some of them with instruments, a violin that needed no tuning, a harp, a cello, waiting for a male guest to wander into their forest, any man would do. They would enchant him with their music, their wordless beauty, and then they would dance him to death, carrying his body with them into another realm when the first sunlight broke through the canopy of leaves, illuminating the dewy threads of cobwebs and the early chrysalis of woodland butterflies. By morning there'd be no trace of the girl-ghosts but the sound of the man's final breathy cry absorbed in a growing symphony of birdsong. They were waiting for *her*, for Sylvie to join them.

'Sylvie?' Greg whispered.

'Mm.' Sylvie shook awake from her light, wine-induced sleep, her eyelids too heavy to open. 'What is it?'

'There's a big Christmas party coming up that Annabel hosts every year.' Greg kissed her on the forehead. 'Will you come?'

Sylvie's eyes flicked open. 'When is it?'

'Next week,' said Greg. 'December the twenty-first.'

'Where is it?'

'Jay and Annabel's, like I said. It normally drags on for ever, but it won't be boring if you come with me.'

'No, it won't,' said Sylvie. 'It definitely won't.'

She closed her eyes again. Her mind swimming with possibilities, with ideas, with revenge, revenge, revenge.

Greg's arms tightened around her, pulling her closer. 'So you'll come?'

'Wouldn't miss it,' Sylvie said. Without a job, without Jay, what did she have to lose?

Act Three

Nineteen

Other People's Husbands

December the twenty-first. Sylvie sat in the passenger seat of Greg's car as it sped down a labyrinth of narrow country lanes in the direction of Jay and Annabel's house. She was dressed for battle in Aunt Jacqueline's fox fur coat, a dark, ruddy auburn that matched her red hair. She wore her aunt's diamond pendant on a gold chain around her neck, diamond and pearl earrings hung from her lobes. Aunt Jacqueline had once said, *Always remember this, my little dove, no matter how dreadful life gets, you must have real jewellery, real flowers and real fur. Vintage if you must but real, always real.* She had her set of tools, her little arsenal, tucked away in her pockets, zipped into her handbag, stashed in her overnight bag. She had one present with her but it was more like a bomb. A small, deceptively harmless-looking package wrapped in cartoonish snowflake wrapping paper that rested by her feet, bumping softly against the side of her boots when the car turned a corner. Its revelation would guarantee devastation, mutually assured destruction for all in the perimeter.

This was it, showtime at last. Sylvie was resolved to have the callousness of a soldier marching into battle but a quick glance to her right-hand side made her doubt herself. Greg. She would miss him. He made her laugh, he draped his heavy arm over her shoulders like a safety blanket when they walked together side by side. She liked to find him asleep next to her when she opened her eyes in the mornings. His presence was as cheerful and undemanding as a golden retriever's. He almost made her want to call the whole thing off, forget about revenge altogether, but she couldn't do that, she just couldn't. She was a Gardiner woman after all and had a grand and noble tradition to uphold. When Sylvie pulled down the car mirror to touch up her lipstick, she imagined her Aunt Jacqueline hovering over her shoulder, whispering, *Give them hell, darling,* into her ear before pressing a ghostly red lipsticked kiss to her cheek. Sylvie knew that after this weekend, Greg would never speak to her again. That was a sacrifice she would just have to make.

Jay and Annabel lived on a long, tree-lined street where the grass was well cut and the trees evenly spaced along it. All of the houses were set back from the road with high electric gates. Blackthorn House was an enormous symmetrical red-brick that looked at once like a wedding venue and an office building. There was something officious and not at all homely about its manicured lawn and stage-prop perfection.

'Don't judge me on this lot,' said Greg. He swung Sylvie's overnight bag onto his shoulder and pressed a kiss to her forehead as they waited on the doorstep.

'Don't be silly,' said Sylvie.

As they waited on the porch, Sylvie felt suddenly overcome with nerves. She hadn't forgotten how completely Jay's presence affected her. She worried she'd feel powerless, too mesmerized by him to speak, much less carry out her plan. He knew she was coming, surely, but how was he going to treat her? He hated her and would undoubtedly send her withering glares and icy jabs all weekend long. How would she hold up under the pressure? Only time would tell, but Sylvie thought just then of Jay's stance when he held up the gun and fired shots into the dark. The chill night air, the burnt asphalt smell, the gravel that had worked itself into the toe of her shoe, most of all his profile swathed in shadow and the blaze, like green flame, in his eyes when he turned over his shoulder and looked at her.

Sylvie's left knee buckled, and Greg reached out to steady her.

'Shit, Sylv, are you okay, babe?'

'I'm fine,' she said. 'Thanks. Babe.'

Annabel answered the door with a pretty, fat, ringletted child in her arms. 'Sylvie! Greg!' she said. 'Welcome, come in. Oh my goodness, Sylvie, you look *fabulous!*'

Annabel was clearly frazzled by the demands of the day. The Lakemores' annual Christmas party, Greg had explained on the journey, was an event of epic proportions. First Annabel bought out the contents of every artisan deli and winery in the county, had the house professionally decorated by the same people that dressed the windows for the Christmas display at Hamley's, and then a homing signal was emitted, which attracted every toff within a 200-mile radius.

Sylvie was pleased to see Annabel's perfection a little disturbed, even if that meant just a crease down the front of her tastefully festive, red jumper. Annabel and the child were both dressed in chic, coordinating shades of red and green. She was also pleased to see that the decorations were minimal and inoffensive to the eye. She was not pleased, however, to have come face to face with the little girl whose existence she'd only recently discovered and which disturbed her immensely. She was so damn angelic-looking and adorable, watching Sylvie with inquisitive doll-like eyes over Annabel's shoulder. She felt herself flush with guilt at the thought of what she was about to do. Guilt really is the most extraordinary enemy to womankind.

The hallway was vast with cherry-mahogany floors and sage walls. A set of wooden building blocks lolled in the middle of the hall. Deep red, velvet bows were pinned to the walls, and reels of hand-shredded tinsel had been strung up beneath them. It was so *real*, the black-and-white family photographs hanging in subdued black frames. Annabel and Jay. Their home, their life that Sylvie had intruded on, infiltrated like a disease. It was unfortunate but necessary, she reminded herself.

'They're in the sitting room,' said Annabel. 'I'll show you.'

Sylvie and Greg followed her to the end of the hall that opened into a formal sitting room with two brown leather sofas positioned opposite each other, either side of a low, dark coffee table. There was a Persian rug and jewel-coloured lamps. Beyond that room there was a wide hallway, with windows that looked out onto the fields beyond. As they walked along it, Annabel first with the little child in her arms, Aurelie looked back over Annabel's shoulder and stared at Sylvie, her little brow furrowed. She didn't look frightened exactly but curious, suspicious. Sylvie tried to avoid looking at her completely.

'I don't think you've met little Aurelie yet,' said Annabel.

'No,' said Sylvie. 'I don't think I have. Cute.'

Sylvie felt Greg's hand on the back of her neck, and she glanced up to see a stupid, tender look in his eyes. God, she thought, at least this little weekend's going to send him running and screaming before any silly ideas about the future have a chance to set in.

Annabel pushed open the sitting room door. Five eager and expectant faces turned to inspect the new arrivals. Sylvie noticed, with a touch of relief, that Jay's was not among them. Not yet at least. There was Hugh and Lily, Verity, Dahlia and Johnny, or Jonno if one preferred. Annabel introduced each of them and they raised their hands, all except Verity, a woman in her mid-thirties with streaky blonde hair who wore an elaborate, sparkly, shin-length dress embellished with ruffles and panelling. She jumped up from her seat and approached, a glass of fizz in her hand which sloshed with each step, dangerously close to the edge of the glass. She threw her arms around Sylvie and then Greg.

'Just *look* at you two!' she cried. 'Absolutely gorgeous. I'm Verity.'

Verity had a full face, with sweet features. Small, upturned eyes, a little button nose and lips that were small and heart-shaped, despite her large mouth, which seemed to contort into several different shapes per second. A very tall woman, she towered over Sylvie who had to crane at the neck to look at her.

'I like this one,' said Verity, looking at Greg. 'Much better than the others, already.'

Greg's ears flushed a violent shade of red and he scratched the back of his neck before casting a nervous eye at Sylvie.

'Oh my goodness, you mustn't take any offence, darling,' Verity gasped, putting her hand on Sylvie's shoulder. 'I only meant to say I liked you already. I'm a brilliant judge of character.'

'It's true,' said Annabel, smiling as she bounced the little child in her arms. 'Verity's never wrong about people.'

Verity let out a loud cackle then, and alarmed by the sound, the three of them, Sylvie, Greg and Annabel, startled with the shock.

'Ha,' Verity went on. 'Do you remember that woman you were seeing a few years ago? What was her name?'

'Hayley?' Annabel offered, her finger trapped in baby Aurelie's fist. Soft-spoken and serenely visaged, it was clear that beneath it all she savoured the gossip. 'It was Hayley, wasn't it, Greg?'

'Yeah,' said Greg. Supremely uncomfortable, he rocked back and forth on his heels.

'Yes, that's it,' said Verity. 'She did six shots of tequila, stripped naked and fell into the swimming pool!'

More whooping laughter followed.

Sylvie turned to look at Greg, whose face was beetroot. 'She sounds like fun,' she said.

'Fun?' Verity bellowed. 'My dear, she was a riot! At the party she suggested all the women give lap dances to the fellows on rotation and when no one else would take part, she took up the mantle herself and volunteered to do them all!'

'Smashing girl, that Hayley! I liked her.' Hugo, red-trousered and be-loafered, raised his glass from the other end of the room.

'Of course you did, darling,' said Lily, who perched on the love seat beside him, taking up about 20 per cent of the space while Hugh man-spread himself across the vast majority of it.

'Well, since then, I've had final approval on Greg's guests,' said Annabel, with a wink in Sylvie's direction.

'Glad to hear I made the cut,' said Sylvie.

'Of course,' said Annabel. 'You're the loveliest girl he's been with by a long way.'

'All right, Ann, that's enough,' said Greg, though he was grinning like an idiot and gripped Sylvie's waist a little tighter.

'I'm just trying to make Sylvie feel welcome,' said Annabel, gently prising back her necklace from Aurelie's grip. 'I want Sylvie to come back next year and save us from another disaster.'

'Hear, hear,' said Verity, tipping her glass at her lips and returning to her original seat via a table laden with platters of party nibbles.

'Right, I'm off to see how everything's getting on in the kitchen,' said Annabel. 'We're having about a dozen more descend on us for drinks tonight, I'm putting together a little spread.'

'Do you need some help?' Sylvie offered.

'No, thank you, sweetheart,' Annabel said, starting for the door. 'You stay here and enjoy yourself. Jay will be down in a minute!'

'She's hired staff,' said Greg. 'Everything all right? It's a lot, isn't it.'

Sylvie told Greg she was fine and just tired, not that she was having an internal panic attack at the thought of coming face to face with Jay. Greg picked Sylvie up by the waist and spun her around, placing her down on her heels very carefully afterwards as if she were a Barbie doll. Then he leant down and kissed her.

'I need a drink after that, how about you, babe?'

Sylvie sank into one of the available armchairs, a high-backed seat upholstered in burnt orange fabric, while Greg poured them glasses of champagne. The conversation recommenced after a second's pause in which the small group bleated their greetings at her. They were all clearly drunk, red-faced and shouting at the person beside them. They were recounting a tale of a Christmas past, when Jonno (Classic Jonno) got absolutely *trolleyed* on Christmas Eve, came downstairs and ate half of the Christmas dinner while everybody slept.

'That's right!' Verity kept interrupting, each time with a little gasp.

'Not a raw turkey?' said Lily, a pretty woman with raven black hair that tumbled, glossy, down her back, and wore an ankle-length, silver sheath dress that was similarly shiny. She had rather bony ankles which stuck out above pointy-toed shoes with little heels and embellished diamanté bows on them, and spoke with a considerable amount of vocal fry.

'No,' said Hugh, turning to her with an incredulous look. 'He did *not* eat the raw turkey.'

'But if anyone could bloody well manage it,' said Jonno, slapping his shirt-encased belly with both his open palms at once, 'it would be me.'

Dahlia, who was sitting just one seat along from Sylvie, turned to her in a rather conspiratorial manner and made her startle. 'Bottomless pits, aren't they?' she said, raising an eyebrow. 'Men. Jolly useful at times, I can tell you. When

Hugh proposed to lovely Lily over there, he had the kitchen staff hide the ring in her soufflé, and the poor girl was full up on two bites and wanted to go for a nightcap somewhere. He had to finish off the soufflé to find the ring, can you imagine it? He'd already had a crème brûleé of his own, ooh and a cheese plate!'

Dahlia was a mousey-haired woman, sturdy-looking in her plain black trousers and blouse, decidedly 'unfussy'. Sylvie said she couldn't believe it, it was indeed miraculous. Greg returned, handed Sylvie the glass of champagne which she drained almost immediately, and sat on the arm of her armchair, essentially trapping her. She wouldn't be able to slip away without notice as she'd hoped.

'But not the *raw* potatoes, surely?' Lily's voice fizzled like an egg in a frying pan.

'No,' said Hugh. 'Not the raw potatoes, darling. Let's see, it was all the vegetable garnishes, wasn't it? The red cabbage, the carrots, the sprouts.'

'Oh, God, those were good,' said Jonno. 'Buttery sprouts with bacon bits.'

'That's right!' Verity gasped.

'You drank a litre of the eggnog,' Hugh went on, his red face reddening as he pointed a finger at Jonno. 'A Christmas pudding, half a yule log and all the brandy cream.'

Quite inexplicably, Hugh and Jonno began to jeer and slap each other around the back like apes. Verity laughed so hard that she finally spilt her champagne all over her skirt and leapt up from the sofa with a squeal.

'Oh, look what I've done!' she cackled. 'Goodness me, goodness me.'

She announced that she was going to the cloakroom to clean up and she stopped off at the snacks table to collect a fistful of cheese straws and put a few chipolatas into her little sequinned purse on the way. The men settled down into their chairs, breathing heavily, and then Jonno's eyes settled on Sylvie as if he had not quite looked at her properly before and the conversation turned to the subject of her ethnicity.

Sylvie pressed her back against the armchair, wishing that she could disappear into it. She felt Greg's hand on her arm, a comforting squeeze; Sylvie watched his jaw tighten, his teeth clench in anticipation of the politically incorrect or offensive comment he could be sure was coming any moment. Sylvie couldn't care less what any of those ridiculous caricatures of human beings thought about her, she only resented having to sit there and listen to it. But it's necessary, she reminded herself, it's necessary to the plan. She began to dissociate around the time that Jonno announced he'd dated a Welsh girl once.

Dahlia guffawed. 'Wales isn't that exotic, is it?'

'Depends,' said Jonno. 'Some Welsh have got terribly dark colouring, practically Italian-looking.'

'Gosh,' said Dahlia.

Sylvie distracted herself by admiring the well-decorated room, cosy, with heavy draped curtains in deep orange either side of the French windows that opened onto the garden. A fire crackled away beneath a dark marble mantelpiece. The room smelt of the embers, bitter and sweet like burnt caramel. In the corner, there was a Christmas tree alive with twinkling warm-toned fairy lights blinking out from the branches that appeared inky blue rather than green in the darkness. It was only afternoon, and yet between the overcast grey of the sky outside and the absence of overhead lighting indoors, it felt much later. All the better for enjoying the light of the fire, Sylvie thought, the rich, familiar smell of burning oak and ash, and the flickering light of the candles which stood like tall, creamy church spires from their holders amongst the glut of spiky holly leaves and berries. But the darkness also brought with it an ominous sense of foreboding and reminded Sylvie that she hadn't yet come face to face with Jay. He was lurking somewhere in the house, right at that very moment, perhaps waiting to rush out at her with his box-cutting knife.

Sylvie poked Greg's leg, gently. 'I need to go to the loo,' she said.

Greg frowned. 'You okay, babe?'

'I'm fine,' said Sylvie. 'Promise.'

He stood up to let her out. Sylvie passed Verity in the hallway who grabbed her by the wrist and bellowed at her, 'Annabel is just *the best* host, wouldn't you agree? She's hand-selected these extraordinary, rare onions for a French onion soup for Jay, all because he doesn't like seafood and won't eat the lobster bisque. They're supposed to be absolutely bursting with flavour, the *queen* of onions, I'm told.'

'Incredible,' said Sylvie. 'Do you know where the loo is?'

Verity flapped her hand in the vague direction. 'Down the hall, second door on your right, or is it left?' She gave a hearty laugh. 'You'll find it,' she said, patting Sylvie's shoulder.

Safely locked behind the *third* door on the right, Sylvie put her hands either side of the basin and leant up close to her reflection in the mirror. She narrowed her eyes, scrutinizing her image for weaknesses. Her diamond earrings glittered from where they nestled in her hair. She'd been so sure of things when she'd woken up that morning, so certain of how her masterplan was going to play out. Now she found herself, not wavering as such but fighting desperately to keep from being swallowed up by nerves. It was Jay. Damned Jay, who always managed to get at her. It was the suspense, the anticipation of seeing him, nothing more. Yes, that was it, she thought to herself.

She opened the window and breathed in a few gasps of cold air, looking at the last of the sunlight peeking out through the dark cloud. At the very bottom of the garden, the tree trunks seemed to glow copper when the orange sunbeams hit the dark green moss. How long had it been since she'd gone for a run in the woods? Too long to remember. She sat down on the toilet for a few minutes. There was a framed foam finger on the back of the wall: GO ANNABEL GO! The ANNA-BEL had been split onto two different lines for the letters to fit. The foam was salmon pink, the lettering was white. Sylvie wondered what it had been for, a marathon perhaps. She could imagine Annabel running a marathon, her sinewy arms pumping hard in a svelte black lycra outfit as she overtook hordes of professional athletes in her mission to raise funds for a children's hospital. She genuinely liked Annabel and took a deep sigh at the great inconvenience of the fact.

When Sylvie thought it was about time to join the group again, she raked a hand through her straightened hair and wiped a faint smudge of lipstick from the skin above her cupid's bow in the mirror's reflection. A few deep inhalations and then she was ready. She could walk back into the sitting room and drink just enough champagne to make it all tolerable and then she would carry out her scheme exactly as she'd planned it, and it was all going to go off without a hitch. She unlocked the bathroom door with a renewed sense of focus, and with her chin high and her shoulders back, pushed the door open to reveal . . . Jay.

'Sylvie,' he said.

His expression was as unreadable as ever. It was a trait that had intrigued Sylvie in the past but now only chilled her to the bone. He wore a black corduroy shirt, black jeans, and a pair of black Nike trainers. The first few buttons of his shirt were undone, and the dark hair just visible at the top of his chest reminded Sylvie of them being in bed together, the whole thing like a fever dream, like an alternate reality.

'Jay,' she said.

'I didn't think you'd actually show,' he said. 'Stupid of me.'

The hostility in his voice, which was barely raised louder than a whisper, sent a shiver down her spine.

'Greg wanted me here.'

There was a short and painful pause in which Jay and Sylvie looked at one another, each reluctant to make the next move.

'What are you going to do?' He asked her this plainly, with nothing accusatory in his voice. As if he'd accepted that the upper hand was hers and that he was at her mercy, for now at least. It was as if he'd accepted that one of his scorned young women would inevitably show up to cause trouble, throwing tantrums in his sitting room like a petulant toddler.

Sylvie felt herself regaining her composure; second by second his power was weakening to nothing. She saw her chance to further his torture and took it.

'I'm not going to do anything,' she said, her eyes wide and innocent. 'I don't want any trouble, I just want to have a nice time with Greg, that's all. We can get along for forty-eight hours, can't we?'

She wanted him relaxed and unsuspecting. She wanted every step of her plan to feel like a stab to the heart. As she moved to brush past him, he leapt back out of her way as if she was going to burn him.

'Are you afraid of me?' she leaned in and whispered.

He glared at her and said nothing. Sylvie walked off and left him standing there. She heard the bathroom door close behind her and the lock turn. Dahlia seemed to appear out of nowhere and she stood in the middle of the corridor, watching Sylvie expectantly.

'You okay?' Sylvie asked her.

'Yes, yes,' said Dahlia, 'just going upstairs to unpack before the party.' Then she gestured in the direction Sylvie had just come from. 'You know Jay well, do you?'

Sylvie felt her stomach twist up into a tight knot.

'Yes,' she said. 'Sort of. I used to work for him.'

'Ah,' said Dahlia. 'That makes sense. But a word of advice, dear – better if one can avoid it, whispering in dark corners with other people's husbands.'

Twenty

Play-Pretend and Tricks

'There you are!' Annabel called out as Sylvie entered the room shortly after Jay. Both of them smiled in an effort not to appear guilty. Annabel, who sat in Sylvie's recently vacated seat and bounced baby Aurelie in her arms, remarked, 'Hope he's not still treating you like an employee, Sylvie. Do I need to have a word?'

'No,' said Sylvie and then she forced an awkward laugh. 'No, thanks.'

'Jay said you found another job?' she asked.

'Yes,' said Sylvie. 'Almost, kind of. I miss nannying.'

'That's so sweet,' said Annabel. 'Well, you're welcome to look after baby Aurelie any time.'

Sylvie winced.

'Thanks,' she said.

Jay stopped at the table of nibbles, to scoop up a handful of crisps. He said hi to Greg from across the room.

Greg put his arm around Sylvie's waist, running his fingers along the skin at the base of her ribcage.

'We've got hours until the party,' he said. 'Everyone's gonna go for a nap probably, shower and get ready and everything. Let's go have a lie-down?'

'Yes,' Sylvie answered, immediately. This was an opportunity to carry out Step One of her revenge plan, and she knew she had to take it.

'Are you all right, mate?' Hugo's shiny red face was screwed up with concern when he approached Jay at the table, glass of red wine in hand.

'Yeah, why?' Jay watched over Hugo's shoulder as Sylvie and Greg said goodbye to everyone and started for the door. He, no doubt, held tightly to the fragile, gleaming thread of possibility that he could escape this little adventure unscathed.

'Nothing, mate, I've just called your name about four times in a row, and you haven't responded. I thought for a minute there you might be having a stroke.'

'Sorry,' said Jay, dusting crisp crumbs from his hands. 'In my own world for a minute there. It's been hectic.'

Upstairs in one of the many guest rooms, Greg began to trace kisses along Sylvie's shoulder and collarbone, grasping at her waist through the fabric of her jumper, pausing to blink at her when she failed to respond. For God's sake, Greg, she thought, I don't have the time for this.

'What's wrong?' Greg was becoming anxious. 'Look,' he said, holding her by the shoulders. 'If you're not feeling this,

I get it, all right? We can leave right now, go home, just the two of us. Whatever you want? I just want you to be happy.'

Sylvie looked up at him, feeling the familiar thaw. She put a hand through his hair.

'Nothing's wrong,' she said. 'I promise, just had a bit too much to drink, feel a bit sick, that's all. I'm gonna go down for a cigarette.'

'I thought you didn't smoke.'

'I always smoke at Christmas,' Sylvie said. 'In remembrance of my grandpa.'

Greg raised an eyebrow but knew better than to laugh. 'Of course you do,' he said. 'Want me to come? We can remember our grandads together.'

'No,' said Sylvie, feeling her handbag through the outside to make sure she had everything she needed. 'No, thank you, I'm just going to have a quiet sit outside, get myself together before the party later. Won't be long.'

'All right.' Greg lowered himself onto the bed with a sigh, kicked off his shoes and lay back with his arms behind his head. 'See you soon.'

He'll be asleep soon, Sylvie thought; he seemed to be capable of napping at any given time. All the better, as she didn't know exactly how long it was going to take her to execute the next step of her plan. As she pushed open the door, she turned back to say goodbye.

'Love you,' said Greg.

Sylvie froze momentarily, and a myriad of possible responses flashed through her brain, none of them good enough. It was all she could do to pretend she hadn't heard and leave the room without turning back.

With the door closed behind her on Poor Sweet Greg and any ill-timed notions of love, a sharp sense of focus returned to her and Sylvie made a mental checklist of the party's whereabouts. Dahlia had gone for a lie-down in another guest room, which was two doors along from her and Greg's room on the right. The door was shut, and nothing could be heard from inside. Fine. The others were downstairs, smoking cigars and having drinks in Jay's study; they'd only just moved into the other room when Sylvie and Greg left them so they could be counted on to stay there for a while. Jay's study was not only downstairs but on the other side of the house entirely. Sylvie couldn't hear any of them, not even Verity, from all the way up here. Annabel had said something about wanting to put Aurelie down for a nap. Sylvie didn't know where Aurelie's room was, but Annabel would probably be coming upstairs some time in the next half-hour. Sylvie knew this was risky, but she didn't know when she'd have another opportunity. It might be hard to disappear once the party had started without Greg or Verity trailing her, or any other number of inquisitive and wine-drunk guests. It had to be now when no one was looking for her. Get in and get out, Sylvie thought to herself, pressing the underside of her arm firmly against the handbag she had pushed up against her armpit.

The cream-carpeted hallway seemed unending as Sylvie picked her way along it. Opening the doors as quietly as she could, she spied guest rooms with sherbet lemon-coloured comforters; a disused office stacked with cardboard boxes full of clothes in plastic hanger bags, an old PC lacquered with dust on a desk in the corner; a sitting room with a floor-to-ceiling bookshelf, inherited old classics organized by colour rather than category, decorative rather than practical.

Finally, Sylvie came across Aurelie's nursery. The room was wide, as large as her bedroom at home, and seemed all the larger for the absence of an adult bed. Pink and white striped curtains hung either side of the window which looked over the garden. The crib was painted white, a blond teddy with curly fur and obsidian black eyes lolled against a pillow with its legs tucked under a crocheted blanket, the wool speckled with threads of glittering opal.

Sylvie shut the door. This meant the next room would be Annabel and Jay's. *Annabel and Jay*. Their life seemed so solid, so tangible that it was hard to imagine Sylvie had once been set on a future with Jay. It had never even been within the realms of possibility, but he had made her feel that it was. He'd done it deliberately – why? Sylvie hadn't figured that out yet. It doesn't matter why he did it, Sylvie thought to herself as she turned the doorknob, only that he did. He broke her heart on purpose with zero regard for the consequences and for that he must be punished.

Annabel and Jay's room was all pale pink and ivory. The wardrobes were French antique with baroque designs on the panelling. A pale pink bedspread embroidered with a lacy pattern, a white fur rug, a sage coloured velvet armchair with a plump William Morris-esque cushion poked into the corner. The lamps on the white bedside tables were blush-coloured satin and ruched at the edges in a way that reminded Sylvie of a bridesmaid's dress. Now that she thought of it, the whole room had a bridal feel to it from the scalloped white edge of the porcelain picture frames that adorned the walls, to the satiny sheen of the floor-length dressing gown that hung from a padded hanger on the outside of the wardrobe.

Sylvie approached the bedspread. She was supposed to be on a mission, but she couldn't help herself. She was distracted by it, all *their* things, their life together. She ran her fingers over the material and lifted it to reveal the pillows and the duvet set beneath. She wondered which pillow was Jay's and which was Annabel's. This was where Jay had come home and made love to Annabel after he told Sylvie he loved her, where he left Annabel sleeping every morning before he came to the office to flirt with Sylvie. Perhaps they had discussed her there, lying close side by side, engaged in intimate marital pillow talk. Perhaps they'd never even breathed her name.

Sylvie tugged the bedspread back into place. Focus, she told herself, Annabel will be on her way any minute. She had to get on with the plan. At the end of the room, on the opposite side to the door she'd come in from, was another door that swung partway open on its hinges to reveal the edge of a bathtub and a stretch of snow-white bath mat. As she entered the ensuite, Sylvie noticed that the bathroom was not exactly sparkling clean but filled with signs of life: a blonde hair on the glass shower shield, a half-melted flurry of foamy bubbles around the plughole. For some reason, this disturbed Sylvie more than if the place had been spotless. She was forced to confront the reality of their toothbrushes together in a porcelain holder in the bathroom, the tiny droplets of spit on the mirror that had been missed. Sylvie imagined them there together, their bare feet on the soft white rug. Annabel in the bath. Sylvie's intimacy with Jay had been nothing more than play-pretend and tricks. All this was achingly, unescapably real.

She heard something then: a child's tired, whiny cry. Aurelie's cry, followed by Verity asking Annabel if she needed any help. They must be in the hallway downstairs if Sylvie could hear them. Annabel was on her way up. Sylvie lurched into action. She zoned in on the aluminium shower caddy, visually sifting through the pearlescent bottles of Kérastase and milky Olaplex containers, searching desperately for something male. If she couldn't find Jay's shampoo the whole plan was over before it started. She spotted something dark grey and was relieved to see a L'Oréal men's shampoo with just over half the liquid left in the bottle. Bingo. Sylvie unscrewed the cap and placed the open bottle on the edge of the bath. Then, she unzipped her handbag and unsheathed the plastic tube of fast-acting hair removal cream like it was a weapon, which of course it was. She squeezed as much of it as she could into the shampoo bottle and watched with horror as the pink, pungent-smelling paste sank down to the bottom of the pearlescent shampoo, the difference between the two liquids starkly visible.

Sylvie picked up a toothbrush from the holder by the sink and stuck the end of it into the shampoo bottle, stirring furiously. She was running out of time and panic made her neck prickle with perspiration and her hands tremble, which was inconvenient when precision was vital. She rinsed off the toothbrush and put it back, screwed the shampoo lid back in place and shook up the bottle as hard as she could. There, she thought, the hair removal cream was undetectable now but hopefully still potent. 'Works in just two minutes!' the packaging promised. Sylvie had been sure to choose 'Extra Strength: for hair that just won't quit'. She'd been inspired by what she'd read in her Aunt Jacqueline's diary about her buzzing off Cornelius's comb-over while he slept. She thought that Jay seemed similarly vain about his own hair, so it was worth a shot. An homage, if you will. She put the shampoo bottle back into the shower caddy and zipped up her handbag.

'Sylvie?'

Sylvie looked up to see that Annabel was gazing at her incredulously from the doorway, as if she'd just watched Sylvie materialize out of thin air or sprout a pair of fairy wings.

'What are you doing here?' Annabel smiled, and her tone was deliberately unobtrusive.

Aurelie, exhausted, rubbed at her red eyes with a balled-up fist and pushed her curly blonde head against her mother's chest.

'Sorry,' said Sylvie. 'I was just looking for some toothpaste.'

Annabel gasped. 'Oh my goodness, I'm so sorry,' she said. 'I thought all the guest rooms had been stocked. There's extras in the cupboard under the sink there.'

'Thanks,' said Sylvie. She bent down and opened the cupboard, reaching for one of a half-dozen tubes of Colgate, lined up like soldiers against the back wall. She felt Annabel's eyes on her, watching closely.

'Sorry about that, Sylvie,' said Annabel. 'Mummy brain, I think they call it. Anything else you need just ask me.'

Sylvie felt herself blush. Annabel gave Sylvie another of her winks.

'Well,' said Sylvie. 'Now I've got everything, thank you.'

She skirted past Annabel and hurried out of the room as quickly as she could.

Back in the guest room Sylvie bounced onto the bed beside Greg, who was naked beneath the covers and already half-asleep.

'You're in a good mood,' he said.

And she was. She was in a glorious mood. She felt positively buoyant. Sylvie wore an enormous smile that she couldn't have hidden if she'd tried.

'Come here.' Greg pulled her close around the waist and kissed her.

It was a deep yearning kiss, the kind that typically gave way to sex, and at that moment Sylvie certainly wouldn't have objected, so she was surprised and disappointed when Greg withdrew and blinked at her. He'd started looking at her like that more often, starry-eyed, as if she were a sunset or a kitten or a baby doing a handstand.

'What?' she asked him, reaching her hand under the covers and stroking his thigh.

'What's your secret?' he asked her, eyes twinkling.

'Excuse me?'

'You don't smell of fags at all.'

Sylvie reached for the unopened tube of Colgate on the bedside table and held it up in his direction. Greg started to laugh.

'Fair enough,' he said. 'Come on, babe, get under the covers with me, we've got hours till the party yet.'

Twenty-one

Enemy Territory

Come nine o'clock that evening, the first of the shiny black four-by-fours rolled onto the driveway. Sylvie, dressed in a black velvet drop-waist dress that Jacqueline had left her and her great-aunt's jewellery hanging from her neck and ears, watched from the window as Greg emerged from the bathroom and shook the water from his hair like a dog.

'Here come the toffs,' he said, drying his ears out with the corner of his towel. 'Sorry, babe, we're in for a long night.'

Sylvie, with her arms crossed over her chest, watched a middle-aged couple emerge from the car. She couldn't really see their faces, just the tops of their grey heads. The woman wore a square-necked velvet dress and a fur stole; the man was dressed in dark blue trousers, a white shirt, bow-tie and jacket. He collected a gift bag so large from the boot of the car that it took both arms to support it, and he staggered under the weight of it as the woman urged him on, beckoning impatiently.

'Those are Annabel's parents,' said Greg. 'George and Christine.'

'And what are they like?'

Sylvie heard Greg zipping up his trouser fly behind her. She didn't take her eyes off the couple on the drive. They were fascinating to her. They produced Annabel, who, despite her outward perfection and wonderful upbringing, had chosen Jay.

'They're . . .' Greg searched for the words. 'They're how you'd expect. I get the feeling they were really hard on Ann, high expectations and all that. They're not Jay's biggest fans but then again, who is? He's so fucking moody all the time.'

'Hmm,' said Sylvie, thinking.

She felt Greg come up behind her, the warmth of his body as he approached. 'I'd bet money that Annabel's mum screamed the house down when she found out they were getting married. They'd much rather their little princess ended up with one of the snobs you'll meet tonight. But you've got to hand it to them, they do their best, they grin and bear it.'

Sylvie felt his hand rest heavy on the back of her shoulder, as she turned to look at him. He was tanned, white-toothed, blue-eyed in a crisp shirt so blinding white that it looked like sunlit snow.

'You look good,' she said.

'You too.' He drew her closer, planting a kiss on her forehead.

She worried that when he put his arms around her, he might somehow dislodge the baggie in her bra. It was so minuscule and contained such a tiny measure of white crystalline powder that it was hard to believe it could have any real impact on a full-sized adult man. It was vital to the next stage of her plan. All she had to do was find the right place to put it.

'Come on,' she said, eager to get going.

'All right, babe,' said Greg. 'Just remember, we can leave whenever you want. I'll make an excuse, we'll come up to bed.'

'I'll be fine,' said Sylvie who was uncertain but determined – and determination counted for a lot.

As they descended the stairs, Sylvie heard the dulcet tones of remastered Christmas classics curl up through the air like gossamer tendrils of smoke. She was reminded of Aunt Jacqueline, the melancholy of that last Christmas season, the only time she'd seen her aunt cry, her eyes reddening around the edges when 'Silent Night' came on the radio. Sylvie thought Christmas was probably the saddest time of year; ghosts seemed to appear everywhere when the Christmas tree went up.

The night before, Sylvie hadn't been able to sleep. Her mind drifted elsewhere, down the hill to the train station and all the way along the track to Richmond, to the Victorian villa where her aunt, the singular most daring and spirited person she'd ever met, was weakening by the hour. The house had been decorated for Christmas when Sylvie came home from Aunt Jacqueline's the night she'd told her she was ill. Jacqueline clasped her hands together, diamonds glittering in the candlelight and said, *I have something to tell you, darling Sylvie. And it's rather serious, I'm afraid.*

Sylvie looked down at the tasteful red bows and candles that Annabel had used to adorn the table in the centre of the hall and said a pleading internal prayer to Aunt Jacqueline and the girl-ghosts. To Giselle herself. She was alone in enemy territory and needed all the help she could get. Jay would have showered by now. When everyone retired to their rooms to freshen up, he would have lathered the spiked shampoo through his luscious dark waves. Sylvie's stomach turned at the thought of a now hairless Jay seething and baying for her blood. Even if he didn't suspect her immediately, Sylvie thought the whole hair removal cream business would certainly have put a damper on his already dreadful mood.

The group, now twenty or twenty-five strong, had gathered in the room with the Christmas tree and lean, youthful waiting staff swayed through the crowd with silver platters of twinkling champagne flutes held high. The atmosphere was frantic, overexcited greetings and loud barking laughter, conversations that sounded more like competitions. The state-of-the-art sound system blasted music from every perceivable direction so that to stand amongst the throng in the middle of the room was like being swallowed into chaos. Annabel, the perfect hostess, called Sylvie over immediately and with a soft, moisturized arm around her waist, touted her around the party, introducing her to the new arrivals. Sylvie couldn't remember any of their names. The warmth of the open fire together with all those bodies, their faces suddenly close, their greetings indecipherable gibberish, overwhelmed her ability to concentrate. She'd become separated from Greg and had been absorbed into Annabel's person like an additional limb. She was close enough to feel Annabel's hair against her collarbone and inhale so much of her Jo Malone perfume that she could taste it, a chemical fruit and floral that turned bitter at the back of her throat.

Finally, she came face to face with Annabel's parents, George and Christine. The enormous gift bag Sylvie had seen them carry in apparently contained 'games for later', Annabel's father relayed with a wink. Sylvie was suddenly reminded that every film she'd ever seen about an extravagant posh party at a countryside mansion had ended in gruesome murder and felt instantly uncomfortable. Jay was still nowhere to be seen. But she was glad Annabel's parents were there, she wanted them to be a part of this. The wonderful plan she had for Jay needed witnesses.

'Right,' Annabel announced when she'd finished the rounds, removing her arm from around Sylvie's waist. 'I'll leave you here with Lily, she'll take good care of you, won't you, Lil?'

Lily gave Sylvie a half-hearted smile. They stood beside a red-faced Hugh who was engaged in lively conversation with a man hunched over onto a coal black cane.

'Of course,' she said.

'Brilliant,' said Annabel and told them she was going upstairs to check on Aurelie and the babysitter. 'And Jay,' she sighed. 'We've had a bit of a grooming disaster.'

Sylvie fixed her face into a picture of inquisitive surprise.

'Do you want a drink?' Lily leant in and raised her voice to compete with the music. 'No, thanks,' said Sylvie.

She couldn't risk drinking until she'd carried out the next part of her plan. It was risky enough as it was, and she needed to be sharp. It was a godsend that the party was already so tipsy they were practically swaying on their feet but even still. The baggie felt like it was burning a hole in her chest, as though it could be seen glowing through the fabric of her dress.

Beside them, Hugh had his hand clamped onto the curved back of the elderly gentleman and he was yelling into his face about soil types (it transpired that Hugh came from a long line of red-trousered, red-faced, toweringly tall farmers, and they'd been breeding woodland pigs for centuries). The conversation appeared completely one-sided. The old man wore circular glasses with spindly gold frames. He had a terribly long upper lip, crinkled with lines, and a small round head over which the skin was thin and liver-spotted, the hair growing sparingly and white around the temples. He watched Hugh with an unwavering, intense focus, as if each word he bellowed was endlessly fascinating. Finally, when Hugh finished his impassioned monologue, he announced 'Sausages!' and set off in the direction of the waitress who had sashayed past with a tray filled with artisan canapés.

The old man with the cane turned to Sylvie and said loudly, 'I haven't the faintest clue what he's been going on about, have you?' And Sylvie and Lily turned to each other and burst out laughing.

'What's funny?' Greg said, having managed to evade Jonno.

'Just Hugh,' Sylvie said.

'Hugh being Hugh,' said Lily and she drained the rest of her champagne and went to search for more.

'Oh my Gawwwwd, Sylvie, Greg, look at you two, you look *divine*!'

Verity appeared out of nowhere in an alarmingly sparkly number with her décolletage flushed shock-pink, and immediately pulled Sylvie and Greg into a bone-crushing, rose-scented embrace. When she released them, she launched into a rave review of Annabel's hosting abilities. The decorations! The food! The drink! The easy atmosphere! And table-settings! Simply to die for! Sylvie half-expected Verity to lean in and remark, her eyes glowing with admiration, that Annabel's farts smelled of lavender and orange blossom and that never (NEVER!) in all her born days had she ever smelt anything quite like it.

Annabel returned to the room with Jay in tow. He looked a fright. Such a fright that Sylvie couldn't help but keep stealing glances at him as he wandered woefully through the party crowd, trailing behind Annabel like a miserable pup. He tried the shampoo then, Sylvie thought, no doubt about that. Gone was the dark gloss of a beard that had added such handsome definition to his face, and instead his face was left bloated, naked-looking and awkward. He wore a baseball cap, presumably to hide the destruction done to his thick, well-groomed head of hair. Sylvie wanted to whoop with joy, do a little dance on the spot but she couldn't, it was important to maintain focus, now more than ever. With Annabel and Jay having just rejoined the party, it was the perfect time to slip away and put her little baggie to work.

'Just going to the loo,' said Sylvie.

She gave Greg a quick kiss on the cheek and disappeared before he had the chance to protest. She started down the hall following the marching ant line of wait staff who entered the door at the very far end with empty trays and reappeared with them replenished. She turned to her right and saw a dining table set for twenty. It makes quite an impact, a table elaborately laid for twenty people. It's a lavish statement, a flaunt. If everything went to plan, it would also be the scene of the crime, and the stage set for the evening's performance. A comedy of errors starring Jay Lakemore.

Twenty-two

The Queen of Onions

Beyond the sophisticated atmosphere of the hallway, the kitchen was pandemonium. There were two chefs, one man and one woman, dressed in black aprons and black hats who fluttered from one dish to another, their hands moving furiously between utensils, stopping every few seconds to dab sweat from their brows. It was *hot*, the windows glossed with steam and so humid that Sylvie could feel the ends of her hair beginning to curl. She was glad though – the more uncomfortable it was in the kitchen, the less likely that the chefs would have the energy to question her presence there. Get in, get out, Sylvie repeated to herself, her mantra for the day.

She needed something, perhaps she could even make a drink. Just something that Jay and only Jay would have. And then she remembered it. Soup. The Queen of Onions.

The rest of them were having lobster bisque but the French onion soup was just for him. He couldn't stand seafood.

'Annabel sent me to have a try of the soup,' said Sylvie. 'The French onion soup? Is that all right? Sorry to be a bother, it's just that her husband's *really* particular.' Sylvie scrunched up her nose then and gave the bemused chefs a knowing look. 'And we don't want him having another episode. Jesus, you weren't at last year's party, were you?'

'No, we weren't,' said the man chef. 'But sure,' he shrugged. 'Go ahead.'

Sylvie thought private chefs were probably used to pedanticism. She could have whipped out a thermometer or a basket full of gold-coated saffron and they wouldn't have blinked. Sylvie approached the simmering metallic saucepan filled with translucent onion slices and the rich, broth-like gravy. The extra special, *royal* onions really looked quite ordinary as far as she could tell. She stood to conceal the pot from view of the chefs who were stationed on the other side of the kitchen, chopping and creaming and prodding.

The onion-scented steam rose up in tendrils and the velvet smoke curled under her nose. She emptied the contents of the baggie into the soup, picked up the metal ladle from the counter and gave it a stir before pretending to taste it.

It was MDMA. It had been relatively hard to get hold of, requiring her to get in touch with Jordan from the warehouse and waiting anxiously as he asked around.

Eventually he'd come back to her with a number and insisted on coming with her to a deserted spot at the back of the train station, where a guy pulled up in a Corsa and put a tiny baggie of white crystals into her palm. Jordan then turned to her with a twinkle in his eyes and asked her if she had a problem, nothing to be ashamed of, he assured her. Sylvie promised him it was nothing, just something she'd been wanting to try. Scientific curiosity, that was the phrase she'd used. That evening she'd crushed the crystals up into a powder with the bottom of one of her old pointe shoes.

'Mm, delicious,' she said. 'Really good! I'd better be off then.'

Sylvie put the empty baggie into her bra and pushed out into the hallway where the air was a cool relief in comparison to the tropical heat of the kitchen.

'Everything all right?' It was Dahlia, who Sylvie thought was beginning to become a bit of a nuisance.

'Everything's perfect,' said Sylvie.

'You were in the kitchen,' said Dahlia, blinking expectantly in a way that seemed to demand an explanation.

'Yes, I was,' said Sylvie. 'I wanted to make sure they knew about my allergy.'

Dahlia blew a stream of air out from her mouth that vibrated her top lip. 'Oh, darling, Annabel would *never* have forgotten something like that.'

'No, but *I* did,' said Sylvie. 'I realized just now that I forgot to tell her, and I didn't want to stress her out so I thought I'd just go and see the chefs myself.'

Dahlia looked annoyed at the fact that she couldn't pick any holes in this premise. She put her hands on her hips and rocked back and forth on her heels for a few exhausting moments after which she gave a defeated sigh, said, 'Very well,' and headed for the stairs.

'Wait a minute,' she said, turning over her shoulder. 'What are you allergic to?'

'Gluten,' Sylvie responded smoothly, raising an eyebrow as if to say, *Anything else?*

'You all right, babe?' Greg appeared at Sylvie's side, put his arm over her shoulder and kissed her on the forehead. 'We're about to go and eat.'

'Perfect,' said Sylvie.

The group began the procession down the hallway and into the extravagant dining room where the music, thankfully, had been turned down. There were plenty of oohs and aahs over Annabel's table-settings, to which she blushed humbly and batted a dismissive hand in the air. Then, they all settled into their assigned seats that were signalled by little name cards written in silver cursive. Each person had a small white and silver Christmas cracker in the centre of their plate and Sylvie picked hers up and shook it by her ear. It was heavy. *Premium* Christmas crackers no doubt, she wouldn't have expected any less. These were probably filled with sterling silver fountain pens and money clips, or some other classic hallmark of the wealthy that had been forged from a precious metal.

Annabel's mother, Christine, said, 'Wonderful job, darling,' in the same scrutinizing tone as an official government inspector.

Annabel pressed a hand to her heart. 'Thank you, Mummy.'

Sylvie had been seated with Greg to her left and Verity to her right, typical of Annabel to deviate from the traditional table-setting structure to make everyone more comfortable. She was almost beginning to resent Annabel's kindness. I mean *really*, what was her *problem*? Sylvie thought to herself. She must be overcompensating for something, an addiction to running over pigeons on the side of the road or something. The thrill of the anonymous kill. How could anyone really be that *nice*? It was so indecent, inconsiderate, *rude* really, come to think of it.

Waiters took elegant promenades along the edge of the table touting bottles of red wine, pouring elegantly with their thumbs in the divot at the base of the dark bottles, and white napkins tucked over their elbows. The soup came out quickly, creamy bowls of lobster bisque, sprinkled with tarragon, and then the onion soup. But hang on a minute, Sylvie began to panic as she watched the waiter approach with his tray. There were *two* bowls of French onion soup, *heavily spiked* onion soup.

'Ah!' Annabel beamed at the waiter and his stony face cracked up into a smile, thawed by the genuine warmth of her delight. 'One for the gentleman just there, please.'

'What's that?'

'We've made you some French onion soup, Hector,' said Annabel, raising her voice and then immediately apologizing about it to all in the immediate vicinity.

Sylvie looked on in abject horror as the first bowl of soup was placed down in front of the elderly man from earlier, the one with the walking stick who Hugh was yelling at. Sylvie felt an ice-cold thrill of fear wash over her like cool rain.

'And the other one here, please.'

The waiter placed the remaining bowl of soup in front of Jay. Annabel picked up her spoon and so did everybody else. Sylvie dipped her polished spoon into the orange-pink of the lobster bisque, its surface swirled with cream. She couldn't bring herself to taste it, she felt ill at the thought of swallowing a mouthful. She watched each of the guests along the table opposite as they discussed Christmas plans and sang Annabel's praises. George's booming voice could be heard above the throng. Jonno was uncharacteristically quiet and hunched over as he slurped up lobster bisque from his bowl with a canine concentration. Sylvie gripped so tightly to the spoon handle as Hector tipped a spoonful of onion soup into his age-lined lips, that she knew she was marking grooves onto the insides of her fingers. She felt Greg's hand come down on her shoulder, a comforting gesture that had grown oppressive.

The woman who was sitting next to Greg was red-haired, in her late forties and very attractive. To Sylvie, everything about her screamed Newly Divorced. From the way her posture responded to Greg's presence – she was like a flower leaning towards the sun – to her demure smile and the way she kept batting her lashes and arching her back in her seat, her eyes flicking nervously in Sylvie's direction. She was trying her hand at an old game and not sure she remembered all the rules.

'Lovely soup,' she squeaked in Greg's direction. 'Isn't it? So silky.'

'What do you think, babe?'

Greg turned to Sylvie and found her staring at Hector, her brow all crumpled with worry. 'What's that?'

'The soup,' said Greg, raising his eyebrows at her in a way that said, *Get this woman away from me.*

Sylvie, quite frankly, couldn't care less about the woman. It might even serve her later if Greg was distracted by someone else and paying less attention to what she was doing. All she could think about now was the enormous quantity of MDMA that the elderly, hard-of-hearing relative of Annabel's had just unknowingly ingested. She tapped her foot impatiently under the table. God, she thought, how long has it been? Half an hour? Twenty to forty minutes for a come-up, that's what she'd read online. She stared at the clock mounted on the wall opposite; the second hand seemed to be spinning around faster and faster. Her heart pumped hard and frantic in her chest. God only knew what the drugs were going to do to him. Surely not *kill* him? Sylvie gave a sharp involuntary gasp at the thought. It was too terrible. She'd be arrested and everyone would know what she'd done. She'd be the psychopath who spiked an innocent old man for kicks. At *Christmas*, no less. But for now, Hector seemed perfectly normal. He'd finished the soup and pushed his empty bowl into the centre of the table, his hands clasped together grandly over the small protrusion of his belly. His napkin was tucked at the corner into his collar in a way only the old and infantile can get away with. His small mouth hung down low like an ageing basset hound and he had the same droopy, reddening eyes.

It was inevitable that Jay's smart shirt and Yankee cap combination would attract some comment during the evening, but no one was quite drunk enough to have a go at poking the bear, at least until the end of the first course. The moment the soup bowls were removed and the napkins refreshed, it was Annabel's father, George, who, with a tone that could have made flowers wilt said, 'My boy, why are you so strangely dressed?'

Jonno piped up from his seat at the end of the table. 'What the hell does he look like?' he said, laughing. 'Trying to start a new trend, eh, Lakemore?'

'A cap at the *table*?' Hugh mock-scolded him, loudly. 'Abominable!'

Everyone started laughing, which Sylvie knew Jay would absolutely *detest*. He was not the kind of person who could laugh at himself. However, he didn't appear to be getting angry, or especially irritated, just uncomfortable. He'd grown pinker in his newly shorn cheeks. Sylvie could see that he was sweating even though his cap was pulled low over his brow.

'It's probably the fashion now, is it, dear?' asked Christine through gritted teeth.

'Something like that,' said Jay.

'And Jesus, mate,' said Greg. 'What the hell happened to your beard?'

'I used Annabel's hair removal cream instead of shampoo in the shower.'

The whole group giggled and gawped.

Greg winced. 'Well, it is *not* a good look for you, mate, I can tell you that much.'

'Yeah, cheers.'

Annabel reached out and gave Jay a consolatory squeeze on the shoulder.

'I don't know how it happened,' she said. 'The bottles are so different. You must not have been thinking. Jay's been working so hard lately.'

'Well, I've chucked it out,' he said with a forced, sparkless smile that begged her to change the subject.

The next course was roasted quail served with honey-glazed leeks and roasted baby potatoes. The conversation moved on to more pleasant topics such as taxes and immigration, which the monied crowd, their tongues loosened by the drink and festive cheer, attacked with gusto. There was no faux-liberalism any more. They were so brutal that Sylvie thought it was like watching a horde of piranhas strip the flesh off a baby goat.

Jay and Greg noticeably abstained from the conversation, as the others attacked migrants, people on benefits and extolled the virtues of privatizing the NHS. Greg put his hand over Sylvie's shoulder, massaging her through the fabric of her dress as if she were his own personal stress ball. Jay focused on hacking away gracelessly at the roasted quail. He's agitated, Sylvie thought, I hope that's not going to affect the high. Knowing what she did about Jay and Greg's childhood, she wondered how he could stand it, marrying Annabel and sitting here with all these people whose hereditary gene code had been untouched by any form of struggle.

Greg leant in and whispered, 'Sorry about this. I don't want you to be uncomfortable.'

Sylvie was in fact supremely uncomfortable, but only because it looked as though Hector's face was beginning to change colour.

She shrugged. 'I've heard worse. It doesn't bother me.' Sylvie had often found herself wafting around the periphery of these kinds of circles, the ballet classes and schools had been full of the offspring of these types. Whenever things got socio-political she'd mentally check out. She'd quickly learnt the script and it was boring.

Sylvie put her hand over the top of her glass when the servers carted the wine around. She watched Jay across the table (it was her luck to be just opposite him), as the candle flames darted across her vision and blurred his features into a smudged impression. She watched him grow slowly redder and tug at his collar. She watched his forehead begin to shine and gradually, beads of sweat were prised from his brow and one rolled, like a single pearl, down the bridge of his nose, where it hung a few seconds from the tip before he wiped it away.

The conversation had, thankfully, turned to the subject of raising children. Sylvie knew enough to realize that Annabel's circle were not really *raised* at all but reared by nannies, au pairs and jolly-hockey-sticks boarding schools in the countryside. All the wealthy girls she'd known at Willow Way had complained about their parents, but secretly wanted to be just like them. As they grew older, they imitated their way of talking and looking at the world. She knew that one day they'd wake up and would have had so much practice that they weren't imitating any more, they were just *being*. That's how people like this regenerated.

Jay put his hand to the back of Annabel's neck and looked at her tenderly. The action, inexplicably, felt like a knife in Sylvie's chest.

'I love you,' he said, loudly, deliberately, as if he wanted the whole table to hear.

The entire table (except for Sylvie) cooed in unison. Annabel, part-alarmed, part-touched, pressed her hand to the outside of Jay's.

'I love all of you,' he said then, looking up and down the table and making startling eye contact with each person in turn. 'It means so much –' he stood up out of his chair, the legs of which shunted loudly against the floor – 'for you all to travel here to be with us at this very, very, very special time of year. Actually, hang on . . .'

Then he strode out of the room, leaving everyone to mutter uncertainly amongst themselves. Annabel clapped her hands together, said, 'Goodness,' and masked her anxiety with a bright, cheerful smile.

'What the fuck?' Greg whispered into Sylvie's ear.

'Sweet, isn't it?' Verity announced. 'To see a person really taken with the Christmas spirit.'

Twenty-three

Blancmange of a Man

The Christmas tree entered the room. Although it appeared to be wearing a pair of black Nike trainers, it shed shreds of tinsel behind it in its wake. The plug for the fairy lights trailed along. The Christmas tree swayed over to the far head of the table, revealing Jay as its puppeteer. He had scooped it up in his arms, so it looked like he was dancing with it when he wiggled it back and forth, trying to set it down in just the right place. He lost his cap in the process and Sylvie watched as he scrambled after it. He looks nothing like himself, she thought. The black shiny hair that he styled in luscious waves, piled atop his head, were long gone.

'Good heavens!' Verity cried. 'He's as bald as a baby.'

'He's like a cue ball,' added Jonno.

'Really, Annabel,' said Christine, as if Jay's baldness was a personal affront. 'What is the meaning of all this?'

'I'm so sorry, Mummy,' said Annabel. 'I don't know *how* it happened.'

Cap firmly affixed in place again, Jay plugged the lights in and then took a few paces back from the tree.

'Darling?' Annabel's searching voice cut through the drunken rumble of the party guests.

'Yes,' said Jay.

Though she could only see half of his face, Sylvie could see from her seat that he was crying.

'Darling?' Annabel's smile had dropped clean off.

'It's so beautiful,' said Jay. 'Isn't it?'

George turned over his shoulder and giving Jay a look of disgust, said, 'Goodness me, old chap, sit down, will you? We haven't finished the quail.'

'Sorry, Daddy,' said Annabel. And then, beckoning to Jay, 'Come and sit next to me, love.'

Jay trudged around the side of the table like a moody child. He miscalculated the position of his seat, or the distance between his arse and the seat, and before anybody could do anything to help him, he was flat on his back with his feet in the air.

'Jay!' Annabel, assisted by a waiter on each side, helped him up.

The drugs, Sylvie thought, are working. She cast a nervous glance in Hector's direction but didn't observe anything out of the ordinary. He seemed quietly satisfied, occupied with eating his meal methodically, cutting off small bite-sized pieces of meat, putting his knife down and changing his fork over to the other hand. Very good, Sylvie thought. He was breathing and she was grateful for that, though her chest was still as tight as a violin string.

'What the fuck is wrong with him?' Greg said to her, under his breath.

Sylvie shrugged.

Jay was perplexed, looking as clueless as a child. He sat down in his seat and Annabel put her hand in his lap and leant in to whisper something to him.

'Goodness,' she said. Cautious as ever of public perception, Annabel was as smooth as a beleaguered politician when she put down her glass and addressed the table with a joyful expression of, 'If you know us very well, which you all do, of course, being our dearest friends, you know that we take festive cheer *very, very* seriously in this house.' A pause for laughter. 'And if I haven't gotten all of you as merry as my wonderful husband here by dessert at the latest, I will have considered myself a failed host.'

She was extraordinary, and the faces which only a moment ago were bemused, almost disgusted, were bright with starry-eyed admiration. Everyone except for George and Christine, that is, who gave each other knowing looks.

Annabel raised her glass of champagne, the same glass she had nursed discreetly since the group first took their seats.

'To Jay,' she said.

'To Jay,' the group echoed.

'For making this Christmas and every Christmas *wonderful*.'

Everyone clapped and cheered. Sylvie too applauded Annabel, who was as graceful a manoeuvrer as she'd encountered in fifteen years of classical ballet.

'I *love* the Christmas tree here, darling,' said Annabel and she kissed Jay, the two of them with tears forming in their eyes.

Sylvie couldn't believe he was getting away with it.

All sense of formality collapsed with the distribution of dessert, which was some kind of black-foresty concoction, all blood red berries and deep, forbidden-looking chocolate cake. The waiters poured port and dessert wine. The air was thick with it, syrupy, rich and strong as sin. The table had broken up into various groups who formed into clusters, their conversation impenetrable, secretive. The music was turned up and various couples took to the floor and began taking clumsy turns around the Christmas tree. Hector danced alone without his stick. Sylvie could only wonder what he was experiencing, what he felt as he performed the same proud flourishes with his arms as she'd seen flamenco dancers make. She thought he'd likely attribute it to the port. It would have to be bloody good port, she thought, half a glass and he'd forgotten all about his gammy leg and was gyrating to Wham!

They were all wasted. Soon she'd better leave and get on with the next part of her plan. That was what she'd come for. Revenge. Though now the word was somewhat duller in her mind's eye. It had lost a little of that sexy lacquer, that gloss that had made it so appealing. Sylvie rested her head back against the tall dining chair headrest and watched Jay and Annabel dance. She felt strange and uncertain. A dull ache between her ribs. It wasn't quite jealousy that she felt. Shame, perhaps, at having been so wrong about a person, a situation. And loss maybe. She would never be the one to slow-dance with Jay at Christmas time. But she didn't want that any more, did she? She hadn't wanted that in a long time. She was being silly, nostalgic and melancholic as a side effect of all this *stuff.* The tree and the lights and the music and the little old man and his minor Christmas miracle. Jay was hanging off Annabel's shoulder, like a rag doll. It appeared as though all the bones in his body had gone soft, as if he lacked the strength to stand up straight. He'd become a simpering, blancmange of a man, all shapeless and pale. Sylvie had sent him straight back to childhood.

'Do you wanna dance?' Greg asked her.

Sylvie shrugged and said sure. She let him turn her in circles around the makeshift dance floor. She felt secure in his arms, as if there was no way she could fall, and he was handsome. What was wrong with her? Why couldn't she just love him?

'I didn't catch your name.' It was George. He was dancing with Christine who fixed her scrutinizing squint on Sylvie.

'Sylvie,' she said.

'Sylvie.' George repeated it. 'That doesn't sound too ethnic, I think I can manage that. I've dreaded asking you all evening.'

'Sorry to disappoint,' said Sylvie.

She detested the way alcohol seemed to embolden bigots the country over, but she knew the only power she held in the exchange was to appear unbothered by the faux pas.

'What did you say, mate?'

Sylvie felt Greg's arm heavy and protective over her shoulder.

'Greg, it's fine,' Sylvie said, making her voice as light and airy as she could manage. 'Honestly, it's fine.'

The last thing she wanted just then was to make a fuss that placed her at the centre of attention, especially over some sort of racial misunderstanding; as the only non-white person there, she already stuck out. George seemed to be enjoying the chaos he'd inadvertently created, a sly half-smile played on his lips, and he released Christine, who wandered off in the direction of a member of the waiting staff with some request.

'Goodness me, old chap.' George clapped a wincing Greg on the back. 'I didn't mean any offence to your lovely lady here. I only wanted to see if the two of you would join us in the next room for a game of tiddlywinks?'

Twenty-four

Kill List

Sylvie managed to escape tiddlywinks by telling Greg she was going for a cigarette and would be back shortly. Sylvie had made up her mind to go through with the plan all the way or be damned. She focused very hard on conjuring the same feeling she'd had when she sat in her darkened room, drinking wine amidst the raging storm outside. That fury had made her feel powerful and otherworldly.

She'd almost reached the stairs when she heard footsteps behind her. A breathy panting voice called out, 'Sylvie, hang on.'

It was Greg, who scooped her into an awkward hug, with her face pressed against his stomach.

'You'll get make-up on your white shirt,' she said.

'It's fine. Look, are you okay, babe? I'm sorry about these pricks, I feel like I never should have brought you here. Fuck it, I hate coming myself. Do you want to leave? Say the word and we'll go wherever you want to.'

Sylvie looked at him, the trace of sweat on his upper lip and his temples, his wide, pleading eyes. He was sweet but also rather inconvenient. The longer she stood there with him in the hallway, the less time she'd have to carry out Phase Two.

'I promise I'm fine,' she said. 'I just want a minute of peace and quiet, to smoke a cigarette and relax, that's all.'

Greg seemed spurned by this, the way he flinched at the imagined rejection.

'Hey,' said Sylvie. She reached up and stroked Greg's cheek with her fingertips. 'I'm fine, honestly. Dumb stuff like that doesn't bother me at all. It's just a bit hot in there, that's all, and my social battery's running low.'

Greg took her hand and kissed it.

'All right, I'll be in the mad house if you need me,' he said.

It was time. Sylvie dashed upstairs to collect her handbag. The bedroom was cast in shadow and for a moment, she panicked that it was gone. But she found it tucked under the edge of her bed. When she put it onto her shoulder, she was relieved by the swishing sound of liquid against the walls of the container as she raced down the staircase. Sodium silicate.

Jay's Jaguar was on her kill list. He loved it, took pride in it, flaunted it, considered it an extension of his person. Therefore, it had to go. It had been the consensus online that sodium silicate was the best thing for the job. It was supposed to crystallize like liquid glass inside the engine and disable it completely. All she had to do was deposit it in the car's system. The cool air was sobering, although she hadn't drunk much. Sylvie was careful to leave the front door slightly ajar so she would be able to find her way back in without calling attention to herself, and she turned her focus to the car. Jay's car. It had a mythic quality about it after all the times she watched it come and go from the office window. It had been the scene of intimate moments between them. Sylvie closed her eyes and remembered Jay's lips on hers, his hand between her legs. She googled the model before she came and found out that the newer models' fuel tanks are opened electronically via a button on the dashboard. However, she should be able to open the petrol cap from outside the vehicle if she could get something under it at just the right angle. She'd packed a mini set of screwdrivers in the inner pocket of her handbag for this exact purpose.

She pulled out a medium-sized screwdriver with a flat head and tucked it under the lip. It took all the strength she had to wrench it open, and she made a nasty scrape on the paint in the process. Her heart raced as she looked at the damage. She spat on her finger and rubbed at the scuffed paint. There was no improvement. Oh, well, she thought, she'd wanted to ruin his car, hadn't she? The petrol cap bounced open, and she untwisted the plastic cover on the tank, and then the lid of the sodium silicate bottle, which had been waiting on the ground by her feet. She didn't know how much of it to use. This was a 500ml bottle. Think, Sylvie, think. How much did it say on the Reddit thread? A whole thread about how to ruin someone's car inconspicuously, and dozens of jilted spouses, stalkers, stalkees and pyromaniacs in the comments. There'd been so many methods to choose from. Sylvie couldn't remember the recommended amount, so she tipped the bottle over the open cap and listened for the glugging sound. She held the bottle there until it was empty.

Then she heard something, voices, footsteps, people walking along the hall and the light flicking on at the front of the house. She could see it in the glass panels either side of the doorway, the door creaking open. Sylvie flung herself into a patch of nearby foliage, grazing her arms and legs on the branches. She felt the prickle of leaves against her cheek. She couldn't see much but she could hear.

'What was that? A fox?' She recognized Verity.

'I've no idea,' said the voice, a man's. It crackled with age.

'All right, well, it was good to see you, my darling. Are you sure you're okay getting home, Hector?'

'Oh, yes,' he said. 'Oh, yes.'

Verity cooed her goodbyes from the porch steps before shutting the door. Sylvie peered through the branches and watched as the little old man held his cane aloft and waltz-stepped down the driveway, humming as he went.

She checked once over the scene to make sure she'd collected everything. Sylvie gathered herself, affixing her handbag in place, dusting off her dress and standing up straight, taming her hair with her fingertips. She pressed the doorbell and a few moments later, Verity answered.

'Oh, hello you,' Verity beamed. 'What on earth are you doing out there?'

Verity peeked left and right over Sylvie's shoulder.

Sylvie held up her handbag as explanation.

'Came out for a smoke,' she said, smiling sweetly. 'But the door closed after me.'

'Come on in out of the cold, darling,' said Verity. 'The *games* are starting!'

Sylvie found the crowd at the dining table, in a state of repose with their chairs rearranged and half the men with their feet up on the table. The music was turned up to deafening volume so that each word of 'Fairytale of New York' seemed to vibrate through the floorboards. They all had ash-marked faces and wide-open mouths as they howled themselves silly over a game of tiddlywinks. The waiting staff were gone and it seemed as though the party had descended into a free-for-all. Jonno returned from the kitchen with a magnum of champagne, which he popped messily, slopping foam onto the rug. Loud cheers followed. Jay, with his head leaning on Annabel's shoulder, drifted in and out of sleep, drowsy as a child up past their bedtime. George and Christine were red-faced, laughing and seemed at last to be having a good time.

Sylvie and Greg sat at the edge of the table and watched the game. Greg held one of Sylvie's hands between his. He thumbed the creases in her palm and the undersides of her fingers as if committing each detail to memory.

'Tired?' he asked her.

'Yes,' she said, yawning for effect.

'Should we go up?'

They said their goodbyes and thank-yous and trudged up the stairs to bed. Lily had already gone up and they could hear her snoring lightly in the room next door.

They slipped exhausted from their clothes and fell into bed without brushing their teeth. Sylvie pretended to sleep first, turning away and burying her head in the pillow. She really, really didn't want to discuss whether she loved Greg back and would have welcomed sleep, but her anxiety kept her awake. She lay very still and stared into the indigo gloom until she felt Greg tumble into sleep, his breath becoming deeper, and then she sat upright with her back against the headboard.

She remembered her final visits to Aunt Jacqueline's house. Eventually she'd been too weak to come downstairs and Sylvie had to see her in the bedroom. Jacqueline wore a silk nightgown and scarf and her face fully made up, like a queen. There were no more cigarettes. No more pink Sobranies but they played gin rummy and watched *Funny Face* on the television. Aunt Jacqueline watched the screen while Sylvie watched Aunt Jacqueline, her eyelids fluttering gently as butterflies' wings as her tired body succumbed to sleep. Sylvie carefully unhooked her hand from her aunt's and looked at her, the peaceful beauty of her face, the delicate wrinkled skin of her eyelids. She reached over and pressed a fairy kiss to her aunt's forehead. She knew then that things would only get worse.

'Can't sleep?' Greg reached over and turned the lamp on.

Sylvie hugged her knees up to her chest and alarmed herself by beginning to cry. She couldn't have said why exactly, perhaps the memories of Aunt Jacqueline. Or maybe it was the plain earnestness of Greg's face in the soft lamplight which made his skin appear so creamy and strangely pure, as if he'd never had a bad thought in his life and was incapable of harm. It made Sylvie feel like a monster beside him, all twisted up and dark inside.

'Hey.' He pulled her closer. 'What's wrong?'

'Nothing,' she said, sniffing back her tears. 'Honestly, it's so stupid, I don't know why I'm crying.'

She let him hold her though she resented it, the velvet of his shoulder against her cheek, his kindness.

'I'm going for a smoke,' she said, wiping her tears roughly with the back of her hand.

'I'm coming with you,' said Greg, not giving her the opportunity to protest.

The party was over and there was nobody in sight. The tinsel hanging over the mantel in the Christmas tree room (now sans Christmas tree) had come loose at one end and dangled limply in the empty space over the fireplace. A few glasses with dregs of champagne and faint ghostly lipstick prints waited forgotten on an abandoned silver tray. The air was active still. It hummed with energy, and Sylvie thought that if she listened very, very closely she would be able to hear 'Auld Lang Syne' played in slow, trudging chords. The French doors were open just slightly as if someone had meant to come back and lock up but had forgotten after passing out from too much brandy and rum-soaked fruitcake. The breeze whistled through the crack and lapped at the edge of a napkin, twisted up and left on the seat of a chair.

It was a clear night and the two of them felt alone in the universe, with just the stars and the unending blackness of the enormous garden. It was darker than dark, the thick, brambly foliage at the edges seemed to have swallowed the abyss and magnified it. Sylvie doubted there was another patch on earth as dark as the edge of Jay's garden. It looked like a black hole, as though you might fall through it and slip into another world completely.

'It's weird being here,' said Greg.

The two of them politely exhaled smoke away from one another. 'When I was a kid, I never could have imagined all this.'

Sylvie nodded.

'We had nothing,' he said, his blue eyes glazed with drink. 'Now we have everything, and it still feels like nothing.'

'That's not true,' said Sylvie, even though she had no way of knowing how Greg felt and only the sense that she needed to protest. 'You should be proud of what you've built.'

'That's not . . . I am, I am proud.' Greg drew closer, his shining eyes reflecting what little light there was, like cat's eyes on a dark road. 'I just mean there's more, things that matter more.'

'More than the Lamborghini?'

'More than the Lamborghini, exactly.'

'Like what?'

'Like family,' he said. 'A real family, and love.' He must have read the fear in Sylvie's eyes because he added, rather quickly, 'Sorry, babe, I'm not trying to freak you out.'

'You're not,' said Sylvie.

'What I'm trying to say is, I think I'm ready for my life to be different, to commit to things, you know?' He wrapped his arms tightly around her waist. 'And I'm really, *really* glad I met you. You're so sure of yourself, so confident, it's sexy as fuck. I meant it,' he said, then, 'when I said, "I love you." I do. I meant it.'

Sylvie kissed him then, mostly to stop him talking though she would have been lying to herself if she pretended to have no feelings for Greg. His mouth was soft and smoky.

He was undeterred. 'Do you want . . . I don't know . . . a future? With me?'

Sylvie put her head on one side and looked at him. 'I've found that wanting something very badly is the quickest way to end up losing it.'

'We're talking in riddles now?'

'I'm drunk,' she lied. 'Let's talk about it tomorrow.'

Greg looked uncomfortable but gritted his teeth and said, 'Sure.' He stretched. 'Are you ready for bed now?'

'Soon,' she said. 'I'll be up in a minute.'

'You want me to stay with you?'

'No,' she said. 'It's fine, I'll come up in a sec.'

Greg gave her a kiss on the cheek before he left.

Sylvie stared out into the dark and lit another cigarette. Aunt Jacqueline had become weaker and weaker until Sylvie's visits were reduced to twenty minutes. Sylvie would sit in a chair by her bedside and talk to her in long disjointed monologues. She thought it must have been terribly painful for Aunt Jacqueline, who always had such wonderful stories to tell, not to be able to speak at all. Sylvie thought she must have been ready to die by then. Aunt Jacqueline looked at her kindly, her blue eyes assuring Sylvie that she knew exactly who she was and that she loved her. She clasped at Sylvie's hands even though her grip was very weak. She no longer wore her diamonds. They'd been shut away in a safe-box. Sylvie did the best she could not to bore her aunt, but it was all she could do to babble incessantly about any old thing she'd read online or seen in the news. Sylvie felt she had to keep talking. She had to keep talking or she was going to cry and that would be selfish of her. It was her aunt who was suffering. Not her.

She did her best though she felt she was too young to be sitting at someone's deathbed; surely this was a job for an adult who'd know just what to say and how to say it. But her aunt didn't make her feel insufficient, she greeted her always with grateful eyes and held her hand until the very last minute. Her aunt had never made her feel as though she wasn't enough. She was the only person in Sylvie's life who'd made her consider that maybe, just maybe, she was perfect as she was. And then she slipped away.

As the New Year approached, her feeling of devastation only grew. The countdown brought her a sense of cool dread that increased exponentially with each decreasing number. It struck her as a very strange thing to celebrate, the passage of time.

Sylvie stubbed her cigarette out under her shoe. Stop it, she thought, snap out of it. Now was not the time for reflection. She had a job to do. Plans for a grand finale. She needed to stay focused. She would hold nothing back; the only thing she wanted in the world was this, no matter what it cost her.

Twenty-five

Naughty Fox

'What the fuck?' Jay's exasperated voice below her window woke Sylvie with a jolt.

'We've slept late,' said Sylvie. 'Everyone's up.' She panicked, her heart pounded, and her palms began to sweat as she racked her brains for any way sleeping in could have jeopardized her plan. She couldn't think of any, *for now.* But she would have to be more careful. Idiot, she thought, you should have set an alarm.

'Who cares?' Sleepy-faced, Greg reached for her over the covers without opening his eyes. 'Let's go back to sleep.'

Sylvie leapt out of bed and practically ran to the window, where a scene was developing on the long, sandstone-coloured driveway around Jay's prized black Jag. Jay sat in the driver's seat with the window rolled all the way down – so that he and Annabel could shout at each other – and pressed down on the accelerator while Annabel stood a way back with Aurelie in her arms. An ominous cloud of tar-black smoke coughed out of the exhaust pipe for a few seconds before the car seemed to short-circuit. Dahlia watched from the front porch with her hands in her pockets.

'Something's going on,' said Sylvie, pressed up to the windowpane where her breath cast a fog onto the glass.

Greg propped himself up on his elbows and rubbed his eyes. 'Like what?'

'I don't know,' said Sylvie. 'Come on, let's go down.'

She rushed over to her suitcase and unzipped it, chipping a fingernail in her hurry to find something to wear. She stripped out of her nightie and into a pair of jeans and a jumper.

'Seriously?' Greg groaned in response to the insistent look Sylvie cast at him. 'Fine.' He brushed the duvet cover aside and sat upright to stretch his arms.

Down on the driveway, Sylvie and Greg's presence was barely acknowledged. Jay (bald head concealed beneath his baseball cap) had the same grief-stricken look on his face as if he'd just knocked down a pedestrian at a zebra crossing. Dahlia regarded Sylvie with the same suspicion as she had the day before, her eyes narrowed in a way that suggested she knew all of her secrets, had guessed them somehow. Impossible, Sylvie thought, you're paranoid.

Sylvie and Greg positioned themselves at a vantage point that was conveniently out of the way and watched as Jay got out of the car and lifted up the bonnet, dropping it once and then a second time on his fingers as he struggled to hoist it into place. Sylvie felt a flush of satisfaction at the helpless look on Jay's face. She was glad she'd gone for the car. She'd struck him where it hurt.

'Gosh, you're all up early!' Verity said brightly as she came out of the front door.

Verity looked unsteady on her feet. Her eyelids were slightly swollen, red and shiny around the rims. There were traces of last night's mascara clinging on to her eyelashes and stuck in the little creases under her eyes. She was dressed in a pair of creased light blue denim jeans, a Christmas jumper with Rudolph embroidered on the front of it. The whole dishevelled ensemble gave the impression she'd dressed in a wind tunnel.

'What's everyone doing out here?' Christine came out onto the drive clutching a mug of tea. It was the trudging, limping walk of someone who would much rather still be in bed.

'Someone's ruined Jay's car,' said Dahlia.

'Unbelievable,' Christine gasped. 'How did they get through the gate?'

'What's all the noise about?' George followed Christine out onto the driveway, dressed in a brown cable-knit jumper and wearing a pair of suede house slippers.

'It's Jay's car,' Christine explained.

George raised his eyebrows as if to say, *What else?*

Annabel bounced baby Aurelie in her arms. The child's pink brow wrinkled as she wondered what her dad was doing kneeling down and rubbing at the petrol cap of his car rather than sitting in the driving seat and driving it.

'Someone's forced it open,' Jay said, through gritted teeth.

Sylvie looked over at the scuffed petrol cap. The scratches in the paint had scraped through to the metal beneath. In the light of day, it looked like the work of a wild animal.

'Maybe you should start it up again?' Verity asked, rather brightly.

'No!' the whole group shouted in unison.

'So strange,' said Annabel. 'Why would anyone want to ruin your car, Jay?'

'And the week before Christmas,' Dahlia tutted. 'Unbelievable.'

Jay's face was typically placid, except for his left eyebrow which twitched just slightly. Sylvie sidled up closer to Greg, clutching his arm.

'Oh, Jay, it's so obvious!' Annabel cried. 'I know just what to do.'

Sylvie clutched Greg's arm tighter but was careful to maintain the expression of someone who was appropriately outraged but not personally invested in the events of the day.

'We've got the cameras,' she said, pointing up at the CCTV cameras affixed to the front of the house and aiming down at them. Small and carefully placed, they were discreet enough to go unnoticed. 'We can check the CCTV.'

'Brilliant,' said Dahlia.

'Are you okay, babe?' Greg looked down at Sylvie, who had just let out an involuntary gasp.

'Fine,' she squeaked.

Sylvie didn't know how she was going to get out of this. She had the urge to run but was unable, she felt as though she were watching herself from the outside.

It was decided that they were going to put the whole matter aside until after breakfast, at which time Jay would review the CCTV footage and if necessary, call the police because as Verity pointed out, 'It could have been a naughty old fox or a badger perhaps!' Annabel was conscious of her party dissolving into some kind of amateur version of *CSI* and didn't think it was proper to set her guests about solving crimes without at least serving them a cup of tea or some coffee first.

'At least it wasn't stolen,' she said, patting Jay's arm as the group began to trail indoors. 'That would have been much worse.'

'A lot of fuss about nothing,' George declared as the party made its way inside.

'George,' Christine half-heartedly chided him. 'He *must* have a cup of coffee, Annabel, before he really gets the grumps.'

'Yes, Mummy, of course.'

Jay said nothing; a dark storm cloud seemed to cover over his countenance and by the looks of it, would remain there for the foreseeable future. Sylvie could practically *feel* the rage simmering off him. She felt him staring at her they walked down the hall. He knows, she thought, and if he doesn't already, then he certainly will when he sees the footage.

Breakfast was served in the Christmas tree room, sparkling clean and returned exactly to its original state as if there'd never been a party at all, Christmas tree included. Cleaners must have come at dawn, Sylvie thought. There was a dining table set with pale green placemats and gold cutlery. In the centre of the table, there were pots of marmalade and fig jam, thinly sliced sourdough toasted golden and lined up on the toast rack, a basket of boiled eggs and a large ceramic bowl filled with neatly chopped fruit. George drank his coffee in three large gulps, Christine requested Annabel fetch her dark rye bread from the kitchen. The group made polite small talk as they sipped tea and hungrily scraped hunks of salted butter across slices of toast. But not Jay. Jay sat under his storm cloud and refused to eat a thing. He only watched with distaste as Aurelie stuck her hand into the jammy, sunset-coloured yolk Annabel had prepared for her and smeared her face with the orange paste.

'Goodness me!' said Annabel, her voice soft. 'We'd better get you cleaned up, missy.'

'I'll take her,' said Jay, hauling Aurelie up from her mother's lap in one swift action.

'Thank you, darling,' Annabel cooed.

Sylvie watched him go. He looked crushed. Her plan was working but she was too worried about the CCTV footage to feel jubilant. With every bite, every sip, every slightly greasy rasher of bacon that Jonno shoved into his chops, they were drawing nearer to the end of the meal, nearer to the grand unveiling of Sylvie as the secret car vandal. She tapped her foot against the bottom of her chair as she thought. Come on, Sylvie, she said to herself, you've got a brain still, haven't you? Think of a way out. But nothing came.

When Jay returned with a clean-faced baby, Aurelie all pink and white again, Sylvie excused herself to the loo. Safely locked in the bathroom she sat down on the closed toilet lid and put her head in her hands. What could she do? Her fate was sealed. In a few moments, they were going to watch the footage. She was caught in 4K. It was a *disaster*. But then she saw it, Jay's phone on the edge of the sink. She grabbed it and put it on silent, her hands shaking as she shoved it into the pocket of her jeans and untucked her jumper to conceal it. She didn't know what she planned to do but she hoped to be able to use it to distract Jay and waylay her public shaming. It was like a gift from Aunt Jacqueline and as she walked the hallway, Sylvie tilted her face up to the ceiling and clasped her hands together in a posture of prayer.

She arrived just as the group had finished their breakfast. The table was full of empty plates, knives and forks pushed together, mugs of tea either finished or gone cold. George clamped his third cup of coffee down onto the tabletop and gave a satisfied grunt.

'I must say, Annabel,' said Christine. 'I do remember the

bread being much nicer – did you get it from the bakery I suggested?'

'Yes, Mummy.' Annabel swallowed her words. Sylvie slid into her seat as Annabel stood up from hers, baby Aurelie in her arms. 'Can I tempt anyone with anything else?'

Verity, who'd been uncharacteristically quiet so far, stuck up her hand. 'One more cup of coffee if you wouldn't mind, darling! I'll need it if I'm going to be any good at catching foxes today.' She winked at Jay.

Jay had a pained expression on his face.

'Mm,' said Christine, disapprovingly. 'Rather.'

'Surely we've had enough of all that car nonsense now, haven't we?' said George.

Annabel's bright white perma-smile quivered slightly.

'Sylvie!' Annabel said her name brightly and Sylvie descended into panic as the whole group turned towards her. 'Will you hold her? I'm going to go and make another pot of coffee.'

'I'm not . . . I don't . . ' Sylvie tried to protest but Annabel walked around the side of the table and shoved Aurelie firmly into her arms before making a swift exit.

Sylvie had taken care of little children before but holding Aurelie just felt wrong.

'She'll be good for you, darling!' Annabel called out as she strode down the hall. 'Back in two ticks.'

Aurelie was heavier than she looked and more cumbersome to hold than she'd expected. Sylvie felt Greg's arm heavy over her shoulder.

'You suit a baby,' he said, low in her ear.

Sylvie forced a chuckle and immediately wandered over to the French doors, holding Aurelie against her chest, keen to put an end to any talk of babies.

'Has anyone seen my phone?' Jay said then. 'It's got the app for the CCTV on it.'

Sylvie was elated. *She* had the phone, of course, and if she was clever about it, she could make sure nobody watched the footage at all. She had to be very careful not to rouse suspicion. She looked around innocuously as if she too was searching for it.

'Oh, yes,' said Verity, 'we've got to have a look at once. Did you ever hear of a fox doing something like this before, Hugh?'

'Wouldn't put it past them,' said Hugh. 'Sneaky bastards. Sneaky, sneaky. The lengths a fox will go to, to get its chops around one of my hens. Pah! It would amaze you.'

'Yes, well, we'll soon find out, won't we?' said Dahlia, a note of relish in her voice.

'Wee!' said Aurelie. 'Wee!'

'Wee?' Sylvie frowned at her. 'I think you're wearing a nappy, aren't you?'

Aurelie crinkled her brow. 'Wee!' she insisted, reaching out her pudgy little arm in the direction of the Christmas tree.

'Oh, you mean tree!' said Sylvie. 'Well, let's go then.'

Aurelie's little face was a picture of delight as she swatted a clumsy outstretched pink hand at its branches.

She touched one of the fairy lights with the tiny tip of her index finger as if she knew it was very delicate and she didn't want to harm it. She looked up at Sylvie with an awed expression. Sylvie thought to herself then that Aurelie really was completely adorable. And she had another thought, a slightly more devious one.

First, Sylvie turned over her shoulder to be sure that no one was looking. Everyone was chatting amongst themselves, moving plates and bowls and mugs as they searched for Jay's phone. Sylvie seized her chance. She knew she would only have one opportunity to execute this and she'd better get it right. She hurled Jay's phone with all her might against the metal foot of an armchair pressed up against the back wall of the room and watched with satisfaction as the glass shattered, scattering over the rug.

'Oh my goodness, what was that!' said Verity, jumping up from her seat as if a mouse had just scurried under the table.

Sylvie turned around and looked at them. 'Aurelie just threw someone's phone. I don't know where she got it. Was that yours, Jay?'

Jay looked at her, barely bothering to conceal his seething hatred. 'You mean you didn't notice she was holding it? Bit strange, no?'

Sylvie shrugged. 'I'm sorry.'

Sylvie felt some trepidation about involving baby Aurelie in her scheme, but needs must. Besides, Aurelie was too young to be affected one way or another. She wasn't yet conscious enough to really remember it, *right?* Baby Aurelie didn't react much to the chaos around her. She was interested primarily in the Christmas tree and then in the reappearance of her mother, who looked as though she'd reapplied her make-up and brushed out her hair before fetching the coffee from the kitchen.

'There you are, Verity dear,' she said, depositing the cafetière on the table. She made a bee-line for Sylvie and collected baby Aurelie into her arms, frowning as the shattered glass caught her eye, the broken pieces reflecting the bright sunlight that beamed in through the French doors. 'What's happened here?'

'Baby Aurelie threw Jay's phone,' Sylvie explained. 'I have no idea when she got hold of it.'

'Yes, that's *very* helpful, thanks, Sylvie,' Jay grumbled.

'Jay!' Annabel was outraged; she reached out and squeezed Sylvie's arm.

'I needed it to look at the CCTV,' said Jay.

'You can use my phone, darling,' said Annabel.

'I can't,' said Jay through gritted teeth. 'It's not that simple. You need to be verified, submit ID, it takes ages.'

'Ah, well,' said Annabel, smiling brightly. 'Let's forget about it for now then and go back to having a nice time.'

'Yes,' said George. 'Let's. This whole thing is becoming rather tiresome.'

'It's supposed to be a party, Annabel,' said Christine. 'I've always tried to demonstrate the importance of being a good host.'

'You have, dear,' said George. 'You certainly have.'

Annabel smiled. 'No more car talk. We'll have the mechanic around after Christmas and that will be that.'

Jay didn't protest. Sylvie could see that he saw Annabel was very serious about this. Her expression was so taut, her smile so strained that it looked like she would explode if anyone challenged her. He gave a defeated sigh and then he glared at Sylvie. She felt his eyes like laser beams scorching through her.

'Just one more day, one more night to go,' said Greg warmly in her ear. 'And then we're free.'

He put his hand gently around the back of her neck and pulled her in to kiss her on the cheek. She'd got away with it by the skin of her teeth, though Jay was definitely on to her.

The penultimate part of Sylvie's plan was the most daring yet. She hoped she would be able to pull it off as she'd intended. The MDMA had been something of a let-down, certainly effective but not as *embarrassing* as she'd hoped. This phase of her scheme involved another substance but not one she'd got from a low-level drug dealer. This time she'd been able to use Amazon. She had the sachet in the pocket of her dressing gown, ready and waiting for the opportune time. As she sat at the breakfast table with Greg, she allowed herself to dissociate to the visions of Jay, humiliated beyond repair.

Twenty-six

Mermaid in the Swimming Pool

'I thought today we could all have a swim and a steam,' said Annabel. 'It might be nice to have a bit of a purge after last night's debauchery.'

Annabel had hardly finished her glass of champagne the previous night, Sylvie knew as much.

'That sounds *lovely*,' said Verity.

Everyone, even George and Christine, agreed that a session in the Blackthorn spa was just what they needed and went off in the direction of their bedrooms to get changed.

'I don't have a swimsuit,' Sylvie said.

'Oh, don't worry, darling,' said Annabel. 'The second drawer down in the chest of drawers in your bedroom there are spare swimming costumes for guests. Take whichever you like.'

As she left the room, Sylvie turned back and looked at Jay, hairless, with his baseball cap pulled low and his arms crossed over his chest. Annabel's smile didn't waver all the while.

'Jay's in a bad mood,' said Sylvie, when she and Greg were back in their guest room with the door safely closed.

'He's not having a great time,' said Greg. 'You know what he's like, and Annabel's parents are real pricks, aren't they? Almost makes you feel sorry for him. He's always been the weird brother. Meanwhile, I'm the handsome, smart one.'

Sylvie laughed.

Greg sat back against the headboard and watched Sylvie strip out of her clothes and step into the brand new Melissa Odabash bikini, tags and all.

Sylvie turned this way and that in the full-length mirror. The pale pink bikini was simple and chic, Annabel's taste without a doubt.

Greg appeared next to Sylvie in the mirror, his hand grasped at her bare stomach.

'You look great,' he said.

'Thank you.' And then sensing that he was readying himself to confess something, another declaration of love perhaps or maybe a proposal of marriage, Sylvie pulled the dressing gown from the back of the door and said, 'Come on, let's go!'

The Blackthorn spa was modern, with low light and dark, coffee-coloured marble. There was a long, narrow, heated swimming pool, a sauna and a steam room each with glass doors and lighting that glowed lilac through the fog. There was a large waterproof crate at the pool's edge filled with games and inflatables, and pool chairs at the edge of the swimming pool. George, Christine, Dahlia, Verity and Lily lay back on poolside loungers, Jonno and Hugh sat opposite one another on the sauna benches, Jay stood outside in a black dressing gown and smoked. There was no sign of Annabel.

Sylvie and Greg were alone in the built-in steam room. Sylvie stretched out her legs and put the heels of her feet over Greg's damp thighs. He squeezed each of her feet in turn, gently kneading the centre of each sole with his thumbs. Sylvie wondered how she was going to administer the contents of the sachet into Jay's drink without him noticing. Then, the idea struck her out of nowhere, as if the mist of the steam room had cleared to reveal a solution, clear and gleaming.

Briefly rinsed by a cold shower, Sylvie trod her way back to the main house in her dressing gown and flip-flops, the sachet bouncing at her hip in her pocket. She hadn't acknowledged Jay on the way out though she could have sworn he called something out after her as she passed. She ignored it, boring on through the cold, crisp December air, the chill of it biting at her shins and collar. She found Annabel, also in a dressing gown, with her hair scraped back to reveal a large pair of diamond studs in her earlobes, feeding Aurelie at a high-chair in the kitchen.

'Annabel, hi,' said Sylvie, realizing as she took a pause that she was partway out of breath.

'Hello, Sylvie.' Annabel beamed. 'Everything all right? How do you like the spa?'

'Oh,' said Sylvie. 'It's amazing!'

'Great, isn't it?' Annabel spooned another small portion of puréed fruits into Aurelie's mouth. Aurelie maintained a perplexed expression, her enormous doll-eyes observing Sylvie closely.

'It's gorgeous,' said Sylvie. 'Just a quick thing, but everyone's a little bit thirsty from the sauna and stuff, so I thought maybe I could make a jug of lemonade?'

'Oh, that's so kind of you! But please don't put yourself out, I can bring a tray of drinks, just as soon as I finish up with this little one.'

'I'd like to do it,' said Sylvie, imitating that beaming smile of Annabel's. 'You've been such a wonderful host, honestly.'

'Sylvie,' Annabel looked at her with a twinkle in her blue eyes that suggested she was genuinely warmed by the offer, 'that is so kind of you. There are lemons in the fridge. I'll get you the sugar in two ticks, and a jug.'

Annabel put down the spoon she'd been holding and collected the utensils Sylvie needed from various places in the kitchen, laying them out neatly on a clean chopping board on the counter. A cluster of clean tumblers, placed on a circular tray.

'Thanks,' said Sylvie, as she washed lemons under the kitchen tap and began to chop them in two, twisting each half back and forth around the glass lemon juicer.

'You know,' said Annabel. 'You really are head and shoulders above every other girlfriend of Greg's we've met.'

'Thank you,' said Sylvie; the guilt she felt made her voice small.

'No, I mean it,' said Annabel. 'I can get along with anybody, you know, it's just . . . it's like he was doing it on purpose, choosing these entirely inappropriate women as a way of avoiding commitment.'

'Maybe,' said Sylvie, tipping the lemon juice into the large glass jug.

'And I just wonder,' said Annabel, 'what you see in him?'

Sylvie froze, baffled by the question and unsure how to respond.

Annabel continued, 'I know he's handsome and all that, it's just, you seem so different, mismatched almost. You're so reserved and refined and he's like a big teddy, isn't he? A bit ridiculous sometimes.' Annabel squinted at her, observing Sylvie's expression, and then suddenly out of nowhere a bright smile sprang from her lips. 'Look at me.' She shook her head. 'I'm one to talk, the number of people who've said the same thing about me and Jay. Gosh, thousands. Suppose there's just something about those Lakemore boys, isn't there?'

'Yep,' said Sylvie, twisting a lemon half against the juicer. She felt there was something Annabel wasn't saying.

'I haven't even had a chance to talk to you properly about leaving the factory,' said Annabel. 'Jay told me you handed in your notice. Nothing he did, I hope?'

Sylvie looked at Annabel's smile and tried to match it.

'Of course not,' she said. 'I miss nannying, that's all.'

Annabel nodded like she understood. 'There's something so refreshing about being in the company of children, isn't there? They're so very honest, so pure.'

Sylvie agreed with her.

'I suppose you must know a different side to my husband than I do,' said Annabel.

Sylvie startled and spilt a little lemon juice on the worktop.

'Sorry,' she said, reaching for the tea towel.

'I just mean, everyone's different when they're at work, aren't they? When they're someone else, outside of the home.'

Sylvie shrugged. 'Maybe.'

'This is me,' said Annabel, wiping Aurelie's face with a damp cloth. 'The only version that exists, I'm afraid. Maybe that's not particularly exciting.'

Sylvie was getting the uncomfortable feeling that Annabel had forgotten she was there and was simply thinking out loud.

'Anyway,' said Annabel, snapping back to reality. 'What am I like? We were talking about Greg, weren't we? He really likes you. It's nice to see. And I like you too. And I hope that if you and Greg stay together long-term that we can get the brothers to be close again, like they were.'

'They were close?'

'Oh, yes,' said Annabel. 'They had an awful childhood, they needed each other.'

'Yes,' said Sylvie. 'I've heard about that.'

Annabel tutted. 'Poor little things.'

The doorbell chimed loudly.

'Watch her for a second, will you?' Annabel said with a wink. 'That will be my turkey arriving.'

Sylvie seized her chance to take the sachet from her pocket, tear it open and empty it into the glass on the far left of the tray. Then she screwed up the wrapper as tightly as she could and discarded it in the kitchen bin. A glance over her shoulder confirmed that Aurelie was watching her. You're paranoid, Sylvie thought to herself, she's a baby. But still, she had the irrational sense that Aurelie was going to snitch.

Annabel returned with her arms full of grocery bags. 'Never stops!' she said. 'Always something going on.'

Sylvie turned over her shoulder and cast her a small smile before returning to her lemonade. She stirred in the sugar with a tall wooden spoon and then poured a small amount in each of the glasses.

'Are you coming?' Sylvie asked Annabel as she collected up the tray.

'Oh, yes,' she said, scraping out the very last of Aurelie's baby food onto the plastic spoon. 'I'll be there in ten minutes or so.'

'Great,' said Sylvie. 'I'll save you a glass.'

'Wait a minute!' Annabel called out, an urgent tone to her voice.

'Yes?'

'Take some ice.' She began to poke about in the freezer for the ice tray, which she added to Sylvie's tray.

The ice cubes were enormous, like something from a trendy cocktail bar.

'Thanks,' said Sylvie. 'See you later.'

Back in the spa, Sylvie arrived just as Jay happened to emerge from the sauna, still wearing his cap. His chest was slick with sweat.

'Here –' she handed him the drink (the *right* drink, the glass on the far left-hand side) – 'Annabel told me to bring you this.'

Jay took the glass from her hand and nodded as if to dismiss her, but Sylvie stayed.

'Shame about your hair,' she said.

'Fuck off,' he said. He pulled the visor of his baseball cap firmly down into place and then thirstily drained the glass in a few gulps.

'Lemonade!' Sylvie called out, placing the tray down on the tiles a little way from the edge of the swimming pool.

Jonno and Hugh attacked the tray at once, their faces pinkened by the sauna heat. Greg waved her over to the pool chairs, opposite where Dahlia and Verity sat draped in kaftans like Greek goddesses. George and Christine lay back on their loungers, with their respective books held up under their noses.

'Where've you been?' Greg asked her as she stripped out of her dressing gown and hung it on the back of the chair. 'I've been going mad with this lot, the sauna and Jonno at the same time is . . .' He made a face.

'Too much to handle?' Sylvie ventured.

'I was gonna say like having teeth pulled but yeah, same sentiment.' He reached out and put a hand on her leg.

'I thought I'd help Annabel out and make some lemonade,' said Sylvie. 'Think I'll have a swim now.'

'That's kind of you,' said Greg. 'Sure, enjoy, babe.'

Sylvie climbed down the marble steps into the water, which lapped warm against her thighs and stomach. She dived beneath the surface to wet her hair before beating a few strong strokes through the water. She spotted Jay alone at the edge of the pool. Wrapped up in his black dressing gown, he stared out of the window, restless without a phone or a luscious head of hair to put his hands through. She began to wade through the water in his direction, peering up at him through wet lashes that were like a dark frill at the edge of her vision. She felt her wet hair lap against her back, mermaid-like, as she rose halfway out of the water's surface, thrusting her chest forward.

'What do you want?' he asked her, gruffly.

As much as he hated her, he could not tear his eyes away from her, from the nakedness of her wet skin and hair, the gloss on her lips like dew on washed cherries. Sylvie knew this. She knew he could be overcome with lust at any moment and she wondered if he ever hated himself for this. Stupid, she thought, stop projecting your own conscience onto him. He feels nothing and cares for no one. His green eyes watched her, lustful but distrusting. She cocked her head to one side and looked at him, really looked at him and wondered if he actually possessed *any* of the qualities that she'd attributed to him over the months.

'Come and swim with me,' she said.

'Yeah, right.'

'Come on,' she said. 'Greg thinks you hate me.'

'Greg thinks right.'

'It's going to make everyone suspicious,' said Sylvie. 'Why would you hate me if you don't know me?'

Realizing that she was right, he stripped very slowly from his black dressing gown and Sylvie pushed back into the water, propelling herself with her feet against the edge of the swimming pool into a smooth, gliding backstroke. Jay did not take off his cap.

'Going for a dip?' Verity called out from her pool chair, her thin lips stretching over an enormous open-mouthed smile. She and Dahlia were talking with Jonno and Hugh. Lily stood quietly uninterested beside them, looking rather like an actual lily in the oversized white dressing gown that gaped around her slight frame.

Jay held his thumb up in Verity's direction and she began to laugh raucously before lying back against the pool chair and recommencing her conversation with the group.

'Greg can't stand these people,' Sylvie said.

'Neither can I,' said Jay.

'But Annabel likes them?'

'Annabel's too nice to say either way.'

'Annabel's a good person,' said Sylvie. She'd halted her backstroke and stood upright, wafting her hands back and forth against the water's surface. 'Not like you and me.'

She lifted her knee to brush against Jay's leg under the water. She knew that he'd surely noticed her nipples were erect and pressing against the thin, water-soaked fabric of her pink triangle bikini. Over his shoulder, she saw Dahlia casting sideways glances at them.

'So, what's it going to take to put a stop to this?'

'A stop to what?'

'Sylvie ...' His voice was soft, a touch of affection perhaps, or just plain old pleading. 'To you trying to get at me.'

'What makes you think I'm trying to do that?'

'I'm asking you to name a price, Sylvie. Any price,' he repeated. 'Anything you want to just go away and disappear from our lives for ever.'

'Our lives? Was this your wife's idea?'

That annoyed him. The vitriol oozed off him. 'No, of course it wasn't my *wife's* idea because she doesn't know what happened between us and she'll never know, right?' And then he gathered himself and took a deep inhale and seemed to calm down before he said, 'Got a pair of balls on you, I'll give you that.' There was half a smile on his lips.

'Maybe I'm in love with him.'

'Shut up.'

'Maybe I am, and so what? He doesn't know about us – no one knows about us, as you've pointed out. You're happy with your wife, who is *lovely* by the way, and I'm happy with Greg.'

'I don't *want* you around, I can't see you all the time.'

'Well, too bad, because I like Greg and I'm planning on being with him.'

'For how long?'

'For as long as I like.' And then Sylvie had a thought. 'Maybe for ever, maybe I'll be Mrs Lakemore and we'll be a family. We'll have to get along then, won't we, Jay?'

'You cunt.'

Sylvie shrugged and turned back to look at Greg who was watching them with a mildly confused expression. Sylvie grinned at him and put up her hand in a wave.

'You don't love my brother,' Jay hissed through gritted teeth. 'Might fool him but you don't fool me.'

'I'm not trying to fool anyone,' said Sylvie. 'I don't like liars.'

Jay made a face, a sudden grimace contorting his features as if he was in terrible pain. It was time, Sylvie decided, for her exit. She wandered around the edge of the pool and started digging in the crate of games where she picked up a pair of rackets and the corresponding ball.

'Hugh, Jay was just saying he's desperate for a game but I'm wrinkly as anything. Why don't you play?' she called out.

'Brilliant idea.' Hugh beamed, getting up from his chair and stripping out of his dressing gown.

'I'll umpire,' George boomed, hastily discarding his book, grateful for something else to do.

'Good chap,' said Hugh.

Christine closed her book too, tucking a bookmark between the pages. She sat up, keen to observe the excitement but careful to maintain a nonchalant air.

Sylvie put the bats and ball onto the water close to Jay, who squinted at her, unsure of what she was trying to do. She was biding her time. She wanted to keep him in the pool long enough for the concoction she'd made to get to work. The medical-grade laxative that boasted of a 'powerful evacuation of the bowels' within an hour.

Hugh and Jay began a game of pool ping-pong, managing only a few rallying shots back and forth at a time. Hugh was determined, grunting and groaning like a professional tennis player at Wimbledon, while Jay wandered about half-heartedly. Still, they had the attention of the room, everyone's eyes firmly focused on the duo, just as Sylvie intended.

'Why don't you give it a bit of gumption, young man?' George cried out from the poolside. 'Where's your sporting spirit?'

Jay looked so miserable it was almost comical, Sylvie thought; if only he knew what was coming next. Surely, by now, he realized something was wrong.

'All right, here we go,' said Hugh, as if he were Roger Federer. 'Best two out of three, starting now. All right with you, mate?'

'Yeah, fine,' said Jay.

'Ooh!' Verity exclaimed. 'It's heating up! Good luck, lads!'

Jonno made a noise that reminded Sylvie of an overexcited chimpanzee.

Hugh made the serve and Jay hit it back. Hugh returned it. Jay missed the ball narrowly with his bat and, losing his balance, he dipped down into the water.

'One to Hugh!' Verity called out.

'I'm not . . .' Jay said, breathless and clutching his side. 'I'm not feeling too well. Think I might need a break.'

'No, come on,' said Hugh, grinning. 'None of your dirty tactics here, let's finish the game. What do you say, folks?'

'Finish – the – game! Finish – the – game!' Jonno beat his fist into the air.

'Don't be a spoilsport, James,' said George. 'You've got to finish what you started, have a little pride.'

Sylvie was at the edge of her seat, as she watched them. Her eyes scanned Jay's face which was slightly grey from what she could make out of it beneath his cap. Surely, it was almost time, she thought. Hugh tossed the ball over his head and hit it hard with the centre of his racket. It made a high curve up through the air and Jay returned the shot quite easily. Hugh hit the ball again and then Jay. Hugh, then Jay, and this time Hugh missed it. The ball bounced off the edge of his racket and plopped into the water beside him.

'All right,' he said. 'Final round!'

Annabel arrived then with Aurelie in tow.

'Ah, Annabel,' Hugh called out. 'You've arrived just in time to watch your husband get thrashed.'

Perhaps emboldened by Annabel's presence in the same way young children feel safest with their mother close by, Jay said he needed a break. He was quite insistent about it, his face contorted and moist with sweat as he complained of a stitch.

'Nonsense,' said Hugh. 'Don't worry, mate, Annabel will still love you if you lose, won't you, Ann?'

'Perhaps she won't,' said George. 'You can use that thought as a bit of motivation.'

'Of course I *will*, darling!' Annabel lifted up little Aurelie's arm in a wave. 'Good luck, Daddy!'

Jay looked at the door, and then at Hugh, and then at the door and said, 'Fine, but make it quick.'

His teeth were gritted together and his jaw wound tight.

Sylvie sat back on her pool lounger, her hair slicked down against her scalp and neck. She picked up her glass and sipped the tart lemonade, ice clinking against her teeth.

And then it happened. The room was suddenly silent enough to hear a pin drop, and then Christine could be heard shrieking, 'Good God in heaven, Annabel!' and there were groans and gasps as the crystalline pool water was polluted by a dark, terrifying bloom surrounding Jay.

'Out!' Annabel shrieked. 'Everybody out.'

The guests were sent to their bedrooms. A doctor was summoned. The party was over.

'Fuck me,' said Greg, as they lay side by side. 'No coming back from that, is there?'

'Hmm,' said Sylvie, who was determined not to give herself away just yet.

'I mean, in a *swimming pool*, right in front of the toffs.' Greg was in disbelief. 'Fuck me, did you see George's face? And Christine. If they didn't think much of him before . . . Jesus.'

'Just one second,' said Sylvie. 'I need the loo.'

'Of course, babe,' said Greg. 'One thing to take away from this – if you ever need the toilet, for God's sake, just get up and *go*.'

Shut in the ensuite, Sylvie grabbed hold of the hand towel and buried her face in it to muffle her laughter. It was a pure and all-encompassing sensation of joyful giddiness. She felt like a tickled child. She wouldn't have been able to stop it if she tried. She dabbed her watery eyes in the mirror, a small involuntary smile playing on her lips. We did it, she thought, a warm sense of pride flooding her body at the sight of her reflection, we did it. We didn't just roll over and play dead. We made him suffer, we gave him a memory he'll shudder at for ever. Sylvie did a tiny little jig on the spot, as silently as she could. She couldn't help it, her body was overcome, there was electricity running through her veins. She'd done it, proven herself as a Gardiner woman, as a force to be reckoned with. If only Aunt Jacqueline were there to see her now.

She had quivered only slightly, when they'd been in the water face to face and she'd looked into his eyes and remembered how alive he'd made her feel and how much she'd wanted to love him, to live for him. It would have been easy to fall back into that easy allegiance had she allowed it, but she'd resisted. And she'd won.

Twenty-seven

Every War has Casualties

Sylvie waited until she had regained her composure before she re-entered the bedroom.

'Are you all right?' Greg asked her.

'Yes,' she said.

'You were in there a while, you're not . . .' He lowered his voice to a whisper. 'You're not feeling ill, are you?'

'I'm fine,' she said. 'I was just taking off my make-up.'

'Ah,' he said. 'That's a relief. Come here.'

She allowed him to pull her closer, to kiss her neck.

'We could probably get out of here now if you wanted,' he said, resting his cheek against her chest. 'No need to stay the last night, everyone would understand.'

Sylvie wasn't quite ready to go for two reasons. The first was that she still had to deposit the present, the final part of her plan, and the second was that she hadn't decided whether or not she wanted to speak to Jay one last time, to tell him it was all her doing, make sure there wasn't any doubt.

'It would be rude to Annabel,' she said.

Greg shrugged. 'All right but dinner's going to be bloody awkward, isn't it, babe?'

Dinner was a disjointed affair. Sylvie wore another dress of Aunt Jacqueline's, silver lamé this time, and diamond earrings; she'd overdone it but felt she owed the dress an outing. Everyone said she looked like a Christmas decoration.

'We should hang you on the tree!' said Verity, who along with Hugh, Annabel and Jonno was among the guests who actually showed.

'Mummy and Daddy wanted to eat in their rooms,' said Annabel. 'They're tired.'

'Of course they are,' said Hugh. 'They've had a shock.'

'As have we all,' said Verity. 'Poor, poor Jay. Goodness me.'

'Where is Jay?' Sylvie asked.

Annabel's smile quivered but remained firmly intact.

'Upstairs,' she said. 'The doctor said he needs some rest.'

Sylvie nodded. The party ate their dinner of salmon and asparagus wearily, all except Sylvie who felt her body humming as if a vital spark had been returned to her. She sat up straighter than she had in recent memory, she saw the diamonds sparkling in the periphery of her vision and imagined that it was not her dress, but she, who was reflecting the flickering light of the tall dinner candles.

She fell asleep beside Greg with the feeling that she had been made over, that all the broken parts, the cracks, her shattered heart, had been restored. Sylvie knew she would leave in the morning and Greg would never see or hear from her again after Annabel uncovered her gift and everything was exposed. She didn't like the thought, but she couldn't bear for any inconvenient questions of conscience to impede on her night of victory. Tonight, she was victorious, powerful and wicked. She fell asleep with the same sated pleasurable drowsiness that she imagined vampires might experience after an evening of indiscriminate carnage, the kind of satisfaction that only spilt blood can achieve.

Sylvie, Sylvie, Sylvie! They came in through the window, their silvery moonlit bodies wafted straight through the glass, and they danced with the tips of their toes hovering in mid-air. Greg didn't stir, they'd come just for her. They danced in a circle over Sylvie's head, their long white tutus like milk-froth. They held out their hands for her to join them and she wanted to. She wanted to celebrate with them, but she couldn't move. She tried with all her might but she was paralysed. The panic rose in her, hot and sudden. *Sylvie, Sylvie, Sylvie!*

'Sylvie,' Greg shook her awake, gently, by the shoulder. 'Are you okay?'

He turned on the bedside lamp.

'Yes,' she said. 'Sorry, I was dreaming.'

'Was it a nightmare?'

She shook her head. 'No, it was about ballet. I'm thirsty, I'm gonna go down for some water.'

'I'll get it,' Greg offered.

'No,' said Sylvie. 'It's fine.'

As Sylvie descended the stairs, careful to be quiet, she noticed there were lights on in the downstairs hallway. Her heartbeat quickened. She silently prayed she would not come face to face with Jay alone in the middle of the night. Which way was the kitchen? She had to concentrate. She crept over the rugs, the polished wood of the floor, as quietly as she could. The kitchen cupboard opened with an almighty creak that made her wince. She filled up a glass with tap water and drank it hurriedly over the sink.

When she left the kitchen, she heard voices and she stopped, straining her ears to listen. The voices were muffled by a closed door, but she could hear the stringent tones of an argument, an agitated back and forth. Sylvie concentrated: a man's voice and a woman's voice. She took a few steps closer to the closed door on her left. Jay and Annabel, it had to be. As gently as she could, she leant in closer, pressing her ear to the wooden door.

'What is happening?' Annabel said. 'Why are you acting so strange? Is it . . . there's something, I know there's something.'

'Stop being so paranoid, Ann,' said Jay. 'I've had enough of this fucking party, all right? And I've had enough of you getting on my case as well. You should have sent them all home this afternoon.'

'I'm not paranoid, Jay,' said Annabel. 'And you know I can't do that. Please, you know what my parents are like. I'm just trying to keep everyone happy.'

There was a whimpering sound, small and pathetic, like a wounded animal.

'Don't cry,' said Jay.

'I'm not crying,' said Annabel.

'For God's sake, we've been through this,' said Jay. 'We've been over this so many times – you're supposed to trust me now.'

'I mean, it's happened before. I'm not crazy,' said Annabel. 'You were sleeping with that girl, the one who moved away.'

'How many times can I apologize for that?' said Jay. 'You know that was because of the pregnancy, you and me were like roommates. I was scared to be a dad, you know, my childhood. I explained all this to the therapist, I explained all this to you. And what did I do? I swore I would never do anything like that again. I swore on Aurelie's life, didn't I?'

There was an indecipherable murmur.

'Didn't I, Annabel?' Jay demanded. 'Or did I not?'

'You did.'

'Exactly,' said Jay. 'I did. You're being irrational.'

'I know what I feel,' said Annabel. 'I know there's something between you.'

Jay groaned. 'Between me and who?'

'Between you and Sylvie.'

Jay laughed. It was a cold, mean laugh and its implication hurt Sylvie, even then.

'Well, now I know you're crazy,' Jay said.

Sylvie had heard enough. She moved away from the door and then down the hall as if she were in one of her old Willow Way ballet classes, as delicately and lightly as she could manage, balancing on the tips of her toes.

The morning light came stark through the gap in the curtains. This was it, the end. Greg looked angelic where he slept on the pillow beside her, his lips pressed up against his hand as if he were waiting to be kissed. Sylvie felt a swell of compassion for him, believing his feelings for her to be genuine and remembering that he had always treated her with kindness. Stop it, Sylvie, she thought, getting out of the bed as smoothly and quietly as she could, you're a soldier, remember? Every war has casualties. She brushed her teeth and packed her things as silently as she could, careful even when she opened the zip on her bag. She froze when Greg stirred. He rolled over onto his side and blinked awake, frowning at the brightness of the room through half-opened eyes.

'Where are you going?' he asked her, his voice hoarse.

'Just for a quick smoke,' she said. 'Go back to sleep, I'll come back to bed when I'm done.'

Satisfied with her answer, Greg dropped his heavy head onto the pillow and within a matter of seconds he was asleep again. Sylvie put her bag onto her shoulder, the wrapped present under her arm. There would be no turning back from what she was about to do, no possible way to ever make amends. She looked at Greg once more, his muscular arm resting over the sheet, the dark hair on his chest.

'Bye then,' she whispered.

Sylvie needed access to the Christmas tree room, and she didn't want to bump into anyone before she'd managed to get there. She didn't want to bump into anyone at all if she could help it.

But Sylvie heard someone running water in the kitchen as she passed by and Annabel's voice called out, 'Good morning! Who's there?'

Sylvie popped her head around the corner, helpless. She had no choice but to adapt her plan.

The smile quivered on Annabel's face, like a flickering bulb. 'Did you sleep well?' she asked her.

'Yes, thanks,' said Sylvie. 'Where is everyone?'

'Still asleep,' Annabel said, shaking her head. 'But Jay's in a foul mood this morning, he's out there with his gun trying to shoot rabbits. I feel terrible for him.'

'Mm,' said Sylvie. 'Me too,' and then she had an idea. This would be her last chance to see him face to face and she'd better take it. 'Think I'll go and get a bit of fresh air as well.'

But before Sylvie could turn around, Annabel called out for her to wait.

'Would you mind giving me a hand with these?'

Annabel held out the stacked plates in her arms with all the reverence of an offering.

'Sure,' said Sylvie, her throat tightening to the circumference of a five-pence coin. She picked up a few empty platters and followed Annabel to the sink.

'I'll wash and you dry?' Annabel smiled a wide white smile at her.

Sylvie was too unsettled to ask if she didn't have a dishwasher. The kitchen was so enormous and grand that it seemed absurd to think that they didn't. The sink itself was almost big enough to bathe in. Annabel dipped plates into the sink, which was filled almost to the brim with soapy water. Annabel stared out of the window as she dipped, her hand working away with the pink foam sponge as if her mind was separate from her body. She passed the still dripping plate on to Sylvie who dabbed at it with the tea towel and set it on the rack. It would have been funny if it wasn't so awkward, the two of them working together side by side.

'I'm going to ask you something,' Annabel said. 'And I just want you to say yes or no. I don't want any more than that.'

She didn't look at Sylvie when she said this and her voice was matter-of-fact and officious, though Sylvie suspected she was trying her hardest to contain a well of messy and embarrassing emotion. Sylvie knew what she was going to ask. There was only one question. Annabel began to run around the outside of a dessert bowl with her soapy sponge. Sylvie waited. The waiting was excruciating.

'Have you had sex with my husband?' said Annabel, passing her the bowl.

Sylvie had to grip it hard to stop it slipping out of her fingers. She started to dry it with the tea towel, and tried to think of the best way to answer. She wondered if it would have been better to lie. She'd planned for Annabel to find out about it when she was long gone. But she found herself saying, 'Yes. I'm sorry.'

Sylvie didn't know whether to prepare herself for a slap or a barrage of verbal abuse. She imagined Annabel was probably too classy to call her a slut though in that moment, Sylvie felt it would be warranted.

'All right,' said Annabel, coughing to clear her throat. 'Well, I'll take over from here. You can go and get that fresh air.'

Sylvie put the tea towel and bowl down and left Annabel at the sink, staring out of the window. It looked like it was going to rain, a mass of black clouds had invaded the sky.

'Annabel,' Sylvie said, as softly as she could manage. 'I didn't know.'

But Annabel didn't turn around.

Twenty-eight

Destiny, Fate, Karma

She was going to get out of there, Sylvie promised herself, she was just going to do this final thing first. Sylvie left the bomb of a present under the tree. Mutually assured destruction. It contained the security tape from the private room of the nightclub the night she was there with Jay and his friends. She'd been through hell to get it, but it was the evidence she needed. She had only wanted to hurt Jay by ruining things with Annabel, but she saw now that she'd been wilfully deceived. Annabel's world would be shattered by this, maybe even little Aurelie's too. But she'd come too far to stop now. This was it, revenge. Final, ultimate, devastating.

Sylvie let herself into the garden through the French doors. She could see Jay in the distance at the bottom of the field, firing his shotgun into the brambly foliage.

What are you doing, Sylvie? she questioned herself as she began to cross the grass, the icy air kissing her cheeks. She felt the rain on her scalp where her hair was parted. Her hands were frozen, and she shoved them deep into her jacket pockets as she trudged towards him, as slowly and ceremoniously as a funeral procession.

When she was only a few metres away, Sylvie stopped.

'Jay!' she called out.

Jay turned around, lowering his shotgun.

'What the fuck do you want?'

Sylvie knew what *he* wanted. It was clear from the look in his eye he wished she was dead.

'You should know that it was me. Your hair, your car, the swimming pool. All of it.'

He didn't seem surprised, his gaze was fixed on the trees a little further on. He took a few paces in their direction, lifting the gun into position.

'Why?' he asked.

'You lied to me,' Sylvie whispered.

She saw Jay's jaw twitch slightly as he moved ahead but he said nothing. She felt her eyes sting with tears.

'Forget about it, all right,' he said. 'It's done.'

'Yes, it's done. There are no more secrets.'

They saw it then, a pheasant fluttering over the path from between the trees. Jay took the shot, and it fell to the ground, the little thing knocked out of the sky. As they approached, Sylvie looked with horror at its wide, unblinking yellow eyes. Jay grabbed it and took a bit of string from his pocket, fastening it around the pheasant's neck like a grotesque collar.

'She knows. Annabel,' said Sylvie.

Jay hoisted the shotgun up onto his shoulder. Sylvie stared down the pair of hollow barrels, her heart rammed against her chest.

'You're going to shoot me?' she said, with a tremor in her voice.

Perhaps this was it. This is what it was all building to, her destiny. She thought that perhaps she deserved it. She hadn't been a good person. All she'd ever done was cause other people pain. She remembered pushing Ffion, after that *Giselle* rehearsal when she'd been so eaten up with jealousy and rage that she could have burnt the whole school to the ground. She'd followed Ffion out of the classroom, grief-stricken, the cheerful bounce in Ffion's gait like a taunt. And then the two of them turned the corner and the long staircase unfurled itself beneath them like a solution to a problem. Sylvie looked at Ffion's back, the knobbled bones of her spine, the tendril of blonde hair curling at the nape of her neck and something in her flashed red. She pushed her, as hard as she could. She could have killed her, she knew this. She could have killed her, that was a risk she was willing to take. What kind of monster, Sylvie thought, was capable of something like that?

'All right,' said Sylvie. 'If you're going to shoot me, at least kiss me goodbye.'

Jay frowned, conflicted by the request, and he lowered the gun slowly. He took a step forward so that he was up close to her face and said, 'Fuck you.' Mutually assured destruction. Sylvie looked at him, the heave in his chest, his eyes wide with fury, the shotgun in his hand. Was he really going to shoot her? She couldn't tell.

She said, 'I know,' and then she reached for him, her hands at the back of his head and though he flinched at first, he let her kiss him. On his lips, she tasted their memories, the love she'd felt, the loneliness, the anger. He didn't taste like hers any more. There was the stench of someone else all over him and she couldn't ignore it. She withdrew from the kiss and looked him in the eyes. She'd imagined him. He was nothing like the person she'd believed he was. Jay hoisted the gun into position, and Sylvie felt the earth's rotation slow down, hyper aware of the shape of each raindrop that passed by her vision, of the beauty of Jay's face despite everything and the burning hatred in his eyes. There was the flavour in her mouth, as distinct as sweetshop candy, of sour cherry.

Sylvie looked at Jay, his burning eyes focused on her, his finger poised over the trigger. Perhaps, she thought, perhaps a part of me always knew it was going to end like this. She waited for the pain. Maybe there wouldn't be any – would she even know she was dying? She wished it had been a sunnier day, for the world to be at its best the last time she'd see it, but instead the clouds were inky black overhead, the rain was icy, her face numb. Jay didn't seem to be moving at all, not even to breathe, there was no detectable quiver of life from him, not even in his chest or his throat.

Perhaps he'd already pulled the trigger, Sylvie thought, the shot had already hit her, shattered her skull, except she was numb and didn't feel it. What if this was hell, or heaven or purgatory, just this image of Jay and his shotgun for the end of time.

'Jay! What are you doing?' Annabel reached for the gun.

She took him by such surprise that his grip had loosened, and she was able to almost wrestle it away from him. She'd arrived like a blonde flash out of nowhere. Her face was ashen, blue eyes bulging from her skull.

'What the fuck are you doing?' Annabel cried out.

Sylvie's shock rooted her to the spot. *MOVE*, she pleaded her legs, *please move.* But she couldn't, all she could do was watch as Jay and Annabel fought over the shotgun. Jay's hands closed into fists over Annabel's. His knuckles were white. It was clear he was hurting her. Finally, Annabel managed to get herself in front of Jay and she pulled the shotgun back with all her might so that it struck him in the stomach and when he doubled over she pulled it back again; this time it was like a battering ram to his groin and he fell to his knees, relinquishing his grip. The gun was hers.

When she'd got hold of the shotgun, Annabel took a few steps backwards before she aimed it at Jay and pulled the trigger. It was an impulse, a reflex, except that it wasn't. It was also something else. It was years of hurt, betrayal. The shot rang out and Jay fell like a demolished building, piece by piece. Then he lay on the ground beside the dead pheasant with the string around its neck.

'Is he . . . ?' asked Sylvie.

'Yes,' said Annabel.

Twenty-nine

Real Magic

Annabel had repeated over and over that she didn't know what had happened; still clutching the shotgun, the rest of her shook like a leaf.

'It was self-defence,' Sylvie said. 'It was self-defence.'

She hated to see Annabel so shattered.

'You need to get my parents,' Annabel said. 'Don't talk to anyone else, just go upstairs to the third room on the left and tell them there's been an accident, and I asked them to come quickly.'

The blood was returning to Annabel's face, flooding her white cheeks with colour, but she couldn't bring herself to look at Jay. She kept her gaze firmly averted, focused on the distant trees. George followed Sylvie out into the rain, dressed in his dark green Barbour and his flat cap. He took the shotgun out of Annabel's grip and sighed.

'It was self-defence,' said Sylvie.

'You leave the semantics to me,' said George, looking at Annabel as if she were a naughty school girl. 'Annabel, I want you to go inside and go up to bed and call the police in thirty minutes exactly, do you understand? Report hearing a gunshot and a scream, say your husband isn't in bed with you and you're frightened. I'll have our lawyers here within the hour. We'll have to helicopter them in.'

Sylvie was struck by his calmness, the absence of any emotion. She knew he'd disliked Jay but to stand over his dead body and barely blink seemed monstrous. He didn't seem worried either. It was like a bit of a nuisance but nothing more serious than that. Sylvie had begun to tremble. She crossed her arms over her chest and stood shaking as Annabel started walking forlornly towards the house.

'You'd better go too,' said George. 'Don't say a word to anyone and if the police come to see you, you give me a call immediately. Where's your phone?'

Sylvie unlocked it and handed it to him.

'This will all be dealt with provided you keep quiet about everything that happened this morning. You had a disagreement with your boyfriend and you left to go home, all right?'

Sylvie didn't have to be told twice.

He returned her phone with his number saved as George V-W and she started towards the house in Annabel's wake. Behind her, she heard George fire the shotgun off a couple of times before emptying out the cartridges. Annabel flinched at the noise.

Sylvie collected her bag and the present from where she'd left it under the tree and walked out of the front door without looking back.

That afternoon Greg called her in pieces, asking where she'd gone. He told her Jay had been shot. Some lunatic had broken into the property and hidden in the garden. The police were asking about business enemies, jilted girlfriends, anyone who might wish him harm. Sylvie could barely make out what he was saying between his tears.

Panicking, Sylvie offered to come over, though George's face hovered in her mind's eye and the sound of the shotgun ringing out played over and over again in her head like a phantom bell. She was frightened of Annabel's family. She wanted to put some distance between herself and Greg.

As it turned out, she needn't have worried. Greg said he had to be alone. He couldn't handle having a girlfriend, he explained, especially one who would disappear when he needed her the most.

'Okay,' Sylvie said. 'Okay.'

She said it over and over again until it was less of a word and more of a sound.

'Who would do this?' Greg said, his voice high and soft like a child's.

She wondered what he would do if he ever found out the truth – she hoped he wouldn't go devoting his life to finding Jay's killer or anything silly like that. Part of her really had wanted to be with Greg, but she knew it was best to disappear. And in any case, it didn't matter any more, the choice was no longer hers. She felt free, in the same way that scorched earth, rid of the past, is free to begin again.

Christmas morning was quiet and frost-laden when Sylvie woke up strangely early. The bright white through the slats in her blinds made her think that it might have snowed but it hadn't. It was only 6:27 and yet she was bolt awake. She crept down the stairs to make herself a coffee. The Christmas tree lights had been left on and blinked blue-white in the dark. Sylvie took the chest of journals out onto her bed and opened one she hadn't yet read. She took a sip of the coffee, hot and strong, and turned to the first page. She recognized the writing, of course it was her aunt's, but there was something different, a distinct change, a perceptible shakiness.

> *I know my time is almost done. After all, I'm an old woman now and I don't mind, my life has been a full one. But I am worried about Sylvie. She is the closest I've ever had to a granddaughter, our relationship has been a special one, a blessing to us both. I worry she has so much ahead of her that I will be unable to see her through. I would very much like to be beside her, to watch as the adventure of her life unfolds but alas, it is not to be.*
>
> *The silly girl has been asking me what I'd like for Christmas – it appears she does not quite grasp the extraordinary value of the gift she has already given*

me. She has seen me not as an old aunt, or a glamour-puss or a fashion-plate, all parts I've played in my time, but as a woman with a great deal of soul and spirit, a person with something valuable to say. I can never repay her for this gift, or the unexpected comfort and joy she's brought me these past few years.

I only hope that my memory will be a comfort to her, that she will imagine me always cheering her on. I hope she will find the courage to make her life a great adventure, to be the orchestrator of her own fate, to steer her own ship, to be wholly unafraid.

I would say to her, 'Darling, you are a true Gardiner woman, just like my mother and I. We are beholden to no one but ourselves. Take your future in hand and by God, don't let them take you lying down.'

In any case it has been a great honour knowing her and I consider myself lucky beyond measure.

Sylvie picked up the framed picture of her aunt from her bedside table and pressed a kiss to her cheek. She dabbed at her teary eyes with the sleeve of her jumper. I'm the lucky one, she thought, where would I be without Aunt Jacqueline? She returned the journals to the chest and decided that a New Year's resolution of hers would be to start a journal of her own. How would she start it? *Welcome to the story of a girl with nothing to lose.*

Sylvie laced up her trainers for a Christmas morning run through the wood. The December sun shone warmly on her face and her limbs felt light as air as she crunched

366

over the crystalline frost of the woodland floor. At the end of the wood before the trees gave way to the open landscape beyond, she paused to catch her breath, taking in welcome lungfuls of fresh cold air. She heard snapping leaves and turned over her shoulder to see a young fawn edging closer towards her.

Struck as she'd always been by the beauty of woodland deer, Sylvie crouched down slowly, frightened of scaring the fawn away with any sudden movements. It only watched her with its enormous brown eyes, and she held out her hand, daring to hope that this fairy-tale creature would allow her to touch it. You should be grown up by now, shouldn't you, Sylvie thought, a fawn in December. The doe – Sylvie thought it must have been a girl – nudged her nose into the centre of her outheld palm and then backed away on long legs for a few careful paces before she turned and bolted in search of her mother.

In the new year, Sylvie called up the number she'd been given for the ballet school in Oxford. It was a job she felt she could do well and, in some way, *needed*. She decided that she was not, as she'd previously thought, ready for a life without ballet. She was ready to rekindle her relationship once more, with her first and truest love.

'Can you start the first week of January?' came the grateful voice through the receiver. The woman had been practically beside herself when Sylvie had recounted her prestigious résumé.

'Wednesday suits me,' said Sylvie, and it did.

The girls in her class were just eight or nine years old, many of them only there because their mothers had dropped them off for a sacred hour alone but there were a couple of precocious girls who were eager to learn and had the same air of seriousness that reminded Sylvie of herself as a child.

'What I want you girls to understand is that what we're doing here is very special. It's like magic,' Sylvie explained as the children spread apart, ready to begin. 'When you dance and everything is just right, every move is perfect and learnt by heart, when you simply become one with the music and let it move you, that is *real* magic. It's the closest thing we have to it. A simple exercise like a port de bras, when you really get it right – and one day you will – should be beautiful enough to bring a grown man to tears.'

As she sat in her Citroën in the car park, she paused beside the darkened driver's seat window and spied her own reflection, flame-coloured hair ablaze under the light of the street lamp. She was relieved to find that she was still a living, breathing girl and not a ghost quite yet.

She decided to go and watch Ffion perform in the Royal Ballet production of *Sleeping Beauty*. Maria had sent an email to all the Willow Way alumni, announcing Ffion's promotion to First Soloist with the Royal Ballet. Ffion had been on her mind more and more of late and she knew that if she didn't go, she'd always wonder.

The Royal Opera House, with the echoey height of its foyer, and the buzz of the bar, the red velvet curtains hanging heavy and grand, gave Sylvie a lump in her throat. She was grateful when the lights went down and no one could see her teary-eyed from where she sat, far back in the stalls. The music began, her heart started to race. Sylvie couldn't believe how long she'd deprived herself of ballet, her first and perhaps deepest love. She was swept away in a trance of beauty, of orchestra music and tutus in pastel colours, arabesques and pirouettes. As she watched she felt the muscles in her legs twitching, her thighs, calves, the sides of her buttocks; her body anticipated the pliés at the end of the dancer's leaps and turns. She danced along with them, subconsciously, from her seat.

Then came Ffion's solo, the wind-chime joyfulness of the songbird solo. Ffion performed the whip-sharp and rapid footwork with flawless execution, her hands tremoring by her face in a balletic imitation of a songbird's quivering wings. The orange-yellow tutu really did look as though a beautiful bird was flitting across the stage. When she was finished, Sylvie clapped until her hands hurt and she was proud. She never thought she'd feel proud but perhaps time and distance had cooled her jealousy. Sitting here and watching Ffion was as close as she was going to get to her once ultimate dream. She was glad that she hadn't ruined it for her. If someone had to live her life, she was glad it was Ffion.

After the performance, Sylvie wrote out a text to Ffion. She didn't even know if she had the same mobile number, but she thought it was worth a try. She tried three different variations of the message and in the end decided not to send anything at all. What good was it now, digging up the past?

Instead she texted Linda, the adult ballet class teacher.

Sylvie: Working on a solo for my Aunt's memorial. Would you mind staying late after class on Thursday to watch and give me a few pointers?

*

'I'm so glad you agreed to do this,' Sylvie's mum, Nadine, said as they arrived at the country club that afternoon.

'Yeah,' said Sylvie. 'Me too.'

Sylvie's dad, Clive, held the front door open for them and huffed as they passed by. 'Bloody hell,' he said. 'This memorial is costing me an arm and a leg, it's the least she could do to contribute.'

Sylvie felt her mum's hand on her upper arm, squeezing gently. 'I know how important she was to you, darling. I know it hasn't been easy.'

'Thank you,' said Sylvie, genuinely.

They waved and mouthed *hello* to the small crowd that had accumulated in the reception. A large portrait of Aunt Jacqueline had been blown up and stood propped on an easel in the corner of the room so that she watched over the gathering with her inscrutable blue-eyed stare.

'You had a special bond,' said Nadine. 'I'm quite jealous, I was always a bit intimidated by Auntie Jacqueline. She didn't think much of me, but she adored you.'

'I adored her too.'

'Sylvie.' Annabel rushed over to kiss Sylvie on the cheek, as Aurelie toddled along beside her. 'It's good to see you.'

Sylvie put her arms around Annabel, holding her close. They'd spoken a couple of times since the incident. Annabel had sent text messages periodically asking how Sylvie was – she wanted to know that she'd kept quiet – and Sylvie had responded that she was very well and she was glad they were friends and would always be friends. Sylvie knew she would always keep Annabel's secret, she owed her that much at least, and her silence made her complicit – it tied them together and if Annabel went down then so would she.

'How have you been holding up?' she asked her.

'Oh, you know,' Annabel said, putting her hand through Aurelie's curls. 'Good days and bad days. Better than I was.'

'Of course,' she said. 'I can't imagine. Thank you for coming.'

'I wanted to see you dance,' said Annabel. 'Aurelie wanted to see you too, she loves ballerinas.'

The crowd was hushed when Sylvie walked out in silence under the silvery light, she saw the dim outlines of their faces from beneath the white veil that covered her like a shroud. The music began for Giselle's ghostly solo. She rose up onto the tips of her pointe shoes and pulled the veil from her face, letting it drift onto the ground beside her. She was whisked away by music, by pure emotion. She felt herself transforming into a daemon of magick just like she used to, all those years ago. And when her eyes fluttered open for a brief moment between turns, she saw her there, Aunt Jacqueline, her face in the dark theatre lighting, eyes electric blue, hair a vivid red and set in waves over one eye. She sat in the front row and looked up and smiled at her. A knowing smile.

Sylvie thought that audiences were overrated perhaps but if Aunt Jacqueline could really see her, as she was then, then she was more than happy. Because *courage is the most important* and Sylvie had rediscovered hers. Sylvie looked back to the same spot, and she was gone.

Acknowledgements

Thank you to my agent Hattie Grünewald. Thank you to my editor Rachel Imrie. Thank you to everyone at Corvus, Atlantic and The Blair Partnership who have had a hand in shaping this story and helping to bring this book out into the world. Thank you to the special ones, my nearest and dearest – you know who you are – for your constant support. And finally, I'm thankful for the story of Giselle and the legend of the Willis for showing us how bad men should be dealt with and doing all of it so gracefully.